Peter Driscoll's *The W...* [...] a successful feature film, established him as an international best-selling author. His most recent novels are *Pangolin* and *Heritage*. He lives with his family in Ireland.

Also by Peter Driscoll

THE WILBY CONSPIRACY
PANGOLIN

and published by Corgi Books

SPEARHEAD

Peter Driscoll

CORGI BOOKS

SPEARHEAD

A CORGI BOOK   0 552 13216 0

Originally published in Great Britain by Bantam Press, a division of
Transworld Publishers Ltd.

PRINTING HISTORY
Bantam Press edition published 1988
Corgi edition published 1989

Copyright © Peter Driscoll 1988

This book is set in 10/11 pt. Linotron Electra by
Goodfellow & Egan, Cambridge Ltd.

Corgi Books are published by Transworld Publishers Ltd.,
61–63 Uxbridge Road, Ealing, London W5 5SA, in Australia by
Transworld Publishers (Australia) Pty. Ltd., 15–23 Helles Avenue,
Moorebank, NSW 2170, and in New Zealand by Transworld
Publishers (N.Z.) Ltd., Cnr., Moselle and Waipareira Avenues,
Henderson, Auckland.

Printed and bound in Great Britain by
Cox & Wyman Ltd, Reading

For Peter and Suzanne Guttridge

Spe·ar-head
I. b. *fig.* A person or body of
persons chosen to lead a thrust
or attack.

Shorter Oxford English Dictionary

PROLOGUE

The cemetery stood on high ground, a forest of gravestones and small marble crosses close to the summit of a windswept hill, and the townships were visible on all sides around it. Row after row, block after block, the tiny, identical, iron-roofed houses stretched away in the mid-morning light to a horizon dimmed by a perpetual haze of smoke. Here and there stood a few sickly-looking bluegum trees or a patch of veld blackened by winter burning, but otherwise it was a landscape almost without features. Like a desert, it impressed by its scale and its monotony.

The funeral procession had been in view all the way from the church, a dark river of people twisting its way up towards the hill, and now they were close enough for the policemen and soldiers blocking the road to hear the sounds they made: the whisper of movement, the murmur of voices, snatches of singing carried to them on the breeze. Sometimes the noise was drowned by the whine and clatter of a distantly circling helicopter.

The hearse was flanked by lines of young men in uniform khaki shirts and black berets, followed by the mourners in a column wide enough to fill the rutted roadway and stretching back two or three hundred yards. Banners and flags swayed above them in the thin winter sunshine, the brilliant colours of the People's Congress standing out with a kind of grotesque carnival gaiety against the drabness of the backdrop.

From a quarter of a mile away, the words of the anthem they sang were now faintly audible:

> 'Nkosi sikelel' iAfrika,
> Maluphakanyisw' uphondo lwayo. . . . '

7

'God bless Africa,' said Corporal Frank Rendle.

'And all who sail in her,' said Nicky Flynn.

It was an old joke, a stock response, and neither of them laughed. Rendle swigged reflectively at the litre bottle of Coke laced with brandy and passed it to Nicky Flynn, then leaned against the dusty side of the Saracen armoured personnel carrier and tipped back his visored riot helmet. He was a big, brawny young man with a nonchalant, self-contained air, and instead of watching the marchers he kept his gaze fixed almost wistfully on the helicopter half a mile away. His eyes were pale blue, and because of their striking contrast to his dark, almost Latin complexion they often seemed icy and indifferent.

Nicky Flynn, the lance-corporal of the squad, was less composed. He drank quickly, then capped the bottle, picked up his rifle and checked once again that it was cocked as well as loaded. He glanced along the slope at the police Land Rover and the three Hippo riot trucks that straddled the road, as huge and ungainly as their name suggested. A couple of dozen cops in pale blue overalls were perched on top of them, protected by their twelve-foot sides of armoured steel, pump guns and gas at the ready, spoiling for a fight.

'Nervous?' Rendle suddenly asked.

'Making sure, Frank.'

'Remember the rule. We're keeping out of this. If the Boers want any zapping done, let them do it themselves.'

You could smell the hatred in the air in this place. That was what Rendle had said once, and after that the rest of his squad seemed to smell it too. He had that kind of effect on them. The smell was mixed up with the fumes of coal and paraffin smoke, the reek of cooking meat and kaffir beer. It rose with the dust churned up by the Saracen's six big wheels on its endless, aimless patrols of the townships. You could see it, too, in the eyes of the idlers and the children who watched their progress sullenly from the sides of the road; and sometimes you could hear it, as now, in the deep defiant singing of the Congress anthem:

'God bless Africa,
Raise up our descendants,
Hear our prayers . . .'

The procession moved closer, the old hearse groaning
along in bottom gear, a dense mass of people close behind it.
Among the banners and festive flags there were placards now
visible as well, most of them identical blown-up photographs
of the same man. It was always the same picture, with never
any need of a caption or slogan. The photograph explained
itself, reminding, reproaching, exhorting. There were more
placards than ever today, for it was this man's wife they were
burying.

Beside one of the Hippos, a red-faced little police major
was fiddling with a megaphone. The rest of the army squad
were shambling back from where they'd been talking to the
cops. Brakpan, the Saracen's driver, looked ludicrously small
beside Lightning, their gangling radio operator. Behind them
came Carver and Fish, Blikkies Steyn and Younis the Greek,
an ill-assorted mob with an easy coherence long established.
Back in South-West and in Angola they'd been in a real war
together, and this stuff by comparison, by common consent,
was a dirty joke.

Brakpan grabbed the Coke bottle off the cowling of the
armoured car and drank thirstily.

'What do those Boers say?' Rendle asked him.

'They don't tell us shit.'

'Uptight bastards,' said Younis the Greek. 'But it looks like
they're going to stop it. One warning, then gas.'

'That major says for us to get in the wagon,' Brakpan said.

'Screw him,' said Rendle easily.

It was the squad's principle to avoid trouble, and they had
only turned up here by chance. Their radio hardly ever
worked, the result of some clever but undetectable tampering
by Lightning, and the Saracen was like a gypsy caravan in
which they wandered more or less at will. For a minute they
stood around it taking turns at the bottle, Rendle still idly
watching the helicopter, the others returning the tacitly

9

hostile stares of the policemen. There'd never been much love lost between cops and troopies – especially since the police had failed, in spite of their guns and gas and Hippos, to impose order on the townships, and the army had been drawn reluctantly into the turmoil. It wasn't what these national servicemen had been trained for, and mostly it wasn't to their taste.

The procession had halted. As if by some agreement between enemies on a battlefield, the hearse and the marchers stopped moving a hundred yards short of the police line. The flags and placards faced them like battle standards. The singing had died away, but now a kind of war cry went up – one word roared by one part of the crowd, the next following it from another:

'*Mayibuye!*'

'*Afrika!*'

The sound was unnerving, more so even than the sheer numbers of the crowd, the way they could be conjured up in their thousands from that bleak landscape like ants emerging on the veld after the first summer rains. Nobody was in charge of them; they seemed driven like the ants by a corporate will. Once in a while the security forces swept through them, spraying gas and shotgun pellets like so much insecticide, leaving a few victims choking and bleeding on the ground, leaving the rest to scatter and hide and form up again somewhere else.

'Attention! Attention!' The major was addressing them through his bullhorn now. 'This is an illegal gathering in terms of the Emergency Regulations. You are not, repeat not, permitted to use a funeral for the purposes of a political demonstration . . .'

'That thing always makes my flesh creep,' Carver said.

'That war cry?' said Fish. 'What's it mean, anyway?'

Rendle and Flynn exchanged a knowing grin. In an earlier life Carver and Fish had been members of a motorbike gang that settled things with brass knuckles and timing chains, but they betrayed a curious innocence when reduced like everyone else to short hair and brown army fatigues.

10

'"Mayibuye Afrika",' said Rendle, 'means "Come back, Africa". It's kind of nostalgic. It harks back to the time when there were no white men around.'

'Like back to the trees, huh?'

'Anybody ever tell you you're an ignorant arsehole, Fish?'

'An illegal gathering . . . ,' the major was repeating through the megaphone, his voice echoing back tinnily from the rooftops. 'The coffin and the clergy and the immediate family of the deceased may enter the cemetery. The rest of you, I give you two minutes to disperse peacefully or force will be used . . .'

'Whyn't they just let them bury the old cow and be done with it?' Lightning wondered plaintively. Nobody answered him. Tension seemed to make the air shimmer between the opposing sides now, the cops watching from the high battlements of their trucks, the mourners massed like a black wall across the road beneath the silently accusing photographs.

For a minute, neither side seemed sure what to do. Then a group of three or four people detached themselves from the crowd, passed by the hearse and began to walk towards the police. They were a deputation, led by a priest and going to argue the case for letting the procession through.

In the distance, the helicopter turned away and receded towards the smudged horizon, like a disappointed spectator who had waited too long for some action. At the same time one of the police Hippos eased its way forward and began to lumber slowly, like some armoured prehistoric beast, down the slope.

To Alex Mzandwile Duma, lingering somewhere near the centre of the crowd, the sight of the approaching riot truck added to a growing sense of unease. There was going to be trouble after all. The presence of the Boers was a provocation by itself. Sometimes they let a political funeral go ahead unhindered, and you would think they had more sense than to interfere on such an emotionally charged occasion as the burial of Elizabeth Kumalo. Well, no, actually you wouldn't

11

think so. They were pig-headed bastards at the best of times, and impervious to the atmosphere in the townships this morning, a feeling that the permanently simmering anger was ready to boil over again. It was a feeling to which Duma's instincts were finely attuned.

He had kept to the middle of the procession and out of view, well behind Nandi Kumalo and the other chief mourners. It was Duma's role to avoid trouble as well, or this kind of trouble at least. Mindless violence – stone-throwing and petrol-bombing – did have its uses but was best left to kids and loafers who cared nothing for their own safety. Comrade Duma, as he was known to some, had more important things to do. Comrade Duma was an officer of the outlawed People's Congress, a veteran of guerrilla training across the border, and for that reason a marked man. Only the size and anonymity of the crowd protected him; only allegiance to Nandi's father and the memory of her mother, and a vague wish to win the gratitude of Nandi herself, had coaxed him out on to the streets at all.

There was something dangerously exhilarating, all the same, about the sensation of approaching conflict. The Hippo was so monstrously ugly that it almost invited attack, and as it drew nearer he found himself craving the weight of a stone in his hand, calculating the chances of braining one of the hateful Boers who peered down over its sides. Duma had his own anger, and his careful political and military training had not quite suppressed the instincts of the street urchin he had been not that many years ago.

There was the tension of a coiled spring in the people all around him. The Hippo stopped twenty yards short of the crowd, and what Duma found tantalizing someone else must have found irresistible. A half-brick went sailing out from somewhere among them, and Duma felt a sense of explosive release, just as though he'd thrown it himself.

The missile arced over the heads of the priest and his deputation and clattered harmlessly off the side of the truck. It made the crew duck for cover, however, and a second later a couple more stones were flung. Duma caught a glimpse of

12

the priest turning to face the procession, mouthing some unheard appeal, and for a few moments nothing more happened. Perhaps the disorder might have ended there, but suddenly one of the policemen on the truck sprang to his feet and fired a gas grenade. Almost before the crack of the Very pistol was audible the shell had struck the ground in front of the delegation and engulfed them in the spreading white vapour of tear gas.

Always there was a thin line between defiance and fury, and it was overrun in a second. Duma felt the restraint of the crowd snap like a physical force. A great roar of anger went up around him. The priest and his companions reeled aside, coughing and sobbing, while the gas drifted towards the main body of people. The undertaker's men scrambled out of the hearse. The mourners in front of Duma parted and scattered, while those behind began to propel him forward.

There were patches of charred veld on either side of the road, and the crowd overflowed on to them. While women and older people fled from the vapour, young men were already gathering stones and hurling them at the truck, the cops bobbing and weaving to avoid them as they scrambled to unleash more gas. The second and third Hippos had started down the slope now, trundling off the road to left and right to outflank the rioters.

Within half a minute the funeral procession had dissolved into chaos. More gas was lobbed; screams were interspersed by the popping of Very pistols, and over them came the sharper bark of shotguns as the police began blasting at the scattered groups of stone-throwers. These had well-practised tactics of their own, fanning out to circle the Hippos just out of range of the guns, then rushing forward in waves to fling their missiles and retreat again.

All the while Duma was being carried along by a solid mass of men eager to join the battle. He tried to push against them, to wriggle out sideways, but was thrust steadily forward. There were shotgun blasts somewhere just ahead and the mob fell back, carrying him helplessly with them. Then he was jammed against the side of the abandoned hearse by the crush of bodies and he saw the first Hippo, moving again, ploughing its way through the crowd and bearing down on him like an ocean liner. For the first time, real fear took hold of him. He felt trapped and exposed in just the way he had sought to avoid, and knew he should never have risked being seen.

Rendle's squad had had a panoramic view of the riot from their vantage-point on the hill. They were still gathered round the Saracen, watching with a sort of detached disbelief, when the little police major marched angrily over from his Land Rover.

'*Wat staan julle ouens hier? Het julle nie my bevel gehoor nie?*'

'We've got no orders,' Rendle said. 'Our radio is out.'

He had spoken in English without apology or deference, and the major stood weighing him up for a second: his manner wasn't disrespectful exaotly, just latently hostile.

'Listen to me, Corporal. Here in the townships you army blokes take your orders from us. And when we give you orders you jump, understand?'

'Yes.' The pale eyes gave nothing away.

'Good. You'll go down there and help pick up the agitators among that mob. Any kaffir who looks like a shit-stirrer or a stone-thrower, you pull him in. Got it?'

'Yes.'

The policeman strutted off. Rendle jerked his head resignedly at the others and within a few seconds they had all piled into the Saracen – Brakpan and Lightning in the two seats at the front of the cab, Rendle in the turret position behind them, the other five in the rear. The Rolls-Royce engine coughed throatily to life, and Brakpan gunned the vehicle down the slope – an ugly, snub-nosed, ten-ton monster for which they had all developed a perverse affection.

Dust and tear gas mingled and drifted on the breeze. Most of the peaceable element of the crowd seemed to have run back to gather their remaining banners and placards among the nearest rows of houses, leaving the open space as a battleground for police and rioters with a clutch of people still around the hearse. Stoning and sporadic shooting continued, and as the Saracen approached a gang of youths converged on it to fling bricks and bottles. Brakpan accelerated and swung playfully towards them, making them scatter.

'Where to?' he yelled at Rendle.

'Oh, we'll look busy for a bit and then piss off.'

Rendle had spoken. It was Rendle who had taught them not to buck the system but to use it, Rendle the busted-down helicopter pilot who knew it made more sense quietly to ignore orders than to disobey them. Nicky Flynn had often wondered about the authority this strangely brooding corporal had over them, and concluded it had nothing to do with his former status or his present rank, or even the fact that he was three or four years older than the rest of them. It came from their recognition that he was a true rebel, while the rest of them had only played at rebellion. He had harnessed their separate disaffections, their dislike of what they were doing, and turned them into something positive. Rendle was the leader of an undeclared but permanent state of mutiny.

For half a minute or so the crowd had kept Duma pressed against the hearse, forced to stare in through its window at the coffin wrapped in its gaudy Congress flag, all thoughts of its burial forgotten. The pressure was released as the last of the mob surged back down the road, but now he saw that one of the riot trucks had swung around behind him, cutting off his retreat.

Duma slithered round to the front of the hearse, ducking beside the grille. There was open ground ahead, and it was only fifty yards to the nearest houses. There the streets would swallow him up, but to reach them he would have to cross a gap between another Hippo and the nearest of the stone-throwing youths. A Saracen armoured car was prowling towards him as well, and he knew he would be horribly exposed, a moving target, but anything was better than waiting here.

His heart pounded. He braced himself to run, then felt a

15

hand seize his arm. He snatched it away and turned in panic to see Nandi behind him: Nandi in her black mourning dress, a black straw hat askew on her head and a stricken look on her face.

'What do you want?' he demanded fiercely. She shook her head as though she didn't understand. 'They won't touch you, Nandi. Don't draw attention to me!'

'Duma . . .,' she said, and took his arm again. Clearly she didn't know what she wanted. Her mother's death, and now the shambles of the funeral, had shocked and confused her beyond any logic. There was a kind of innocence about Nandi that he usually found beguiling, but now it made him angry.

'Get lost, Nandi!' He thrust her away from him and ran.

He raced diagonally away from the road, across blackened stubble littered with stones. Ahead of him, the young men were giving up their attack on the Hippos and retreating towards the nearest houses, some of them hit by pellets and supported by their comrades. One of the trucks had been dangerously close when he started out, but now he was widening the gap. He had covered most of the distance when, risking a glance over his shoulder, he tripped and sprawled on the ground. He stood up, smothered in the ash of burnt grass, and began to run again.

He was only yards from the entrance to a lane between two rows of houses when he felt a kind of sharp tug at his left shoulder and was lifted off his feet by some unseen force. His feet pedalled the air and his arms flailed, and the crash of the pump gun reached him as he hit the ground.

He rolled to the foot of an iron fence at the corner of the lane. He was winded, gasping for air, and only when he caught his breath again did he feel the sticky warmth of blood and the spreading, scalding pain in his shoulder, as though a hot iron had been pressed to his skin. He got to his hands and knees, crawled a few yards into the lane and collapsed again. All he could think, before a dim shadow spread over his consciousness, was that he'd been a bloody fool.

*   *   *

16

The Saracen had made a wide circle around the stranded hearse, its wheels crunching over the burnt veld and the debris of rioting: stones, tear-gas shells and abandoned placards. The shooting had stopped quite suddenly, and across the open space policemen were descending from the Hippos. Most of the rioters had managed to slip away, but half a dozen wounded youths were being helped to their feet and herded to the trucks. Like the end of a game cull, Rendle thought.

From his position in the turret he caught a movement to his right and saw a woman in a black dress and hat running purposefully towards an alleyway between some houses. Just inside it she stopped and bent over a figure lying on the ground. For no reason he could think of, Rendle yelled to Brakpan to follow her.

In a few seconds the vehicle was pulling across the entrance to the alley, blocking it. The woman was kneeling now, beside the prone form of a man in jeans and a bomber jacket. She looked up in fright as Rendle called down to her.

'Is he dead?'

She shook her head numbly.

'Badly hurt?'

She went on staring for a moment, then seemed to recollect herself. 'Let him go,' she said. 'He'll be all right.'

Rendle scrambled out of the turret clutching his Uzi gun. He dropped to the ground and went over to the injured man. The left shoulder of the jacket had been torn off by birdshot, and his left arm and back were soaked in blood. He seemed unconscious, but when Rendle bent down and turned him on his back he snarled in pain. His glazed brown eyes came into focus, sharpened on the uniformed man leaning over him and narrowed with fear and hostility.

'Just let him go,' the woman repeated. 'Please.'

The appeal was made with dignity, and Rendle looked her over curiously. She was young, slightly plump and quite attractive, with strong Zulu features that reminded him vaguely of someone else. Her English sounded fluent and educated. Something in the soldier's manner must have reassured her; she stood up and faced him, then glanced in the direction of the open veld and the police who were scouring it, cut off from view by the Saracen. 'I don't think those police know he's here,' she said. 'They don't have to know, do they? It will go badly with him if they take him.'

'Who is he? What's he done?'

'His name is Duma. He's my friend. He's done nothing that I would call a crime, but they will beat him and torture him all the same.'

Rendle shrugged. 'He needs patching up. He needs a doctor.'

'That can be arranged, if you'll just allow him to go.'

'He won't get far like that.'

'Then will you help him?' she asked quietly. 'Take him out of here?'

Carver, Fish and Nicky Flynn had spilled out of the Saracen. They had heard the question as well and they stared at Rendle, who seemed oddly unsurprised. It was as though he understood the woman's sudden need to trust them, her taking for granted that they were different from the police. On the ground the man called Duma groaned and shifted, trying to sit up. Rendle said to the woman, 'Who are you, anyway?'

'Nandi Kumalo.'

He raised his eyebrows and his gaze went back towards the hearse. 'Her daughter?'

'And *his* daughter.' She indicated one of the fallen placards, the stern and reproving face of the Congress leader. 'The Boers won't touch me, but they'll take Duma. Are you going to help?'

Rendle looked back down the lane, and the others caught the glint of distant amusement in his eyes that was always his response to a challenge. It could be done, of course; the police had either missed Duma or assumed the soldiers were picking him up, and either way it would make no difference to anyone but the victim himself. His fate was in the squad's hands.

Rendle took a decision. 'Get him into the wagon,' he said

to the others, and to her: 'This conversation never happened, right? As far as you're concerned we just took him away. Where does he live?'

'Everywhere. Nowhere. You know Dr Sithole's clinic in Meadowlands? They'll take care of him and ask no questions.'

Only Nicky Flynn demurred. 'We're supposed to take him in, Frank. That major said—'

'He said to pick them up. He didn't say what to do with them.'

Nandi Kumalo knelt beside the wounded man again, propped him into a sitting position, and let Carver and Fish drag him to his feet. He winced with pain and looked round in bewilderment as they staggered with him to the Saracen, manoeuvred him through the doors and pushed him on to one of the rows of seats that faced each other along the sides. The three of them hopped in after him. Nandi Kumalo stood by the doors.

'Thank you.' She gave the soldiers one of those sudden, wide, natural African smiles that banished any thought of mistrust. 'Our people will remember you for this.'

'I'd rather they didn't, frankly.' Rendle slammed and bolted the doors and shouted instructions to Brakpan, and a moment later they were moving, rocking over the burnt grass and on to the road. The policemen around their Hippos glanced at them casually as they turned northwards, and the major up on the slope watched their departure with only brief puzzlement. Bloody soldiers were worse than useless out here, he thought, his mind already occupied with the account he would give to his superiors of these events. The kaffirs had started it, of course, and the police response had been as restrained as circumstances allowed. He could almost have written the press announcement himself; happily no reporters were allowed into the townships these days to provide their own distorted, malicious versions of events.

In the wagon, the troopies looked Duma over curiously. His token Afro hairdo was patched with grey ash. He was quite conscious, though still bleeding and clearly in pain, and gradually his panicky stare gave way to a more aware and calculating look.

'You one of the comrades?' Blikkies Steyn demanded. 'One of the militants?'

Duma did not reply, and two or three other tentative questions got no response either. He seemed almost like a captured wild animal, offering no thanks for being saved and waiting only for a chance to escape. When Younis offered him the bottle of brandy and Coke he took it without a word and finished it off in one long swallow.

Again it was Nicky Flynn who sounded a dubious note. Nicky worried at times about the way they carried on, wondering what Rendle might lead them into next. 'This bloke is wanted, Frank. He's political. What if there are questions?'

'Then we'll say we handed him over to a police patrol. But nobody's going to ask.'

'But why are we doing this?'

'Because we had to make a decision. Because fooling around like we do is just a way of avoiding things.' Rendle sounded annoyed. 'Sooner or later, somebody always asks you to choose which side you're on.'

Duma listened in silence. Soon they had left the wreckage of the funeral behind and were driving through streets where sullen peace prevailed. There were a couple of police roadblocks through which Brakpan charged at speed, offering the cops no opportunity to stop them even if they'd tried. In ten minutes they reached the township of Meadowlands, relatively prosperous, with tarred roads lined by not a few neat, middle-class bungalows. At the end of the street where the clinic stood the Saracen halted. Rendle opened the doors and signalled to the black man to get out.

'You'll manage on your own?'

Again Duma said nothing. Again there was the hunted-animal look about him, as though he still feared some trap. When he had eased himself out of the vehicle and found his feet, he turned and simply walked away. He had left a bloodstain against the bulkhead where he'd been sitting, but otherwise he might never have existed.

PART ONE

THE OPPORTUNITY

1

The commandant's chauffeur stopped the car in front of the prison's main entrance. He got out at once to open the rear door, but one of his passengers had already alighted and was striding towards the great steel gates, leaving little Dr Els to scramble out and hurry after him. The habitual brisk walk of Dr Louis Rose was not that of someone anxious to keep appointments, but of a man who deemed his own time to be precious. People waited for him but he rarely needed to wait for them, and doors had a way of opening magically at his approach. Even here he did not need to announce his arrival; it had been observed through a television scanner, and the narrow door set into a hatchway in one gate swung open to admit him.

Dr Els caught up with him in the reception hall, a place of chilly gloom after the warmth of the November morning. The prison medical officer was short and harassed-looking, and Dr Rose was tall and distinguished, immaculately groomed and tailored, carrying a black medical bag in one hand and an expensive calfskin briefcase in the other, and his arrival had an unsettling effect on the three or four warders present. He drummed his fingers on the counter and studied his drab surroundings with disfavour while Dr Els spoke to the men in Afrikaans and a telephone call was made. Finally the sergeant in charge put down the phone and said: 'We'll take you up right away, gentlemen.' He handed a lapel tag to

21

Dr Rose. It was the usual green visitor's tag, but under earlier instructions he had written no name on it. He glanced at the doctor's bags.

'May I examine those, sir?'

Dr Rose gave him a withering look. 'Certainly not.'

'It's regulations, I'm afraid . . .'

'I'm here by invitation, young man. I do not expect to be treated like one of your inmates.'

'*Dis glad nie nodig nie . . .,*' Dr Els hurriedly intervened and got into an argument about the regulations. The sergeant looked to the other men for support; getting none, he made a surly face and signalled to one of them to escort the arrivals into the inner fastness of the building.

'Sorry about that,' muttered Els. He was a nervous man who'd been apologizing for one thing or another ever since they'd met at the airport. 'Some of these chaps aren't too bright, and they treat their rules like Holy Writ.'

The hospital was in a new wing connected to the main prison block. It had no separate entrance, and access to it was up some stairs, through a maze of passageways and a series of steel doors, each opened and then locked behind them by a different section warder, their progress monitored every step of the way by television cameras. Not for nothing was Pollsmoor Prison considered the most secure in the country. Past one more barrier, glass doors opened into a well-lit lobby and a more conventional hospital atmosphere, apart from the bars on the windows and the prison khaki of the orderlies who hurried about.

Even this was not the end of the journey. Down a quiet hallway was a gate that was unlocked to give access to two more flights of stairs. Then they were in yet another passageway of the vast prison, lined with steel doors, smelling of disinfectant and eerily silent, like a corridor in an empty hotel. Outside one door at the very end a warder was posted. He knocked on it at their approach, and another man examined them through a peephole before unlocking it to let them in.

The object of all this attentive isolation was sitting up in a

22

high hospital bed that looked too small for him, smiling a welcome.

Thirty years of medical practice had trained Dr Rose never to show surprise. Yet even this professional conditioning could hardly prevent his gaping at the vision of a man he had somehow never expected to see in the flesh. Like every legendary figure, he had always seemed more real as a myth than as a live human being. He was a picture on the placards of demonstrators; he was a name uttered with reverence by millions of people, by no means all of them black. In a dozen African countries streets were named after him; in Europe and America prizes and honorary doctorates had been heaped on him. He was the very embodiment of the struggle for racial justice; he had come to be seen almost as holding the future of this country in his hand – and now there was something incongruous in seeing him here, confined in this tiny bare room, guarded by men who hardly knew enough to sense his significance. He had been in jail for twenty-five years, and he was perhaps the world's most famous prisoner.

'Good morning,' he said.

'Lincoln Kumalo!' Dr Rose turned to Els. 'You might at least have warned me.'

'I did say it was highly confidential,' the little man muttered uncomfortably.

When they returned to the hospital lobby half an hour later three men were lined up formally to greet them, as though in response to Dr Rose's own tyranny over time. Dr Els made the introductions: the prison commandant, a Mr Van Straaten and a Colonel Prinsloo. The commandant was the only one in uniform. Dr Rose shook hands briskly with each of them.

'We're grateful to you for coming all this way, Doctor, and at such short notice.' That was Van Straaten, a slight and dapper man of forty or so with gold-framed glasses, a pale grey suit and an unexpectedly studious look. 'I trust everything has gone smoothly?'

'Thank you.' Rose made it clear that he was not interested

23

in small talk. Nor did he see the point of this elaborate reception. 'I have to say I find all this subterfuge a little distasteful. . . .'

'But perhaps now that you've seen the patient you can understand why. He is, after all, a security prisoner . . .'

'Or what some of us would call a political prisoner.'

Van Straaten winced slightly at this sarcasm. 'Please try to understand, Dr Rose. His health is of great concern to us. Dr Els recommended calling you in because you're the best in your field. Depending on your diagnosis, decisions may have to be taken at the highest level. In the meantime the matter is delicate. Rumours could be damaging, you understand? Although he lives in isolation here, we can take no risks. That's why you were asked not even to reveal your identity to him.'

Colonel Prinsloo, a tall, gangling, dyspeptic-looking man in his fifties, had been glancing uneasily about the lobby, and now he spoke in Afrikaans to Van Straaten. The younger man in turn looked at Els. 'Where can we talk?'

'My office.' He led them a little way down the hallway, past doors marked *Radiography* and *Dispensary*, to a smallish room into which they all crowded rather awkwardly. The place had a makeshift air – a bare, barred window and spartan furnishings – and Els was being apologetic again, talking about this being only his temporary quarters; a heap of paperwork was piled high on his desk all the same, and there were tatty notices smothering a board fixed to the wall. An untidy mind, Rose noted, and thought he caught a disapproving look in Van Straaten's eyes as well. Whoever Van Straaten was, he was clearly in charge of the occasion.

They all remained standing. Colonel Prinsloo shut the door and stood beside it as though to guard it. Rose set his bags down on the floor.

'Well, Doctor,' said Van Straaten. 'If you'll let us have your diagnosis?'

Dr Rose glanced questioningly at Dr Els. Medical protocol required him to report to the colleague who had consulted him, not to these laymen. 'Go ahead, go ahead,' Els said

24

hastily, and the visitor unclipped his briefcase and began to spread out X-ray plates and dossiers among the clutter on the desk.

His examination had only confirmed the conclusions he had reached by studying the plates and medical notes he had been sent. It had been a very conscientious examination all the same. Although they had not said much to each other, the doctor had been aware at once of an extraordinary magnetism in his patient's personality: a quality of easy authority, inner strength and absolute conviction. It was he who had put the visitor at his ease, joking wryly about the pains in his abdomen and the trouble he'd had peeing, accepting philosophically what Rose had to tell him, asking only a few pertinent questions. It wasn't possible to be totally impersonal with any patient, of course; Rose remembered that the man's wife had died only three months ago, and offered his condolences, regardless of the nervous presence of Dr Els and the strict warning he'd been given to discuss only medical matters.

Now that it was over it seemed faintly unreal, as though the man had been replaced by the myth again. Yet the man had an illness that was real enough, and Rose was going to give it to his captors with a vengeance. He was contemptuous of these people: they were frightened of Lincoln Kumalo, deep down, but they were even more frightened of his dying on them from neglect or incompetence. He understood now that they wanted him, Dr Louis Rose, not just because he was the country's leading urologist as well as an eminent surgeon and the owner of a small but famous clinic, but also to show that their own hands were clean. They wanted his integrity as much as his medical skills, and this gave him a satisfying sense of power over them.

'Very well.' The material was laid out in front of him. 'Now that I've seen Mr Kumalo—'

'Please . . .' The interruption came from Prinsloo. 'Not the name, if you please. Officially he's still anonymous.'

'Now that I've seen this anonymous patient, then,' said Rose with sarcastic emphasis, 'I have found nothing to contradict the opinion I formed after scrutiny of the X-rays. Without doubt he is suffering from cancer of the prostate gland. He's going to need surgery.' He spoke now without looking at Dr Els. 'Frankly, I'm surprised that it wasn't diagnosed sooner.'

Phineas Molefe was four feet nine inches tall and weighed slightly less than one hundred pounds, and had long ago learned that the key to his survival lay in giving no offence. He threatened nobody and did not make a satisfactory victim. In his four years in Pollsmoor, both prisoners and warders had tended to patronize him, and some would even defend him against the occasional threatening lout. Phineas had also learned to keep his own counsel: he had not forgotten that it was only the stupidity of an accomplice that had landed him here in the first place, and that otherwise he might still be creaming off fifty rands a week from the takings of the dairy in Salt River where he had once worked as a clerk.

Because he gave no trouble and did what he was told, Phineas had been made a trusty. Because of his Standard Eight education he had been given a clerical job in the prison hospital. He had worked quietly and efficiently in the dispensary for three years now, and was as inconspicuous as the low stool on which he squatted behind the counter. Since people took no notice of him, they had a way of assuming he paid no attention to them. His boss, the government pharmacist employed in the prison, considered it a matter of principle to make a fuss once in a while over something Phineas had done, or not done, but otherwise largely ignored him.

His job was monotonous, but it involved no physical hardship and it kept him warm and dry in winter, unlike the other poor *mugus* from his cell block who were out on the prison farmlands in all kinds of weather. Phineas counted off the years and months and days to his release, and knew exactly what he would do when it came. He was going north to join the liberation army of the People's Congress. He would take part in the struggle pioneered by the great Leaders

26

who were kept here, in this very prison. There would be no more stupid petty crime for him; he was going to help kill some Boers, and his contentment was that of a man with a purpose to live for.

The dispensary was divided by the counter facing the door. Some way behind the counter was a separate room in which the pharmacist worked, surrounded by shelves laden with pills and potions. This room was always kept locked in his absence, for it was an Aladdin's Cave of drugs – prison currency which half the *mugus* in this place would give an arm or a leg for. Uppers and downers, phennies and bennies, it didn't matter: they would guzzle aspirins and drink cough syrup if they got the chance, they would swallow anything they thought might refract reality for an hour or two, and not even trustworthy little Phineas could be expected to remain immune for ever to temptation.

This morning, to all appearances daydreaming as usual, Phineas listened with slightly more than his usual idle interest to the drone of voices from next door. A quirk in the way the rooms had been rearranged along the corridor gave him this opportunity to eavesdrop. At one time the adjacent office had been a kind of anteroom to the dispensary, connected to it by a small hatch through which drugs and medicines were issued. This opening had merely been screened by a noticeboard put up on the far side of the wall, and Phineas sat next to it. Through the thin partition he could often hear Dr Els talking on the telephone, or moving about, or holding discussions with members of his staff. These were usually incomprehensible to Phineas, but he was bored enough much of the time to find almost any distraction welcome.

This morning he had been alerted by the arrival of a group of white men in the hospital. Their voices had come drifting down the corridor, and then they had walked past the dispensary door: the prison commandant himself, with Dr Els and three other men, all strangers to the prison. Phineas had speculated that someone important had been taken ill. Until now he had taken his thoughts no further than that.

He heard the white men assembling in the adjacent office, and heard the door closing behind them. It happened that the pharmacist had left the dispensary for a couple of minutes, and Phineas was able to press his ear close to the partition.

Dr Els took out cigarettes, offered them around and was refused. With a guilty air he lit one himself. The commandant, whose uniformed presence seemed to have been purely ceremonial, had excused himself and left a minute ago. Van Straaten and Prinsloo were giving Dr Rose their full attention, as though Els no longer mattered.

'The symptoms first described six weeks ago,' said Rose, 'were difficulty and frequency in urinating. These followed a series of earlier urinary infections resulting in more or less chronic inflammation of the prostate. This is the classic symptom of prostate hyperplasia, or enlargement, by no means uncommon in a man of his age, which I understand is sixty-eight.

'In addition, however . . .' He switched on the desk-lamp and held one of the plates up in front of it. 'Here in the first series of X-rays you'll see a group of quite substantial calculi – stones, that is – in the left lateral lobe. These result from inflammation and are not unexpected. But here among them, something else.' He took out a gold fountain pen and pointed with it at a tiny pale smudge on the plate, barely distinguishable. 'You noticed this, of course,' he said to Els. It seemed not to be a question, but it sounded like one. 'It's masked by the stones, and it could be taken for just one more of them. But this faint aura around it suggests the beginning of damage to the epithelial cells. In other words, the signs of an early carcinoma. Very early, and so not difficult to miss.'

Not difficult when you were a hack prison doctor, was what he meant. The single crumb of comfort he had thrown to Els was hardly worth having, and if he hid his embarrassment behind a show of deference that would not prevent his feeling jealous, possibly resentful.

He picked up two more plates and indicated, in turn, what

seemed little more than a pair of faint thumbprints. 'Now, when we look at the pictures taken last week, we see that the tumour has grown quite substantially. It was at this stage that you sought my opinion.' He paused. 'Luckily, these prostate cancers do not usually progress very rapidly. At present this one is a matter for concern rather than alarm. It's not yet close to spreading to other organs, and that's where the real danger lies. If it had been left for another month, however . . .'

Rose left the sentence unfinished. 'What can be done about it?' Van Straaten asked.

'The treatment is surgical removal of the gland, though that depends very much on the general condition of the patient. Assessing that was the main purpose of my examination, and I can tell you now that he's in superb shape. He has the constitution of a man twenty years younger.'

'You'll operate, then?'

'Yes, but not immediately. In a case of simple prostate enlargement I would say the sooner the better, just for the sake of relieving his discomfort. With a tumour, matters are more complicated. My approach is to begin with a course of hormone treatment which will reduce the size of the carcinoma while also preventing its spreading. That, in turn, will minimize the trauma of surgery. In a man of his age the healing process is slow, no matter how fit he may be. This is a major operation, not complicated but delicate; to put it crudely, the less of him that has to be cut out, the faster he'll recover. I would say four to six weeks from now, depending on the success of the hormone tablets. In fact, if we set a date now for about six weeks hence, I'll guarantee that he'll be in the best possible condition to undergo surgery.'

Van Straaten looked a trifle pained, as though he felt he was being hurried along too fast. 'As I mentioned, Dr Rose, this has to have approval higher up.'

'Then get it quickly. You can't play politics with this man's life. The synthetic hormones will have only a temporary effect. Eventually the cancer will spread – first to the bladder, and then via the bloodstream to the bones, possibly to the lungs and liver. Within four months or so his condition might be quite irreversible.'

The bluntness of this statement reduced them to silence, giving Rose the opportunity to follow through. 'Another thing. I understand that this hospital isn't equipped for major surgery. You may know that my clinic near Johannesburg specializes in precisely these disorders, among a few other things. I also have a thoroughly modern operating theatre there, and the services of perhaps the best surgical team in the country. That is where I propose to operate.'

Colonel Prinsloo began to protest at once, but Van Straaten put a restraining hand on his arm. 'Is that really necessary, Doctor? Surely there are quite adequate facilities here in Cape Town?'

'Of course. But if you intend to let me have full control, then this is the only way I can exercise it. I have a reputation to protect, after all.'

'The security problems—' Prinsloo began.

'Will be your concern, Colonel. And you'll have plenty of time to solve them.' Van Straaten did not seem put out. 'If that's what you require, Doctor, then I have little doubt that the relevant persons in government will approve. They are just as concerned as we are that the prisoner should have the best that's available. However, this does make the matter of secrecy even more vital. We must guard against . . . well, indiscretions.'

Rose smiled thinly at the idea that he might be indiscreet. 'My dealings with this patient are covered by medical confidentiality,' he said. 'Besides, if you're looking for privacy, you can't do better than the Woodvale Clinic.'

'I'm afraid we need something a little more concrete than that.' Van Straaten took a folded sheet of paper from his pocket, opened it out and placed it on the desk. Rose fished out his reading glasses and picked it up. It was a printed form, headed *Act 16 of 1956: The Official Secrets Act (As Amended)*. Beneath the heading was the text of the law and its amendments, followed by a declaration of agreement to be bound by its terms. His name and address were typed in, and there was a space at the bottom pencil-marked for his signature.

'Quite ridiculous!' Rose was at his most arch and scornful. 'Why on earth should I agree to this?'

'It reflects no lack of trust in you, Doctor. But we must have a guarantee.'

'And if I refuse to sign?'

'Then, regrettably, the matter will end here and now.' Van Straaten's small brown eyes were suddenly sharp behind his glasses. 'The security laws in any case require you to forget everything you have seen and heard in here. We'll find some-one else.'

Someone of the calibre of Els? Rose wondered. He rarely found himself in a dilemma, but suddenly two sides of his own nature seemed to be in conflict. On the one hand, he wasn't used to having terms dictated to him, least of all by government officials who were the instruments of policies he disliked; on the other, he had guessed from the beginning that more would be at stake than the health of some anonymous prisoner, and there was a challenge here that he relished.

He realized he was at another disadvantage with these two. He was a man in every sense at the peak of his career and reputation, a man whom people tended to orbit around, and he rarely found the time or the need to see them in more than one dimension. Prinsloo and Van Straaten he had classed as a pair of bureaucrats, and left it at that: Now he took stock of them again and saw Prinsloo as a more particular type, a hard-boned Afrikaner policeman of the old school, Van Straaten as something more elusive, possibly even sinister, a warped intellectual maybe, with a pale ascetic face and humourless eyes.

'We'd prefer it not to come to that, of course,' said Van Straaten now, soothingly.

'Perhaps I should have asked,' said Rose, 'exactly who you mean by *we*.'

'Ah. I thought you might have guessed that, Doctor. Colonel Prinsloo is an officer of the Security Police, entrusted with special responsibility for this prisoner. And I have the privilege to be Deputy Director of the National Intelligence Service.'

2

Phineas Molefe saw Dr Els and one of his visitors leaving the hospital as he walked back along the corridor. He was carrying a tray from the kitchen and he stepped nimbly aside to let them pass, talking quietly as they headed for the lobby and the exit. They didn't notice him, and he was quite happy to seem insignificant.

He went into the dispensary, still mulling over what he had learned in the past forty minutes. He had heard the conversation next door only in snatches, and not a lot of it made sense. Only one thing stood out like a beacon among the fog of words, one electrifying name that they had mentioned right at the beginning. Kumalo. The greatest of the Leaders. Without doubt it was Kumalo who was sick upstairs, and it was him they had been discussing.

Now he remembered something else; another small piece of the puzzle fell into place. The man he had just seen in the corridor seemed in every way a more noble and refined person than Dr Els, and his looks fitted the clear, authoritative voice Phineas had heard addressing the others. One of them had said his name: Rose. He was Dr Rose. He had spoken in a haughty and scathing manner to Dr Els, which it had given Phineas some pleasure to hear. Many of the words he used had been incomprehensible, but Phineas gathered enough to understand that this was an important doctor brought in from outside. The discussion had been complicated, and Phineas was just beginning to get the drift of it when the pharmacist sent him out to fetch his morning coffee.

Now he carried the coffee and biscuits to his boss in the room at the rear, and returned with his own tin mug of tea and hunk of brown bread to the counter. He was sorry not to have learned more, even though there was nothing he could do with the knowledge. The Leaders were kept rigorously apart from everyone else, never seen by any ordinary *mugu*, although all were deeply conscious of their presence. A story like this, about one of them being sick, would get around the prison in a flash and almost inevitably be traced back to him.

Phineas fell to daydreaming again. Maybe he was, after all, too small to be a guerrilla fighter. But he was sure they could find use for him up in the north, with his quick wits and his Standard Eight . . .

He heard a sudden subdued laugh from behind the partition and realized, almost with a shock, that there was still someone in the room next door. It had somehow never occurred to him, once he'd seen the two doctors leaving, that anyone else might have stayed behind. Now he heard two voices, speaking in low tones and with an odd secretive intensity. They spoke in Afrikaans, which Phineas did not understand as well as English. The pharmacist was tinkering in the back room now, so he dared not move right up to the hatch. He sat very still where he was and strained every nerve to listen.

The window in Dr Els's office looked out across a gloomy courtyard to a blank stone wall, but if you stood close to it and to one side there was a glimpse of the nearby mountain slope and the cultivated prison lands that lay below it. Tertius Van Straaten had been gazing out at this ever since the two doctors had left, while Colonel Prinsloo moved about the room like a big restless animal, the other man's silence making him uneasy.

Finally he said, 'Well, what do you make of him? Typical arrogant Yid, in my opinion.'

'Then I suggest you keep your opinion to yourself,' Van Straaten rebuked him mildly. 'We need him more than he needs us now.'

'I wonder about that,' said Prinsloo. 'You seem to be letting him take a lot of decisions out of our hands.'

'Why not? Don't you sometimes get tired of making decisions?'

'This business about taking him to Jo'burg. Flying him all

that way for one simple operation. I have to remind you that
I'm responsible for the security aspects. . . .'

'And I'm sure you'll do a fine job. We'll keep it all under
wraps until it's over.'

'It just isn't necessary. Think of the scale of the thing. For
what? A sop to this bloody man's vanity?'

Van Straaten gave a brief chuckle, of condescension rather
than of amusement, and turned at last to face him. 'Don't
undervalue his vanity. It's very useful to us. That and his
position, his background . . .'

'Limousine liberal,' said Prinsloo with a snort.

'Exactly. A man above reproach, unlike our good Dr Els.
I'm all for giving him all the responsibility he wants. That
way, any mistakes will be down to him as well.'

'Why should there be any mistakes?'

Van Straaten gave him a curious look. 'You know that
expression the English have, about giving a man enough
rope to hang himself?'

'I'm afraid I don't follow,' said Prinsloo, a trifle impatiently.

Van Straaten did not enlighten him. His mind seemed to
have turned to something else. Suddenly he said: 'It's time I
told you about an idea of mine.'

Prinsloo said nothing. There were a lot of these academic
types in Intelligence these days, and they conferred their
ideas on you like blessings.

'There's a wonderful opportunity here, Prinsloo, if we're
up to grabbing it. The first opportunity we've ever had of
solving this whole problem without getting mud on our faces.
It's going to need permission from the top, friends at court,
but after what I've heard this morning I know it can be done.'

Prinsloo listened without interrupting. Van Straaten could
not know it, but the colonel's range of prejudices was quite
wide enough to include him as well as Dr Rose. Prinsloo
liked to think of himself as a simple policeman, and he
distrusted intellectuals – whether of the rich and supercilious
Jewish variety or of the ambitious professorial type like Van
Straaten. Above all he distrusted this style of sophisticated

34

games-playing, in which there was too much room for error. And yet, as he listened, a certain bizarre logic seemed to take shape from the younger man's words, the outline of a scheme so imaginative that it fell just a little short of the fanciful. If it worked, it would work brilliantly. If it didn't . . . There was just enough doubt in Prinsloo's mind to leave him silent again at the end, and Van Straaten took this for acquiescence.

'Well?' he demanded. 'You see it, don't you? We have a date set now, we've got six weeks to play with. A lot can be accomplished in that time, a lot of ground prepared.' He looked at Prinsloo earnestly. 'It's going to need both of us – me to work at my level, you at yours. You know his daughter; you mentioned she was coming for a visit soon?'

'Next Tuesday.'

'A happy coincidence, Prinsloo. It's a perfectly natural occasion for an approach from the top. We don't want to make it seem too easy, of course; we just want to sow some seeds, and see how they take root.'

Prinsloo suddenly gave a coarse laugh, a kind of defensive reaction against the other man's seriousness. 'You haven't been in this business for too long, have you, Mr Van Straaten? There was a much simpler way of doing this kind of thing in the old days, you know. It was called *shot while trying to escape.*'

Van Straaten looked scandalized. He had no sense of humour at all.

'Phineas!'

The pharmacist was standing in the doorway of the back room, bawling at him, and he realized it was not the first time his name had been called. The voices next door went abruptly silent, and Phineas recollected himself. In order not to give way his presence to those on the other side he did not reply at once, but hopped quietly off the stool and walked back the several yards to where his boss stood.

'My baas?'

'*Wat sit jy daar en slaap, Phineas?* You're asleep again,

my boy. Don't you know it's stocktaking tomorrow? We've got work to do.'

Phineas meekly followed him into the back of the dispensary, took out the record-books and began to go through the routine of preparing for the monthly stocktaking. After a minute or two the edges of his apprehension were blunted. Nobody came from the next room to investigate his boss's shout: presumably they took it for just another of the random harsh yells that echoed through the prison. If anyone had come, they would have seen only a tiny black prisoner hunched over the table behind the counter, intent upon his work.

Behind his mask of frowning concentration, Phineas was deeply troubled. Once again he had not understood all the words that had been spoken, only enough to grasp that he had eavesdropped on a ghastly secret.

The smell of the prison was something Dr Rose hadn't really noticed while he was there, but which had somehow lingered and clung to him afterwards: a combination of cement dust and carbolic and sweat-stained cotton that seemed to have infused his own clothing the way tobacco smoke did other people's. Even now, in the ventilated cabin of the jumbo jet winging northwards, he thought there was still a trace of it about him.

The smell, or his imagination of it, reminded him of the only other time he'd been into a prison, back in – 1971, was it? – to visit his cousin Joshua when they were holding him under the 180-day law. Funny the way they had brought up Joshua's name today – hesitantly, as though they'd expected a strong reaction from him. That was Afrikaaners for you: people of extreme likes and dislikes, and worse than the Jews with their monolithic sense of family unity. Perhaps they'd thought he would either stand up for Josh or condemn him, and were puzzled that he'd done neither. Difficult to explain to people like that that you'd grown apart long before Josh had skipped the country, that you'd had no real contact since, hardly even thought about him for fifteen years. Judith had written him the odd letter, Louis seemed to remember; but then his daughter would do that just to be perverse.

That was what all that Official Secrets Act stuff had been about, anyway: they were nervous about this distant family connection. Nervous of him, Louis, as well, perhaps, because he was not one of them: not a true believer in Separate Development, Plural Relations, or whatever the latest euphemism was for white supremacy. As though being a liberal made him automatically a potential subversive.

Well, he'd signed the damned thing, if only to show that he wasn't scared of them, but under protest. Colonel Prinsloo, in his gravelly, ominous, policeman's voice, warning him of its meaning: 'A penalty of fifteen years' imprisonment for communicating information prejudicial to the safety or interests of the Republic. You may not disclose to anyone anything you have seen or heard here, sir, or anything whatever in connection with this prisoner. . . .' As if he was likely to. Though he wouldn't give them the satisfaction of knowing it, Rose would do nothing to jeopardize his chances of operating on Lincoln Kumalo. Few surgeons, no matter how rich or respected, would turn down the opportunity of having such a luminary as a patient. Besides which, it might well make the Woodvale Clinic world-famous.

Rose was still in a slightly euphoric, self-congratulatory mood as the plane neared the end of its two-hour flight and began the long descent to Jan Smuts airport. The rich spring greenery of the Cape seemed like a distant dream as he gazed down at the dusty brown of the Highveld. He hoped Judith had passed on the message to have the driver meet him: it was just the sort of thing she was likely to forget. Although he chided himself for it sometimes, he could not help thinking of his daughter with a certain irritation.

Phineas's day continued on its humdrum way: requisitions for drugs were brought to his counter; he took these to the pharmacist, and when the orders were made up he took them back. He recorded each order in the day-book and filed a copy of the requisition. All the 'controlled' drugs that left the dispensary – the narcotic and addictive groups, including some stimulants and depressants – had also to be entered in a separate register. This was the pharmacist's own responsibility, but he was an indolent man and in practice it fell mostly to Phineas. In between all these things he carried on filling out the stock returns for the check that would be conducted tomorrow by a clerk from the Department's central stores.

He carried out these functions automatically, his mind in a turmoil of doubt and confusion. He wished he could seek advice, confide in someone about the things he had heard. But there was no one. The Leaders were inaccessible. As for his fellow-*mugus* in Cell Block C, they were thieves and violent criminals, for the most part stupid and not to be trusted.

Phineas took no risks and asked no favours. It had not, for instance, escaped the notice of the others in his cell block that he was sitting on a gold mine in this job: a handful of pills could have bought him anything from extra food to a month's supply of cigarettes, or even sexual favours if he'd been so inclined, but he had resisted all pressures and blandishments to steal. He knew that once he began there would be no stopping, and his future plans were too important.

All of which made it difficult now to know what to do. That he had to do something seemed beyond question. If he could talk to no-one in here about it, perhaps he could get a message out – but to whom? The Leader's daughter? They had mentioned that she was to visit him next Tuesday. But Phineas could not possibly gain access to her and she would have no reason to trust him anyway. Besides, what could such a message actually convey? Perhaps the only real fact at his disposal was the date: several times the white men next door had referred to a date, a day which had a significance of its own and on which a terrible thing was planned. Of the thing itself he had no knowledge. Everything had been innuendo, and yet Phineas was as strangely positive about its meaning as he had ever been about anything.

A warning. That was all the message needed to contain. If a warning reached the right people, they would know how to act upon it. If it was intercepted, however, that would only make matters worse. The thing was to conceal its origins yet somehow show that it was authentic.

He had pondered over these problems for the rest of the morning, and over the lunch of soup and bread that was brought to him at twelve o'clock. As a trusty he was permitted to eat in the dispensary instead of returning to the cell block for the frantic scramble of the food queue. Afterwards he brooded again in the patients' lavatory where he could move his bowels in privacy and smoke a surreptitious cigarette. He led a privileged life here, he reflected, and wondered why he even considered risking it all.

His final job, before the prisoners were herded back to their sections at four o'clock, was to file the drug prescription dockets that had accumulated during the day. This had always seemed a pointless task; the dockets were flimsy duplicates, seldom if ever needed again and thrown out at six-monthly intervals. There was one that was difficult to read, written in the shapeless scrawl of Dr Els, a prescription for a substance Phineas had never heard of. Stilboestrol? He hadn't seen the form earlier in the day, so presumably the pharmacist himself had dropped it in the tray. *Stilboestrol 3mg × 30*, it said: thirty tablets of three milligrams each. It carried today's date, November the second, and Dr Els's signature, and . . .

Phineas stood by the filing-cabinet and stared at the docket as though hypnotized. Against the printed notation that said *Name of Patient*, Dr Els had written: *Prisoner 4008*.

At once everything seemed to fall into place. Everyone in here knew who Prisoner 4008 was. Presumably those outside – or those who mattered anyway – would recognize the number as well. This was a prescription for the drug, the hormone treatment, the Leader was to have. This bit of paper could make the messsage authentic.

Down the corridors, warders began yelling for the trusties and orderlies to form up for the march back to their sections and cell blocks. Hastily Phineas stuck the docket into the file: he could retrieve it whenever he wanted. Now he could see a solution to his problem. Now he could plan.

3

At the western edge of the great sprawl of townships known collectively as Soweto, the road back to the military camp at Lenz led past a number of small farms. Down a track between two of these, in a fold among the mealie fields, Rendle's squad had several weeks ago discovered a small irrigation dam. It had been almost empty then, its muddy bottom hard and cracked at the end of the dry winter months. Now it was half-full after the heavy spring rains, waist-deep with murky brown water, and this afternoon they swam in it. They stripped off their uniforms and went in bare-arsed – all except Lightning, who sat on the roof of the Saracen, rolled himself a joint of dagga and watched the others. Lightning was often the butt of their jokes, and they taunted him as they wallowed and wrestled in the shallows.

'Hey, Lightning, you scared of water?'

'Can't you swim, or what?'

'You ever seen the sea, Lightning?'

''Course I seen the fucking sea,' he retorted. 'Went to Durban once.'

'What, on your old man's yacht?'

'You know I got no old man, Brakpan, you cocksucker. Went with the fucking orphanage, didn't I?'

Their banter was cruel but essentially good-natured, in the way of people who have nothing left to hide from each other. Their time in the bush together had exposed all their strengths and weaknesses. Only Rendle maintained a certain necessary aloofness, and only Nicky Flynn was serious – or conventional – enough to flinch at their crudeness.

Nicky had had enough horseplay after a few minutes, and he left the water and sat naked on the rear deck of the armoured car, letting the late-afternoon sunshine dry him off. Lightning reached down and offered him his *zol*, which Nicky took and puffed at just to be sociable. The stuff had never really turned him on, and he couldn't understand Lightning's passion for it.

Lightning was called that because outwardly he was slow-witted, while inwardly he was a kind of genius. He'd been an orphanage boy, an apprentice electrician and an amateur radio enthusiast, and could work miracles with busted transistor sets and burned-out wall sockets. It was he who had 'bent' the Saracen's VHF transceiver, by switching its circuitry around, so that it worked only when he wanted it to – a fault which a dozen Signal Corps technicians had scratched their heads over. Otherwise Lightning was a gangling uncoordinated oaf who couldn't drill and barely understood the workings of a rifle. He was a standing joke in the barracks, but his strength was that he didn't care: he had a stubborn singlemindedness through which no sense of external order could penetrate.

In silence the two of them sat and watched the antics of the others.

Back in the rookie camp, the Afrikaner instructors had had a name for people like them. They were *kakdroogmakers*. Shit-driers. Troublemakers. Each of them had brought his own kind of trouble with him from home, and they had drifted together the way dissenters paradoxically will, defying the rules imposed on them but creating a set of their own. That was before Rendle had been put in charge of them – Rendle, whose authority they respected because he was the greatest *droogmaker* of all.

Nicky turned to pick his clothes from among the jumble of uniforms in the back of the wagon and saw a solitary black man standing at the edge of the mealie field, about thirty yards away. He stood quite still, as though he'd been there for some time, watching them. When he saw that he'd been spotted he came forward without hesitation. He was young and slender, dressed in jeans and a dark T-shirt and carrying a plastic shopping bag. He stopped a few feet away from the soldiers and smiled.

'Hello. You remember me?'

They didn't. They glanced at each other. The newcomer

41

reached into his plastic bag and, mysteriously, took out a bottle of Viceroy brandy. He tossed it to Nicky, who fumbled and then caught it, two-handed.

'I owe you that, white boys. Remember now?'

It was Lightning who recognized him first. 'Hey! Alex Duma? From that funeral?'

Duma was still smiling. 'I've seen you guys here before. I was waiting for a chance to show my thanks.'

Almost certainly they wouldn't have known Duma if they had passed him on a township street. He was affable and self-possessed, quite different from the wounded, frightened animal they had helped out of trouble on that day back in August.

'You get yourself patched up?' Nicky asked.

'Sure. Got a souvenir to show for it, though.' Duma pulled up the left sleeve of his T-shirt to expose the upper arm and shoulder. Against his brown skin was a rash of darker spots where the flesh was peppered with the unmistakable tiny craters of birdshot. 'Soweto confetti,' he said with a grin. 'Almost like a war medal these days. You going back to your camp now?'

'In a few minutes.'

Nicky set the bottle down and began to get dressed. Duma, clearly in no hurry to go anywhere, sat down on the ground and watched the others horsing around in the water. He knew he was safe enough out here, away from the townships where darkness was his only protection. Sometimes he had to get away from the anger and tension, the constant fear of a knock on the door of one or other of the cramped, crowded houses between which he moved. Sometimes he came out to these fields and just lay about for a whole day, soaking up the sun. That was how he had spotted and recognized this Saracen car and its crew a fortnight ago.

His first instinct had been to lure them into a trap.

Whatever fleeting gratitude he had felt for their pulling him out of danger three months ago was easily cancelled by the knowledge that they were still on the same side as the Boer policemen, still basically his enemies. A party of comrades, an ambush carefully laid . . . there was a wealth of weapons to be captured, and even now his gaze lingered covetously over the R4 automatic rifles and the corporal's Uzi gun stacked beside the vehicle. He had abandoned the idea, however, not least because he was by no means sure it would work. The icy-eyed corporal was anything but a fool. Besides, Duma liked to think of himself as a strategist: the loyalty of these white boys was shaky, and there was something to be said for trying to cultivate them.

Lightning scrambled down off the Saracen's roof and picked up the brandy. 'You saving this for Christmas, or what?' he said to Nicky. He uncapped the bottle, drank some and passed it to Duma.

'You guys don't take your work too seriously, ha?'

'We try to avoid aggro, that's all.' Nicky finished dressing and sat down beside him. 'We mark time. We take any fun we can find.'

'It would be good if there were more like you. Why should you do the Boers' work for them?'

'We don't make the laws, you know.'

'But also you don't enforce them if you can help it. I've watched you. Apartheid is finished, you know: the quicker it is killed off, the better for all of us. You and I, we're all young. Why should we fight over the mistakes old men have made? What's in it for you, except a chance to die sooner than you need to?'

Nicky didn't reply. Watching the others beginning to leave the water and drift back to the Saracen, he knew it was a question they all asked themselves from time to time. Even Carver and Fish, whose thoughts rarely stretched beyond motorbikes and screwing and fighting. Even Brakpan, whose passion for driving fast cars – other people's cars – had had him in and out of reformatories from the age of fifteen. Even Younis the Greek, the tough son of a deported Cypriot nightclub owner, whose ambition was to retire on his poker winnings before he was thirty.

As for Blikkies Steyn . . . it was harder to know what Blikkies thought. As the only Afrikaner in the squad he was the one most at home in the bush, with natural gifts of fieldcraft and camouflage, yet otherwise he had no respect for the traditions of his *volk*. Off on his own as usual, he'd been searching for snakes among the savanna grass at the edge of the dam, the way he always did when he was out in the veld. Hunting with the skill of a mongoose for the den of a ringhals or a puff-adder, pinning it down with the blade of the panga he always carried, teasing it for a while before letting it go. Once he had kept a black mamba in his locker as a deterrent to thieves, and at times he seemed to have more affinity for snakes than for people.

Among this group, Nicky Flynn himself was an odd man out, gratified that they accepted him. They scoffed at his middle-class fastidiousness but looked up to him for his education, casting him in the role of barrack-room lawyer. They gave a hearing to his ideas in a way which his unhappy, hidebound parents never had. It was he who had articulated their grievances along something approaching political lines, though like every political theorist he had found that it took someone else, a leader, to put ideas into effect.

That left Rendle, wading out of the water now, running both hands back through his short black hair to squeeze it dry. Rendle let you know only as much about himself as he wanted to. His family had been British settlers who had moved south from Kenya ahead of the tide of black independence, inhabiting a world of golf-club blazers and sentimental loyalties that he had come to despise. All Rendle had ever wanted to do was fly, and he'd joined the South African Air Force, got his wings and piloted helicopters in Angola. The story about his refusal to destroy a native village had emerged only in bits and pieces, not because he was ashamed but because it was the background to a deeper resentment. Getting kicked out of the air force didn't exempt him from national service, so he'd had to start out all over again as a buck private in the army. In spite of all that there was an odd defiant pride in him: earning promotion, licking this squad into shape, were ways of showing the shitkickers that they hadn't beaten him.

They came back to the wagon in ones and twos, gathering in a naked, dripping circle around their visitor. All of them remembered Duma once he had re-introduced himself. The incident in August had stuck in their memories, as though it marked the point at which their quiet little rebellion had taken its first serious turn.

Rendle, the last to arrive, glanced suspiciously at the brandy bottle now being handed around.

'Just returning a favour, Corporal,' said the black man with a grin. 'Showing that someone appreciates you, ha? Your job must be frustrating.'

'You reckon,' said Rendle neutrally.

'You know you have no real control in the townships. The people may be afraid of your guns, but they have no respect for you. It's the People's Congress they look up to. Nothing personal, my friends, but you are on the losing side. It's part of an inevitable process. Who will ever thank you for standing against it?'

'Nobody, I dare say.' Rendle took a drink from the bottle and passed it along. He fished out his underpants and pulled them on. 'But what's the choice? The People's Congress isn't all sweetness and light. There've been bombs in supermarkets. There've been people burned to death with rubber tyres around their necks because somebody fingers them as police informers.'

'The Congress leadership doesn't approve of such things,' Duma said. 'But there are times when people take matters into their own hands. Excesses are committed in every war. They don't alter the basic justice of our cause.'

'Well, we prefer to stay neutral.'

'Nobody can be neutral in a struggle like this! Some day you'll have to make a choice.'

'What would you like us to do?' said Younis sarcastically. 'Blow our officers away? This isn't the Russian Revolution or something.'

'Or maybe you'd like us to desert,' Brakpan said. 'Duck over the border and go live on coconuts in one of your jungle republics up there.'

'Oh, I know it's not easy for you.' The half-empty bottle had reached Duma again. 'But just consider your own futures. During the guerrilla war up in Zimbabwe, white boys like you were doing more and more military service until they were spending six months of every year in uniform. That's how it could go here, for ten or maybe twenty years. What sort of career does that leave you with? What sort of future? How much of it can you take?'

Half way through dressing, several of the soldiers glanced at each other in silence. Duma knew he had struck a chord familiar to at least some of them, but it was Rendle who said, unexpectedly, 'There is a third choice, and that's just to get out. Leave the country legally and quietly, leave all this shit behind. That's what I'm planning to do.'

'You serious, Frank?' That was Carver, surprised. 'You going to take the gap? The chicken run?'

'There's nothing chicken about wanting to live your own life. If you guys had any sense you'd think about it too.' Rendle sounded faintly irritated, as if regretting that the conversation had taken a personal turn. He was fully dressed now and he glanced at his watch. 'Time to go.' To Duma he said, 'If you came here to indoctrinate us, I think you're wasting your time.'

'Not at all. We were discussing your own interests. What if there was something in it for you?'

'Something in what?'

'Oh, I don't know. I'm just talking loosely. I really came only to thank you. Maybe I'll see you again, white boys.'

'Maybe.' Rendle gave him a curious look. The brandy bottle was in his hand again after doing another round, and he tossed it to the black man. 'Thanks,' he said.

The soldiers gathered their weapons and piled quickly into the Saracen. As it reversed and swung on to the track, Duma stood up and waved. He drank off the remaining inch of brandy and threw the bottle away among the mealies. That had been a good investment, he thought. Contact had been made, a barrier crossed. He'd had a feeling that these white boys were all drifting, looking for something without knowing

46

what. With the right inducement they might yet be very useful.

Judith Rose got back from the clinic to find that her father was already home from his trip. Thank God she'd remembered at the last minute to send the driver to the airport; otherwise she'd have got another of those pained little lectures about inefficiency. Louis Rose had just had his evening swim – thirty vigorous lengths of the twelve-metre pool, never more, never less – and was coming in from the terrace in his bathing trunks, rubbing himself dry. He was in superb physical shape for a man of his age, which was fifty-seven, and his body was almost as firm and certainly as lean as she'd ever known it.

She gave him a perfunctory kiss on the cheek. 'How was Cape Town?'

'I didn't see much of it.'

'What does it take to make Dr Louis Rose travel fifteen hundred kilometres to see a patient? Must be somebody pretty special.'

'Special enough.'

'Give us a clue. A Cabinet minister? An oil sheik? Must be loaded, whoever he is.'

'You know my patients are my own business, Jude. Why don't you go for a swim?'

'I don't think so.'

'You should get more exercise, Snow White. It would put colour in your cheeks.'

She made a face at his retreating back as he padded off through the big drawing room. Even without meaning to, he could always find something to criticize about her. For some years now their relationship had been an uneasy one, with antagonism never far below the surface of the idle banter that formed most of their conversation. It had started, of course, when she had dropped out of her law studies and gone to live with her current lover in a commune of young radicals. The fact that the affair hadn't worked out seemed only to justify her parents' disapproval. Never by word or deed had they suggested that they were disappointed in her in a wider sense – heavens, no, they were far too civilized for that – but it was implicit in some of their attitudes. It really *was* time she got off her backside and found a new place of her own to live.

Judith went to the drinks tray, poured herself a stiff Scotch and slumped into an armchair, staring out at the view across the garden through the open french windows. Her mother, in a straw hat and armed with a trowel, was discussing something with the gardener beside her fearsomely disciplined border of flowering shrubs. Soon she would be coming in to check with Sophie, the maid, on the progress of the dinner, before going upstairs to change. She would ask Judith whether she'd had a good day at work, in the same automatic way she asked her husband, without really listening to the answer. No, Judith would have liked to reply, I've had another day of boredom and frustration doing a shitty little job that Daddy invented for me. I don't know what I was cut out to be, but working as a so-called administrative assistant at the Woodvale Clinic isn't it. I can't even understand the bloody computer that's supposed to be the mainstay of the whole thing, and it looks as though I never will.

Ah, but Mummy wouldn't understand. She would only be hurt and baffled. Why couldn't I settle for being a memsahib myself, Judith wondered, with all my certainties in place? Mummy had never seemed less than content to be a wife, mother and hostess, the gracious companion of a successful and accomplished man. Her life was fulfilled. Perhaps she mildly regretted the absence of her other children – Judith's older brothers were both doctors, one working in New York, the other in Melbourne – but exchanging visits once or twice a year kept them closely in touch. If anything, their being abroad only emphasized the fact that her parents remained saddled with Judith, the youngest and least satisfactory one.

They were not so naïve, of course, as to expect her to settle down and marry some agreeable yuppie from the Anglo-American Corporation. On the other hand, such an attitude would seem more justifiable to them if she were actually pursuing a career of her own. Her trouble, her father had complained more than once, was that she never completed anything she began. First there'd been her abandoned legal studies, then the three years of working as the secretary of a down-at-heel students' union, now this job in the clinic that she was working up the courage to ditch . . . Hell! There was something degrading, at the age of twenty-seven, in living with your parents *and* working for your father. It had been eighteen months now since the commune had broken up and she'd returned – temporarily, to sort herself out, as she had envisaged it – and sheer inertia had prevented her from moving on.

She stood up, poured another whisky and wandered with it out on to the terrace. Her mother had gone indoors, but the gardener was still out there, setting the sprinkler going on a lawn as smooth and perfect as green baize. There was much that was seductive about this life, about shutting up and closing your eyes, though others had rejected it long ago. Uncle Joshua, for instance – not really her uncle but her father's cousin and her godfather, who had still sent her birthday cards until a few years ago, forwarded through London from wherever he now hid out. She'd been only eleven when Joshua had slipped out of the country, and she'd felt angry and betrayed at first, not really old enough to understand the circumstances: the denial of a passport, the several arrests, the twilight world of the banning order under which he'd lived. He had always seemed more fun than her father – more relaxed, less aloof – and even today it was difficult to think of him as a revolutionary. The Joshua Rosenblatt mentioned sometimes as one of the few white men prominent in the liberation movement seemed quite a different person from Uncle Josh – the discrepancy in their surnames merely reinforcing the impression. He had explained once that he'd reverted to using the family's real name not because he wanted to make anything of being a Jew, merely because it seemed less affected. Possibly it also made him sound more proletarian.

Her father naturally disapproved of Joshua and his politics, though he was above being embarrassed by either. Daddy was an old-fashioned liberal, a man of impeccable anti-racist views and unassailable logic: Judith could never win an argument against him. He was what her erstwhile radical friends, and possibly Joshua, would scorn as a man who didn't mind rocking the boat as long as there was no danger of capsizing it.

And herself? Judith couldn't honestly say that she knew where she stood any longer. Her political passions seemed to have fizzled out. She wondered frequently, as she did again now: Why am I so lazy? Why am I so indecisive? Often she sensed as well that the time was approaching for a radical change in her life, but she had no idea what form it might take.

When she returned to the drawing room she found her parents sipping their pre-dinner sherries. Her father was scanning a medical journal, her mother was lost in the arts pages of the *Observer*'s airmail edition. I might as well not be here, she thought. They could lead their chic, cultivated lives quite easily without me. She went to the drinks tray and poured another Scotch.

'Is that your second or your third?' her father suddenly asked.

Judith stood with the decanter still poised over her glass. 'I haven't been counting. Have you?'

'Of course not. I just can't help noticing that you're drinking rather more these days.'

She turned to face him. 'Too much? Is that what you're saying?'

'It was just an observation, Jude. But, since you ask, it isn't considered wise nowadays to drink spirits on a daily basis.'

'Are you talking from a medical or a moral point of view?'

'A medical one, of course. It's a habit that becomes hard to break, even if it doesn't lead on to anything.'

'Into your Drunk Tank at the clinic, you mean? Christ, at the rate you go on I sometimes think you're going to drive me there!'

'Jude, Jude. . . .' That was his misunderstood tone, supported by a shake of the head and the closing of the eyes behind his reading-glasses.

'Judith, don't be so aggressive,' cautioned her mother mildly.

'Well, for Christ's sake! I'm twenty-seven years old and I won't be treated like a child!' She slammed down the glass and marched back out to the terrace. Standing there, staring out at the darkening garden, she felt tears of frustration pricking at her eyes but forced them back. Once again her father had goaded her into an almost adolescent response to what was, on the face of it, an eminently reasonable point of view. That's what you were when you lived with your parents – little more than an overgrown teenager. Perhaps she could put up with that, she thought, if only her father wasn't so monumentally bloody pleased with himself.

Her musing was interrupted by Sophie, emerging cautiously on to the terrace to tell her that dinner was served. She went in to find her parents seated at the table, and the meal proceeded in ritualistic silence. They really don't want me here, she thought, any more than I want to be with them. Tomorrow, without fail, she would start hunting for a flat.

4

The weekly meeting of the State Security Council had been in progress for half an hour before Deputy Minister Frans Hoeksma was called in. Knowing his item was fifth on the agenda, however, he had arranged to be notified in his own office just before he was needed, and so had spent only three or four minutes awaiting his summons in the anteroom beside the presidential chambers. It didn't do one's standing any good to be seen waiting about like a petitioner, and Deputy Minister Hoeksma was strongly conscious of his dignity. He had the kind of plump, pink, youthful looks that were difficult to take seriously; to compensate, he had cultivated a sense of self-importance. While secretaries and clerks wafted and whispered about him, he sat studying a folder from his briefcase with the air of restrained impatience suitable to a man who has no time to waste.

When the Cabinet Secretary called him into the conference room, however, Hoeksma had to mask a certain selfconsciousness. The room was a large one on the top floor of the Union Buildings, overlooking Pretoria. Its walls were panelled in stinkwood, its floor was thickly carpeted. At one end, above the President's place at the head of a long mahogany table, the country's coat of arms, carved in oak, was flanked by flagstaffs bearing its colours of orange, white and blue. This, conspicuously, was the cockpit of the country's power; here, more and more over the recent years of internal crisis and international pressure, decisions crucial to its future had been made. Over the heads of Parliament and even Cabinet, the State Security Council deliberated the grand strategy of the Republic. The dominant smell in the room was of fine polished wood; to Hoeksma it held the tantalizing aroma of power.

He was aware, as he entered, of the critical scrutiny of the dozen older men grouped around the table. For the opinion of the two in uniform – the Commissioner of Police and the Commandant-General of the Defence Force – he did not need to concern himself. Besides the President himself, eight of the others were politicians, and like all of their profession they were wary of young lions in their midst. When Hoeksma had been persuaded to give up a professorship in economics at Stellenbosch University to stand in a safe National Party seat three years ago, it had been on the understanding that early promotion would follow. It should be only a matter of time before he had a full ministerial portfolio; perhaps then to take his place in this room by right, instead of waiting to be invited. What he had to say here this morning might well make a critical difference to his career.

He stopped just inside the door as it closed behind him, inclining his head slightly towards the top of the table.

'Mr President. Gentlemen. Good morning.'

There were a few murmured replies. The President himself merely glanced at him through his rimless spectacles and continued a quiet conversation with the Minister of Justice on his left. Hoeksma walked briskly to the vacant chair beside

52

his own minister and sat down. He took out his folder and waited, attentive and respectful. He had dressed carefully for the occasion in a dark pin-striped suit, tailored like all his clothes to disguise his paunch, a pale blue shirt and a Stellenbosch tie. The tie announced that whatever his reputation as a reform-minded young technocrat – each of those terms suspicious in itself to some of the men gathered here – he remained part of the Afrikaner establishment, a product of the same training ground that had provided the party's intellectual élite since its foundation.

The President faced the table, commanding their attention. He was a heavy-featured man who didn't smile easily, and there was something faintly intimidating about the way the glasses enlarged his gaze.

'Item five on the agenda,' he said. 'Subject: Lincoln Kumalo.'

Hoeksma cleared his throat, but still waited for the invitation to speak. He knew the procedure by now. For the past two years, the matter of Kumalo had been on the agenda at least once a month, though it was only on the last four occasions that Hoeksma had been invited to attend. At the first such meeting he had been asked to take personal control of the case, to familiarize himself with every aspect of it, to report, to recommend, and – by implication, for nobody had said so in as many words – to find a solution.

The plain fact was that the Government for several years had been in a gigantic dilemma over Kumalo. When they had put him in jail all those years ago it had been fairly safe to assume that he would soon be forgotten, a black rabble-rouser who had broken the law and paid the price. Immured behind the grim walls of Robben Island prison, permitted only one visitor every six months, he would soon become a distant memory even to his most ardent followers. So went the theory. In fact precisely the opposite had happened: Kumalo had become famous. In prison he was an embarrassment; out of it, he would be dangerous. Nobody knew what the hell to do with him, and the buck had been passed to Hoeksma. He sensed they had chosen him for the same

53

reasons they were wary of him: he was young, his outlook was modern, he could speak his mind in an uncomfortably realistic way.

They had also given him a brilliant assistant named Tertius Van Straaten. Like Hoeksma himself, Van Straaten was a fashionable young academic plucked from Stellenbosch to be made Deputy Director of the National Intelligence Service. Besides having much in common, each had instantly recognized the usefulness of the other: Hoeksma could advance Van Straaten's career while taking political credit for his ideas. It was just such an idea of Van Straaten's that he was about to put to the test.

'Deputy Minister Hoeksma,' said the President, 'will bring us up to date.'

'Thank you, sir.' He paused. 'First, the matter of Kumalo's health. I am assuming you have all received a copy of the report prepared yesterday by my office.' Several of them nodded. 'Then you'll understand that it's necessary for him soon to have an operation: not a risky procedure, I gather, but a fairly major one. I believe you'll appreciate that it's important to demonstrate to the world that Kumalo is being treated humanely and is receiving the best possible medical care. As it happens, the specialist we have engaged insists on performing this procedure at a private clinic near Johannesburg. I think we should go along with that proposal, subject only to having a government doctor present as an observer—'

'The security problems . . .' He had been waiting for the first objection, and it came from the Commissioner of Police.

'They are in capable hands,' said Hoeksma, 'and I think are thoroughly outweighed by the advantages of doing this as openly as possible. Kumalo's daughter and his lawyer will of course have to be informed that an operation is pending, and I expect a certain number of rumours will get around, but there's no reason why the date and place of the operation shouldn't be kept secret until the last minute. There is another reason, which I'll come to later, for asking you to agree to this. But now I would like to address some of the wider issues which it raises.'

54

He had their full attention. He was well aware that these men had pinned their frustrations as well as their hopes on him and, consciously or not, they identified him with his subject. Like a messenger bearing bad news, he ran the risk of suffering for it.

'As you know, gentlemen, Lincoln Kumalo has been in jail now for twenty-five years. And, as I hardly need to point out, we have been under considerable pressure, both domestically and internationally, to release him. Over the past four years we have made several informal offers to do so, and all of them have been rejected. In the light of these new circumstances, I believe the time is now appropriate to reconsider the position.'

Hoeksma sensed a restless stirring around him, but plunged on. 'In each case he turned down the offer because we attached conditions to it. We said we would let him go into exile, up in Zambia among his comrades in the Congress. We said he could stay here if he agreed not to engage in any political activity. In each case the reply conveyed by his attorney—'

'Ibrahim Khan?' That was the Minister of Justice, forcefully crushing out a cigarette in an ashtray already half-full. 'That bloody Indian has always been a fly in the ointment.'

'Carry on, Mr Hoeksma,' said the President tartly.

'The reply from Kumalo was roughly this: He was jailed under an unjust law, framed by a government whose legitimacy he does not recognize. To accept any form of conditional release would be tantamount to admitting his guilt.

'Let us now look at the reasons why he was jailed: for planning the sabotage of some electricity pylons and for conspiring with others to begin a rebellion which in fact never took place and would have had no chance of succeeding. In view of events that have happened since, in the black townships and elsewhere, these offences look almost insignificant. All the same, he was sentenced to life imprisonment, and under our system that means what it says: life. There is no remission for political offences—'

'I think we all know the background, Frans,' his own minister interrupted, a trifle edgily.

'What I'm getting at is this. . . .' Hoeksma had this off by heart and needed to glance only occasionally at the notes in his folder. 'The whole political climate has changed since those days. There were no Arab terrorists blowing up planes then. There were no bombs exploding in the streets of London or Paris, or even Beirut. No Red Brigades, no IRA. Acts of political violence were the exception rather than the rule. The crimes of a Kumalo could be seen as very serious then, and his political attitudes as revolutionary. Today, in comparison with others on the international scene, Kumalo is a moderate.

'Perhaps it was a natural response to jail him for life, but it tied our hands indefinitely. It's become quite obvious that he's no longer being punished for his crimes, but is being held because we don't know what else to do with him. Every day of his detention he becomes that much more of a living martyr. He's a hero to those people, whether we like it or not.'

They didn't like it. He could feel the groundswell of hostility growing, but he went on.

'We moved him four years ago from Robben Island to Pollsmoor Prison, here on the mainland. That was done for practical reasons of security, but it created a climate of expectation that we were moving towards his release, a belief that this was the first step in that direction. You see, whatever the law may say, it's psychologically almost impossible to believe that a life sentence really is for life. He knows that as well as anyone. The initiative has passed out of our hands and into his.'

'I'm not buying that,' growled the Minister of Justice. 'You seem to be saying that circumstances, outside pressures, are forcing us in a direction we don't need to take.'

'Not quite, if you'll just hear me out—'

'Kumalo has been offered one concession after another. He's been virtually handed the key to his own cell. If he refuses to take it, that's his problem.'

'Respectfully, I beg to differ. It's a problem we have helped to create for ourselves. The longer we do nothing about it, the bigger it will grow.'

'If we let him out unconditionally we'll have a revolution on our hands,' said the Minister of Defence.

'And you think a revolution hasn't already begun?' There. He had spoken as harshly as he dared. 'Out in the townships they believe they are part of a revolution, and Kumalo is their hero. He has their support, almost unanimously – and I don't mean only among the activists and so-called "comrades". Young men who weren't born when he went inside are already repeating his name to their children—'

'All right, Frans,' said his own minister tersely, and he sensed that he was getting carried away. Perhaps he himself had fallen a little under Kumalo's spell.

'What I'm trying to suggest—'

'You seem to be making an excellent case for keeping him where he is,' the Commissioner of Police put in drily.

'No. What I'm saying is that his importance as a symbol cannot be overstressed. But there's another side to that coin: without the symbol, this revolution would lose much of its coherence. We are engaged on our own programme of racial reforms, which in time we hope will cut the ground from under the more radical black elements, those who seek to end white rule altogether. We need to buy that time, gentlemen, and in order to do so we've always known that Kumalo would have to be removed from the equation.

'Up to now our strategy has been to effect his release upon certain conditions – in effect, to let him go while seeing to it that he is politically neutralized. He has seen through that strategy and rejected it. That seems to have left us with two alternatives: to keep him in prison indefinitely or to release him on his own terms and face the consequences. In view of the situation that has arisen over his health, I believe we now have a third choice.'

He paused again, a little theatrically, glancing round the table at their heavy, serious faces. He had primed them well, he thought. They had been stuck for too long in this impasse, while all their instincts favoured *kragdadigheid*, the Afrikaner doctrine of power through action. They were eager to be shown a way out.

'We have an opportunity here,' he said, 'through a set of circumstances that will never arise again, to achieve exactly what we want without appearing to influence events at all. In fact we could seem to be losing rather than gaining. In the meantime it's going to be necessary to eat a certain amount of humble pie. I'm going to ask you here and now to give me a mandate' – Hoeksma took a deep breath, then expelled it – 'to let it be known that Kumalo will be freed by the end of the year—'

The storm of raised voices was like a sudden gale, swamping his words. The Minister of Justice was actually on his feet, almost shouting: 'A ridiculous suggestion . . . grotesque . . .'

'A recipe for disaster!' said the Minister of Defence.

'Gentlemen!' The President's voice was stern, level, penetrating. 'Order, if you please. Let's hear Mr Hoeksma out.'

'I used the words "let it be known", and I used them advisedly,' said Hoeksma with dignity. 'The key to this enterprise is to let him think he has beaten us. In a roundabout way, of course: it can't be made too easy. Anything that happened after that would be coincidental, outside our control.'

'How do you persuade him that he's won?' asked the Commissioner of Police suspiciously.

'We don't have to, General. We have only to convince a few others, beginning with his daughter. How much more do you really want to know, gentlemen?'

It was on that Friday afternoon that Phineas Molefe put his plan into effect.

As he had always known, it was not greatly difficult to steal from the prison dispensary. In the outer room in which he worked was a metal cupboard, usually left unlocked, containing minor medical accessories which he could have pilfered with ease. He was not one of those fools who stole things just

because they were there, however, and he had never considered the risk worth taking. As for the controlled drugs, they
were accounted for down to the last milligram, and sooner or
later would inevitably be missed. The reprisals then would be
severe: solitary confinement, spare diet, a loss of remission
and of his trusty status.

These consequences he had decided to face up to.

At one o'clock, the pharmacist went to lunch in the staff
canteen, locking the back door behind him as usual but
thankfully not bothering even to close the door of the store
cupboard in the outer office. Left to himself for half an hour,
Phineas made his preparations.

He went to the bottom shelf of the cupboard and pulled
out one of several cardboard boxes of empty tablet phials that
were kept there: small brown plastic tubes with snap-on lids
that were used by the hundred every week. From a box
already half-empty he took one of the smallest type, two
inches long by half an inch across. Then he went to the
cabinet where the prescription dockets were filed, and took
out the one that Dr Els had made out for Prisoner 4008 two
days ago. This, too, was something unlikely ever to be
missed. He folded it in two, then rolled it carefully into a
cylinder of just the right size to go into the tablet phial, one
tube fitting snugly around the other. He capped the phial and
slipped it into the pocket of his prison blouse.

Back at the store cupboard, he opened one of the big
hospital-size jars of Vaseline that were kept on an upper
shelf. He skimmed a good-sized blob of the jelly off the top,
smoothing the surface carefully down again before he
replaced the lid. Then, with the Vaseline concealed in his
fist, he left the dispensary and went down the corridor to the
patients' lavatory.

There are few places to hide things in a prison, and none
that are totally secure, but for a couple of hours this would
have to do. Standing on the lavatory seat, Phineas was just
tall enough to lift the lid off the old iron cistern. He scraped
the Vaseline off his hand so that it stuck to the inside edge of
the metal, above the water-line. He dropped the phial into

the cistern and left it to float there. He replaced the heavy lid, flushed the lavatory, left the cubicle, washed his hands and returned to the dispensary.

The next stage would be much trickier. Although Phineas never spent more than a few minutes at a time in the back room with the pharmacist, he knew the exact location of almost every type of drug in the place. He also knew the functions of many of them. After the stocktaking yesterday he even knew how many pills or capsules were contained in each of the big white plastic wholesaler's jars that lined the shelves.

He knew that there were ninety-four five-milligram Dexedrine tablets on a shelf just inside the room to the right. The number hadn't changed for several months.

Dexedrine was an 'upper', one of the amphetamines, still used to treat certain forms of epilepsy but otherwise rarely prescribed nowadays because of its addictive properties. The chances that some of these tablets would be missed, at least until next month's stocktaking, were remote. They were in a screw-top container right across the narrow gangway from the table at which the pharmacist worked. There was no chance of sneaking the jar out, so Phineas would have to depend on creating a diversion: on just the sort of incompetent behaviour, in fact, that his boss expected of him.

He worked on as usual through the afternoon. One of his daily chores was to sweep out the dispensary, and today he had left it late. At a quarter to four he was wielding the broom awkwardly in the narrow space when, with a clumsy swing of the handle, he swept a dozen plastic jars off the shelf beside him.

·The containers were unbreakable. They simply clattered and bounced all over the floor, the pills inside them rolling noisily about. '*Phineas, jou kakhandige doos,*' the pharmacist swore at him mechanically. '*Verskoon, baas, verskoon,*' Phineas pleaded, abandoning the broom, going through a pantomime of apology and amends-making by gathering the jars and dropping half of them again in his haste to replace them. He grinned in embarrassment, bobbing up and down.

On his hands and knees in front of the table, he was below the line of his boss's sight. It took only two or three seconds to unscrew the top of the Dexedrine jar and spill a bunch of the tiny white tablets into his hand. He transferred them swiftly to the pocket of his blouse, replaced the lid of the container and stood up.

He put the Dexedrine container and the others neatly back where they belonged; then he resumed his sweeping, going about it more slowly and methodically than usual to quieten the hammering in his heart, the tablets feeling as though they were burning a hole in his pocket. The pharmacist, counting out some capsules, had long ago lost interest in him.

At five to four Phineas pleaded an upset stomach and asked to visit the lavatory before the return to the cell blocks. Locked into the cubicle, he retrieved the tablet phial from the cistern. Hastily, with fingers made clumsy by fear, he transferred the amphetamines one by one from his pocket into the tube. He replaced the snap-on lid, sealing the tablets in together with the prescription docket. Then he got the blob of Vaseline down from the tank and smeared it evenly all over the phial. He pulled down his shorts and, with practised care, inserted the tube in his rectum.

It was a practice known to every *mugu* as 'bottling'. Only a rigorous strip-search would locate a 'bottled' object, and these were far from routine. Nevertheless, Phineas remained ultra-cautious. There was no going back on what he had done, and it would be stupid to be caught now, before he had begun the second phase of his plan.

He fastened his shorts, flushed the lavatory and trotted out just in time to join the march back to the cells. Now he had a way to authenticate his message, and the means to pay for sending it out. It remained to select a messenger.

5

There was a gaggle of reporters on the platform when Nandi Kumalo's train arrived in Cape Town that Monday evening, but luckily Ibrahim Khan was waiting for her as well and he brushed them aside in his peremptory way, seizing her arm and marching her off as though she herself were a prisoner under escort. On the whole she was grateful to her father's lawyer, even if she found his brusque and quarrelsome nature trying at times. He had a way of getting things done, and that was all that really mattered. His young assistant would follow them with her baggage, he informed her; in the meantime they had an appointment to keep.

For the photographers who ran in front of her she gave a shy, helpless smile. Outside the station there was a small pro-Kumalo demonstration – half a dozen young people, black and white, holding up posters – which the police for reasons of their own, probably connected with the presence of the press, had not broken up. They cheered; Nandi waved, but barely got a glance at them before Ibrahim Khan had steered her to his Mercedes.

She would never get used to these flurries of publicity, she thought, all the more nerve-racking for happening only occasionally. Her mother had handled it all so much better. Her mother had embraced the role cheerfully, with all the courage and defiance that had made her almost as famous a figure as Lincoln Kumalo himself. Since her death, Nandi had felt herself incapable of the same responsibility, perhaps not even worthy of it.

Ibrahim drove in one of his grim silences into the rush-hour traffic of the Foreshore. The last time she had been here, in May, there had been one of those unpleasant Berg winds blowing that produced odd suffocating pockets of warmth within the chill of autumn, but now spring had settled over the Cape. Flowers bloomed on the traffic islands along Adderley Street, and the air was balmy. Nandi remembered that just such an evening had greeted her and her mother the previous November, and the November before that, and she had a sudden depressing awareness of how repetitive one aspect of her life had become. She would make these journeys alone from now on, and how many more of them would there be? How many years would continue to pivot around these six-monthly pilgrimages? She could hardly pretend to enjoy them, and this made her feel awash with guilt. In the popular imagination she was no doubt regarded, since her mother's death, as her father's sole emotional support, but there was a basic flaw in the assumption. She loved Lincoln Kumalo and she was sure he loved her, but he didn't need her in the way he had needed Elizabeth. Nandi had been only one year old when he had first gone to jail; twenty-five years later, it was only an idea of each other that they shared, images seen and spoken to for half an hour through a wall of armoured glass. In a way she dreaded the day when he might be set free, when they would discover that they were strangers to each other.

'Bloody lunatic!'

Ibrahim abruptly ended his silence to yell at a motorcyclist who had swerved in front of him. It was only now that Nandi realized he was driving them in a strange direction. Instead of heading for his office behind the Parade or his house at Elsie's River where she was to spend the night, they were travelling out along the Table Bay shore towards the white suburb of Sea Point. She recollected that he'd said something about an appointment.

'Where are we going, Ib?'

'To see a representative of our esteemed government. A deputy minister, no less.'

'You might have warned me!' she said indignantly.

'I got a call just this morning. There was no way I could let you know.'

'Well, maybe I don't want to see any deputy minister. What does he want anyway?'

'Now, now, don't be hasty, Nandi.' Ibrahim had known

63

her since she was a young girl, and sometimes talked to her as though she still was. 'His name is Hoeksma. Know anything about him?'

She shook her head sulkily. The name was vaguely familiar, nothing more.

'He's one of their bright young men, supposedly. A so-called *verligte*, one of the forward-looking ones. It seems he has a particular interest in your father's case. He happens to be in Cape Town and he'd welcome the chance to meet both of us, strictly informally and off the record.'

'Ib, I have just spent twenty-eight hours in a train and I was looking forward to relaxing. I have no wish to exchange pleasantries with my father's jailers.'

Ibrahim said nothing for a few moments. They were stuck in a traffic jam. He fished in his pockets for cigarettes and lit one, then flicked on the radio, *boeremusiek* blaring out at full volume from Radio Good Hope. He glanced at her and put a warning finger to his lips; the cantankerous surrogate uncle was also a crafty lawyer, the veteran of dozens of political trials and well used to subterfuge. It was not the least bit unlikely that his car was bugged.

He eased the Mercedes forward. He spoke very quietly, beneath the squawking of the radio rather than over it. 'Actually, I don't believe a word he said. I think they've got something up their sleeves. I have a feeling they're going to make another offer.'

'To . . . release him?'

'Maybe.'

Nandi felt her heartbeat quicken. She stared at Ibrahim as though searching for hope in his beaky Indian profile.

'Well?' She spoke too loudly, and he hushed her again. 'Well, Ib, tell me more.'

'There's nothing I can put my finger on. I just thought I should warn you. You know his health hasn't been of the best lately, and it could be tied up with that. You mustn't expect them to offer anything realistic, Nandi. You mustn't expect it to be anything Lincoln could accept. Every time they've produced conditions. Every time they've used different words to say the same thing. They want him politically castrated. If you'll forgive the expression,' Ibrahim added in a sudden moment of Muslim prudishness. 'However, we have a duty to listen to what they say.'

She sagged back in her seat. Of course. What else should she have thought? Even the surge of hope she had experienced made her feel somehow unworthy again, as though it were a tacit betrayal of what her father had fought for. Other, lesser men, his contemporaries in the struggle, had accepted conditional release over the years as they felt their lives trickling away from them, as they yearned to end their days sitting in the sun. But not Lincoln Kumalo. Twenty-five years had done nothing to blunt his will. It was that which had earned him the unstinting devotion even of the young township radicals like Duma.

Perhaps she would be happier herself if she could share that singleminded obstinacy. Nandi had had an oddly sheltered upbringing, her mother seeking to shield her from the harsher realities of her own life: the bannings, the arrests, the midnight knocks on the door. There'd been the boarding school in Swaziland, the college in Zambia, postgraduate studies in Baltimore and Edinburgh: with a name like hers, you could pick up grants and scholarships like acorns. Now, pursuing her career as a social worker in Soweto as unobtrusively as her circumstances allowed, she was fashioning a life for herself that did not depend on her being the daughter of Lincoln Kumalo. It was something of which she found herself surprisingly jealous.

They were driving along Beach Road, tall hotels and the apartment blocks of white people on one side, the sun melting into a darkly glittering sea on the other. Suddenly she said: 'Why does this Hoeksma want to see me?'

'Why not?'

'I mean you've always handled the negotiations over my father before. They've never consulted me. What's different this time?'

'I suppose we'll soon find out,' said Ibrahim, lighting

65

another cigarette. He always smoked a lot more when he was nervous.

Because they were not political, or 'security' prisoners, the forty or so inmates of Cell Block C, Black Male, were permitted an hour each evening of free association. This meant that after their supper and before lock-up time they were allowed to wander in and out of the four large cells that made up the block and to mingle in the corridor that connected them. This was the high point of the day, a period in which gossip was exchanged, friendships and sexual alliances were formed and enmities were sharpened. There was also frantic trading in prison commodities: tobacco for chocolate, soap for jam, sugar for sewing thread. Smuggled dagga changed hands for hard cash. Some prisoners played cards, others mended their clothes or listened idly to the blander kind of township pop music that was piped through the loudspeakers. The literate ones might read for the hundredth time the last letter that had filtered through to them from the censor.

In Phineas Molefe's cell a deadly serious poker school met each evening to win or lose a fortune in cigarettes. Phineas rarely joined in. Tonight some of the players observed him lying on his bunk paging through the Gideon Bible, the only printed reading matter in the cell.

'Suddenly you have found religion, Phineas?' one of them chaffed.

'You think God going to get you out of here?' called another. The little man ignored them. Attending to their game, they did not notice that he was not just reading but copying from the Bible, concentrating furiously, cross-referring from one section to another and writing with a chewed pencil-stub on a small yellow sheet of paper. When he had finished, with ten minutes to go before lock-up, he studied his efforts critically. Then he rolled up the paper, stuffed it into a small plastic tube and put the cap on. From among the few possessions he kept under his mattress – practically the only storage space that existed in the cell – he

66

took a battered half-used tube of toothpaste that had been rolled up from the bottom. Equipped with these two items, he stood up and strolled out of the cell.

Phineas had done much quiet research since Friday in preparation for the next stage of his plan. By subtle questioning he had learned something of the routines of the gangs who laboured outdoors in the prison grounds, for he needed not only a messenger but one who could be guaranteed to be in the right place at the right time; a man, as well, who could be trusted not to talk foolishly afterwards. Now he made his way past the gossips in the corridor to the cell at the end, stood in the doorway and called to a man who lay on his bunk in the corner, staring vacantly at the ceiling.

'Bobbejaan!'

The man sat up, blinking at him. Phineas beckoned, and he got off the bunk and shuffled out, frowning. Bobbejaan in fact looked more like a gorilla than the baboon for which he had been nicknamed. He was not tall but immensely strong and very black. His shaven head rested on a neck so short and thick it was almost invisible. His body was barrel-shaped, two hundred pounds of sheer gristle, and his hands could have strangled an ox. Everyone was wary of him, even the warders; although his temper was generally mild, he was reputed to be like a furious bull when roused. He had been a stevedore in the Cape Town docks; it was said he had gone berserk there once, almost killing a white foreman who had pushed him too far, and that it had taken eight policemen to subdue him.

'I greet you, Bobbejaan. Are you well?'

'I'm well, little Phineas.' They spoke in Sotho, their mutual language, not much understood by the other prisoners who were mostly Xhosas.

'There's something I want you to do for me, Bobbejaan. I'll pay you well for it, provided it remains a secret between us.'

'What thing is this, little brother?'

'I'll give you this, now, to show that I trust you.' He opened his palm to show the crumpled toothpaste tube. 'There are forty pills in here, Bobbejaan. Forty Dexies.'

67

'Forty?'

'And forty more when you've done what I ask. As long as you're careful what you do with them.'

Phineas had been rather alarmed, when he counted them, to find he had stolen eighty-one of the amphetamines, leaving only thirteen in the container. But there was no way of replacing any. Working under the blanket on his bunk, he had divided his hoard and concealed it in two separate batches. He had slit the toothpaste tube open, squeezing out some of the paste to make a pocket large enough to take half the tablets. The other half he had wrapped tightly in a twist of paper and sewn into the hem of the blanket.

Bobbejaan's gaze had brightened with astonishment. He was an animal, a slow-witted but a cunning one. His sexual appetite was voracious, and when he'd come to jail he had redirected his desires without a second thought from women to attractive young men. Eighty Dexedrine tablets would buy him untold favours.

'What is this thing you want?' he asked, and Phineas began to explain. Five minutes later, when the section warders returned and began to yell at everyone to return to their cells, the deal had been struck. To any casual watcher it looked like an ordinary cell-block barter. Bobbejaan took the toothpaste and the innocuous tablet phial with its bit of paper inside; he had his instructions, though he was ignorant of their purpose.

'One other thing,' said Phineas sternly. 'These are important people that we do this for. If you fail, or if you only pretend to do what I ask, they will know. It will go badly for you.'

Bobbejaan seemed impressed at this bit of bluff. As for Phineas, he went back to his cell as satisfied as he could be. There was a chance that he would be considered no more than a madman, but he had done what he could for the Leader. Now he could only mark time before retribution came.

The sitting room of the top-floor suite in the President Hotel was dominated by a vast picture window. The view over Table Bay was splendid in spite of the failing light, and dead in the middle of it was the dark hump of Robben Island, where

Lincoln Kumalo had spent the first twenty years of his imprisonment. That they had chosen this as a meeting place seemed to confirm something Nandi had always thought about Afrikaners: they had no sense of irony. And, then, as if to reinforce the point, Colonel Prinsloo had been present.

Long ago, Prinsloo had haunted her childhood like a bogyman. It was he who had been responsible for enforcing her mother's various banning orders, he who knocked on their door in the night, never discourteous but always with an air of menace beneath his grudging politeness. He had watched over her family like a malevolent spirit, and now here he was again, seeming oddly out of place in these surroundings, in the company of little Mr Hoeksma. She had frozen at the sight of him and should have walked out right then, but somehow the moment had passed and she'd found herself being steered to a seat at a coffee table. Luckily, Prinsloo seemed no more talkative than she was, and all the conversation had been between Hoeksma and Ibrahim. But whose idea of a friendly chat was this? And what was its purpose?

'Of course,' Deputy Minister Hoeksma was saying, 'I have never had the privilege of meeting Lincoln Kumalo, but I sometimes feel as though I know him rather well. I've studied him at a distance. Speaking in a personal capacity, I have to say that it's a matter of profound regret that a man of such brilliance should languish in prison.'

'Then, why not just let him out?' demanded Ibrahim.

'If it were left to me . . .' Hoeksma made a helpless gesture as if to say: Who knows what might be possible? 'The political reality is that he's made it very difficult for us.'

'The way he sees it is that you've made it impossible for him.'

'There were conditions, of course. There had to be conditions.'

If there was any point to this discussion, Nandi thought, they were not yet close to it. They had been here fifteen minutes and the deputy minister had stuck to generalities, politely parrying the lawyer's sharp little barbs. Yet Ib's

69

prediction that this was to be more than a casual meeting had been borne out by the manner of their reception. A terribly polite young white man had met them as they parked their car, led them to a side entrance of the hotel and whisked them up in a private lift. There was no sign that anyone was living in the suite, so it had been booked for this purpose alone. The young secretary, if such he was, had served them drinks from a bar in the corner, and then vanished.

In a different frame of mind she might have found the contrast between Hoeksma and Prinsloo comical, the one small and plump, the other tall and lean. Endomorph and ectomorph. Hoeksma had been at pains to welcome them and thank them for coming, and certainly he was an unlikely-looking antagonist, with his pink cherub cheeks and his prim little cupid's-bow mouth. Like most of his breeding and generation he spoke precise faultless English, and he looked as though he might be more at home in a European drawing room than in the parlours of his Cape rural constituents.

Prinsloo, sitting on the sofa beside him, on the other hand, was one of those lanky, narrow, taciturn Afrikaners who looked so much like hillbillies that they sometimes surprised you with the sharpness of their wits. He had big bones and coarse peasant features, and his eyes were brown without warmth. They were angry eyes, Nandi thought, steady, knowing and cynical. Again she wondered what he was doing here.

'Mr Kumalo,' said Hoeksma judiciously, 'has always rejected our conditions. But it's struck me that he has never really said – or at least you as the intermediary have never said – what he found wrong with them.'

'What was wrong was that you tried to impose conditions at all. His position remains what it always has been: either he comes out as a completely free man or he stays where he is.'

'But politics is the art of compromise, surely? If we can shift our position, why can't he?'

'He doesn't see that you've made any shift, fundamen-tally.'

'Come on, Mr Khan! Three years ago we were offering to free him provided he left the country—'

'And he said he would catch the first plane back.'

'A year later we made another offer. We said: All right, go free, stay here, just don't engage in any political activity. That, too, he rejected. We've gone more than halfway towards meeting him. The Government has taken political risks with its own electorate . . .' Hoeksma suddenly looked deeply despondent in the way only a fat man can. 'Are you sure he's really in touch with what's been going on outside that prison? Twenty-five years is a long time. If he knew of the improvements that have taken place, the repeal of so many discriminatory laws—'

'He sees them as so much cosmetic surgery,' said Ibrahim with a shrug. He lit another cigarette. 'Measures designed really to strengthen and perpetuate the system rather than end it. To hide its essential ugliness.'

Hoeksma sighed, as if aware that they were talking across an unbridgeable gulf. He took a sip of his whisky and turned to Nandi. 'How do you feel about all this, Miss Kumalo?'

'Naturally I would like to see my father go free. But only on his own terms.'

'You know, I believe there is always some middle ground between two points of view. There is always something, no matter how small, on which opponents can agree: a starting point. You're due to visit him tomorrow, not so? Would you convey a message to him?'

Was this where the conversation had been leading? She said stiffly, 'If you think I have any influence over him, you're wrong.'

'I don't think that. There are personal circumstances involved, and the message might be better received from his closest relative than through official channels.' Hoeksma leaned forward, straining to show his sincerity. 'What I am saying now must not go beyond the four of us in this room – unless, that is, you agree to convey it to Lincoln Kumalo. Is that acceptable?'

71

She glanced at Ibrahim and got an encouraging nod. 'All right.'

'You know that his health has been causing some concern?'

'We know that he has prostate trouble,' Ibrahim answered for her. 'I've tried to get more details from the prison authorities and met with a good deal of obstruction.'

'We haven't wanted – we still don't want – alarmist rumours to get about. Besides, the diagnosis was only confirmed a few days ago. The position is that he has a tumour . . .'

Nandi gasped. 'Cancer?'

'Please don't let it frighten you. It's not as serious as it may sound. It's a small tumour, it's been detected in good time and it will be operated on before the end of the year. There's every reason to believe he'll make a full recovery. That's as much as he knows at present, and as much as I'm at liberty to tell you.'

Nandi sat rigid. 'That's ridiculous!' Ibrahim protested. 'We have a right to more information than that.'

'Actually you don't, Mr Khan, but that's not an argument I want to get into . . .'

'You're going to carry out an operation on him in secret? You need permission from his next of kin, at the very least.'

'There are questions of security involved,' Hoeksma said, with a faint uneasy glance at Prinsloo. 'And you should know, Mr Khan, that since all prisoners are the legal responsibility of the Government no permission is required from their relatives for any medical procedure. They may be consulted as a matter of courtesy, but they have no *locus standi*.'

'But . . .'

'Please let's not get sidetracked. What I have to say is this. After the operation there will be a convalescent period of up to two weeks. In similar circumstances in the past, where a prisoner has served the bulk of a long sentence, and where it appeared that his age and overall condition warranted it – in these cases, consideration has sometimes been given to his release on medical, or humanitarian, grounds.'

Nandi gave Ibrahim Khan a startled look. It was he who was quicker on the uptake. 'What are you saying? Unconditional release by another name?'

'Please don't put words into my mouth, Mr Khan. I'm saying that there are precedents for the release of a prisoner under these conditions. Let me ask you this, Miss Kumalo. Leaving all other considerations aside, does your father in his heart and soul not want to get out of that prison? Isn't he trapped there by circumstances which are not, in a way, of his own making? Just as we are prevented from releasing him on his own terms? A discharge on medical grounds could, subject to certain understandings, solve the dilemma for both of us.'

'That would be your own decision,' said Ibrahim. 'You wouldn't need his agreement.'

'In ordinary cases, no. From him, we would want an assurance that he would accept this for exactly what it would be: a medical discharge, nothing more or less. We'd want no talk of an unconditional release.'

'But that would be a condition in itself,' Ibrahim objected. 'I can see that it would save face for you, and for that reason I can't see him agreeing to it.'

'Ib, surely . . .' Nandi stifled her words at a look from Ibrahim. He said calmly to Hoeksma, 'You spoke of certain understandings. What would they be?'

'All we ask for now is an agreement in principle that he would not say no if he were officially offered a discharge after his operation. In due course we could come to a wink-and-nod arrangement permitting him to engage in any political activity that was within the law.'

'The same law that sent him to jail?'

'You know things have changed since then, Mr Khan.'

'In theory, perhaps.' She knew now that Ibrahim was being querulous merely on principle. She couldn't think why, but he seemed oddly pleased with himself. 'In practice, Lincoln Kumalo has always maintained that the only real change will be a change to majority rule, and that means black rule. Are you saying you're ready to face that possibility, Mr Hoeksma? Are you, Colonel Prinsloo?'

Prinsloo stirred his long frame on the sofa. He looked as though he disliked Ibrahim. Perhaps he just disliked everyone, but certainly in a man of his make-up there would be a natural

73

antipathy to smart-talking Indian lawyers. He spoke for almost the first time.

'All that interests me, sir, is safeguarding the security of this country. Lincoln Kumalo has come to seem a safer bet than the crowd who run his Congress from up in Lusaka. The external leadership of such a movement is always more extreme than those on the ground. The Congress is also infiltrated by communists up there, who have far bigger ambitions than majority rule.'

He lapsed disconcertingly back into silence, almost as though his speech had been a set-piece, rehearsed for the occasion. Hoeksma took up what seemed to be the thread of his argument: 'We're not as short-sighted as you may imagine us to be. We recognize that fundamental change must come. We don't even ask any longer to dictate the process of that change, simply to prevent the process from falling into the hands of extremists. Miss Kumalo . . .?' He directed all his attention to her, sensing the hope that had fluttered again like a trapped bird inside her. 'We want your father's co-operation. We recognize that he can't afford to compromise, and we're no longer asking him to. Is it worth years more of wrangling over his future for the sake of one small concession? I ask you to put it to him as a human being: Does he want to breathe free air again? Will you ask him that?'

She nodded numbly. 'I'll ask,' she said.

Three minutes later they were leaving the hotel. In the lift on the way down they did not speak, and in the darkness of the car park Ibrahim seized her arm and turned her to face him.

'We're going to get him out, Nandi!'

'But you said he would refuse . . .'

'Of course he'll refuse to go along with this piffling arrangement! Why should he agree to it? Don't you see? They've played their last card, and it's a loser. Once he says no to this they'll have nothing more to offer!'

'They can always keep him in jail,' she said pragmatically.

'They didn't even threaten that! They've made up their minds. They've finally decided that Lincoln Kumalo is more trouble in prison than out of it. I'm certain of it. They're going to let him go. They'd rather it looked like a magnanimous gesture than a defeat, that's all.'

Ibrahim's mood remained buoyant all the way home. It affected Nandi as well, lightening her spirits , but she worried over why she couldn't share fully in his optimism. Ib had never been wrong in his assessments of these matters, and she trusted his judgement completely. Maybe after all these years she simply couldn't dare to believe in this.

6

Judith Rose pecked tentatively, one-fingered, at the keyboard of her computer terminal.

She typed in her initials and user's password and saw them appear on the status line at the bottom of the screen, giving her access to the system. She tapped the control and the command key for the computer's main directory and got a list of headings on the screen. She tapped A, the command key for Accounts, and was presented with a second list of subheadings. So far, so good. Today was the day she'd promised herself she would master the bloody thing.

Although there was plenty of high-tech medical equipment in its operating theatre and small laboratory, the Woodvale Clinic had until recently managed without a computerized office system. The clinic had only twenty-four beds, including eight in the separate building that housed the Substance Abuse Unit: the Drunk Tank, as Judith referred to it. It stood in two hectares of gardens twenty-five kilometres north of Johannesburg, and her father liked it to have the atmosphere of a well-run country hotel, with modern comforts but old-fashioned standards. Personal service was one of the things that appealed to its patients, many of them elderly, all of them well heeled.

Eventually, however, the pressure to simplify and speed up the administrative work had become irresistible, and once the system was installed Dr Rose himself, naturally, had learned

75

it inside out in the course of a weekend. Like all people who assimilate knowledge without effort, he was impatient of anyone who couldn't.

It was, after all, as he took care to point out to Judith, a simple 64K database system of the sort kids were using in school these days. Well, not at the kind of classy little girls' academy she had attended, they weren't. Far from making her work easier, the computer had so far merely complicated it.

Take this business she was about to attempt now, of moving data from one file to another. Patients who didn't settle their accounts on departure – and no one at the Woodvale Clinic was so discourteous as to insist that they should – had their names transferred to a different file that was programmed to issue bills at the end of each month. Well, she thought, here goes.

She used the cursor to select a subheading: PATIENT ACCOUNTS, CURRENT. She tapped the READ key, and the screen obligingly produced an alphabetical list of names and addresses. She hunted for SWITCH, and found it, and the list moved to the left of the screen. She scrolled it up and down a couple of times, in a sort of victory roll at this success.

At the top of the list was Mr Ahlers, who had been discharged yesterday. He would have to be moved to OUT-STANDING.

She had begun celebrating too soon. How the hell did you call up the OUTSTANDING file without losing the CURRENT one? She pressed the CONTROL key and the one marked HELP.

The screen went blank.

After a second a flashing message appeared near the bottom: USER ERROR. TRY AGAIN.

'Shit!' she said aloud.

Yvonne came through from the reception area with a knowing smile on her face. Yvonne was a nineteen-year-old Coloured girl whose work hardly involved the computer but who seemed to have an intuitive grasp of its functions.

'What is it this time?'

'This bloody thing is going to give me a nervous breakdown.'

76

Yvonne sat down beside her and deftly manipulated the keys. She got the two lists lined up side by side on the screen and explained: 'You got to use DELETE BLOCK and INSERT. But first you've got to define the block of materials you want moved.'

Under Yvonne's guidance she got the entry lined up for transfer. She pressed a sequence of keys. Mr Ahlers and the details of his stay in the clinic vanished from one side of the screen but did not reappear on the other.

'You've done it in the wrong order. You've lost Mr Ahlers!'

It was true. When they went back to the beginning and repeated the sequence of commands, Mr Ahlers had disappeared from the register. They began to giggle. Mr Ahlers was a frequent resident of the clinic's eight-bed Substance Abuse Unit, and now there was no record of his latest stay.

'Mr Ahlers no longer exists!' chortled Yvonne. 'Mr Ahlers has gone to the great cocktail bar in the sky!'

'Oh, well, nobody will miss the old piss-artist.' They were hysterical as schoolgirls. 'Now, before I kill off anyone else . . .'

'Better try something simpler. Try keying in some reservations.'

Yvonne found the BED AVAILABILITY file for her. It held daily bed-reservation charts for the next three months and could be moved back and forth at the touch of a button. But now Judith's fingers were all thumbs, and instead of tapping the SCROLL key she touched SEND. The Epson printer in the corner began to buzz, and an endless sequence of pages started rolling up the screen. She had ordered the computer to print out ninety sheets of totally useless information. There was no stopping it until it reached the end.

Yvonne sighed. 'Let's face it, Judith. You really aren't computer-literate.'

'*Now* what have I done?'

The screen was still scrolling up pages, but in this particular batch there were blank spaces between them, with a single word that kept rolling from bottom to top: DELETED – DELETED – DELETED. It happened eight or ten times before the charts moved forward once more in their regular sequence.

Puzzled, Yvonne went over to the printer. She waited till the machine caught up with the backlog of material it was processing, then said: 'It's nothing you've done. Someone has cut Ward A out of the reservations schedule for a while. Eleven days, in fact. From December the fifteenth to . . . yes, the twenty-fifth. Looks as if your father is closing the ward down over Christmas.'

'Whatever for?'

'Who knows? He was working on the computer yesterday, while you were out flat-hunting. Putting stuff into his personal file, I assumed. Maybe he deleted those pages then, or simply transferred them for his own use.'

'It would be nice if he'd let us know these things.'

Yvonne looked baffled. Judith shrugged. Her father would no doubt clear up the mystery when it suited him.

Yvonne went back to reception and Judith returned to safer pastures, preparing handwritten invoices for the outstanding accounts. So much for technology. Any further thought that she might have given to the missing ten days in Ward A's schedules were banished by a phone call a few minutes later. It was from one of the estate agents she had been to see yesterday. There was a flat that might interest her, over in Northcliff, available at the end of the month.

One mile short of Pollsmoor, Ibrahim Khan's Mercedes was admitted without formality through the first of the outer security barriers. At the next one, guarding the inner precincts, he had to turn into the visitors' car park and leave Nandi to walk on alone to the big stone gateway.

It was an improbable setting for a prison, she had always thought. Rich and gentle scenery lay all around it. Vineyards and orchards climbed the slopes of the mountain in the background, and the prison itself did not disgrace the view. At least, not from a distance. The main building looked like a great country house, a château perhaps, positioned well up the mountainside the better to overlook its estates. Even the gangs of convicts in the fields might have passed for contented peasants labouring in a beautiful landscape. It was only when you drew closer that you saw the bars on the windows and the machine-gun positions on the roof and the whole place, its very existence, seemed incongruous.

She was frozen with apprehension. For the first time she would be seeing Lincoln Kumalo without her mother present. For the first time all his attention would be on her, and she wondered what he would make of her. Against this the question of how he would respond to the offer Deputy Minister Hoeksma had made, even Ibrahim's belief that he would soon be released anyway, had almost faded into the background.

In the office beside the gates she produced her authorization to visit and went through the rigmarole of recording her name and address and being issued with a visitor's tag. The warders knew quite well who she was, and their manner was icily correct. A white wardress examined the contents of her handbag and gave her a brisk body-search before escorting her to a minibus for the next stage of the journey, to the wall surrounding Maximum Security itself. Here she passed through another control post where two more warders took charge of her, leading her across a concrete-paved gap overlooked by watchtowers and in through a grim steel doorway. This was a prison within a prison, and once she had penetrated this far into the place she sometimes had the uneasy feeling that she might never get out. The door was opened, then slammed and locked behind them. She and her escort were surveyed by a television monitor before someone deep inside the building pressed a button and another steel door rumbled automatically open in front of them. They stepped through into the familiar passageway that led to the visiting area. The door slid shut behind them.

At the end of the passage she was admitted to a room where the cheerful middle-aged head warder who was usually in charge here wished her good morning and nodded a dismissal to her escort. She was suddenly too nervous to speak, a lump in her throat and her legs turning to jelly. The room was long, narrow and bare, with cameras high up in the corners, divided exactly down the middle by a counter with a partition of thick bulletproof glass rising to the ceiling. Half a dozen chairs were drawn up to face the counter. To allow conversation, a telephone handset was placed in front of each chair, its cable connected to another behind the glass. It was assumed that everything said would be automatically recorded.

She was the only visitor, and there was only one prisoner sitting behind the barrier, with a single warder for an escort. Lincoln Kumalo rose to greet his daughter.

Nandi was always oddly surprised to rediscover what a big man her father was. Well over six feet tall, deep-chested and wide-shouldered, he dwarfed the little white warder who stood behind him. A century ago he would have been a splendid Zulu warrior; in his sixties now, he still had an aura of sheer physical power that was undoubtedly part of his magnetism. He was a lion of a man, still revered by the young in a way that could never have happened if he'd been some dry little intellectual.

He gave her a grin of delight. She stumbled forward, weak-kneed, and they mimed a kiss through the glass.

'Nandi . . .,' he mouthed, and then, realizing he couldn't be heard, seized hold of the telephone. 'Nandi . . .'

The longing to hold him, the surge of affection that couldn't be physically expressed, was always the worst part. She sat down hastily, fumbled for the telephone receiver, clamped it to her ear and heard his rich Zulu chuckle, oddly disembodied but as light as ever. 'Nandi, how are you?' And then, suddenly, as had happened before, she found herself with nothing to say. Tears welled from her eyes and ran hotly down her cheeks. All she could think, for the moment, was: I am not worthy.

Outside, in the car park, Ibrahim Khan supposed that he ought to be enjoying the fresh air. He wandered restlessly around the small enclosure in the sharp spring sunshine, smoking and glancing every few minutes at his watch. A bundle of raw nerves most of the time, Ibrahim had never been much good at waiting. He also found it difficult to compromise, which was not good for a lawyer. It had lost him more battles than it had won, but it had made him the natural choice as the defender of causes that were half-lost already. His reputation had been made almost solely in political trials: very often a process of taking one step forward and two steps back. No sooner had you blown a hole in one of their security laws than they passed another to fill in the gap. It wasn't even a paying business.

While he paced the carpark, Ibrahim had been idly watching a gang of convicts moving towards the fence across the nearest of the vegetable plots. They were black men, half a dozen of them in the charge of a single white warder; low-security prisoners, no doubt, dressed in khaki shorts and blouses, and barefoot. They were planting potatoes, two of them at the head of the line using spades to open a neatly furrowed drill, two more on hands and knees behind them, setting and covering the tubers in the soil, while another pair brought up the rear with a wheelbarrow. They chattered and laughed as they worked, seeming more carefree than they had any reason to be.

Ibrahim turned away, glancing at the sinister bulk of the prison half a mile off, checking his watch again. Nandi's visit would be halfway through, and he didn't relish meeting her afterwards. She would be emotionally drained, and like most men he was not very adept at dealing with a woman's feelings. Besides, he knew she was not entirely convinced by his arguments; she had been inclined to take Hoeksma's offer of a medical discharge for her father at face value, and would be upset when Lincoln turned it down.

'Mister!'

The voice came from behind him. Not quite a whisper, low but clear, a bass African voice raised just loud enough to draw his attention. He turned in surprise and saw that the group of convicts had worked their way closer to the fence. One had moved ahead of the others, digging faster than they could plant, and was only twenty feet away, leaning on his

81

spade. He stood facing Ibrahim but kept glancing back at the rest of the gang and the warder dawdling behind them.

'Mister! Come to the wire.'

The man spoke in the same level tone, suppressing urgency beneath his words. He had a shaven head, a heavy, simian face and a stocky, powerful body. As Ibrahim stared at him, he went on throwing backward looks at the others. One of the men with the wheelbarrow said something to the warder, diverting his attention briefly. The convict left his spade and trotted quickly towards the fence.

'Mister!' He called openly and loudly now. 'You got cigarettes, mister?' His expression was serious, at odds with the casual nature of the request. Ibrahim moved towards the man, but within a second the warder was yelling from behind him.

'*Bobbejaan! Wat maak jy daar?*'

The man reached the barbed wire and thrust his hands out, palms up in a begging attitude. 'Mister, you got cigarettes for a poor *mugu?*' He glanced round at the warder, loping down the furrow now, pulling the truncheon off his belt.

'*Kom weg van daai draad, Bobbejaan! Weg!*'

Ibrahim regained his presence of mind. His work had made him alive to the uses of subterfuge, and he understood that within this man's odd behaviour there was a core of logic. The convict was trying to tell him something. Whatever it was was connected in some way with his plea for cigarettes.

Ibrahim hastily pulled out his packet of twenty Rothmans and began to tip smokes into his palm.

'The packet, man, the packet!' the convict hissed. The warder was almost on top of him now, roaring and swearing. Ibrahim thrust the whole thing at him, spilling cigarettes on the ground, spotting as he did so something the man held in his hand, a little brown plastic tube clasped between his thick index and middle fingers. He slipped it into the flip-top box and closed it just as the warder swung his truncheon and fetched him a crack on the side of the head.

'*Jou moer, Bobbejaan!*'

The prisoner lurched back from the fence, dropping the packet. The warder grabbed him by the shirt collar and hit him again. The convict staggered, regained his balance and for a moment seemed about to retaliate. His nostrils flared and his bloodshot eyes were dilated with rage. The warder stepped back a pace, but went on yelling at him.

'*Jy gaan kak vreet, hoor jy . . .?*'

'He was only asking for cigarettes,' Ibrahim protested.

'It's not allowed.' The warder glared at him through the wires. 'It's not allowed, and he knows it.'

The prisoner was an awesome figure, his bare feet planted firmly apart in the soil, his huge hands bunched into claws. He looked as though he could have broken the warder over his knee, but he didn't move. Blood was running from a gash above his ear. The Rothmans packet lay a foot inside the fence, Ibrahim not daring to draw attention to it.

The rest of the convicts had gathered round them in a cautious semicircle, and now they parted as someone else approached. He was a sergeant who had crossed the field from another work gang. He exchanged some words in Afrikaans with the warder, then spoke to Ibrahim.

'Don't you know you can't give anything to a prisoner without permission?'

'He asked me for cigarettes. I didn't see any harm in giving him a few.'

'He'll be put on a charge for talking to you. We could charge you as well. What are you doing here?'

'I gave a lift to a visitor.' Ibrahim had all his wits about him now. It was obvious that neither of these two knew who he was – why should they know? – and there was no point in enlightening them. It would only cause complications. Although his instinct was to quarrel with them, he said humbly: 'I didn't know about your regulations. I'm sorry.'

The two white men gave each other a look. 'All right, forget it this time,' said the sergeant. 'But remember it well for the future. Go and wait in your car. That way you'll keep yourself and others out of trouble. *Gee hom t'rug sy sigarette,*' he said to the warder.

The man picked up the Rothmans packet and passed it through the wire. Ibrahim took it with a suitable show of gratitude. The prison officers turned and herded the convicts away from the fence, the big man called Bobbejaan shambling off among them without looking back.

Back in his car, he sat for five minutes doing absolutely nothing. He had to consider the possibility that there had been more to that scene than had met even his eye. It might have been a set-up. Even now someone might be watching him from a distance, to trap and incriminate him. In what, or why, he couldn't imagine, but you could not always expect logical behaviour from these people. They were divided among themselves. There were some among them who hated the very idea of Lincoln Kumalo so much that they wouldn't hesitate to make life difficult for his lawyer.

Finally he could resist no longer. He took the Rothmans packet from his pocket, removed a cigarette and lit it. Keeping the packet well below the level of the dashboard, he took out the little plastic tube that the convict had inserted in it. It had been quite a clever ploy, that – giving in the guise of taking. He flipped off the lid of the tube and saw a slip of paper rolled up inside. He glanced around quickly, finding no one within sight, before teasing the paper out and unrolling it.

The message had been written in pencil on the back of a small official form of some kind. It was in the bold capitals of a not over-literate hand, the words spaced out with care as though each one had an importance of its own. It read:

AS THE LORD GOD IS MY WITNESS THIS THING IS TRUE. AND ALL THE PEOPLE SHALL SAY AMEN (Deuteronomy, 27:24).
BY THE RIVER OF NCOME THE APPOINTED TIME, AND THE DESERT SHALL REJOICE AND BLOSSOM (Isaiah, 35:1). WHO SHALL DELIVER HIM? (Romans, 7:24).

He read it through half a dozen times. Then he tried staring at the block of writing as a whole, as though like one of those optical tricks it might reveal a pattern or a picture

84

within the words. Finally he gave a snort of laughter. Had that whole charade been for the sake of these . . . absurd religious ravings? Was Bobbejaan trying to alert the world to his personal vision of the Apocalypse? If so, why choose someone like himself to spread the word, a nominal Muslim who couldn't make sense of these biblical references? Even he could tell that one of those was wrong, though: It was *By the rivers of Babylon*, wasn't it? Ncome was an African name, but not one that meant anything to him either.

Ibrahim took out his lighter. It would be best to burn this rubbish here and now. Only a second's hesitation, while he wondered how to accomplish this inside the car, made him reconsider. Experience had taught him to take nothing in the devious business of underground politics at its face value. The author of this message was not necessarily Bobbejaan. And, although its contents seemed nonsensical, someone had put considerable thought into the means of delivering it. Well, there could be method in the madness even of a religious freak, he supposed . . . yet perhaps he was falling into a trap designed for someone else. There could be a subtle mind at work here. What if the writer *wanted* this to sound like the harmless rantings of a religious lunatic, just in case it fell into the wrong hands? Within it, just possibly, was another message shouting out to be heard.

He decided to keep the message. He would give it some thought later, once he was safely beyond the prison boundary. If it should be a trick, if he should be searched and it was found, he could still plead ignorance.

It was only as he was refolding the slip of paper that he thought to glance at its reverse side. It was a printed form bearing the coat of arms of the prison service. It seemed to be a carbon copy of a doctor's prescription. It bore several lines of hasty scribbling, only one of which was easily legible. Opposite *Name of Patient*, it said *Prisoner 4008*.

7

'You've got five more minutes,' the head warder said behind her.

The words were spoken neutrally. Nandi scarcely heard them. All her concentration was on the figure behind the glass, on the still strangely disembodied voice that came to her through the telephone, as she sought to imprint every possible moment of the visit on her memory. It was he who had done most of the talking, almost as though he were bringing news of the outside world to her. Their conversation was artificial, of course, outwardly avoiding things like politics and conditions in the prison, forbidden by the regulations, yet it was still possible for them to send signals to each other in a code that had evolved itself over the years, that had no key other than their knowledge of each other, the emphasis they gave to certain words and phrases.

Thus she learned, in the course of some innocuous anecdotes, that there had been no change in his circumstances since she had last been here. He was still kept in what amounted to a comfortable solitary confinement, allowed to mingle for only an hour each day with other 'politicals' similarly isolated from the rest of the inmates. He was permitted some books and an occasional newspaper, after they had been through the censor's hands, and his hungry intellect seemed to absorb and assess every scrap of information that reached him. Again she felt inadequate in his presence, and even this he seemed instinctively to understand, telling her he knew things could be harder for her outside than for him.

She had told him in detail about her mother's funeral, circumspectly describing the way the police had broken up the procession and the way the burial had had to go ahead in private. He told her about his health and the visit of the anonymous specialist, the hormone treatment he was getting and the prospect of an operation. This led them back, with time running out, to the matter she had raised at the beginning, of Hoeksma's offer. He shook his head sadly, anticipating her disappointment.

'It has to be no, Nandi. I'm sorry.'

'I'm only their messenger. Ibrahim warned me what to expect.'

'But you hoped?'

'Yes, I suppose I hoped a bit.'

'I've had twenty-five years to think about these things, sweetheart. I've anticipated every possible option they could offer me, and there's only one I could accept.'

'Unconditional release? Those very words? They've gone as far as they can without actually using them.'

'There are no degrees in a thing like this.' He grinned at her. 'It's like chastity. You either are a virgin or you aren't.'

His flippancy slightly, unexpectedly, annoyed her. 'Are you really prepared to go on like this indefinitely? Until . . .?'

'Until I die, do you mean? It's true that I'm not getting any younger, and I have no particular wish to be a martyr. But to leave here on their terms, to go along with this sham of a medical release, would be to negate all the sacrifice.'

'Ib seems to think. . . .' She didn't know how to say it. Apart from the fact that there was a warder listening in on either side of the barrier, these surroundings had further diminished what confidence she'd had in Ibrahim's judgement. 'He says . . .'

'I think I know what Ib is thinking.'

'Do you agree with him?'

'You obviously don't,' he parried.

'I don't know what to think.'

'One more minute,' the head warder called out.

' 'I'll tell you this, Nandi. Ib can afford to hope on my behalf. Hope doesn't cost him anything. In this place, it's a dangerous commodity to deal in.'

'But' – she glanced involuntarily over his shoulder at the warder behind him – 'do you think it's possible?'

87

'It looks as though the signs may be pointing that way. I'd prefer to wait and see.'

'And if Ib is wrong? Then, it could be another five years, or ten. . . .'

'Yes, by then it could be too late,' he said with an air of harshness. 'Too late for me, perhaps, but not for millions of others.'

Nandi was silent for a few moments, unable to utter a thought that was almost sacrilegious; unwilling, really, to acknowledge it. No one could call her father selfish, and yet all dedicated men must be selfish in a way. Someone had to suffer for their singlemindedness.

'Time up now, please.'

'Oh, Daddy . . .' She was stricken suddenly by despair and had to bite back her tears, not wanting to leave him upset.

'I love you, Nandi. I know you're brave, Nandi. You don't need to convince me.'

'Say your goodbyes now,' the head warder urged them, not unkindly. Inside the glass cage the other guard was moving the switch that controlled the telephone. Kumalo stood up, still holding the handset in his left hand, clenching his right fist and raising it in the Congress salute.

'Goodbye, Nandi. Remember: *Amandla!*'

'*Amandla!*' she repeated, returning the sign: Power – just as the plug was pulled on their subversive exchange. He mouthed another kiss at her through the glass, and he was standing there smiling as the head warder touched her elbow and turned her away.

Hoeksma, when they met him an hour later in the same suite at the President Hotel, seemed more resigned than actively disappointed. This was strange, given his impassioned pleading of the night before, but no doubt the Security Police had listened in to the conversation in the prison and had already relayed the substance of it to him. There was just a slightly offended air about him, as though he felt that his good nature had been taken advantage of.

This time there was no Prinsloo present, and no offer of drinks. The meeting had the air of a brief, distasteful formality to be got quickly out of the way, which suited Nandi. Only Ibrahim seemed to have any interest in prolonging the proceedings, fussily dissecting the reasons for Kumalo's refusal and raising new questions.

'Well, I did warn you, Minister. You aren't, then, prepared perhaps to define any other circumstances in which his release might be considered?'

'Mr Khan, you heard the terms of the offer. It was the only offer on the table.'

Ibrahim shrugged. He was all calm affability again. 'I merely want to be clear about where my client stands now.'

'The offer is now withdrawn. Can I be clearer than that?'

'And will not be renewed?'

'Certainly not. The matter is closed.'

'The matter of Lincoln Kumalo won't be closed until it's resolved, Mr Hoeksma. I think we both know what the logical next step is. But I won't press you on that. We'll perhaps be talking again after his operation. When will that be?'

'I think I made it clear that the details cannot yet be disclosed.'

'I find that most unsatisfactory. It suggests you have something to hide.'

Hoeksma regarded him coldly. Even the most genial Afrikaners, Ibrahim thought, could show an officious streak when scratched. 'The Government is fully aware of its responsibilities with regard to Mr Kumalo's health. For practical reasons it remains an internal matter at present. You'll be kept informed as and when it is practicable.'

'That really isn't good enough—'

'Ib, leave it alone,' Nandi interjected wearily.

He turned and snapped at her, 'Your father's health is as much my concern as his legal affairs are!'

'And do you think I don't care?' she flared at him. 'You behave sometimes as though he were your personal property, Ibrahim. What matters to me is that he's still in prison. He's not concerned about the operation. He told me he was quite satisfied with the treatment he was getting. It's going to be some time before they can operate. Why must you invent problems before they arise?'

'Quite so,' agreed Hoeksma, glad of this momentary ally. 'You don't imagine, surely, that he's getting anything but the best of medical attention? Doctors of the highest integrity? As I've said, you'll be informed in due course. And now, if you'll excuse me . . .?'

Once again they left the hotel by the side entrance. Ibrahim was in one of his little huffs again, driving ill-temperedly through Green Point and into the city. There was an hour and a half to go before her train left for Johannesburg, and she'd assumed they would stop at his office. Instead they seemed to be off on another mystery tour, up the mountainside and through the white suburb of Oranjezicht. This time she didn't ask where they were going, both masking annoyance behind indifference to each other.

Eventually he turned up a steep, winding slope signposted Signal Hill, a conical, pine-covered outcrop among the chain of mountains that girdled the city. Near the summit the road ended in a level patch of tarmac laid out as a viewing point and a car park, all but deserted. He stopped the Mercedes and got out, slamming the door. He walked to the edge of the terrace, turned, frowned at her and then beckoned. For the first time she sensed another meaning in his silence. In the self-centredness of her own anger she'd forgotten the possibility of bugs in the car.

She slipped out of the Mercedes and joined him. He took out his cigarettes, lit one and stood staring in silence over the city a thousand feet below. When he spoke it was quietly, unemphatically.

'They're going to go ahead. Let him go. I'm more convinced than ever.'

'It didn't sound that way to me. The matter is closed, he said.'

'They've got to talk tough. Even an oily little man like

Hoeksma. That's *kragdadigheid*. All right, they've been slapped in the face; it'll take them a while to get over the sting. After that they'll see quite clearly that there's only one solution left.'

'Daddy said he'd prefer to wait and see.'

'I don't think he'll have long to wait.'

Ibrahim smiled at her and fiddled with his cigarette packet. He took out the brown plastic tube and handed it to her. 'Tell me what you make of that.'

Nandi plucked the message out of the tablet phial and read it, as he had, several times in silence. He told her to look at the back as well. Finally she said, 'What *is* this?'

He told her briefly of his encounter with the convict at Pollsmoor. 'I know it reads like a lot of rubbish, but I'm sure now that it has a hidden meaning to it. What convinced me was the paper it's written on. A prescription form, obviously from the prison hospital, with Lincoln's prison number on it.'

'You don't think it's the prescription itself that's significant? That the message, so-called, is intended to distract attention from it?'

'Ah! A good notion, but I think you're being over-subtle. It's dated November the second, which was only last Wednesday. Presumably this is the hormone they've started him on. No, I go for the number as the clue: it wouldn't mean anything to more than a handful of people outside the prison. In fact, to anyone else casually picking this up it is just a bit of scrap paper that's been used to write a lot of gibberish on. That, I think, is exactly what it's meant to look like. The number tells us different.'

'It tells us this is a message about Daddy. Is that right?'

'Yes. And that's why it was given to me. But I'm damned if I know what it means.'

They began to stroll along the edge of the terrace, Nandi still studying the paper. 'We'd need a Bible to look up these references, for a start,' she said.

'Don't look at me.'

'It's a kind of code, obviously, that can only be cracked

with the help of a Bible. That makes some sense: the Bible is often the only reading matter that they're allowed inside.'

'Perhaps we're overlooking another possibility,' said Ibrahim.

'That it's a plant?' Nandi was quick to grasp his meaning. 'It wouldn't be the first time. But if they'd wanted to send you a false message this would be a very uncertain, roundabout way of doing it. You might not have taken it seriously.'

'True.' Ibrahim was impressed by her deductive powers. He had refrained from mentioning that he'd almost burned the paper. 'I'm still not sure I do take it seriously, to tell the truth.'

A grey squirrrel hopped out from among the pines and sat watching them expectantly from a few feet away. They had nothing to give it. Lost for any means of making sense of the message, they fell back to speculating on who might have sent it.

'I can't see this prisoner Bobbejaan as the originator, somehow. For a start, he didn't look a very subtle type. And, then, whoever did write it has gone to some pains to hide its origins. There are clues here all right, but none to his identity.'

'Except the prescription form. Who would have access to such a thing? Someone who worked in the hospital?'

'And who knew Lincoln was sick. Perhaps that's all he was trying to tell me, not realizing that I already knew. *As the Lord God is my witness this thing is true.*' Ibrahim had taken the paper back and was reading from it aloud. '*And all the people shall say Amen. By the river of Ncome the appointed time.* . . . That one struck me as really nonsensical.'

'Ncome?' Nandi grabbed the message from him and studied it again. When she looked up at him there was a triumphant gleam in her eyes. 'Ncome! I knew there was something familiar about it. It was only when I heard you say it. . . .'

'That quote is a distortion. Isn't it *By the rivers of Babylon, there we sat down, yea, we wept . . .*?'

'Yes, yes,' she said impatiently. 'But of course you wouldn't know what I do about the history of our people.'

'What people?'

'The Zulus. The battle of 1838, in which the Zulu nation

92

was finally defeated by the Boers. They haven't allowed us to forget about it since.'

'The battle of Blood River? Of course I know about that.'

'But perhaps you don't know that the Boers only gave it that name afterwards, because the water ran red with Zulu blood. Before then the river was known as the Ncome. It's an obscure little stream, really, in northern Natal.'

'Well . . .?' Ibrahim was nonplussed. 'Why should I be expected to know a thing like that?'

'Not you, Ibrahim.'

The penny dropped. 'You think the message is for *you*?'

'Of course it is! If this Bobbejaan wasn't its originator, isn't it just as likely that you weren't really meant to be the recipient? One thing we haven't asked ourselves is how he knew you would be there this morning, in the prison car park. The answer is, he didn't. But he knew somehow that *I'd* be visiting. He knew that Bobbejaan would be well placed to deliver a message to me.'

'And so Bobbejaan saw us arrive together, perhaps, but couldn't get close enough to the fence at the right time. So he did the next best thing and gave it to me. All right, I'll buy that; but what more does it tell us?'

'*By the river of Ncome the appointed time,*' she quoted again. 'It sounds like a rendezvous of some kind. But why "time" and not "place"?'

She stopped walking and held up the slip of paper, looking at him earnestly. 'You don't mind if I take this home, do you? I'd like to try to make sense of it.'

'Do you really think you should be taking it that seriously? Even allowing it does concern Lincoln, the chances are that it's just a crazy message from some Jesus freak.'

'It's worth trying to find out, surely?' Although Ib would only scoff at her, it was the last line of the message – *Who shall deliver him?* – that she found ominous. It sounded like a warning of some kind. 'It might be possible to trace this person. I have friends in Jo'burg who might help.'

'Congress people? The underground? You'd do well to stay away from them, especially at a time like this. You've always

93

kept your nose clean politically, and the police have left you alone. In a few more weeks everything could be different.'

'But if not?' Before he could answer she had turned and begun to walk briskly back towards the car, leaving him to hurry after her.

'What's the rush? We've got plenty of time.'

'I want to get hold of a Bible, of course. To study on the train.'

'Listen, girl. I've got your father's interests to consider. I can't stop you doing whatever you want to, up in Jo'burg, but if you have dealings with illegal contacts, then I don't want to know.'

In the car on the way down Signal Hill Ibrahim looked discouraged, as though one more burden had been added to his load of worries. No doubt he wished he had never even mentioned the message. However – perhaps because he couldn't resist showing off – as he was seeing her off on the train he ventured a small theory of his own.

'You know there is a rendezvous at Blood River every year? It's December the sixteenth, the anniversary of the battle. It's the day the Afrikaners commemorate their victory. Do you think that could be your appointed time?'

Countless hours later, Nandi sat staring out at the dark wasteland of the Great Karroo. An angry red sun had set behind the Hex River Mountains as the engine strained up the final gradient on to the great African plateau; after that the train had gathered speed and now it thundered steadily over the flat semi-desert country, its carriages rocking with a gentle hypnotic motion.

Nandi had a headache. Long train journeys often did that to her, though she preferred them to flying. She wasn't much of an adventurer, she thought, though this particular headache probably had more to do with the hours of concentration she had put into trying to solve the puzzle that lay spread out before her on the small folding table.

The coloured conductor had brought her some aspirins. He had also, without being asked, given her a couchette compartment to herself; it was part of the silent conspiracy of sympathy that surrounded her name. She supposed she ought to feel guilty about accepting it, but found herself glad of the privacy.

She turned from the window to address the puzzle again: the message from Pollsmoor, the scrawled pages of notes she had made, the Pocket Oxford edition of the King James Bible bought at Garlicks bookshop on the way to the station. The exasperating thing was that she still didn't know whether she had solved the riddle or not. If there was some hidden coherence in this message, it still eluded her.

The three quotations attributed to the Bible had been easy to look up. It was only when she had studied their contexts, however, that she realized that each was part of an incomplete verse. Set out in full, the verses read:

> Cursed be he that smiteth his neighbour secretly. And all the people shall say Amen. *Deuteronomy*

> The wilderness and the solitary place shall be glad for them; and the desert shall rejoice, and blossom as the rose. *Isaiah*

> O wretched man that I am! Who shall deliver me from the body of this death? *Romans*

It had struck her that the significance of each sentence might lie in the part of the verse that had been *left out*. The real message could be in the missing words: that would tie in with the writer's allusive approach, the substitution of *Ncome* for *Babylon* in that other distorted quote. And what was she to make of that? If Ibrahim's theory was correct, it referred to a date: December the sixteenth. It was a public holiday: Dingaan's Day, it had once been called, in memory of the Zulu king whose army had been routed at Blood River. Now it was the Day of the Covenant, supposedly because of a deal the Boers had made with God. If He gave them victory, they would ever after honour the day in His memory.

The opening sentence – *As the Lord God is my witness this thing is true* – was biblical in style, but did not appear to refer to a particular passage. It could be just a way of setting a crackpot religious tone to the message, at the same time urging the reader to believe it.

Translated into a more specific set of clues and allusions, the message might read:

> This thing is true:
> Cursed be he that smiteth his neighbour
> secretly;
> December 16th;
> The wilderness and the solitary place shall be
> glad for them/as the rose.
> O wretched man that I am/the body of this
> death.

She had tried extracting what seemed to be the key words from this, to see whether they formed some pattern: *true – smite – neighbour – secretly – December 16th – wilderness – solitary place – the rose – wretched man – body – death.*

Beneath this list she had noted:

1. Two references to death;
2. *Solitary place* = prison?
3. Who shall deliver *me*? in Bible; deliver *him*? in message.

She pondered this last point. In the other place where he had misquoted the Bible – substituting *Ncome* for *Babylon* – it had been done deliberately, for a purpose. The same was probably true here. She had no doubt now that the writer was trying to warn her of some danger. He was also making it clear that it was not he who was being threatened but somebody else. *Him.* Who else but Prisoner 4008? And what was the danger? Death.

Nandi sighed and gazed out of the window again. The whole thing could still mean anything or nothing. It was like trying to piece together some disturbing but far from vivid dream. For all her head-banging, the only thing she had resembling a positive clue was the one that Ibrahim had given her, about the date. The Day of the Covenant was no cause for celebration among black people. It marked the event that had led to a century and a half of domination, and God had clearly had somewhat less to do with the Boers' victory than the superiority of muskets and cannon over stabbing spears and oxhide shields. Was something that involved her father due to happen on that day, *the appointed time*?

December the sixteenth was thirty-eight days away.

She pulled down the window blind and began preparing for bed. What all this needed was a fresh pair of eyes. Perhaps she would ask little Alex Duma for help. For all he was a hothead, he was intelligent. He was also constantly trying to impress her, and so would be glad to do her a favour. Duma had the right contacts to take the puzzle one stage further.

8

When he had nothing better to do, which seemed to be a lot of the time, Virgil would hang about the Woodvale Clinic's reception area trying to chat up Yvonne. Virgil was one of the security guards, an overweight young English immigrant with an over-eager smile. He knew Judith disliked him and so always tried to wind her up.

He was leaning over the reception counter when she returned from the city that Thursday afternoon.

'Three o'clock,' he said, ostentatiously checking his watch. 'Long lunch, eh? All right for some people, isn't it?'

She ignored him. 'I got it!' she said triumphantly to Yvonne.

'The flat? Hooray!'

'The one I told you about, over in Northcliff. Furnished, as well. I've got it on a year's lease. I can move in on the first of next month.'

'Congratulations.'

'Inviting me to the housewarming party?' said Virgil with a leer.

She went round the counter and into the admin office.

She settled at her desk, opened her handbag and briefly inspected her make-up in a tiny cracked mirror. Just lipstick and a touch of eye-liner: anything more made her pale bony face look like a death-mask under its cascade of black curls. All her features were bold, her father's Roman nose managing, on her, to look more like a Jewish *schnozz*, giving the lie to his WASP pretensions. Maybe that was what really disappointed him about her: she was a throwback. Well, she'd be out of his hair soon, apart from working hours, and that should make them both happier. She was excited about the flat but also apprehensive, a little taken aback by her own decisiveness.

She could barely afford the rent, but what the hell? Maybe it would give her the incentive to find a better-paying job in the city, to make the final, overdue break with her parents.

She heard Virgil's adenoidal Birmingham voice droning on outside as she sorted through a pile of mail. When she had finished she carried three letters out to reception.

'Government inspectors, my eye,' he was saying. 'When did government inspectors go round checking the perimeter fence, for God's sake? No, I'd know the look of those blokes anywhere . . .'

She slapped the letters down on the counter in front of him. 'Take these over to Dr Clooney in the Drunk Tank.'

'Here, what am I, a messenger boy?'

'I don't know what you are, but with a name like yours you should have been a cop in a Californian TV series.'

'I nearly became a cop,' he said with dignity. 'It's what my father was, for thirty years. West Midlands Police. That's how I know the look of them: it's the same everywhere.'

He took the letters and went off, grumbling. Judith and Yvonne rolled their eyes at each other.

'Why do you put up with him? What was all that about, anyway?'

'There've been two government officials looking the place over. Department of Health, I suppose. They're in with your father now. Virgil maintains they're actually from the Security Police.'

Judith snorted. 'Conspiracy theories. He's a real Boy Scout.'

'Actually, they *were* behaving a bit oddly. They went through the buildings thoroughly and even looked all around the grounds. And they've been checking the personnel files.'

Judith looked at her blankly. 'How do you know?'

'I'll show you,' said Yvonne with a secretive smile. 'Strictly between us.'

The coloured girl led her back into the office, to the computer terminal. She switched it on, tapped herself into the system, pressed the RAPID ACCESS key and then P for PRINT RECORD. The screen produced a string of headings, an alphabetical list of the clinic's staff, each surname preceded by a series of code numbers and letters.

'You know how this works?' asked Yvonne. Judith shook her head. 'Every time one of the printers is used the computer keeps a record of what it's printing. I suppose it's so bosses can be sure their employees aren't moonlighting with the system. It's easy enough to delete the record, mind you. That's what I was doing an hour ago – trying to kill all that rubbish you ordered up the other day – when I spotted this.

'The personnel records are held in your father's private file, accessed by his personal password. It's the computer equivalent of keeping them in a safe with a combination lock. But he's been making hard copies on the printer in his office – obviously for his two visitors to look at.'

'Bit of a cheek, asking for those.' But Judith was looking at her own name, two-thirds of the way down the list. The heading read: *PR02 10/11 1351 PERS Rose J Pers No 54*.

'That means my file was copied on printer number two at nine minutes to two this afternoon. Even I can work that out.' She gave Yvonne a look. 'Does this mean *we* have access to the files?'

'Well, we could have, just for as long as this stays on the screen. I'm sure he'll be deleting it shortly.'

'Go on, let's have a peep at our own.'

Yvonne looked uncomfortable. 'I said we could, not that we *should*.'

'Let's see if the old bugger has any interesting notes on us.'

'It's a terrible breach of confidence, Judith.'

'It's regarded as a civil right in some places. Go on!'

Reluctantly Yvonne pecked at the keys, lining the cursor up against Judith's name and pressing the READ button. A page in document form, like a completed questionnaire, flashed up on the screen. Judith read through it. It was all very ordinary and impersonal: date of birth, education, previous experience and so on. There was a space near the bottom for comments, but it was blank. She was vaguely disappointed. Everyone was curious, or egocentric, enough to want to know what others thought worth recording about one.

'Try yours now,' she said.

'Hold on. There's something else at the bottom.'

The document was rather too long for the screen to hold in full. Yvonne scrolled it up a little.

At the bottom of Judith's file were two more brief lines:

SECURITY RATING: Negative.
ACCESS TO INDUNA PROJECT: Nil.

'Jesus Christ,' she breathed. She could hardly believe her eyes. 'Jesus Christ, a *security* rating? What sort of shit is this?'

'Keep your voice down,' Yvonne hissed.

'Like hell I will! What does he think he's doing? I'm going to demand an explanation!'

'You can't. . . .'

'I bloody sure can. What's more, I'm going to confront him with the evidence before he gets rid of it.'

She leaned across the panic-stricken Yvonne and attacked the keyboard. Miraculously she hit the right sequence of keys and the printer began to hum.

'Judith, you bloody fool! You've gone on to Print Record. He'll know.'

'He's going to know in about twenty seconds from now anyway!'

The printer took only a few moments to copy the document. Judith ripped it off the machine and marched out of the office. Fat Virgil, shambling back into reception, halted and gaped as she stalked down the corridor towards her father's office. She was halfway there when the door opened and he led his two visitors out.

She halted in front of them, no longer quite so certain of herself. Both the men were big in different ways, one tall and slightly stooped, the other of average height but broad and strongly built. They had unmistakable Afrikaner features and wore nondescript suits.

Her father looked displeased to see her, raising an inquiring eyebrow. 'What is it, Judith?'

'I need to see you,' she said tersely.

'Can't it wait until later?'

'Not really.'

'You'll have to hang on a minute, while I see these gentlemen out . . .'

'No, no, we'll leave you here,' said the taller of the two politely. He was looking at Judith with speculative interest and suddenly he thrust out a powerful paw, introducing himself in the abrupt Afrikaner way.

'Prinsloo,' he said. She shook his hand numbly.

'Booysen,' said the other man, also offering his hand. Neither of them gave any further explanation of himself. Booysen had prominent blue eyes and a mighty jaw. He looked like a dance-hall bouncer.

'My daughter Judith,' said Dr Rose rather grimly. He seemed ill at ease, anxious not to prolong the conversation, and the man called Prinsloo took his cue.

'We'll be off, then, Doctor. We'll be in touch again. Goodbye, Miss Rose.'

Prinsloo and Booysen marched away. 'Come in,' Dr Rose said ungraciously, still annoyed with her, and she followed him into the office. By the time he had closed the door she had regained her own anger and she thrust the computer printout at him. He glanced through it, flinched and looked up at her.

'What's the meaning of this, Judith? You've been tampering with confidential records!'

101

'I think it's you who owes me the explanation, Daddy. Security rating? Induna Project? What sort of sinister nonsense is this?'

'Keep your voice down,' he warned her.

'I want to know what all this is about! Who are those people anyway? Why have they been snooping about here?'

'I don't actually see that it's any of your business.'

'Well, I do. What entitles them to see confidential information about me?'

'Now, look here, Judith . . .' He was trying to be stern but he was also on the defensive. He relented a little. 'You may find this hard to take, but I'm not in a position to answer any of your questions. Not yet.'

'Well, if you can't tell me, they will have to. They can't have left yet.'

She turned towards the door, but he put a restraining hand on her arm. 'Don't do that, Judith. You could get me into trouble.'

She swung round to face him. 'Trouble? You?' she said incredulously. Then she realized that perhaps Virgil had been making sense for once. 'Were those men from the Security Police?'

'Colonel Prinsloo and Major Booysen,' he muttered.

'What the hell did they want with you? And why were they interested in me?'

'It's not just you. They were making a routine security check on the staff. I agreed to it, and I can promise you there was nothing conspiratorial about it.'

Even he did not seem convinced by this bland, official-sounding assurance. Judith could sense that he was uncomfortable. There was much that was arrogant about her father, but he would never arbitrarily refuse to discuss anything. Now he tried to sound reasonable. 'Listen, Judith, I don't like this part of it any more than you do. But the fact is that I've taken on a particularly sensitive job for those people and I've had to sign the Official Secrets Act. I'm not allowed to discuss it with anybody. Since you've stumbled on one aspect of it, though, I can only take you so far into my confidence as a warning not to let it go any further. Will you promise to be satisfied with that?'

It was late that night before Nandi and Duma finally admitted defeat.

For more than four hours they had racked their brains over the Pollsmoor message, sitting at the kitchen table in her little house in the Orlando section of Soweto. Still they had got no further with the mystery than Nandi herself had taken it on the train two nights before.

'I don't know.' For perhaps the hundredth time Duma scraped back his chair, stood up and prowled around the room. He was dressed in a leather lumberjacket and dark suede trousers, the original Black Panther. 'Maybe there is no mystery, Nandi. Maybe it's vague because the information this guy picked up is just that: vague. And – let's face it – maybe it's a hoax.'

She nodded. She was grateful to Duma tonight, though she did not always welcome his nocturnal appearances on her doorstep. The Security Police, the successors to Colonel Prinsloo, had taken no apparent interest in the house since her mother's death, and she was content to keep it that way. There were still informers about; social calls from a wanted militant would not go unnoticed for ever. Besides, whatever work it was that Duma did for the Congress, he clearly didn't keep the same arduous hours she did, trailing lifelines to the old and destitute of Soweto for six long days a week. He wanted to talk the nights away; she wanted to sleep. He wanted to make love to her, and still didn't think she meant it when she said no.

Nights were the safe times for Duma, when the Hippos and Saracens had pulled out of the townships and the only danger came from an occasional prowling police car. Where he came from on these visits and where he returned to were questions she never asked and didn't want answered.

'Yes, it could be a hoax, Duma. Some elaborate joke by the police themselves. There's just something about it that has the ring of genuine urgency to me. *Who will deliver him?*

103

We have to remember that the writer of this couldn't choose the exact words he wanted. He had to stick to biblical quotations, more or less, and hope that we would sort out what was significant. That's why I tried to make something of what I thought were the key words. "Smite." "Secretly." "Solitary place." "Rose." Why "rose", for heaven's sake?'

'Well, what are we left with, Nandi? A warning of some unspecified danger to your father, possibly occurring on the sixteenth of December. It could have come from a soothsayer. The Ides of March.'

'Caesar didn't listen to the soothsayer. Look what happened to him.'

'You'll be consulting a *muti*-man next. A witchdoctor. We've left all that mumbo-jumbo behind us.'

Nandi smiled, partly to disguise a yawn. Duma liked to think of himself as totally detribalized, a citizen of Africa, though he was as full-blooded a Zulu as she was.

'Ibrahim Khan thinks they're going to let him out, you know. Unconditionally.'

'*What?* You didn't tell me that.'

'Perhaps because I'm reluctant to believe it myself. It would be odd if it happened on December the sixteenth, wouldn't it? Yes, Ib is convinced they're going to release him after his operation. They've played their last card, is what he said.'

'Well? Tell me more!'

'They made another offer, through me, which he rejected. But I can't go into the details. I have given my word – to a deputy minister, no less.'

'Ha! You've been keeping some bad company down there. Well, I'll wait agog for further news.' Duma ceased slinking up and down the kitchen and gestured at the pages of notes that smothered the table. 'You know what I think you should do? Give all this stuff to me. Let me send it to our friends up north, see if they can make any better sense of it.'

'In Zambia? What help could they be?'

'Who knows? They have other sources of information. They sit on their backsides in Lusaka and the world comes tripping to their doorstep. Seriously, it can't do any harm. Keep the original message yourself, and we'll continue to work on it. I'll put out some other feelers among the comrades, see if there's any way of working back to its source.'

She shrugged. She couldn't see much point in the idea, but she was too tired to argue. She stood up, yawning openly this time as an indication that Duma might find this a tactful moment to leave.

For once he did not seem unwilling. He gathered the notes, folded them and stuffed them inside his lumberjacket. Nandi turned off the gas lamp before cautiously opening the kitchen door. The township night was silent but for the distant howling of dogs.

At the door he kissed her on the cheek. 'One of these nights, Nandi . . .'

'I know. One of these nights you think I will invite you to stay. Will you be all right out there?'

He grinned. 'I am a fish in a sea of men.' He hopped down the steps, trotted across her back yard and in a moment was absorbed by the darkness.

9

Joshua Rosenblatt looked up from his typewriter, grateful as ever for a distraction. The first tentative cloudburst of the rainy season had blotted the dust on the window of the motel chalet, and through it he had seen Harry Makibani's old Toyota enter the driveway from the Lusaka road. At the gate a Congress sentry, not too effectively disguised as a Zambian militiaman, had stopped the car and then waved it through. Bouncing on worn springs, it squelched through the muddy potholes and came to a stop outside what had once been the motel's reception office. Harry levered his bulk out and blundered through the downpour to the shelter of the porch. The morose figure of J. K. Govender had come out to meet him, and for a minute they stood gesticulating to each other

105

like puppets – Mr Punch and the Negro Servant? – giving expression to what they were trying to say over the drumming of the rain on the iron roof. Eventually they disappeared into the office. Joshua, without enthusiasm, addressed himself again to the sheet of paper wound into the Olivetti.

Chapter Three, he had typed. *The Evolution of the People's Congress.* And that was all. With only an hour to go before they had to leave for the airport, he didn't know why he was bothering, but maybe that was just it: a brief salve to the conscience allowing him an excuse for further delay. The book, tentatively entitled *South African Nemesis: An Insider's Story of the Revolutionary Struggle*, was already unconscionably overdue for delivery, so another fortnight could hardly matter. He had often been tempted to abandon this project, but for several reasons felt that he couldn't. There was the advance already paid by his publishers in London, and already spent: J. K. Govender, that old Trot, would probably laugh at such a bourgeois sense of obligation, but to Joshua it was real enough. More seriously, though, he believed he had something genuinely important to say. He wanted to explain the aims of the Congress in a way that would capture the understanding and sympathy of Western readers. He wanted to explain that it was not a bloodthirsty terrorist organization, but a national movement that was more than seventy years old, that had resorted to armed resistance only when every peaceful avenue had been closed to it. In a sense he wanted also to vindicate himself, to expunge a certain sense of guilt as well as acknowledging the honour of being the first, the only, white man to reach a prominent position in the movement.

His feelings of guilt could be summarized thus: he could have stayed on. He could have faced up to the bannings and arrests, possibly the torture, that were still inflicted on those who had remained. Instead, he had run for safety. It was something they all felt up here in their not uncomfortable exile, but that Joshua was more aware of than most. Being white, he'd had a fairly pampered existence down there. He was not psychologically hardened against punishment. He was not heroic material in the mould of Lincoln Kumalo.

Life for the executive committee of the Congress was not entirely carefree, of course. The grapevine said there was a price on the head of each of them: fifty thousand rands in Joshua's case, on permanent offer from the South African National Intelligence Service to any freebooter who could locate and eliminate him. He could not help thinking he was rather over-valued. As the treasurer of the movement he had administrative control of its funds, but only a limited say in how they were used.

He abandoned the typewriter, stood up, stretched, and walked to the window at the rear of the chalet. It looked out over the wreckage of a back garden. Elephant grass had supplanted the lawn, and in the flowerbeds cannas and poinsettias were being strangled by monstrous tropical weeds. It was vastly inefficient that the Congress executive should have to keep moving to and from places like this, that it had no permanent base, but that was the result of lessons learned over the years. They paid only fleeting visits to the movement's official headquarters, an office off Cairo Road in Lusaka where a bomb had been planted just five months ago. There'd been other bombs, and other headquarters, and even blatant air raids on the camps of their guerrillas deep in the bush, before the executive had taken to moving about like nomads, pitching camp week after week anywhere within a fifty-mile radius of the town. Joshua couldn't bring himself to call Lusaka a city, not after Johannesburg.

He returned to his desk but did not sit down, standing and staring at the sheet of paper, still blank but for the chapter heading. What was it he was trying to say? That for most of its long history the People's Congress had conducted a peaceful struggle on behalf of South Africa's disfranchised black majority. That only in the late 1950s had it begun to attract a mass following, as independence came or was promised to the colonial territories in the north and the reverberations were felt in the remotest tribal village of South Africa itself. The difference was that there was no colonial power here to pack its bags and depart, but instead a settled white minority determined to hold its position. The mood of the blacks became more militant, and the policies of the Congress reflected this mood, especially after 1958 when a dynamic young lawyer, Lincoln Kumalo, became its president.

Two years later the movement was outlawed. Those of its leaders who escaped arrest either went underground or fled abroad. Even then, they were slow to adopt violent tactics against a regime now determined to destroy them by every possible means. Their first symbolic acts of sabotage were seen not as a warning but as proof of ineffectiveness, yet when Kumalo and a number of other militants were captured they were sentenced for their part in these acts to life imprisonment.

Since then, the development of the Congress from a mildly subversive organization to a revolutionary movement that had won a degree of international respect had been a long and sometimes painful process. The Western powers distrusted them because they accepted some grudging aid from the Russians. Their hosts, the Zambians, treated them at times like embarrassing relatives that custom obliged them to welcome at their hearth.

Things had changed notably after the so-called children's rebellion in Soweto in 1976, when protests by school pupils were savagely repressed and possibly hundreds had died in a month of near-anarchy in the townships. It led to an exodus of young men from the country, filtering northwards to pump new life into the movement and forming the core of its guerrilla army, now several thousand strong. By the dozen every week they were seeping back into their homeland, organizing others against the regime, attacking its exposed parts and, perhaps more importantly, its nerves.

Joshua caught a movement in the window. The rain had stopped and Harry Makibani was bustling across the motel courtyard towards his room, beer belly straining against the buttons of a white safari jacket. Coming to check that he was ready for the trip, Joshua supposed. It wasn't a journey that he relished: twelve hours or so to Algiers in some bone-shaking military aircraft. He turned to look over his luggage again: one suitcase, one briefcase. It would probably still be warm in North Africa at this time of year, but he would need his couple of staid business suits for his meeting with finance ministers and government officials. The Conference of Non-Aligned Nations, at which the People's Congress would have observer status, was notable for Savile Row tailoring on the one hand and flamboyant national dress on the other. Last year there had been Colonel Gaddafi in his brilliant green robe, Fidel Castro in a combat jacket, but these were trademarks no one else could successfully imitate.

He considered again whether to pack the notes for his book and its two completed chapters, and decided not. There was no realistic hope of getting any work done on it during the conference. Equally superfluous was his old family photograph album, but he'd got into the habit of dragging it around wherever he went. Joshua had never married; he had no real home. The album was practically the only link left with his former life, and he had grown superstitious about it.

He had just slipped it into his briefcase when Harry Makibani appeared in the doorway. Harry was their public affairs officer. Although he never looked quite comfortable in a tropical climate, he was an energetic man who moved as though he were always trying to work off his excess weight.

'Josh! Before we go . . . something's come up. Something we ought to talk about.'

Joshua realized Harry was not alone. J. K. Govender, the Congress secretary, had followed him across the courtyard and now he slithered past Harry into the room. Temperamentally the two men were almost perfectly mismatched, an exuberant, impatient African and a gloomy, doctrinaire Indian, and they were forever at loggerheads. Just behind him came Lawrence Gumbi, a tall and taciturn black man, a practitioner of guerrilla strategy who for the past three years had headed the armed wing of the Congress. Had they acknowledged any military rank they would have addressed him as General, the commander of five thousand well-trained men whose influence within the leadership was expanding in line with the growing extent of the armed struggle.

'Pahlani is coming in a minute,' Harry said. 'He's just on the phone to London.'

That would make five of them, practically a quorum for a meeting of the executive. Joshua said: 'What the hell is up?'

'We've had a message. It's about Lincoln.'

Lincoln. In any gathering of this group there was always, metaphorically, an empty place. Lincoln Kumalo, their president, hovered like Banquo's ghost at the head of their table. In their deliberations they even unconsciously included him, each wondering how he would vote on an issue and adjusting his own views accordingly. Those old feelings of guilt could account for part of it; he was in jail, after all, and they weren't. But beyond that, Joshua had come to realize, it was Kumalo who gave them their coherence, who in some way held them together. They buried their differences for his sake; their squabbles seemed petty and shameful in the light of what he had endured.

'It's like this,' said Harry. 'You know the courier system that brings us stuff from Jo'burg?'

Joshua nodded. Like every clandestine organization, the Congress needed an effective means of communicating with its agents and operatives within the country, of exchanging directives and reports. Radio, telephone and even postal links with South Africa were highly vulnerable to interception, so much depended on slow, old-fashioned but reliable courier arrangements.

'Well, I've just picked up a pile of dispatches that got into town this morning,' Harry went on. 'There's one from a comrade called Duma. Dated Friday, so it's only two days old. Duma is close to his daughter—'

'Whose daughter?'

'His, man. Who do you think? Lincoln. And what he says is this: she's got hold of some notion that they may be going to release him soon.'

Nobody spoke for several seconds. Joshua felt a thrill of apprehension and sensed the same feeling ripple through the others. It was J. K. Govender who broke the silence.

'Just whose notion is this?'

'It comes from his lawyer, Ibrahim Khan. It seems Nandi saw both him and Lincoln last week. It's only conjecture so far, but nobody is closer to the situation than he is.'

'Ibrahim Khan,' said J. K. with disapproval, 'has never been one of us.'

'He's had to keep his distance from us, that's all. He's been doing his job, representing his client.'

'And Nandi Kumalo? How reliable do you consider her?'

'All right, she's not a Congress activist either, but she *is* his daughter.'

'If she was half the woman her mother was she'd have felt it her duty to inform us of something like this, instead of letting it reach us as a secondhand rumour.'

That was J. K. for you, Joshua thought. It wasn't enough that your heart was in the right place; you had to commit your soul to the struggle.

'Look,' said Harry in exasperation, 'she sees her first duty as being to her father. Just like Khan. He's the only thing that stands, in a legal sense, between Lincoln and the Boers. He can't do anything to damage his standing with them. And Nandi . . . well, if she wants to lead a quiet life, I suppose that's her privilege. Not everyone is born to be a political animal. The point is, coming from sources like this, the story can't be treated as just another rumour.'

'What about this Duma fellow?' asked Lawrence Gumbi.

'I know him well. He is a little excitable but dependable also. He went through one of your own military training courses, but his talent is more for political organization. He slipped out of the country four years ago and has been back there since early this year, organizing cells among the youngsters. There's another thing—'

'So supposing there is something to all this,' Joshua interrupted, conscious that time was running out, 'what can we actually do about it?'

'Start making some contingency plans,' Harry said. 'We're all going to be stuck in Algiers for the next fortnight, and we're going to look pretty silly if something like this takes us by surprise. I'm sending a message back to Duma asking him to find out anything more he can. He can use the London courier route to reach us if necessary. But there are more important things to consider. If they really are thinking of letting Lincoln out unconditionally, then it's only logical that they must soon start thinking in terms of talking to the movement that he leads. Reaching some accommodation with us. We have to be ready for that.'

'All this on the basis of one man's conjecture?' J. K. was about to launch into a new argument when the door opened and Godfrey Pahlani entered. The acting president of the Congress was a dapper, dignified figure with a crop of thick white hair surrounding a shiny brown bald crown. Glasses with thin gold rims added to his naturally rather severe and ascetic look.

'I was filling them in,' said Harry, 'on this story about Lincoln.'

'Yes. I've been talking to Moses Mohaila. He's heard nothing.'

Pahlani still held in his hands one of the portable scrambler units that Congress officials used whenever possible to make their phone calls more secure. The idea that their respresentative in Britain might know something they didn't was by no means absurd. London was a major listening-post for all kinds of news from South Africa, and it was frequently available there sooner than in Lusaka.

'There's something else we ought to discuss,' Harry said. 'While Ibrahim Khan and Nandi Kumalo were visiting Pollsmoor last week, some kind of garbled message was smuggled out to them. It doesn't make a lot of sense, but she seems to think it was a warning of some kind. Some danger to Lincoln. Duma has sent us a lot of notes, asked if we can figure them out. There's nothing specific about the message except, maybe, the date: December the sixteenth.'

'The anniversary of Blood River,' Pahlani mused. 'Well, we can talk about that later. Right now we have a plane to catch.'

'I think this is important. The plane will wait.'

'Harry, a lot is at stake for us in Algiers. We have fought for

112

a long time to prove that we are serious and reliable people. Let us at least try to be punctual.'

'Let's also try to help people on the ground down there when they ask for something,' Harry said angrily. 'No wonder they think we sit around picking our noses up here!'

'Please keep your temper,' Pahlani said evenly. 'We can discuss all this on the plane.'

Harry gave an exaggerated shrug of resignation and threw a glance at Joshua. Pahlani is a pedantic arsehole, was what it said. Pahlani was certainly a time-keeper: a rare enough quality among Africans, Joshua thought. And a time-server? He had had that unkind notion, too, sometimes. Pahlani was a natural bureaucrat, in effect a caretaker for their absent president. He'd been a compromise candidate for the acting leadership, acceptable both to the left-wing members of the executive like Gumbi and Govender, and to those like Joshua and Harry Makibani who considered themselves moderates. Who could doubt that, if Lincoln Kumalo were freed, Pahlani would be eclipsed? Wouldn't they all be, for that matter?

As the others filed out of the room he pulled the beginning of Chapter Three out of the typewriter, stared at it wistfully and then tossed it into the wastebin. The bloody thing would never get written.

As it happened, all thoughts of Lincoln Kumalo were swept out of their minds by a more immediate event.

For reasons of security, the Congress leadership rarely travelled by scheduled airline flights, especially international ones. They used the services of private charter companies or, more often, courtesy planes laid on by sympathetic governments. They were, as Joshua had once said in a cynical moment, professional freeloaders on the conscience of the world.

For this journey, a small Tupolev-134 jet transport of the Algerian air force had come to fetch them and was parked well out of sight of the main terminal at Lusaka's international airport. Thanks to the status that the Congress enjoyed with the Zambian government, there were also arrangements allowing them to avoid the public areas of the terminal and pass directly through the VIP channel.

The rain clouds had vanished, and with them the short period of cool they had brought. A relentless moist November heat had returned by the time the group had cleared the brief formalities and were led out on to the apron for the long walk to the aircraft.

They were about halfway there when Joshua, bringing up the rear, became aware of an odd commotion off to his left. Glancing round, he saw a line of passengers who'd been queuing to board a Zambia Airways plane breaking up and scuttling back towards the airport building. No sound reached him over the distance of two or three hundred yards, and it was impossible to tell what had disturbed them. What did seem clear was that they were not just in haste; they were in panic. All across the airfield, he saw now through the shimmering heat haze, mechanics and security men had been startled from their usual lethargic walk into a run, all heading for the terminal. On its roof, Sunday sightseers were shading their eyes and gazing up into the sky.

The rest of the group, also aware now of the distant confusion, had halted in bewilderment. Suddenly the walkie-talkie in the hand of the escorting Zambian police inspector burst incomprehensibly to life, and Joshua had a presentiment of what the panic was about.

'Gentlemen! Get back! Quickly!'

They heard the planes before they saw them: a sudden explosive boom followed by the harsh scream of jet engines, rising to a howl, tapering away. Looking up, feeling dreadfully exposed, Joshua caught a twin flash of bright metal against the hard blue of the sky, a glimpse of two dark shapes with swept-back wings, already a mile beyond the airport, banking and turning into steep curve.

'Back inside!'

The police inspector had seized Godfrey Pahlani by the sleeve and was hustling him back towards the terminal. The others followed, breaking into a run, awkward and stumbling.

All at once they were diminished to a group of frightened middle-aged men, in flight from some random impersonal violence. It seemed to take an eternity to cross the expanse of baking concrete, but nothing more happened until they reached the door of the VIP area. Then there was another deafening boom as two more Buccaneer bombers came in, very fast and low, one slightly behind and above the other, the cumbersome clusters of bombs and rockets slung beneath their wings making their speed seem that much more astonishing. For just about a second before they swept on towards the airport perimeter, the orange-white-blue tail markings of the South African Air Force were visible against the camouflage paint.

The police officer bullied them into the building.

'It's the fucking Boers!'

Harry Makibani was the last to arrive, panting and sweating, looking scared and not caring who knew it.

'It's us they're after. Isn't it? Isn't it?' J. K. Govender had lost his cool as well, but his panicky demand got no reply. The sound of the jets had faded away, and they stood staring at each other, trapped in a silent cocoon of ignorance. It occurred to Joshua that if the South Africans really had gone crazy enough to bomb the airport the five of them were in at least as much danger here inside the building as out of it. On the way through the VIP lounge he had spotted a flight of stairs leading to the viewing deck, and now he ran towards it. 'Wait!' called the police inspector, but the rest of the group were already following.

They scrambled up two flights of stairs and out on to the roof. The midday sun struck violently down on them. There were a hundred or more people up here, necks craning as they hunted for the planes on every horizon, from the featureless bush in the north and east to the languid sprawl of Lusaka to the south. Somebody exclaimed and pointed. High above, they saw the fighter escorts, four Mirage F-1s trailing thin streams of vapour as they circled the city almost lazily, on the lookout for any opposition from the lightweight Zambian forces. Harry Makibani was shaking his fist at them, shouting: 'Boers! Bastards!'

Far beyond the town a fierce red blossom appeared among the grey-green bush, followed by another close by and then two more, each eclipsed in turn by a great mushrooming gush of black smoke. It took perhaps five seconds for the noise of the bombing to reach the watchers on the rooftop, the crump and roar of high explosive diffused by the hot, heavy air. By then the second pair of Buccaneers was attacking, just visible as they skimmed the treetops, and the same sequence repeated itself: flash, flame, smoke, bang. It was like watching a wartime newsreel, Joshua thought, appalling and exciting at once, spectacular as destruction always seemed at a distance. Lightened of their bomb load, the jets seemed to dance in the haze as they climbed in two steep arcs to meet their fighter escorts high above the plain.

'Hey, man!' Harry was at his elbow, shouting over the noise, and Joshua caught the reek of a fearful sweat from him. 'You know what they're hitting?'

'One of our camps?'

'Like hell! It's the fucking motel!'

Joshua came out of his trance. He put the scene into a perspective of scale, distance, landmarks: the dark ribbon of road running south to Kafue, the site of the explosions a little way east of it. The buzzing of the airport had been a mere playful diversion. Even as he understood the truth of what Harry was saying, he could not quite detach himself from the spectacle. The Buccaneers were gaining altitude, and now the Mirages were taking their turn, two of them dropping in a long, screaming, almost perpendicular dive, levelling out at the last moment and firing their rockets. There were brief bursts of smoke, aerosol squirts from their wing pods lancing down to reduce what remained of the motel and its surrounding bush to a fiery rubble.

'The motel, Josh! Our headquarters.'

The fighters rose steeply to rejoin the other pair, high above the helpless capital, arrogant in their command of the air. The Buccaneers had grouped into parallel pairs below them, and all eight planes banked together in perfect formation, turning south-westwards, heading back towards their

116

bases in Namibia. The Mirages waggled their wings in defiance before disappearing into the haze.

Joshua and Harry finally turned to face each other.

'How did they know, Josh? We'd only been in the place four days. Who told them?'

'I can't begin to think. Who knew we were there?'

'Apart from us, maybe a dozen others. Most of them probably dead now.' Harry was thinking of the Congress soldiers who had guarded them, the cooks and functionaries who had worked for them. 'Don't you see how close they came to getting us? All of us, in one place at one time.'

The other three joined them at the edge of the roof. Pahlani and Gumbi looked stricken with shock, but J. K. Govender accosted Harry angrily.

'These are the people you think are ready to talk to us? People you talk about negotiating with? That is the language they speak, my friend!'

'Leave it out, J. K. What I want to know is how they found out.'

They were still arguing as they descended the stairs. To Joshua the immediate post-mortems seemed suddenly irrelevant. It had just occurred to him that *South African Nemesis* had been rather symbolically incinerated before it had got to Chapter Three.

10

In Algiers, early the following Saturday evening, Joshua was passing through the lounge of the Aletti Hotel when he spotted Harry Makibani sitting glumly on his own in a corner. No doubt he was waiting, or hoping, for the bar to open. Getting a drink in Algeria was a haphazard business, and self-denial had never been a strong point with Harry.

Joshua went over to him and the black man greeted him like a long-lost friend. They hadn't in fact seen much of each other in the six days they'd been here, their separate duties and engagements taking them on paths which seldom crossed.

'How are things, Harry?'

'Could be better. Not enough for me to do. Another week in this place and I'll be a basket case. Sit down, Josh. They tell me the bar is opening in a few minutes.'

'I was just going up to my room. . . .'

'No, no, sit down. I've been wanting to have a chat to you.'

Joshua pulled a chair up to Harry's table. 'Where are the others?'

'Around and about. Up at the gabfest, probably. Not my idea of a Saturday evening's entertainment.'

Joshua smiled ruefully. It was true that the debates of the Non-Aligned Conference up at the Palais du Peuple had often degenerated into a series of predictable squabbles. The Indian delegation had walked out on a speech by the Pakistani representative; Libya had withdrawn because Egypt was attending; and Iran and Iraq had turned a discussion on oil prices into an exchange of verbal missiles. On some points the conference could be safely expected to agree: there would be ritual condemnations of American imperialism, Zionist aggression and the West's continuing, if increasingly reluctant, support of South Africa.

For the South African People's Congress, the main reason for being here was to lobby for funds from sympathetic governments, and in this respect Joshua had had a rewarding week. Most of his business had been done in private meetings away from the main conference, and he had come away with promises of just over seven million dollars in immediate aid for the coming year, an increase of one and a half million on last year. Stated like that, it sounded like a lot of money, but it hardly came close to meeting the movement's rapidly growing needs.

While Joshua panhandled, J. K. Govender and Godfrey Pahlani had sat stiffly through the debates, Gumbi had vanished on mysterious missions involving the supply of arms, and Harry had put in token appearances at the conference.

'I've had time to think, Josh,' the black man said, 'and I'm

118

worried. I'm worried about important things that we should be talking about and aren't. Like that air raid. Somebody tipped them off about where we were, Josh. That was supposed to be a secure headquarters, and we'd been using it for exactly four days. Somewhere there's a leak in our security the size of the Victoria Falls. I really don't know who to trust any longer.'

'Why are you telling me, then?'

'I'm backing a hunch. I have faith in you, Josh. We share a certain – what can I call it? – lack of ideological blinkering? That's why you and I have to stick together.'

'You aren't suggesting that one of the others . . . on the Executive . . .?'

'Is an informer? No. If only because all five of us would have been fried in the same pan. The entire Executive, apart from Moses Mohaila in London. And even forgetting that he's a good friend to you and me, he'd have had nothing to gain from it either.'

'Somebody else inside the headquarters, then?' Joshua suggested, but Harry was shaking his head. When they'd driven back to the rubble of the motel that Sunday afternoon they'd found six Congress soldiers and workers dead, another four seriously injured.

'Those Boers weren't playing games, Josh, they were trying to kill us. They knew precisely where the motel was and what it was being used for. The only thing they didn't know was that we'd already left for the airport. They couldn't have told us in plainer language that there was an informer in the movement. Either they don't care if he's exposed or they know he's so secure that he never will be. No, I'm not pointing any fingers. I'm just saying the others are not taking it seriously enough. That's bad security in itself. They've got their priorities wrong. They've got too caught up running the organization and they're forgetting where the real action is. Take this story about Lincoln. Rumours that he's going to be released have even reached here, you know. I've had half a dozen people asking me whether they're true, and I've had to say dumbly that I don't know any more than they do.'

'No more news from down south?'

'Not a word. Another thing we haven't managed to discuss is that message that was sent out of Pollsmoor.' He tapped the breast pocket of his jacket. 'I've been carrying it around with me, breaking my skull over it and all those notes we were sent, but got no further. I really don't know how much it matters. I just think we're letting people down by not even trying.' Harry glanced at his watch and looked hopelessly around for a waiter. 'I don't believe this bar is ever going to open. Listen, why don't we have dinner together? I've found a place where you can get a decent bottle of wine if you're early enough. We can talk some more.'

They stood up and went to the reception desk. With his room key Joshua was also handed a letter, postmarked London.

'Who knows you're staying here?' Harry asked suspiciously.

'It's only my publisher. I phoned him when we arrived.'

'Not good, Josh. Security.'

'It really can't matter. I had to let him know about my manuscript.'

'Meet you down here. Twenty minutes?'

Up in his room, Joshua delayed opening the letter until he'd had a quick shower and changed his clothes. He was a little nervous of the letter. Perhaps his long-suffering publisher was about to become less tolerant. On the phone the poor fellow had sounded incredulous, and who could blame him? A manuscript destroyed in an air raid? In Bloomsbury that would sound like a pretty far-fetched excuse.

The envelope was bulky, a size larger than usual, and when he'd opened it he understood why. Besides a note on his publisher's stationery it contained another letter, sealed in an airmail envelope but without an address or a stamp. There was just his name, handwritten in a vaguely familiar scribble, and the heavily underlined instruction, *To be forwarded urgently. Private and Confidential*.

He ignored this mystery for a moment. The publisher's note was brief and reassuring. Much sympathy on the loss of

Nemesis. Quite understand the further delay. No hurry. At the bottom he had written: 'The enclosed has just arrived, under cover of a South African envelope addressed only to us. Thought I should get it off to you soonest.'

Joshua tore open the second envelope and extracted several sheets of airmail-weight writing paper. There was no address at the head of the letter, just a date: 11 November. That was eight days ago.

It began:

Dear Joshua,
I don't know when, where or even whether this will reach you, but I have to write in the hope that it will find you somehow, and soon.

It must be ages – 3 or 4 years? – since I last heard from you, and even longer since I wrote to thank you for the birthday cards you used to send. Ungrateful cow. Nowadays I'd rather forget my birthdays. You had such a lot of cover addresses over the years that I lost track, and now I can't find the last one you gave me.

As it is, I feel I'm firing this off into a vacuum. I recall you saying you had a commission to write a book. I remembered the publishers' name and got their address from the flyleaf of one of their titles.

Why I'm writing is this. No. First I should warn you that it's just possible that I'm being watched, so whatever you do don't try to contact me. Daddy has got himself involved in something I think is sinister and ugly. He's going to operate, in secret, on someone at the behest of the Security Police . . .

Joshua sat down slowly on the end of his bed, gripping the pages tightly, staring hard at the breathless scrawl.

I discovered something about this by accident and confronted him with it. He told me just that and no more, and swore me to secrecy. He was at great pains to explain that there was nothing illegal or underhand about it, but somehow I can't believe that. You know

121

how they torture and ill-treat people, how they take them into custody and make them just disappear. The point is that for some unfathomable reason he's letting them use him – his position, his reputation – to do their dirty work for them. I think in a way he sees this himself, but believes he's in control of the situation. His vanity is monstrous! Of course he won't discuss the thing any further, but I can see that if this is some dirty trick that goes wrong he'll be nicely set up to take the blame.

This probably sounds paranoid as hell. I think anyone would feel the same in the circumstances. I'd be skinned alive if anyone knew I had written this. There are all sorts of laws they can use. What I want to ask is whether you could find a way to expose this somehow before it's too late. Maybe not you personally, but the People's Congress, without of course attributing any of it to me. There's nobody here I could risk approaching, and the newspapers aren't allowed to touch this kind of thing now. Of course I don't know the name of the patient (or victim) but they've got a code-name for this project. It is INDUNA. He doesn't know I also found this out, but the operation is scheduled for the 15th or 16th of December.

I do feel vaguely disloyal. God knows why he is doing this. I don't see eye to eye with Daddy about many things but I hate to think of his integrity being compromised. Mummy of course is oblivious to everything but her dahlias . . .

'*Induna*,' said Harry half an hour later, taking a grateful gulp of wine. 'You know what that means. An *induna* was the leader of an *impi*, a Zulu regiment, back in the old days. Apt enough. Tell me who she is again.'

'My cousin's daughter. Judith Rose. Actually she always called me "uncle". I'm also her godfather.'

'A Jew can be a godfather?' Harry said quizzically.

'Not strictly speaking, I suppose. But, then, Judith and my

cousin Louis aren't really Jewish. He had a Gentile mother. That's why he calls himself Rose, even though our fathers were brothers—'

'Why don't you start at the beginning?' Harry suggested.

They sat in a crowded restaurant in the Rue Ben M'Hidi, a dilapidated vestige of what had once been the elegant Rue d'Isly in French colonial times. Harry had drunk the best part of a bottle of Monts du Zaccar with their first course, and then ordered another. 'Panic buying,' he explained. 'You never know when they're going to stop serving it.' He had also read Judith's letter three times, and now he sat listening intently to Joshua.

'You didn't know I had a cousin in Jo'burg? Louis is a urologist, a specialist in urinary diseases. He's also a highly respected surgeon and the owner of a small private hospital called the Woodvale Clinic. A fat cat, in other words, and a liberal up to a point.

'Our fathers were the Rosenblatt brothers, Abie and David. They grew up in Frankfurt, but went out to Johannesburg together as young men in the nineteen twenties. They were both tailors. They set up shop in Jeppe – you remember Jeppe? – and came to be known as the Rose brothers. The name stuck to them vaguely, especially to Abie when he married a Gentile girl who didn't convert. There were some social advantages in not being too obviously Jewish in Jo'burg in those days. Well, later David got married as well, in his case to a Jewish girl. Abie's wife had one son, Louis, and I was David's boy. There were no other children.

'The families were pretty close, as you can imagine. The brothers' only relatives were still in Germany, and virtually none of them survived the concentration camps. Louis and I grew up more like brothers than cousins. Our fathers had prospered. We both were sent to a rather posh school: High Anglican, Jewboys not quite the thing at that time, so the surname Rose came in quite handy. I can't say I distinguished myself there, but the older cousin, the high achiever, not only swept the board academically, but also out-WASPed them all: rugby colours, cricket captain, head boy, the lot. He also did brilliantly at medical school, while I sort of blundered into accountancy.

'Well, he became Dr Louis Rose, high flying young medical specialist, got married, had three kids: all the right things. I remained plain Mr Rosenblatt, the balding bachelor. All our parents were dead by the time we were in our thirties, and there wasn't much left to hold us together. I think Louis was always driven by a need to escape from his background, while I tended to backslide into mine. I don't think he minded that I got involved in politics, and got banned and put under house arrest. He just thought that going to jail was a rather vulgar thing to do.

'I always got on well with his family. Especially Judith. She always had the makings of a tearaway. I gather she hasn't really settled down to anything much since she left school, and it seems from this letter that she's been working lately in her old man's nice exclusive clinic. Well, that's the background. The letter explains itself.'

Harry had been eating a beef daube as he listened. He mopped up the last of the sauce with a crust of bread, chewed judiciously for a minute and took a large gulp of wine. He sighed, sat back and looked at Joshua.

'Yes, Josh. It does explain itself. It also solves the mystery.'

'What mystery?'

'The message from Pollsmoor, man.' He took the sheaf of notes from his pocket and flattened them on the table beside the letter. 'All these biblical quotations I told you about. Nandi Kumalo was on the right track: it's the key words that contain the meaning. But there were a couple that she missed, that she hadn't a hope of figuring out without more information. Look here. It's this middle sentence that made the least sense of all.' He quoted: '"The wilderness and the solitary place shall be glad for them; and the desert shall rejoice, and blossom as the rose." Isn't it obvious?'

'Not to me, I'm afraid.'

'As *the rose*, Josh. Just put a capital *r* on that you have the name of your esteemed cousin. Dr Rose.' He watched Joshua's face with satisfaction. 'You want more proof? Cut out this middle bit about the desert rejoicing, because that was just there to guide us to the real thing, and the key words you are left with are "wilderness – solitary place – rose". For "wilderness" read *wood*, for "solitary place" read *vale*. Vale of tears, and all that. Wood. Vale. The Woodvale Clinic.'

Joshua was incredulous. 'You're saying Louis is going to operate there, on Lincoln Kumalo?'

'And on December the sixteenth. Just as the message says, and just as your little niece or whatever she is has confirmed. Only she's got the wrong end of the stick, or was given the wrong end. She imagines some sinister medical experiment, a lobotomy or something being carried out under the orders of the police. The truth is simpler. They are keeping the identity of the patient secret, no doubt for reasons of security.'

Harry leaned back again, a smug, black Sherlock Holmes to Joshua's plodding Watson, awaiting the next question.

'All right. Assuming your deductions are correct, then the message from the prison was accurate. Does it change anything?'

'Of course it does. We've now had independent confirmation that parts of it are absolutely authentic. That means we must take the whole thing very seriously indeed. Without knowing it, your little Judith lady is quite right: there is something sinister going on. Just look at all the key words we have now.' He stabbed a finger at the papers. '"True – smite" – let's leave out "neighbour" – "secretly – December 16th – Woodvale – Rose – wretched man – body – death." You don't have to be a cryptographer to work out that something pretty nasty is on the cards. All right, it's not very specific, but whoever sent this had to be careful. He was relying on Nandi, or somebody, to put two and two together and come up with five. The meaning of that sum is that Lincoln is in some deadly danger, Josh. And it's got to be stopped.'

'What do you mean, stopped?'

'*Who shall deliver him*, Josh?' Harry spoke with a sudden tipsy solemnity. The second bottle of wine was by now well punished. 'You and me, Josh, that's who. We're the only

125

ones who know. We've got the two matching halves of the ticket, and we're going to keep it to ourselves. We're going to find out what's going on down there, Josh, and we're going to stop it. If necessary, we're going to get Kumalo out!'

He fell silent as a waiter appeared and removed their plates. Two crême caramels were placed in front of them. Harry tucked in to his with relish and drank some more wine.

'You're not making sense, Harry. Even if such a thing were possible, the rest of the executive would have to agree—'

'Bugger them!' Harry waved his spoon carelessly. 'They'd hum and they'd haw, they'd raise objections. Besides . . .' He became confiding. 'I told you I wasn't happy about our security. Apart from that business of the air raid, you and I know quite well that there are people in our movement who pay lip service to the idea of having Lincoln back as our leader, while all the time they know that he'd threaten their own positions. He's safer where he is, as far as they're concerned.'

Joshua shrugged uncomfortably. 'All this is highly hypothetical.'

'Maybe. But a lot could be hanging on it. It needs to be checked out, and quickly. December the sixteenth is less than a month away. What we need is our own man in there. Yes, that's it – somebody who knows what he's doing, who can find out what needs to be known and act on it if necessary. A complete outsider, in fact, who'd report directly to us. Somebody they won't connect with us or with the Congress. Somebody above suspicion, who's also tough and capable . . .'

This was getting absurd, Joshua thought. 'A man of action, and yet a dreamer withal?' he suggested sarcastically. 'Come off it, Harry—'

'You're not taking me seriously!' the black man snapped. If the wine had made his thinking grandiose, his wits were still sharp. 'We're in the business of revolutionary politics –

a thing you perhaps forget when you're buried in your account books. I'm talking about a professional intelligence operation, possibly also a military one, and we need a skilled professional to take charge of it. Though I don't like to admit it, he'll probably have to be a white man.'

'A mercenary?'

'Shit, Josh, you don't believe any of that Rambo rubbish about mercenaries, do you? Let me tell you that they are a bunch of cut-throats, criminals and psychopaths who'll take money from the highest bidder to kill the next-highest. Especially if he happens to be black. They are also, on the whole, a bunch of remarkably stupid men. No. We need someone smart. Someone for whom money is an inducement but not the decisive factor. Someone who's actually willing to take our side.'

'Assuming you could find such a paragon, he'd still have to be paid,' Joshua pointed out.

'We've got money,' Harry said dismissively. 'We've got seven million dollars.'

'You know that isn't ours to play with.'

'We wouldn't be playing with it. We'd be investing it.' Harry gave a sudden mischievous grin. 'Just you and me, Josh. A small private investment. I think it could be done.'

The restaurant did not serve coffee. Harry tried to order a third bottle of wine, but fortunately was refused; the place was closing in a few minutes, though it was barely nine o'clock. As they walked back towards the hotel through streets already almost deserted, the cool November air seemed to sober Harry up, or at least to curb his volubility. For this Joshua was grateful. Harry was a persuasive character, and his enthusiasm was infectious: Joshua had felt himself beginning to be bludgeoned into a kind of belief in this extravagant scheme.

The respite was brief, however. As they turned on to the boulevard above the dark waterfront, Harry said: 'This money we've just been pledged – how soon will it be paid?'

'Within the next week or two.'

'What are the mechanics of it?'

127

Joshua felt he was on safe ground. 'Well, as you know, we keep our main holding account at the Union Banque Suisse in Zurich. I'm making separate arrangements with each of the governments that's contributing money, to pick up the cheques in person at their various embassies in Bern. I'll deposit them at once in the UBS.'

'Which then invests the money for us?'

'They put it into liquid securities: gilt-edged stocks, treasury bonds, that sort of thing.'

'All those securities are readily convertible to cash, aren't they?'

'Yes, but—'

'And any other Swiss bank could give us a similar service, presumably. What's to stop you depositing some of that money in a new account, a different bank?'

'There's no earthly reason to do that, Harry.'

'Stop thinking like an accountant, Josh. Can you or can't you?'

'I could, but only with the agreement of the full executive committee.'

'But, as you well know, it's the finance committee that handles these things on a day-to-day basis. And you and I constitute two of its five members. If we get one more to agree, we'll have a majority. All the executive needs to know is that we've decided to establish a relationship with a second bank, to diversify our investments a little. As long as there's no urgent call on the money for a couple of months or so, nobody needs to know exactly what's been done with it. Do they?'

'Well, you still couldn't do anything without that third vote.' Joshua spoke with finality, but also with the uneasy feeling that he was being drawn into a trap.

'There's Moses Mohaila in London. I trust him, and I'm sure I could get him to agree. It's not as though we'd be stealing the cash,' he added soothingly. 'We'd just be keeping control of it for a while. And by the time the executive finds out . . . well, they may have no choice but to consider it money well spent. The thing is, I can't go to this man empty-handed. I've got to have something to put up front.'

They had reached the entrance to the Aletti Hotel. Joshua stopped and turned. 'This man? You talk as though you'd already chosen him.'

'As a matter of fact,' said Harry, 'I think I have.' He paused. 'It may take me some time to find him, but if I can, then he's the only one for the job.' He gave his conspiratorial grin again. 'I'm not really needed around here, you know. I think I'm going to take a little trip to London.'

'Just a minute, just a minute.' At some point this conversation had got out of control, Joshua thought. 'You can't go committing us to anything. We haven't even talked about the money. I mean, how much money?'

'Oh, half a million dollars or so initially,' said Harry airily. 'And we should have another couple of million in reserve, of course.'

PART TWO

THE MAN

11

A dozen times that Tuesday morning the Labrador bitch had flushed pheasants from the long wet grass, but Patrick Marriner had taken the trouble to shoot only twice, bagging a fat hen each time. There was no point in killing more than could be eaten, and he had a whole winter's shooting ahead of him. He wasn't out for serious sport anyway, he was inspecting the cattle fences for damage and loose wire; he took the gun with him mainly because it pleased the Labrador to see him with it and encouraged her to search for birds.

Marriner always enjoyed these three-mile tramps around the perimeter of his farm. They gave him a reassuring sense of possession. For a man who had rarely been settled in one place for more than a year or two, there was still enough novelty in the idea of his owning this land to please him. Ownership being, of course, a relative term; the farm was still heavily mortgaged after the depredations of his Uncle Ham, but at least he had managed to turn its perennial losses into a modest profit and keep it from the clutches of the bankers.

His way home led across sloping fields where some of his Aberdeen Angus herd munched contentedly on a rich growth of grass. The weather had been good this past summer, with just the right combination of sunshine and rain, cutting down on the need to buy winter fodder. He had taught himself to farm, and no doubt he was far from perfect at it,

131

but he had always found satisfaction in doing things for himself. His neighbours in this hilly South Cork country were charming people who had been genuinely concerned that a novice would make a hash of the whole business. They were also mostly dairy farmers, doubtful that old Hamilton Marriner had ever been wise to stick to his beef herd. In time they had come to regard his nephew with baffled admiration. Ballygarron had become a viable farm again, and this proved an unexpected source of pride to those who remembered its history.

Patrick Marriner had also discovered that farming wasn't quite the time-consuming business that everyone made it out to be. After a couple of years of really back breaking work while he rescued the land from a decade of neglect, he had found that the system he'd established functioned smoothly enough to require more supervision than actual labour on his part. Especially at this time of year, with the mature bullocks sold for slaughter, the hay cut and stored and the silage made, he found time fairly easy on his hands.

He saw a car approaching the house when he was still two hundred yards short of it. The Labrador saw it as well, and stiffened and growled. It was a newish red Ford Fiesta, one that he didn't recognize, and just the faintest flicker of apprehension sent the adrenalin threading through his veins. He felt automatically for the spare shotgun cartridges in the pocket of his Barbour jacket, then told himself he was being ridiculous. If trouble ever came to Ballygarron, it would not arrive in broad daylight. He had no need to be concerned about the attitude of anyone in the locality; of that he was absolutely certain. But there had always been the possibility that the wrong people in Dublin, or even Belfast, would pick up word of his background and put too simple a construction on it. The odds were perhaps a thousand to one. The chances of their choosing to do anything about it were infinitely more remote, but they were something of which one tiny corner of his mind was constantly aware.

He saw now that the Fiesta's driver was unfamiliar with the surroundings. The elm-lined avenue that led from the

Bandon road approached Ballygarron House from the side, so that it was difficult at first to see where the front door was. The driver hesitated at the junction, then made the right choice and drove on to the gravelled forecourt, disappearing from Marriner's view. The car had appeared to have only one occupant.

He walked on, ordering the bitch to heel. He had a lean but muscular six-foot frame and a rangy outdoor look that made him seem younger than his age, which was forty-three. No amount of Irish sunshine could have accounted for his colouring, which was tawny in the permanent way of fair-skinned people who have spent years in hot climates. His hair, once bleached almost yellow by the sun, had returned to a palish brown, speckled nowadays with grey. Thoughtful blue eyes and a small firm mouth gave the suggestion of a trim disciplined man, content within himself but perhaps not too easy to impress.

In the yard behind the kitchen he leaned his shotgun against the wall and stripped off his gumboots and jacket. Mary O'Leary, his housekeeper, came to the door.

'There's a man wanting to see you, Major. I've put him in the library.'

'Thank you.' He handed her his game bag with the pheasants in it. 'Hang these for me, will you? Oh, and will you get a couple of those sea trout out of the freezer? Mrs Swanson is coming for dinner.'

'Ah, that'll be nice for you.' Mary approved of Jenny Swanson, in spite of some possible reservations about the code of behaviour to be expected of a widow woman. 'Will I stay on and do the dinner, Major?'

'Thanks, Mary, but I can just about manage to cook a fish. Who's the man?'

'A Mr . . . Mac-something?' she said hopefully.

'Did he say what he wanted?'

'No. He . . .' There was an odd note of curiosity in her voice, but she stopped herself saying whatever she'd been going to and disappeared into the house.

Marriner followed her, pausing beside the door to slip on

his shoes. He laid the shotgun, broken open, on the table in the vast old kitchen and stopped at the sink to wash his hands. To no avail he had tried to discourage Mary and her husband Mick, the farm foreman, from addressing him by his army rank. There was much respect for that sort of thing ingrained in people of their generation, and no doubt they considered it suited the traditions of Ballygarron House.

It was a classical four-square Georgian farmhouse that had been in his family since the early 1800s and was still much as his uncle had left it, a bachelor establishment for the past forty years with its décor badly neglected. It was stuffed with heavy old furniture and gloomy paintings, though anything of real value had long since been sold off to keep Uncle Ham's creditors at bay. Ham had been born in the wrong century, that was his trouble. His passions had been fishing, shooting and whiskey, increasingly the latter in his last years, and he had been emphatically a gentleman first and a farmer second. Only the loyalty and hard work of Mick O'Leary had saved Ballygarron from bankruptcy years before Uncle Ham succumbed to a long-standing liver complaint, leaving the estate and its debts to his nephew.

Marriner's first inclination had been to sell the farm for whatever it would fetch, but then he had reconsidered. Although he had spent most of his life abroad and had no sentimental attachment to the place, it seemed a pity to surrender it in such adverse circumstances. Then, as well, the inheritance had come at a critical point in his own life, just as he was nearing forty, facing up to the reality of a failed marriage and wondering whether twenty years in the Army wasn't long enough. He had resigned his commission and decided to make a go of Ballygarron.

His friends in the Parachute Regiment had said he was crazy, that he had a bright future ahead of him. A battalion command was the logical next step, and all his experience in special operations, the SAS and military missions abroad had shown him to have just the kind of talents that an efficient, pared-down British army needed at the top. The Military Cross he had won in the Falklands would be no disadvantage either, though it had seemed a hollow honour at the time. It was not in a spirit of triumph that he had returned from the bloodiest battle of that brief conflict, but with a sense of its savage futility.

He walked from the kitchen, down the long hallway with its threadbare carpet and faded wallpaper, to the library. He'd never had the spare money to do anything to the house, and the Widow Swanson was always saying that her hands itched to redecorate it. Maybe one day he would let her at it; all that stopped him was a feeling that it would give her too much of a stake, not in the house, but in him.

His visitor was standing by one of the bookshelves, paging through an old leather-bound volume he had picked out. He looked up and beamed with pleasure, and Marriner had to hide his surprise.

Mr Mac-something was black.

He wore a grey three-piece suit with rather a loud pale stripe. He was fat in a solid way that made it seem natural to him: *portly* was probably the word. He was about fifty, and his face was familiar from somewhere: Marriner could get no nearer than that.

'Major Marriner!' The man's smile was vivid. He snapped the book shut. 'Please forgive the intrusion. I meant to phone first, but on impulse I decided just to turn up. We have met, but there's no reason why you should remember. It was at Beira, in Mozambique – oh, seventy-eight or nine? Makibani. Harry Makibani.'

He stuck out a hand and Marriner shook it. Recognition came. Beira, formerly a sleepy, steamy little East African port, had been a hotbed of intrigue in those days. The Marxist government of Mozambique had given refuge there to the Rhodesian liberation movement, ZANU, then still engaged in its bush war against the white rebel regime across the border. Harry Makibani, as a fellow African nationalist, had been a frequent visitor to ZANU's headquarters. He was a liaison officer, or 'fraternal delegate' or some such, from the South African People's Congress based in similar exile in Lusaka. He was usually to be found drinking dark Laurentina

135

beer in the cafés where the 'boys' hung out – the guerrillas in between missions, the young politicians and theorists of revolution. Always engaged in some amiable argument, Makibani had had less reason to be inconspicuous than Marriner.

'I do remember. It's a surprise to see you, all the same. My housekeeper thought your name was *Mac*–something.'

The black man chuckled. 'She's not the first one. Perhaps I have Irish or Scottish ancestors. Picked up a tan in the colonies, eh?'

Marriner smiled, feeling a twinge of nostalgia for the easy, self-deprecating African humour. 'You aren't living here now, surely?'

'No, no, just visiting. Still in Lusaka, still in the same business.'

'Sit down. Some coffee? Or maybe it's time for a drink?'

Makibani glanced appreciatively at the bottles arrayed on a table in the corner. 'It *is* time for a drink,' he said firmly. 'Cork Dry Gin? I think I should give that a try.'

'With tonic? I'll go and get some.'

Marriner left the room and Harry Makibani lingered by the bookshelves, grateful for a minute in which to arrange his thoughts. His reception had been friendly; he was over the first hurdle. Marriner hadn't immediately asked why he was here, which was further encouragement; it could be allowed to emerge naturally, while they weighed each other up. Harry had told only one small lie: he had never had any intention of telephoning before his arrival. A voice on the phone is easier to dismiss than a presence in your sitting room, as every insurance salesman knows.

His host returned, carrying tonic, an ice-bucket, slices of lemon on a saucer. Harry approved of his style, though he was glad to find that his surroundings tended to confirm what he had managed to learn about Marriner: that he was not exactly flush with money. He knew enough of European standards and conventions to recognize shabby gentility when he saw it. Everything was old here, but nothing was valuable.

To forestall questions while Marriner mixed their drinks, he said, 'I was a little surprised to learn that you were living here. With the trouble in Northern Ireland, an ex-British Army officer . . . couldn't you be at risk?'

'From the IRA? It's a slight possibility, but only from those who don't know their history. I'm Irish, you see. Well, Anglo-Irish. It's part of our tradition to serve in the British Army, but it's also understood that I belong here. My grandfather was shot by the Black and Tans. Right in front of this house, actually.'

'He was a rebel?' Harry asked with interest.

'Far from it. He was a Unionist gentleman. He disliked the Tans because they were scoundrels and thugs. They turned up here one night in nineteen-twenty to arrest two of his labourers who they claimed were Sinn Feiners. He went out and challenged them, full of whiskey and belligerence, and they shot him. And so he died for Ireland. Around here, what your grandfather was is often more important than what you are.'

'I'm afraid all that is a bit beyond me,' Harry confessed.

'You'd need to live here to understand it.' Marriner handed him his drink. 'Well, cheers.'

Harry took a hefty swallow of gin and they sat down, facing each other, in a pair of cracked leather armchairs. Marriner's silence was a tacit invitation to his visitor to state his business, but Harry wasn't quite ready for that yet.

'Beira, Major—'

'Do call me Patrick.'

'All right. Patrick. I suppose you haven't been back to Beira? It used to be a nice little town. You should see it now. It's almost cut off from the rest of Mozambique by a rebel army trained and supported by the South Africans. No water, no light, no food. Rubbish littering the streets, kids going hungry. South Africa is systematically destroying the economies of its neighbours to force them into a state of dependence. It's not good, Patrick.'

'I follow the news from there quite keenly,' Marriner said neutrally.

'Those are countries whose armies you helped to train. Whose independence you were helping to defend, really. Zambia. Mozambique. That *was* what you were doing in Beira, wasn't it? You and about half a dozen sunburnt Englishmen trying hard to look like tourists?'

'I was in charge of a small British military mission. It was quite legitimate, but it had to be kept very unofficial. The Mozambicans didn't want to jeopardize all the Russian aid they were getting by being seen to flirt with us Western imperialists. We were assessing the needs of their army.'

'And keeping an eye on the Russians? That's what we suspected, anyway. Never mind. Everybody was snooping on somebody else in Beira.' Harry smiled to show it was of no importance; but there was no avoiding the main issue now. He said, 'Patrick, I can't say I know you well, but I think you're the sort of man who would appreciate frankness. I'd made up a story about being in Ireland on other business, about hearing your name by chance and deciding to look you up, but . . . well, I've decided it's best not to pretend. The truth is, I went to some trouble to locate you.'

'I'd worked that out already,' Marriner said coolly.

'When I was visiting London a few years ago I saw your name in a newspaper. It was the *Daily Telegraph*, I think. It was just a few lines near the back, mentioning that you'd resigned your army commission to take up farming. The only thing that made it in any way newsworthy was that you'd recently been decorated for heroism in the Falklands campaign.'

Marriner nodded slightly. Harry went on: 'Three days ago I happened to remember that newspaper item. I came back to London to try to find you. I didn't want to make any enquiries through official channels, so it was a matter of hunting through telephone directories and voters' lists. No luck there, but I did try phoning a few of the Marriners at random, and one of them told me he thought there was an Irish branch of the family. We have a few friends over here: Congress sympathizers, and some members of the Anti-Apartheid Movement. I located you, and had a few discreet enquiries made. Without, of course, revealing why.'

Marriner was amused. Harry was about the least likely private detective he could imagine. 'Well, you haven't told me why yet.'

'Patrick, if all I've heard about you is right, you've spent quite a large part of your military career doing cloak-and-dagger jobs of one kind or another. Special and covert operations, intelligence work, delicate missions in foreign countries. You were also brought up in Southern Africa, and your soldiering took you back there quite a lot. That means you know it from the inside. I think you also have sympathy for its problems. That's quite a unique combination of qualities.'

Marriner looked at him curiously. 'You make me sound like a colonial romantic. Well, it's true that in some ways I feel more at home out there than anywhere else.'

'That's good, Patrick. I want to know if you'd consider going back there for a short while. And doing a job for us.'

'For the People's Congress? What kind of job?'

'Just the kind you're equipped for. Covert intelligence, and quite possibly a rescue mission. I won't beat about the bush: at best it will be tricky, at worst it will be bloody dangerous. It's also extremely urgent.'

For all his cheeriness, Harry Makibani could be businesslike and even forceful. Marriner found himself readjusting his defences. 'You need another drink,' he said.

Harry's gin and tonic had disappeared at amazing speed. As he got up and busied himself with the bottle and glasses, Marriner was struck by his own lack of surprise. You didn't walk away from a background like his all that easily. Maybe it was something like this, and not the IRA, that he'd really been waiting for every time he saw a car approaching the house or wondered at the look he was getting from a stranger when he visited Bandon or Cork City.

He gave Harry his drink. For himself he'd poured only tonic water this time. Alcohol addiction had run like a deadly virus thorough two generations of his family, and although he'd never felt himself in danger of dependence he was always wary.

'I know that your first inclination will be to back off,' Harry said, 'so I'll tell you straight away that the money will be good. The money could be damned spectacular, in fact.'

'In proportion to the risk, do you mean?'

'The money is no problem, Patrick. But we also need a man who will put his heart into it. I know you're right for this job. I'll tell you just as much as I can afford to at the moment. In return I won't ask you to commit yourself right away, just to agree to take it one stage further. Do I need to add that this is entirely between us?' Marriner shook his head. 'Very good. You're not married, Patrick?'

'I used to be.'

'Children?'

'No. She stayed in England when I moved over here. We had different ideas about our future.'

'So you have no family commitments? Nobody you have to give an account of yourself to? I mean, it wouldn't look terribly strange if you went away for three or four weeks at fairly short notice, would it?'

'Now hang on, Harry.' The man needed firm handling; he would have made a fortune selling encyclopaedias. 'It's not a question of what it would look like. You don't imagine this farm runs itself, do you?'

'Of course not. But, unlike some of my more idealistic friends in the Congress, I have great faith in the power of money to solve certain problems. This sounds like one of them. However, we're still talking hypothetically. All I want to know now is whether you could manage a trip to Zurich, just for twenty-four hours or so, some time within the next couple of days. No catches. No strings attached.'

'Why Zurich?' Marriner asked suspiciously.

'Because that's where the money is, Patrick. That's where we'll take it a stage further, and ask you to say yes or no. We'll pay all your expenses, naturally, but also we don't expect you to give us your time for nothing. You're a professional, after all. There'll be – what shall we call it? – a consultancy fee. And also a sign of our good faith. How does five thousand pounds sterling sound?'

It sounded astonishing. Marriner tried to hide his surprise, but Harry gave him a knowing grin. 'That's just hello money, Patrick. We'll be talking much bigger numbers. We're very serious about this.'

Marriner stood up and went and stared out of the window. He was far from reassured. Five thousand pounds was a ludicrous figure, clearly intended to overwhelm him, to blow his critical faculties to hell. Whatever Harry's talk about there being no strings attached, accepting it would place him under an obligation. On the other hand, perhaps it was they and not he who had lost a sense of proportion. He could certainly use the money, and if they were prepared to throw it around he would be foolish not even to consider picking it up.

'How would it be paid?' he asked.

'I have a cash cheque already made out, Patrick.'

'That was jumping the gun a bit, wasn't it?'

'I don't have time to mess around. I told you it was urgent.'

He made a decision. He went back to his chair. 'All right,' he said. 'I'll take it, but strictly on a sale-or-return basis. I'll fly to Zurich and talk to you, but I won't decide until then whether to cash the cheque or not. I want to know more about this first. If I don't like what I hear, I'll give you the money back.'

'If that's what you wish,' said Harry equably,' 'then that's fine by me. I want no mistrust or friction between us.' He took a plain white envelope from his breast pocket and placed it on the small table between them. Marriner left it there. 'How would Thursday suit you? The day after tomorrow. If you can get yourself to Dublin, I'll have a ticket waiting for you at the airport for the first flight out that morning. I'll get a travel agency to make the arrangements and advise you.'

Harry looked pleased with himself. His glass was empty again, and this time he simply handed it to Marriner to be refilled. There was nothing coy about Harry.

'Well, now that's out of the way,' he said, leaning forward, 'there are one or two things I can tell you.'

12

Jenny Swanson turned on the bedside lamp and reached for her cigarettes. When she had lit one she lay back, blowing smoke contentedly and staring at the ceiling.

'You really ought to get that moulding restored,' she said. 'It could look quite lovely.'

Marriner grunted. Post-coital reflectiveness was unknown to Jenny, and it no longer surprised him that a minute after ardent lovemaking she should be mentally redecorating his bedroom. In another woman he might have found this disconcerting, but her attitude to sex was as natural as it was to everything else.

'Maybe I will fix it up,' he said. 'The trouble with this house is that renovating one part would make all the rest look twice as shabby. Once I started I wouldn't be able to stop.'

'Like me, h'mm?' She leaned across the bed and nuzzled his ear with her lips. When he had first come to South Cork and before he had even met Jenny he had heard her described – snidely and unoriginally, but with a grain of truth – as the Merry Widow. It wasn't that she was promiscuous; her vivacious nature was simply mistaken by people without imagination for availability. Jenny was rather amused at her own reputation, and rose above the gossip with a proper ascendancy disdain. Her conscience was clear. She had loved her husband, but she had been only thirty at the time of his death in a car crash, and she wasn't going to spend the rest of her life grieving for him. That he had left her extremely well off was beside the point. She managed her four hundred acres with an effortless efficiency that still allowed her time to ride to hounds, play tennis, collect paintings and visit Paris, Florence or Vienna two or three times a year. She had style and she had energy. It had seemed almost inevitable that she and Marriner should drift together.

Tonight they had been too impatient to wait until dinner

was over. Within ten minutes of her arrival they had made love, quickly and greedily, on the moth-eaten hearthrug in front of the drawing-room fire. Then they had eaten his sea trout and drunk a bottle of Bourgogne Aligoté and gone to bed properly.

'What if I were to give you a free hand with the house?' he said. 'I mean, invited you in to do whatever you thought it needed. Within financial reason, of course,' he added quickly. 'What would it cost?'

'Oh, well, you'd want the floorboards sanded and polished. New wallpaper and paint throughout. Some plasterwork and some other small repairs, inevitably. I suppose three or four thousand?'

'I know these things always cost more than one expects.'

'Not with me in charge.' Jenny had the thriftiness of her class as well as sureness of taste. She spent money but never wasted it. 'You aren't actually serious, are you? You'd let me arrange all that?'

'I'd pay you for it, of course. We could work something out. It's possible that I may be going away for a few weeks. It would be a good opportunity to get it done.'

He would have had to warn her sooner or later, and this seemed the best context in which to do it. Perhaps it hadn't quite sunk in, however; she lay looking into his face as if searching for a new meaning to his words.

'Why do this all of a sudden? You've always said you couldn't afford it.'

'Maybe now I'll be able to.'

'Jolly good. There's something I can say to you now, Patrick. I've always suspected that you felt if you let me do anything like that for you I'd also be taking you over. I don't want to possess you. Silly.' She poked him in the ribs with her finger, stubbed out her cigarette, then threw back the bedcovers and padded over to the bathroom. Exercise had kept her figure as firm as a young girl's, and even given her a slight muscularity that suited her.

'Where are you going, anyway?' she called over her shoulder.

'As I said, it's only a possibility. Some business that's far from definite yet. Africa.'

He did not specify where, and she didn't ask. Jenny could have guided him around two dozen cities in Europe, but he knew that Africa to her was merely a vast amorphous landmass, a place she had never visited and had no interest in.

She disappeared into the bathroom. Maybe he didn't appreciate her enough, he thought. She was clever, she was good company and she made no emotional demands of him. There were also unstated rules of privacy about each other's personal affairs, and he was glad he did not have to lie to her.

In an unsatisfactory way, he and Harry Makibani had talked that morning about a possible cover story.

'Business, Patrick. You'd be going to South Africa on business.'

'What business? What if I'm asked? I don't know the first thing about business.'

'We'll have to work something out for you. What occupation does your passport show?'

'Army officer. I've had it for eight years.'

'Mmm. Not helpful. And there's no time to renew it – at least, not without going through a lot of explanations. You can't call yourself a tourist, certainly. Tourists head for the game reserves and the beaches. You're going to have to hang around and poke about in places where they don't go. It's best to tell as much of the truth as possible. You never know when they might decide to take an interest in you, and for no particular reason. Somebody at the airport may not like the look of you and decide to check out your movements. You're going to have to lie low and do nothing untoward for two or three days. That's another reason to get you there as soon as possible.'

'Harry, whatever I do, whatever I call myself, do you really expect me to go in there and walk out with Lincoln Kumalo in my luggage?'

It was the name of Lincoln Kumalo that had come as the real shock of Harry's visit. He'd been on his fourth gin at that stage, had warmed to Marriner and become more confiding than he'd set out to be. Up to then, he'd painted a scrappy but not unconvincing word-picture of an anonymous black political figure under threat, the need to find out more, the possible necessity of springing him from a hospital bed. Such things had been done at other times and places. It was when he let slip the name that the whole scenario seemed to become absurd. Marriner had realized he should have been warned by that figure of five thousand pounds. He'd been tempted to hand it back right then, and still couldn't work out why he hadn't.

'Now who is jumping the gun?' Harry had demanded. 'All we ask is that you go there and look around. We will give you the contacts you need. Find out how true this thing is and, if it is, study the feasibility of getting Kumalo out.'

'All within three weeks?'

'I know the time is short, but we have no choice. You are a foreigner they will not suspect; a white man who can move freely among them, who can set the springs. Do you realize the significance of this, Patrick?' Harry had asked with a rhetorical flourish, waving his glass. 'The People's Congress is sometimes called the spear of the revolution. You can be our spearhead, Patrick!'

Jenny reappeared from the bathroom. She sprang on to the foot of the bed, lithely naked, and walked forward, straining the bedsprings, until she bestrode his chest. She smiled down at him like a playful female Colossus, her spread thighs teasing and inviting him. He took hold of the backs of her knees and pulled her down.

They coupled indolently, without urgency, Jenny murmuring as she moved slowly on top of him.

'There. Yes, that's nice. I want to make this last. You aren't going to screw a lot of black ladies out there, are you?'

'I doubt it.'

'Keep your hands there. Yes. There's a lot of AIDS in Africa, isn't there? Is that the deterrent?'

'No.'

'What is, then? Do you mean you're going to be faithful to

145

me? Oh God, do that again. That means I'll have to be faithful back.'

'Anything wrong with that?'

'Only the frustration. Doesn't it occur to you that I'm going to miss you, you bastard?'

Later, while Jenny lay in a sated sleep beside him, Marriner's mind drifted back to thoughts of Africa. He'd only just missed being born out there, and more than half his life had been inextricably bound up with the place. His return to Ballygarron had in fact completed a great vagabond circle that could be traced back to that night in 1920 when his grandfather had been murdered by the Black and Tans.

For twelve years after that his grandmother, a woman of spirit, had managed the farm until the elder of her two sons, Hamilton, was old enough to take over from her. The younger, Patrick's father, followed in the family's military tradition by joining the Royal Engineers in 1935. After sustaining a leg wound at Benghazi in 1942 he was removed from front-line duty and spent the rest of the war in South Africa, helping to train their sappers in bridge-building and airfield construction. He fell in love with that part of the world and incidentally with an English WAAF officer who was also stationed there.

They were married in Durban. When the war ended they returned home for just long enough to resign their commissions, see Patrick into the world and secure a passage back to South Africa. Britain in the postwar austerity years had little appeal to anyone who'd had a taste of life in the sun and open spaces.

Patrick's father was taken on by one of the biggest civil engineering firms in the subcontinent. For the next fifteen years the family moved from one construction project to the next, all over southern and central Africa, never for more than a year or two at a time. It was an exciting, if unsettled, childhood for Patrick. Even when he was sent to boarding school, at Michaelhouse in Natal, he never knew where he would be spending his holidays. It might be in the

Transvaal or the Cape; Northern Rhodesia, Uganda or Nyasaland. Once it was the Belgian Congo.

Only an army career had seemed to offer a chance of perpetuating the nomadic existence he had become used to. After Sandhurst and his commission in the Parachute Regiment, however, the army in which he found himself was one with contracting global commitments. Independence had come to the African colonies; they needed British officers to train their armed forces, and he was a natural candidate for the job. Periods of secondment had followed, to Nigeria, Kenya, and Zambia. There'd been other, less visible, periods as well, of attachment to the Intelligence Corps at Ashford, in Kent, where he learned that rather more was expected of him during these sojourns abroad: intelligence assessments for perusal by anonymous persons in London; reports on political and military figures, above all on the waves that the Soviets and Chinese were making on these not always peaceful African backwaters.

His two-year stint of duty with the élite Special Air Service Regiment had been shrouded by an almost equal level of secrecy. Sabotage, commando operations and behind-the-lines reconnaissance were among its specialities. Finally had come the Falklands, providing a definitive test of everything for which he had been trained. Eight days spent lying on a freezing hillside above Port Stanley with an SAS patrol, observing Argentinian strengths and dispositions; then, after being reassigned to the Second Battalion of the Parachute Regiment, the attack on Goose Green: thirty-six hours of savage close-quarter fighting, at a cost of seventeen British deaths in exchange for killing two hundred and fifty Argentinians. These chilly statistics still seemed meaningless. There had been no rejoicing among the men of his company, merely a sense of relief that the awfulness of it was over.

For the first time Marriner understood what the veterans of other campaigns had meant when they'd said that nothing as important could ever happen to them again. He'd taken the dissolution of his marriage philosophically. Even his mother's death shortly afterwards had seemed a much less

147

painful experience than watching his father go five years earlier, a victim at the age of sixty of a lifetime's heavy drinking, compounded by hard work in harsh climates.

Marriner dozed for a while himself. At three o'clock Jenny awoke and got ready to leave. Although their affair was hardly a secret, she had an old-fashioned sense of decorum and didn't want to embarrass the matronly Mary O'Leary by making it obvious she had spent the night with him. He offered, as he had done before, to escort her home, but she refused. She blew him a kiss as the wheels of her Range Rover scattered gravel from the drive, and then she was gone.

He went back to bed and slept. He had forgotten to set his alarm clock, and it was twenty minutes to ten when he was wakened by the telephone. A sprightly Thomas Cook voice informed him that he was booked on an eight o'clock flight to London the next morning, with a connection to Zurich. A room was reserved for him at the Dublin Airport International Hotel for tonight, and another at the Meilenhof Hotel in Zurich for tomorrow.

The call reminded him that he had done nothing to prepare for the journey. When he had bathed and dressed he drew up a list of instructions for Mick O'Leary to carry out in his absence. Mending the fences was a two-man job and would have to wait until the weekend, but there were plenty of other bits of work to be done. After lunch he packed an overnight bag, and once he had made a few other arrangements it was time to leave.

Together with the farm, Uncle Ham had bequeathed to him an ancient Wolseley, eaten by rust but with a still powerful engine. Without actually telling any lies he had left it to be assumed that he was merely visiting Dublin for a couple of days, and it looked more natural to drive there than to fly. To Jenny in particular he had been careful not to mention Zurich, if only because she would not be beyond inviting herself along and he could offer no innocent reason for refusing.

At the Wolseley's leisurely pace it took him just under four hours to reach Dublin. When he had settled into the hotel and had dinner he felt vaguely at a loose end. He was tempted to phone one of the dozen or so friends he had in the city, but decided against it. They would feel obliged to invite him round, or perhaps join him for a drink. Explanations would be necessary, and complications might set in. Already a furtiveness had crept into his behaviour. There was something a trifle melodramatic about flying to Switzerland to discuss secret plans with African revolutionaries. He contented himself with one whiskey at the bar and went to bed with a book, leaving instructions to be called at six-thirty in the morning.

13

The Swissair flight touched down at Zurich-Kloten airport at eleven o'clock, and Marriner was clear of Customs and Immigration fifteen minutes later. He took a taxi into the city, marvelling like any first-time visitor at its impossibly beautiful lakeside setting, its chocolate-box backdrop of distant snow-covered Alps sparkling in the autumn sunshine.

The Meilenhof Hotel turned out to be a modestly elegant little building tucked away in a side street off the Limmat-Quai on the right bank of the river. The room to which he was shown was chintzy and restful, an impression disrupted the moment he had dumped his bag on the bed by the ringing of the telephone. Somebody must have been watching for his arrival.

'Patrick?' It was Harry, of course. 'Did everything go smoothly? That's good. Whenever you're ready, leave the hotel, turn left and take the first turning left. There's a little pub called the Aurora about halfway up the street. We'll meet you there.'

He didn't hurry. Faintly irritated by Harry's hustling tone, he unpacked his bag, freshened up and changed from his casual travelling clothes into a dark worsted suit before leaving the hotel.

The Bierstübli Aurora was three minutes' walk away, a

place of heavy oak beams and latticed windows, seeming the essence of cosy Swiss respectability. Its low-ceilinged interior was gloomy and quiet, and Marriner at once saw Harry's bulky shape rising from a corner table to greet him. He was wearing another of the emphatic suits he favoured and he was in the company of a middle-aged white man.

'Patrick! Good to see you!' Harry beamed, squeezed his hand and slapped his shoulder. It might have been a reunion of war veterans. 'Patrick, I want you to meet Joshua Rosenblatt, the treasurer of the People's Congress. Josh, this is Major Marriner.'

Rosenblatt stood and offered his hand rather diffidently. He was a balding man in his early fifties. What remained of his hair was black and untidy, and his features were globular, unremarkable, vaguely Jewish. There was a hint of shy humour behind the heavy-framed glasses, however, and his smile was warm.

'I'm glad to meet you.' His accent was South African. 'Harry's told me a good deal about you.'

Harry bustled about them. There was a coffee cup and an empty beer glass on the table. 'Patrick, sit down. What will you drink? Josh, more coffee? *Bitte ein Bier, zwei Kaffees,*' he called in an atrocious accent to an approaching waiter. 'Now,' he said, settling in his chair, 'I suggest we get our business out of the way first, then have an early lunch in this place. That will leave us plenty of time to go to the bank—'

'You're about three jumps ahead of me again,' Marriner said firmly. He looked at the other man. 'I hope it's been made clear that nothing is agreed.'

Rosenblatt nodded uncomfortably. He looked as though Harry constantly embarrassed him. 'Of course. I must tell you quite honestly that I'm in some doubt myself about the wisdom of this scheme.'

'Josh!' Harry protested. 'What sort of sales talk is that?'

'I'm not a salesman, unfortunately. I'm the one who has to justify the expense,' he explained to Marriner.

'Accountants never make good gamblers,' Harry said dismissively. 'At heart they do not believe that taking a risk ever pays off. This is a gamble, I'll admit, but in my opinion the odds are acceptable. Do you feel any better about the idea now, Patrick?'

'There's a hell of a lot more I want to know first. About your own security to begin with. How many people are in on this?'

'Yes, you're entitled to know that. There are just the two of us, and one other. He is Moses Mohaila, the Congress representative in London. He had to know for procedural reasons that I won't bore you with, but I can assure you he's trustworthy.'

'Only three of you? Does that mean that your full leadership isn't aware of this plan?'

It was Harry's turn to look uneasy. 'It happens that Josh and I are the only ones with the information, and we've decided to keep it that way for now. I'm not going to pretend to you that the security of the Congress is watertight. However, since Josh and I also have control of the money, the decisions are ours to make.'

They fell into silence for a few moments as the waiter arrived with the beer and the coffee. This was not a good beginning, Marriner thought. He had the distinct impression that this was all Harry's show and that Rosenblatt – and he himself, for that matter – were being dragged along in his wake.

'Patrick, I'd better mention that there are rumours getting around that Lincoln Kumalo is to be released soon. You're bound to hear them yourself sooner or later, and so wonder whether there's any sense in what we're doing. I can only say that we have no way of knowing whether there's any substance to the story. One piece of information we have – a flimsy piece, admittedly – suggests precisely the opposite. Taken literally, in fact, it suggests that they're going to kill him. In which case the rumours have been started as a blind.'

Harry paused to let this sink in. He drank some beer. 'As I explained, Patrick, we want you initially to look around, to check out this information. On the other hand, it will be necessary to make plans from the start for a rescue operation.

151

That means getting him out of that clinic, and out of the country. Such plans can always be called off, but they certainly can't be cobbled together at the last minute.'

'Three weeks is almost no time as it is,' Marriner said. 'Have you any idea of the complexity of such a project? To be mounted in what amounts to hostile territory? Against horribly efficient security forces? Perhaps the SAS, or the Israelis, or the South Africans themselves, could pull off a stunt like that, but you're asking a freelance like me to arrange it? With what resources?'

'We'll come to that in a minute, Patrick. Try to look on the positive side. This clinic can only be what you would call a soft target – much softer, anyway, than Pollsmoor Prison. You'll also have the advantage of surprise. The South Africans don't know there's been a leak.'

'What makes you so sure?'

'The nature of the information we have makes it impossible for them to know. It will all be explained to you.'

'All right. Supposing for a moment that it was feasible. I would need all kinds of back-up facilities. A base to operate from. Communications, weapons, supplies, possibly a plane to fly him out of the country, which in turn means a pilot. Arrangements for a safe reception somewhere across the border. Above all I would need a team of men, trustworthy and experienced men. Where do you suppose I would find them?'

'I was coming to that,' Harry said. 'In their own army there are many disaffected men. We keep a lookout for them, as a source of possible sympathy to our cause, even as potential Congress agents and fifth columnists. They are young white men, conscripted against their will, who either don't like what they are made to do or are fed up with it. They are fighting for something they don't believe in. They are armed, and they often have combat experience.'

'What am I supposed to do? Advertise for some in the papers?'

'Of course not.' Harry ignored the sarcasm, and Marriner regretted it. 'One of our comrades out there is aware of one particular group that he feels might be persuaded to go along with something like this. He incidentally has some limited knowledge of the threat against Kumalo. He would be in touch with you soon after you arrived. It will be a matter of making your own assessment, Patrick – and, if you think it will work, doing it.'

'How about financing all this?' said Marriner, still sceptical. 'Do you realize how much it's going to cost?'

'Your department, Josh,' said Harry.

'A lot of it is guesswork, really.' Rosenblatt adjusted his glasses. He looked unhappy even at the mention of money. 'All the arrangements must be made here in Switzerland, partly because there are no exchange-control problems, partly because their banking system is efficient and confidential. However, forget all the nonsense you've probably heard about numbered accounts. They've fallen into disrepute, and they are really more trouble than they're worth. As far as payment to you is concerned, I would propose opening a current account in your name into which an initial deposit would be made, followed possibly by a subsequent one. There would be a separate account over which I would have control . . .'

'For God's sake tell the man how much!' Harry interrupted.

'Well, you've had an advance of five thousand pounds,' Rosenblatt said. 'We would add forty-five thousand to that on your acceptance of the proposal.'

'That's fifty grand just for saying yes,' Harry elaborated. 'Just for going out and looking around. Guaranteed. Unconditional.'

'In addition, should the project be successfully completed, we would deposit another two hundred thousand pounds in your account.'

'That's a straight quarter of a million in all if you get Kumalo out. And the whole thing can be arranged this afternoon,' Harry said triumphantly.

Marriner leaned back in his chair and studied them both critically. Harry's stare was eager; Rosenblatt looked nervous.

A quarter of a million pounds. The figure was almost meaningless to him, so far outside the scope of his experience that it had no reality. Had they said a million, or two million, the effect could hardly have been different.

'As well as that,' said Harry by way of further encouragement, 'you'll be able to draw on a separate fund to cover the cost of the operation. There'll be another million pounds in it. Money for the other participants—'

'That's a figure we haven't agreed,' Rosenblatt snapped at him.

'I'm not saying we have to spend it all. Patrick has to know what's available, so he can budget. You'll have to open a bank account over there, Patrick, and send to Josh for money as and when it's needed.'

'How do I explain an influx of money on that sort of scale?'

'Who will you have to explain to? It's your own money. It will be processed through your own account. It could be an inheritance or something that you're planning to invest out there. In fact. . . .' An idea came to Harry, and he grinned. 'We were having trouble thinking of a cover story for you, remember? Well, here it is. You're a farmer. Why don't you buy a farm? Or at least let it be known that that's what you've decided to do? That will explain your presence there for an indefinite period. It will also account for the money.'

Marriner considered. This at least wasn't a bad notion. There'd been dozens of times in his life when he'd had to pretend to be something more or less than he was, and the roles in which he'd felt most comfortable were those he could identify with. It wasn't at all implausible that a man who'd spent half his life in Africa should have a hankering to go back there and take up something he was familiar with.

Perhaps Harry sensed the drift of this thoughts. 'You have nothing to lose, Patrick,' he coaxed, 'and at least fifty thousand pounds to gain. Now, why don't we have some lunch and give you time to think it over?'

By half-past one everything was settled. In spite of his misgivings, Marriner had come to the simple conclusion that

154

he would be a fool to turn the offer down. He would regret it for ever if he did, and nothing of the sort would ever come his way again. Fifty thousand pounds would go most of the way towards paying off the debts at Ballygarron. With the other two hundred thousand. . . . But he refused to think about that. He was convinced that the idea of springing Kumalo was far too ambitious. If he could prove this to his own satisfaction, he would have done an honest job and could pocket the fifty thousand with a clear conscience. The money was in proportion to the risk; it was time to stop having middle-class reservations about it.

At two o'clock they took a taxi across the river to Talstrasse and the headquarters of the Handelsbank Bauer. It was one of the smaller Zurich banks, located in what had once been a large private house, and the office of its investment director, Dr Buchmann, might have been an elegant drawing-room but for the desk with its two telephones and its computer terminal. The procedure was a model of discretion and simplicity. Marriner produced his passport, provided two specimen signatures and was allocated two account numbers. Into the first, Rosenblatt deposited a cheque for forty-five thousand pounds drawn on a sterling account at the Union Banque Suisse. Into the second he transferred one million pounds from an account he had already opened with the Handelsbank Bauer. Marriner was to be the nominee holder of this second account, while Rosenblatt remained its signatory.

Dr Buchmann's only questions were purely procedural ones. At length he sat back and said in his impeccable English: 'The arrangements are clear, then, I trust. The funds in the first account are entirely at Mr Marriner's disposal. All transactions on the second account will be in his name, but will require the signature of Mr Rosenblatt only. From time to time Mr Rosenblatt will instruct us to transfer funds in Mr Marriner's name to an account nominated by him in another country.'

'That's correct.' Rosenblatt turned to Marriner. 'In effect, any money you need can be made available to you within twenty-four hours, forty-eight at the most, except over weekends. Is that about right?' he asked Dr Buchmann.

'All instructions to us are carried out immediately, of course, but I cannot speak for the efficiency of foreign banks. It varies from country to country.'

Rosenblatt and Harry exchanged a glance. 'This will be South Africa,' Rosenblatt said.

'Then there should be no difficulty. It would expedite matters if you were able to deal direct with our correspondents there, who are the Standard Bank of South Africa. Their foreign branch in Johannesburg can release funds on our instructions and charge them to our account. Well, gentlemen, if that covers everything . . .'

Their day's business was not yet over. Before they left the bank Rosenblatt used his new account to buy three thousand pounds' worth of sterling traveller's cheques in Marriner's name. Then they took another cab into the Unterstrass district, to the north, where Rosenblatt had rented a service flat in a modern block. Zurich was a city with a large floating population of business people, and there was plenty of this sort of short-term accommodation: anonymous, without character, ideal for anyone wanting to remain inconspicuous.

Harry had insisted on stopping on the way to buy a bottle of Scotch. They opened it and sat down around the table in the small dining-alcove, and began to talk.

They talked for two and a half hours. They covered everything that had happened, or everything they knew had happened, since the day Nandi Kumalo had received the message from Pollsmoor. They speculated all over again on its meaning, and on the implications of the letter from Judith Rose. If one thing was clear to Marriner at the end, it was that this girl held the key to one large part of the puzzle. In spite of her warning against making contact with her, that was one of the first things he was going to have to do.

'She's obviously as nervous as hell,' he said, 'and she'll have no reason whatever to trust me.'

'Take the letter with you?' Rosenblatt suggested. 'If you showed it to her, it would be proof that you'd spoken to me.'

'Too risky to carry about. And she might be more inclined to think it had been intercepted and I had come to threaten her.'

'There may be something else.'

Rosenblatt got up and went to a suitcase, still only half-unpacked, that lay on the sitting-room floor. He came back with an old leather-bound photograph album. From a page in the middle he carefully loosened a picture from its mountings and handed it over.

'She'll know this can only have come from me. It's nine or ten years old, but it's the most recent I have.'

It was a black and white portrait, a bit larger than postcard size, showing a girl in her late teens with short curly dark hair, strong features and an almost comically determined expression. She was wearing a plain blouse and a necklet with a pendant in the shape of the letter J.

'Turn it over.'

There was an inscription on the back, in the same big impatient writing as that in the letter. *To Joshua*, it said, *Me facing up to my matric exams. Nil desperandum. Love, Judith.*

Marriner nodded. 'That should do nicely. What's she like?'

'Heaven knows. She was a little girl when I last saw her. I think later she had a sort of teenage crush on me. In my absence she could build me up into a romantic, notorious figure. She has a lot of spirit, obviously, but I suspect that she lacks self-confidence. Louis was always a hard father to please.'

From earlier events they moved on to considering future ones. There was no point in trying to make plans for the projected springing of Kumalo from the clinic, since that was something Marriner would have to work out on the ground. There was, however, the equally vital question of getting him out of the country afterwards. Here it was Harry who seemed to have been doing his sums.

'You've got several choices, Patrick. If you could find an exceptionally safe hideout, you could hold him there for a while and smuggle him out later, when the heat is down a bit. Or you could break straight for the border, either overland or by air. It's going to be your decision, but personally I wouldn't consider any option except flying. The moment the stuff hits the fan, the ground is going to be crawling with police and troops. They'll scour the townships. They'll seal off every possible exit route. Plus, you've got to consider that Kumalo is sixty-eight years old and not in the best of health. Not a stretcher case, maybe, but not up to an arduous journey or a long period in hiding.'

Harry produced a Bartholomew's map of Central and Southern Africa and spread it on the table. 'Look here. The two nearest borders are those of Botswana in the west, Mozambique in the east. Botswana is closer and may look more tempting, but that doesn't make it safer. Its government is edgy about its relationship with South Africa. It doesn't encourage our people to operate there. Getting there is also just the start. It's a long dangerous haul to the north, travelling close to the South African frontier, before you reach safety in Zambia.'

'Safety being a relative term,' said Rosenblatt drily, remembering the air raid of eleven days ago.

'OK, Josh,' Harry said with slight irritation. 'It's true that there is nowhere in this region that's immune to attack and reprisals. But Mozambique at least has always been willing to stick its neck out, to shelter our people and even to suffer the consequences. Mozambique' – he stabbed a finger at that long narrow slab of territory lying between the Transvaal and the Indian Ocean – 'is a much better bet. It is as hostile to South Africa as it can afford to be. It is easier to hide in. It will welcome Lincoln Kumalo as an honoured guest.'

Marriner had been studying the map with interest. He used a ballpoint pen as a ruler to measure a rough distance, then held it against the mileage scale. 'It's about two hundred and fifty miles from Johannesburg to the Mozambique border, as the crow flies. That's travelling roughly east-north-east and aiming straight for the capital, Maputo. If you headed due east instead, though, you'd reach the border of

Swaziland first. That's fifty or sixty miles closer. Overflying Swaziland *en route* to Mozambique would cut down on the time spent in South African air space.'

They all stared at the tiny, roughly rectangular outline on the map that represented the landlocked kingdom of Swaziland. It was surrounded on three and a half of its four sides by South Africa but shared a border of perhaps sixty or seventy miles with Mozambique.

'That's good thinking, Patrick,' said Harry. He gave Rosenblatt a nudge. 'You see what we're paying the man for?'

'Swaziland is almost totally dependent on South Africa,' Rosenblatt objected. 'Its king is an autocratic traditional ruler and not friendly to us.'

'We're not going to ask for his help, Josh. We're just going to take a quick hop over his territory, and he has nothing to stop us with.'

'There's nothing to stop the South Africans from doing exactly the same. They don't hesitate to cross any of these borders whenever it suits them.'

'Joshua, you're being negative again!' Harry had grown more exuberant as the level of the whisky bottle fell. 'It makes it that much more difficult for them, which is all to our advantage.' He addressed Marriner again, tracing a line with his finger eastwards across the map. 'Once you've crossed Swaziland, Patrick, you're over southern Mozambique. It would be ideal if you could make a landing somewhere there, well away from any towns. With the help of the Mozambicans we could be ready to receive you and whip Kumalo quietly out of the way.'

'I visited that area once,' Marriner said dubiously, looking at the strip of country south of Maputo. 'It's pretty wild, all bush and swamp. There are very few roads, mostly unusable in the rainy season. I doubt if there's even an airstrip.'

'I'll check it out for you. I'll be flying back to Lusaka this weekend, but of course we will stay in touch. Which brings us to the question of communications.'

Marriner came back to earth with a sense of relief, reminding himself that all this talk was theoretical. Harry's knack of sweeping people off on the magic carpet of his own imagination could be dangerous.

It appeared that while Harry planned to return to Zambia with the rest of the Congress delegation from Algiers, Rosenblatt had found excuses for remaining in Zurich. He needed immediate access to the money in the Handelsbank Bauer; in addition, this flat and its telephone would serve as a link between Marriner and Harry. It would be far too risky to attempt to communicate directly between Johannesburg and Lusaka. As an added precaution, they would use a telephone scrambler system.

Rosenblatt showed him the apparatus. It was a DTS/AX portable security phone, packed into a black vinyl box the size and shape of a hefty book. The receiver was attached by a spiral cord to a cradle with a dial. The receiver had a hole near the mouthpiece fitted with a small plastic plug, cylindrically shaped like an old-fashioned electric mains fuse.

'This one you'll take with you. I have another one here. This is its brain, so to speak.' He pulled out the tiny plug. 'It's a code-key plug. There are thousands of different codes, and you can use a new one for every call provided the user at the other end inserts a matching key. It will work anywhere, including a pay phone. You put the handset of the ordinary telephone into this cradle. It encodes your voice at your end and decodes it at mine.'

Marriner regarded it with some misgiving. Years ago he had used similar but far more sophisticated equipment.

'I can promise you it's effective,' said Harry, guessing his thoughts again. 'And, just as important, it attracts no attention. Businessmen carry them around these days to prevent their calls being bugged.'

'I'm supposed to be a farmer,' Marriner reminded him.

'I assure you that the Customs never give them a second glance,' Rosenblatt said. 'I've enclosed a dozen code-plugs, numbered from one to twelve. That should be plenty, though I suggest you phone only when it's strictly necessary. Use them in their numbered order and discard the plug after each call. For extra security, to guard against any possible traces, you should ideally use a different phone each time.'

Darkness had fallen, creeping through the gloomy little flat, by the time they had said all that seemed to need saying. Harry, who'd been drinking steadily for most of the day, seemed reluctant to let the party break up and proposed a night on the town. He was disappointed when Marriner refused; no doubt he would cajole the luckless Rosenblatt into accompanying him.

They wished Marriner good luck in a low-keyed way, not making too much of it, and he left the flat carrying his dubious souvenirs: the telephone scrambler and the photograph of Judith Rose. Outside, the night air was cold, sharp and suddenly dizzying. He'd drunk three whiskies, one over his usual limit, while Rosenblatt had had a couple and Harry had demolished the rest of the bottle. Harry was a pernicious influence in more than one way.

To clear his head and give himself a chance to think, he set off to walk at least part of the way into the city centre. It turned out to be closer than he'd imagined, and he was back at the Meilenhof Hotel in half an hour.

From his room he telephoned Swissair reservations. He had decided on a change in his itinerary. He already had a seat on a plane leaving for London at midday, with an immediate connection to Dublin. He managed to switch these for flights at nine o'clock and six-fifteen respectively. He needed a few hours in London. There were some cards in this game he wanted to deal for himself.

14

'So you've heard the rumours, too?' said Fred Dyce. 'I was thinking of writing a piece about it, if only I could harden the information up a bit.'

'No idea of its source?' asked Marriner.

'Well, it certainly doesn't seem to be a leak from the South African Government. Not directly, anyway. My contacts out there say it seems to have spread from the townships. Kumalo's lawyer is in touch with the Government quite regularly, of course, but he's a cagey old bugger and never says yea or nay to anything the press ask him. There's Kumalo's daughter, Nandi, but she keeps well clear of any controversy as well. It's tempting to believe, of course. It's what a lot of people out there *want* to believe. No smoke without fire, is what they'll be thinking.'

'Do you think they would seriously consider releasing him?'

'That is one of the great questions of our time, old son. Let me get you another.'

'Just a Perrier this time.'

Marriner had phoned Fred Dyce as soon as he'd arrived at Heathrow airport that morning, and luckily found him at home. They had been at Michaelhouse School in Natal together, had bumped into each other again in Zambia a dozen years ago and remained occasionally in touch. Dyce had made a good career for himself in London as a freelance journalist of mildly left-wing views, a specialist on Southern African affairs who wrote for the serious weeklies and was much in demand as a participant in television panel discussions. He had a lunch appointment that day, but had agreed to meet Marriner for a drink at El Vino in Fleet Street beforehand.

Marriner had said he wanted some advice. He was thinking of going back to South Africa, possibly to take up farming. He wondered what Dyce, as a close observer of the scene out there, thought of the country's future.

'Buying a farm?' the journalist had said. 'Well, you're a braver man than I am, Patrick. Nobody is investing money there these days. On the other hand, if you're prepared to take a gamble, I suppose you could get a pretty good deal. The price of land is depressed at the moment, I gather. In ten years' time, say, you might either sell it for a fortune or find it's quite worthless, depending on how the wind blows.'

Marriner was glad to find his cover story was not greeted with complete incredulity. He had said nothing of his trip to

Zurich or his dealings with Makibani and Rosenblatt, of course, but the conversation had led quite naturally to the People's Congress and Lincoln Kumalo.

'In a way, Kumalo holds the key to the country's future,' Dyce said now. 'From the Government's point of view, a time must eventually come when letting him go will seem a lesser evil than keeping him locked up. What's really interesting is the question of what that would do to the Congress leadership.'

'How so?'

'Like all those African liberation movements, it has dissension at the top. While they all agree on the need to overthrow the system, they differ quite fundamentally over what to put in its place. The South African Government is fond of saying the Congress is really a tool of the Communist Party, that victory for them will inevitably be followed by a Marxist dictatorship. That's a distortion, in fact, but it's true that there are Marxists, or at least extreme left-wingers, among its leaders. Men like J. K. Govender and Lawrence Gumbi, who would favour nationalization and extreme socialist policies. It's their influence that would wane if Kumalo were free.'

'And who would stand to benefit?'

'The moderates. People like Mohaila, who's their man here in London, and a fellow called Harry Makibani. Harry I would call a materialist, and I don't mean a dialectical one. Kumalo himself is a social democrat: you have only to read some of the speeches he made before he went to jail. His generation were steeped in democratic traditions. They're looking for equality and majority rule, of course, but they're not totalitarians. I think your farm would be quite safe under them. Are you sure I'm not boring you with all this?'

'I'm fascinated,' Marriner said.

Dyce said hello to a couple of colleagues passing the bar. He sipped at his glass of hock. 'Well, loyalty to Kumalo is the glue that holds these disparate elements together. If he came out and took charge, there would certainly be a shake-up. If there's anything to these rumours, then perhaps that's what the Government is gambling on: Kumalo as a moderating influence rather than a menace. Personally, I'm not sure they're ready to face that.'

'He's not getting any younger, is he? What if he died in prison?' Marriner inquired casually.

'I hate to think. It would throw the leadership into disarray, for a start. There'd be a pretty vicious power struggle. Whoever came out on top, it would certainly take their minds off their work for a while.' Dyce glanced at his watch. 'God, I'm late already. Well, good luck, Patrick. Invite me to your farm some day.'

'After the Revolution,' Marriner said with a grin.

He took a bus from the wine bar, down the Strand to Trafalgar Square and South Africa House. The embassy had the look these days of a building permanently under siege. Two policemen stood guard at each of its two entrances; another four were keeping an eye on a small demonstration across the road, between the bronze lions flanking Nelson's Column, bobbies and demonstrators looking equally cold on this raw November day. Among the placards being held aloft were half a dozen carrying blown-up photographs of Lincoln Kumalo.

Marriner recalled that the consular offices had been on the first floor. They were adjacent to a reading-room with a rather clubby atmosphere where he had come occasionally during his Sandhurst days for a nostalgic browse through the South African newspapers. Now, a porter informed him at the door, consular services were handled at an office across from the square, in Charles II Street off the Haymarket. The embassy itself was no longer open to the public.

He made his way to the consulate-general, outlined his request to a woman at the inquiry desk, filled in a form stating his name, address and business, and was asked to wait. No doubt Harry Makibani would have a fit if he could see him now, but Marriner had worked out his own approach to one particular problem. There was no point in having a cover story unless you could make it stand up, and that meant letting yourself be noticed a little bit.

In a couple of minutes a pleasant sandy-haired young man from the commercial section came out to meet him and they talked in a public room lined with colour posters of lions and giraffes. No, he was not aware of any restrictions on foreigners buying or leasing land in South Africa, the official said. Certainly, any amount of capital could be imported for such a purpose. When Marriner mentioned a figure and asked what grants or tax concessions this might qualify him for, the young man at once became apologetic.

'I'm afraid I have to say I simply don't know. Incentives to commercial and industrial investors, yes, I could tell you about those, but this is the first inquiry I've had about agricultural land. We've always had a settled farming population and we've never had to give land grants to immigrants the way they used to in places like Kenya and Rhodesia. But of course any investment is welcome, and I can certainly send for the information . . .'

'I'm in a bit of a hurry to get out there and look around.'

'Then by all means go and see the Department of Lands in Pretoria.'

'It would help if I could have a letter of introduction to someone.'

'Oh, I don't know . . .'

'It might open a few doors more quickly, mightn't it?'

'Well, it isn't really necessary, but . . .' But it was rare enough to meet someone with the confidence to sink money into the country these days, was the young man's unspoken thought. It was a harmless request, and he might gain some credit for himself by obliging this obviously well-heeled potential settler.

He disappeared for a few minutes. When he came back he was carrying not only a letter addressed to the Secretary of the Department of Lands, but half a dozen back numbers of *Farmers Weekly* magazine culled from the Information Bureau.

'I thought you might find these helpful,' he said with a smile, escorting Marriner to the lift. 'They advertise farms for sale, and they have the addresses of a lot of agents and so on. What line of farming are you in?'

'Beef cattle.'

'Then the Transvaal is where you'll be looking, from what I know of it. Good luck, Mr Marriner.'

He'd been wished a lot of good luck lately, he thought as he emerged on the street. Perhaps some of it would stick. He had drawn some harmless attention to himself, which was a good way of deflecting the other kind, and in return he had a letter on consular notepaper helping to establish his bona fides.

He took a taxi to the South African Airways office in Regent Street and booked a flight to Johannesburg for Sunday evening, leaving the return date open.

The weekend was predictably hectic. Although this was a slack period on the farm, there suddenly seemed to be at least a hundred jobs that needed doing, and even more to be planned for during his absence. Indoors, Jenny Swanson was taking over with the team of painters and handymen she had already conjured up from somewhere. Marriner had finally succumbed to Jenny's pressure; he was letting her do up the house.

On Sunday she brought over a picnic lunch, which they shared in the kitchen once he had finished packing. For the first time Marriner looked at the cheque for five thousand pounds that Harry Makibani had given him last Tuesday. It was, as Harry had said, made out for cash and therefore anonymous. It had been drawn on a branch of the National Westminster Bank in Islington in London and carried two illegible signatures.

'Better pop this in your own account,' he said to Jenny, 'and draw on it when you need to. Try to leave me some change.'

She slipped the cheque into her handbag. 'All right. Is there anywhere I can reach you out there? There will be things we'll have to discuss.'

Marriner hesitated. He did have the name of a hotel in

Johannesburg to which Harry had directed him. There was no need to make a secret of it, but something cautioned him against being so specific. As far as Jenny or anyone else here knew, he was still just on his way to 'Africa'.

'I don't know when I'll be in touch, frankly,' he said. 'I'm not really sure of my movements yet.'

At five o'clock she drove him to Cork airport for his connecting flight to London. He felt vaguely guilty towards her as she kissed him goodbye, admonishing him once again to stay clear of black ladies and AIDS. Sitting back in the steeply climbing Aer Lingus Boeing 737, it was with a sense of ignoble relief that he looked down on the dwindling scattered lights of the south Irish coast.

At Heathrow he transferred smoothly between terminals 1 and 3 and checked in for the Johannesburg flight. It was only when he stepped aboard the SAA jumbo jet and heard the familiar South African accents around him that he began to have any real sense of foreboding.

At about the time Marriner's plane was lumbering into the dark autumn skies over London, six thousand miles away in the beautiful Eerste River Valley inland from Cape Town, Deputy Minister Frans Hoeksma's open-air *braaivleis* party was just getting into full swing.

His house was a gracious white gabled Cape Dutch mansion that had been in his family for four generations, and the guests had been invited to arrive before sunset, the better to appreciate the spectacular view of the valley smothered in vines and the distant purple mass of the Franschhoek Mountains.

There were eighty people present, just enough to fill the gardens without making them seem crowded. About a dozen were prominent National Party members from his constituency, whom the Hoeksmas were more or less obliged to invite, but the occasion was deliberately non-political in tone. Many of the guests were academics from Stel-lenbosch, a few were business and professional people, others were senior civil servants. They amounted to a fair cross-section of the Cape Afrikaner élite, people easily at home in these surroundings and glad to be considered cosmopolitan. Few would be surprised to encounter each other on a Swiss ski-slope or in a theatre crowd in London or New York.

The only ones significantly out of place were Colonel Prinsloo and Dr Els. Prinsloo had driven them out from the city and they remained together like some awkward couple new to the neighbourhood, lingering at the edge of the lawn, accepting glasses of wine from the coloured waiters. They didn't talk much to anyone else and they watched with a pretence of distant amusement the younger people who cavorted in the swimming pool before dinner. Els seemed a little overawed by it all and was drinking too fast, while Prinsloo found himself disguising a certain rebellious anger. He had nothing in common with any of these people, and knew he would never have been invited for his own sake. He watched fat little Hoeksma and his wife, also on the podgy side, wafting about among the people they thought worth talking to, and said loudly to Els: 'How do you think they fuck?'

'What?' Els gave him a startled look.

'They're such a pair of little porkers. How does he get it into her?'

Els gave a dutiful snigger. Maybe Prinsloo in his own crude way was trying to put him at his ease. Els knew he was not here because of his social standing either. He had been a government doctor ever since he qualified, underpaid, undervalued, accustomed to being pushed around by the likes of Prinsloo and yet never before needing to feel afraid. Somehow he had taken for granted the protection they had given him for all these years, had never considered they would chalk it up as a favour he still owed them. Now, he knew, the moment of reckoning had come. Fortified by several glasses of wine, however, he told himself he wasn't going to make it easy for them. He was not the pushover they thought he would be. There was still a spark of integrity in his soul.

Els had glimpsed the pale unsmiling face of Tertius Van

Straaten across the lawn earlier on, but he had disappeared by the time dinner arrived. It came in relays of *sosaties* – skewers of barbecued lamb marinated in a spicy Malay sauce – together with lengths of *boerewors* sausage and T-bone and fillet steaks, baked potatoes and heaped platefuls of salads, all washed down with more excellent wine and eaten out on the lawns. A deep, warm darkness enclosed the floodlit gardens. The gleaming surface of the pool was broken only by the fluttering wings of downed flying ants. Eventually the elliptical shadow of their host moved across the grass to fall on Prinsloo and Els where they sat.

'Gentlemen. I've been neglecting you. Shall we go in now and have our chat?'

The inside of the house still held some of the heat of the day. From the front door a wide, stone-flagged hall led past the main living rooms to the rear of the eighteenth-century farmstead, to an annex beyond the kitchen where domestic slaves had once been quartered. Here a comfortably converted room served Hoeksma as a private office. Its windows and shutters were closed, making it stuffy but ensuring its seclusion from the guests who wandered about outside.

Van Straaten was already in the room. When Hoeksma had shut and locked the door he waved them all into chairs around a small table, joining them there instead of presiding from behind his desk. Four balloon glasses and a brandy bottle were on the table: none of your Cape KWV, Prinsloo noted sardonically, but five-star Remy Martin. Hoeksma poured them all a good measure, then took up his own glass and swirled the Cognac in it with his plump delicate hand. He had greeted Dr Els briefly on his arrival, but now he took serious notice of him for the first time.

'Doctor, I understand that you may be in a position to help us on a rather delicate matter of some importance to our national security. I think I need hardly spell out the details?'

Els glanced at Prinsloo and Van Straaten in turn. 'They've been made clear to me, yes.'

'I understand also that you have some objections to the part you have been asked to play in this. Now, I haven't asked you here to put pressure on you, Doctor, merely to try to emphasize the importance of what we're asking. You'll understand that in my position I must confine what I say to very general terms. I've been made aware of your background, and it seems to me you are a true Afrikaner—'

'Oh, he's a *Boereseun* all right,' said Prinsloo heartily. Hoeksma cocked a disapproving eyebrow at the interruption.

'It seems to me,' he said, 'that you're a man who might be able to see the cause of this nation as more important than any narrower loyalty.'

'Loyalty to my medical ethics, you mean. I don't see why I should have to make such a choice.'

'But you make choices all the time, Dr Els.' Hoeksma moved into what sounded like a well-rehearsed argument. 'Every doctor does. You took the Hippocratic Oath, which commits you admirably to saving life, but what happens, for instance, when there's a disaster and the emergency services can't cope with all the casualties? A train crash? An earthquake? What happens in wartime, for that matter? Some have to be left to die in order that others may be helped. You have to play God. Now I can appreciate that that must be hard, but you'd do what any practical man in the circumstances would do: work for the greatest good of the greatest number.'

'It's a false comparison,' said Els, lighting a cigarette. He was rather surprised at his own nerve. 'I can't stop this going ahead. I just don't want to be part of it.'

'I'm trying to make you see that there are wider considerations, Doctor. Do you know that forty thousand children die every day in Black Africa? Every day. And why do they die? Because they live in countries that can't afford to feed them. Countries with governments that are corrupt or inefficient, or that spend their money on futile wars and useless social experiments instead of on food and medicines. It's because we don't want this country to become like that, Doctor, that I'm putting this to you. It's because we want the time to make peaceful and orderly progress, without pressure or interference.'

'If I thought you could guarantee that. . . .'

'Of course I can't,' said Hoeksma smoothly. 'I can only tell you it's the best hope we've got.'

Els wondered why he was being so stubborn. To protect his job and his pension he had compromised with his conscience many times; perhaps this had brought him to a weary sense of honesty. He felt that he had this much in common with Prinsloo. What had all the dirtying of hands and dubious death certificates achieved? There was a kind of dangerous naïveté behind the ·cunning of people like Hoeksma and Van Straaten, who still sought solutions through manipulating people.

He took a defiant swallow of brandy. 'Supposing I say no?'

'I'd rather it didn't come to that,' Hoeksma said.

'Go on, just supposing. I want you to tell me what would happen.'

This was too much to ask of fastidious Mr Hoeksma. Like a kindly man pushed towards desperate measures, he glanced at Van Straaten.

'Nobody can force you to do anything.' The intelligence officer spoke up for the first time. 'Equally, nobody was forced to protect you over the death of Matthew Mthembu.'

Though not fully unexpected, the mention of the name was enough to make Els flinch. 'They were protecting themselves as well,' he said. 'They'd have made me the scapegoat if it had suited them.'

'All the same, he died because of your negligence. At least, that's the way the Medical Association would see it.'

There was no denying this. Matthew Mthembu had been a young political prisoner who suffered from valvar disease of the heart. On three successive days Dr Els had given permission for the Security Police to remove him from the prison for interrogation. On the third day they had brought him back dead. By falsifying the records it had been possible to show that the authorities were unaware of his condition, and Els's role went completely unmentioned. The inquest had attracted much attention, but had ended with a verdict of accidental death.

171

The Mthembu case had been the gravest of his errors under pressure, but it was not a matter that would be easy to revive. 'It happened eight years ago,' he said. 'Any proof there might have been was destroyed.'

'Any written proof, you mean. But there were witnesses, Doctor. There were two warders and a prison nurse who were willing to keep quiet at the time. They were aware that you knew of Mthembu's condition, and they heard the orders you gave. They would now be happy enough to testify against you if necessary. I ordered a little homework to be done on this case, you see. The Medical Association have long memories. They're especially sensitive to this sort of thing, and it would look all the worse for having been hidden for so long.'

Els was shaking his head, half-incredulous, half in a kind of self-mocking admiration. 'What a lot of trouble you go to! For somebody you've always been so sure of, always had in your pockets.' He turned to Hoeksma. 'No pressure, you said? What exactly do you call this?'

The deputy minister spread his hands apologetically. 'This wasn't the way I wanted it, Dr Els. But you understand what it means to you? This thing is too important to allow us to take chances.'

Of course he knew what it meant. He would be struck off the medical register without hesitation. The Prisons Department would have to dismiss him, probably with a suitable show of horror. No job, no pension, and at fifty-three no prospect of picking up the pieces. A sudden surge of anger washed over him, and he drained his glass and thumped it down on the table. 'All right. It obviously hasn't crossed your mind that I might call your bluff. That I might say to hell with you and walk out of here and tell the whole story. Maybe to the foreign press.'

'But what story, Doctor?' Van Straaten's chilly, meticulous tone hadn't changed. 'I don't believe we have discussed anything but generalities. And there are three witnesses here, including a deputy minister, who will deny everything you say. What credibility would you have if the Mthembu

172

case came to light? It's true that you could cause some inconvenience, but another way would be found to complete our project, Doctor. A way that would not depend on you. Nobody is indispensable.'

Els stared at each of them in turn. Hoeksma still looked regretful. Van Straaten blandly sipped Cognac, and Prinsloo wore a cynical smile. Between the three of them they had stitched him up from the start. He had never had any choice, whatever he liked to tell himself.

It was Hoeksma who broke the brief silence. 'I suggest you get some fresh air, Dr Els. Go back to the party for a while. Here, take some more brandy. Think over what has been said. Take your time. And then let us know.'

He unlocked the door and Dr Els left, walking like an automaton. When he rejoined the others at the table Hoeksma allowed himself a small, satisfied smile.

'I believe he will see the sense in co-operating.' He poured them all more brandy. 'Dr Rose has agreed to have Els present at the operation?'

'Under some protest,' said Prinsloo. 'I gather it's all right as long as he doesn't touch anything.' He grinned. 'A bit of a prima donna, is Dr Rose.'

'But he's co-operating?'

'Oh, yes. He's also a devil for efficiency. He's devised a whole computer program to cover his arrangements, reorganizing the routine of the clinic and so on. He insists it's safer than leaving papers lying about. No, I don't think we have to worry about Dr Rose, though I did have reservations about that old family connection of his.'

'With his cousin? Rosenblatt? Well, there seems to be no harm in that, and it helps to establish his credentials. A man who positively dislikes our policies and even has a relative who's active in the Congress: there could be no better proof of his independence from us.'

'A family like that will never be anything but a part of the liberal Johannesburg establishment,' Prinsloo said. 'The richer and more comfortable they get, the more their hearts bleed for the suffering masses. Once in a while one of them, like Joshua Rosenblatt, will actually stick his neck out and become a real live Marxist, but the rest will just go on quietly bleeding.' He paused. 'There is a daughter, Judith, who used to be tied up with the radical student movement. She doesn't seem to have been very active politically, though. The only thing that bothered me slightly is that she actually has a job in her old man's clinic.'

'You consider her a security risk?' Van Straaten asked.

'I don't think so,' said Prinsloo after a few moments' reflection. 'Like other people at the clinic, she'll probably get an inkling sooner or later that something is going on, but nobody will really know anything until the last minute. We've kept an occasional eye on her. I also actually met her briefly when I was up there.' He paused again and grinned. 'I think she would run scared. I think she's a bleeder.'

15

It was four in the morning by Marriner's watch, still set to Greenwich Mean Time, when a blood-red sun began to rise over the African landmass ahead of the airliner. An hour later breakfast was served, and not long afterwards the Boeing began its long descent.

Johannesburg came suddenly into view beyond the starboard wing, a glittering mass of skyscrapers rearing abruptly from the brown earth, bordered to the south and west by the strange pale shapes of mine dumps, fringed by mile after mile of suburbs with motorways coiling through them like a nest of snakes. There had been a time, back in his boyhood in rural Natal, when this had seemed like the ultimate city, and even now he felt a tug of excitement at the idea of seeing it again. As its citizens would tell you, this was the true capital of South Africa. Anything that was really important happened here first, in this brash upstart of a place that made the two official capitals, Cape Town and Pretoria, seem staid and provincial. It pretended to no charm and invited few philosophical reflections. It was a city that never relaxed, and it could seem glamorous and menacing in equal proportions.

The passengers stepped out of the plane just before eight o'clock local time, into thin Highveld air already warmed by the sun. There were glamorous tanned policewomen in pale khaki uniforms on the tarmac, cops with guns, black loaders lounging stylishly about in T-shirts and baseball caps. The whole image was new to Marriner, with something faintly Californian about it.

The terminal building was vast, functional and un-crowded. At Passport Control a man in summer whites carefully studied Marriner's entry card.

'You're a farmer, Mr Marriner? Your passport says you're an army officer.'

'I used to be. Nowadays I run a farm.'

The official made a note on the card. '"Length of stay: six weeks. Purpose of visit: business,"' he read out. He glanced up. 'That's rather a long business trip.'

'I may be buying some land here. I need time to look around.'

The lie tripped easily off his tongue now. He was tempted to show the letter from the consulate-general, but felt that would be explaining too much. As it was, the man looked quite impressed. 'Buying land? Well, good luck,' he said. He stamped the passport, snapped it shut and handed it back. He even managed a small smile.

So far, so smooth, Marriner thought. He collected his baggage and took it as a further good omen when he passed through the green Customs channel without being stopped, thus facing no awkward questions about the telephone scrambler. He cashed some traveller's cheques at the airport bank and emerged from the terminal feeling more relieved than he somehow thought was justified. As he walked towards the taxi rank he stopped deliberately and took several deep breaths of the familiar intoxicating air of Africa. He was still trying to convince himself he was here.

The Windsor Hotel was just the sort of faded, pleasantly

old-fashioned place its name led you to expect. It was in Plein Street, in the heart of the city near the railway station, five storeys of sandstone façades and little wrought-iron balconies maintaining their dignity among the surrounding monsters of steel and glass. Inside, it retained the air of an English commercial hotel from the twenties or thirties. There were potted palms in the lobby, a marble-topped reception desk, and mulligatawny soup on the luncheon menu pinned up beside it.

Yes, said the woman at the desk, they had a room reserved for him. As he filled in the register he asked casually who had made the booking. She wasn't sure. Just a telephone call, by the look of it. No written confirmation would have been needed.

The hotel corridors were wide and high-ceilinged. His room on the third floor was also of an impressive size, sharing the threadbare elegance of the rest of the building. Besides the big double bed and other standard furnishings, it easily accommodated a sofa and a pair of armchairs with faded William Morris print covers, forming a kind of sitting-room alcove by the window. The fittings in the bathroom were archaic but functional. By the time he had unpacked his bags he was feeling further reassured. There was a certain, no doubt spurious, sense of security about a hotel room: it was a base, a haven, an anonymous home from home. He also found that his appetite had returned, and when he phoned room service they told him he was still in plenty of time to have breakfast sent up.

On a shelf beneath the telephone was a set of directories for Johannesburg and the Witwatersrand. Out of curiosity he looked up a couple of entries. Dr Louis Rose, Surgeon, with a string of initials after his name, lived in Houghton Drive. Easily one of the smartest two or three spots in the city, Marriner recalled. The Woodvale Clinic's address was given simply as Woodvale. It wasn't an area he had heard of.

His breakfast was brought by a small stocky Zulu with a splendid moustache, clad in a khaki drill uniform with braided epaulettes. 'I am Nimrod, sir,' he announced when

176

Marriner had signed the bill and tipped him. 'I am your floor boy. I am available for anything you require. At your service. Sir.'

Nimrod retreated with parade-ground ceremony. When he had eaten his bacon and eggs Marriner found himself restless. He'd had only a few hours' sleep on the plane but he wasn't tired enough for bed yet. He was, as Harry had advised, going to lie low for a couple of days; but there was no harm in getting a few necessary and innocuous tasks out of the way.

He showered, shaved and changed into lightweight clothes, then went downstairs, handed in his key and left the hotel. At the bookshop a few yards down the street he stopped and bought a map of Greater Johannesburg and a larger-scale street plan of the city. The latter he studied for a minute to refresh his memory and get his bearings, and then set off. The streets were much as he remembered them, noisier and more crowded if anything, but the big difference was the presence of black people in far greater preponderance than he had known before. Whatever their political and economic disadvantages might be, there was a new assertiveness about them that was instantly noticeable. There were no more barefoot country boys or mammies in *doeks* and blankets ogling the shop windows, but harassed-looking executive types in business suits and fashionable strolling girls in designer jeans and teased-out hair. On the yellow T-shirt of a youth wired into a Walkman he was startled to see the legend *Free Kumalo*.

The western end of Fox Street was at the heart of the financial district, and a longer walk than he had reckoned on. Here the huge mining conglomerates that had generated much of the country's wealth all had their offices within a few blocks of the Stock Exchange, and among them was a slender skyscraper housing the headquarters of the Standard Bank of South Africa. At the reception desk Marriner stated his business to a sun-kissed blonde and was led to the office of Mr Jepson of the foreign department.

Jepson was a cheery, ruddy-faced, outgoing man whose

three-piece suit made no concessions to the weather. He also wore a cricket club tie dotted with stumps and bails. His accent was South African, but his speech was peppered with incongruous, outdated English jargon, as though he'd just walked off the set of a Battle of Britain film.

'Just got in from Blighty, Mr Marriner? Couple of years since I was over there. Always try to make my trips coincide with the County Championships, fit in a few days at Lord's, what? Well, you just visiting, or planning to peg out your tent here?'

Marriner explained that he had come to look around, that he was thinking of buying a farm, that he had money in Switzerland that he could send for if and when he found what he was looking for. The more often he told this story the easier it came. He'd been recommended to come here by the Handelsbank Bauer, he said. He had the equivalent of several thousand rands with him at present, and was interested in opening a current account.

'No problem at all, old boy. Never turn away anyone with a spot of the ready. More bods wanting to take it out than bring it in at the moment. Of course the best cattle country is well north of here, so you may want to transfer your account to another branch eventually. If I were you, I'd be jolly careful about putting all my eggs in one basket, though. If you wanted to start in a more modest way, I've noticed that a lot of small farms are for sale to the north-west of here, over towards the Magaliesberg. You might even talk one of the owners into leasing or renting it for a while.' Jepson became confiding. 'Between you and me, you've got to be careful of these old Boers. They can be a lot craftier than they make out . . .'

Half an hour later and after much more gratuitous advice, Marriner left the bank equipped with an account number, a chequebook and a promise that a cheque card would be forwarded to him within a couple of days. He had deposited two thousand rands in the account, which should be enough to cover all his immediate expenses. The time spent listening to Jepson's babbling had not been entirely wasted; it had given him an idea.

What he needed next was a car. In a phone booth near the Stock Exchange he hunted in the classified directory and picked out a hire firm a few blocks away in Main Street. He walked there and was invited to choose from among several models, settling on an inconspicuous grey Ford Orion with eight thousand kilometres on the clock. He paid a deposit of two hundred rands and two weeks' rent in advance. There was one form to fill in, requiring little more than his name, address and signature for insurance purposes. The man barely glanced at the details and didn't even ask to see his driver's licence, which made Marriner half-regret that he hadn't used a false name. That would not have been wise, he thought. Harry had warned him of the chance that someone might decide to take an interest in him. There didn't even have to be a reason. Though it was hard to believe in such a possibility, his behaviour had to remain completely above suspicion.

He drove off into the chaotic city traffic. On his street plan he had picked out a multi-storey parking garage off De Villiers Street, close to the hotel. He left the Orion there after being assured that the place was open day and night, then headed back to the Windsor. Over lunch, for the first time he paged through the copies of the *Farmers Weekly* he had been given in London, studying the descriptions of farms for sale and noting the names of the agents who advertised them. He was almost beginning to believe his own cover story, he thought. At half-past two he returned to his room, earning a smart salute from Nimrod, the floor boy, whom he passed in the corridor. By three o'clock he was catching up on his sleep.

The next morning, refreshed and rested, he set off early to go exploring.

He drove northwards, against the flow of rush-hour traffic pouring into the city, out along the main artery of Louis Botha Avenue and from there on to the motorway that led to Pretoria. The route took him past miles and miles of leafy white suburbs, reaching much further than he remembered, before opening out into bare veld surmounted by woody ridges, some of it farming land but some still residential. Off to the left here somewhere, among the straggling outer limits of Johannesburg, he had located on his map the area called Woodvale, but he intended to avoid it for the moment. He was still on legitimate business.

Once finally clear of Johannesburg, it seemed hardly any time before he was nearing Pretoria, its approach marked out by the vast granite monolith of the Voortrekker Monument among the low hills south of the city. Here, Afrikaners on their feast-days came to relive their history and reaffirm their allegiance to the *volk*. Soon after that he found the turning he had spotted on the map, the secondary road leading west towards Brits and Hartbeespoort, two of the several little settlements scattered about among the hills of the Magaliesberg. This was the area Jepson had been talking about yesterday.

From the beginning he had known this: if it did become necessary and prove feasible to spring Kumalo from the Woodvale Clinic, then the first thing he would need was a secure base from which to mount the operation, and possibly to use at least as a temporary refuge afterwards. All other considerations were secondary. Even the problem of getting him out of the country would have to be solved within the limitations imposed by this first criterion. The base would have to be somewhere extremely private and secluded, but within a reasonable distance from the clinic.

After he'd listened to Jepson, two things had struck him quite forcibly. The first was that a small farm, of just the sort that the bank official had mentioned, might be the ideal place; once his map had shown him how close the clinic was to this rough country to the north-west, the idea had begun to seem even more attractive. The second point was that he hadn't the remotest hope of buying such a farm within the time available, which was now only eighteen days. Buying land in any country was a complicated business involving lawyers, the transfer of deeds and the registration of ownership. Possibly his letter of introduction to the Secretary of Lands might help speed up the process, but even so he could not see it all being settled in less than a couple of weeks.

Renting or leasing a farm, on the other hand, as Jepson had suggested he might, ought to be a much simpler business. Provided he could find one that was suitable, and even that was asking a lot in so short a time.

Marriner had given much thought to the problem since yesterday. He had set out with a cover story that offered a reasonable explanation for his presence in the country. He'd planned to keep up the pretence, to the extent of showing an interest in acquiring some land but not of getting involved in any serious negotiations. Now it seemed that the lie had almost become a reality. And why not? He had the money, and he had his bona fides well established. All he lacked was time.

Gradually but emphatically, the countryside had changed within a few miles as he slipped down from the high ridge of the Witwatersrand to the lower altitude of the Bushveld Basin. Grassland had given way to low scrub, thorn trees and acacias, and the rolling expanses of the veld were replaced by rocky bush-smothered hills. The land was settled wherever it could be cultivated, but otherwise it had the authentic feel of the old Africa about it. The day grew hotter as he meandered along the little-used country roads, not quite certain what he was looking for but sure that he would know when he found it. The car was handling well. He enjoyed the feeling of air rushing through the open windows, of sweat making his shirt stick to his back, of the great sense of space in the distant views of the hills. He kept a careful eye on the driving mirror, and several times he pretended to miss a turning and doubled back for a couple of miles. Had anyone been following him he would certainly have known.

Mr Labuschagne was a pleasant, urbane young man who offered Marriner tea and then expounded on what seemed like a familiar theme.

'All of us Afrikaners are peasants at heart, I think. We all have a hankering for a bit of land to call our own. So what happens? A man who may have been born and bred in the city, a professional or business man with a nice house in the suburbs, the minute he's got a bit of spare cash he buys himself a few hectares within easy driving distance of town, somewhere he can go at weekends and sit on his stoep and call himself a farmer. It was the dream of every old Boer to live where he couldn't see his neighbour's chimney smoke, and that goes far to explain why we're determined to hold on to what we've got. But now I'm talking politics. Forgive me.'

Marriner had driven by a circuitous route back towards Johannesburg to reach the village of Muldersdrift, on its outer north-west fringe, at four in the afternoon. In the course of his wanderings he had seen a dozen or so promising properties with FOR SALE notices at their gates, and half of these had been advertised by the firm of Labuschagne & Son, of Muldersdrift. It was also a name he had seen in some of the ads in the *Farmers Weekly*, so clearly this was the market they specialized in. He guessed it was the son who was now addressing him.

'Well, these are mostly the people who are buying up these small places. Weekend farmers. Replacing the old fellows who can't make a living out of them any longer. I'm not saying some of these farms aren't viable: they can run to fifty hectares or more, mostly of rough grazing, but it's a full-time job to make them even marginally profitable these days. The weekenders don't want that. They keep a few cattle, maybe some chickens or ducks, and have a boy to look after them. No, if you want real farming, Mr Marriner, you'll have to go out a good fifty kilometres or so. We have some good sizeable places on our books as well . . .'

'I'm not sure I'm ready for that big a risk,' Marriner said. 'I want to take it slowly, learn from my mistakes. That's why it struck me as ideal to try out one of these small places for a while. Perhaps get a lease for six months or a year, with an option to buy as a further incentive.'

Labuschagne looked doubtful. 'These vendors are usually looking for hard cash. On the other hand, the market is sluggish, so it's just possible that one of them might agree to some letting arrangement. It will take a while, of course. A lot of them aren't on the phone. It will mean my writing to them, or calling in when I have the time.'

'I wouldn't mind doing some of the legwork myself.'

'I don't think that would help. Many of them don't have much English, and they'd be suspicious anyway of some foreigner walking in to look their farms over.'

Marriner finished his tea. He could understand the agent's lack of enthusiasm: a deal like this was probably more trouble than it was worth. He said: 'Do you mind telling me what your commission is?'

'I take ten per cent of the first year's rent from the lessor. It won't cost you anything.'

'What if I threw in another ten per cent from my side? Plus a bonus of five hundred rands if you could come up with the right place inside, say, a week?'

Labuschagne was taken aback. 'You *are* in a hurry, aren't you?'

'Staying in a hotel is costing a fortune. The money is well worth it if I can get settled quickly.'

'Some of the houses on these farms may not be up to your standards of comfort.'

'Oh, I've been known to rough it before.'

Considerably animated, Labuschagne stood up and shook hands. 'That's a deal, then. I'll get to work on it at once. It may still take a couple of days to organize, but I'm sure I can come up with something to offer you.'

Marriner left the office after arranging that the agent would telephone him at the hotel as soon as he had some prospects lined up. He was beginning, like Harry, to acquire some faith in the power of money.

16

On his third morning in Johannesburg, which was Wednesday, Marriner decided to address himself to the problem of approaching Judith Rose. What he'd accomplished so far had been useful groundwork, nothing more. Harry's contacts in the People's Congress had made no attempt to get in touch with him; he presumed they were avoiding him deliberately for a while. As for himself, instincts sharpened by training had been powerfully alert for the past forty-eight hours and had detected no suspicious vibrations around him. He knew that his hotel room had not been either bugged or searched. He was as sure as it was possible to be that he was not being watched. The time had come to expose himself to a few small risks.

Before collecting his car from the garage he did some shopping. After trying two bookshops he was directed to a third, smaller one in Bree Street that had a specialist map section catering for hikers and mountaineers. Here he found a Trigonometrical Survey sheet covering the section of the south-central Transvaal that interested him. Its scale was fifty thousand to one, and it showed in great detail an area of about fifteen hundred square kilometres, bounded in the east by the northern areas of Johannesburg and a section of Pretoria, in the west by the towns of Brits and Hekpoort.

One block from there he found a camera shop where he bought a pair of Zeiss 8×30 binoculars. Neither of these purchases could count as unusual for a man of his concerns.

Once again he drove northwards on to the Pretoria motorway. He had the photograph Rosenblatt had given him in the glove-box of the car, but it was out of the question for him to approach Judith Rose directly with it. She thought she was being watched; she would suspect a trick. A telephone call would be just as risky. Whatever means he finally chose, he was bound to scare the hell out of her. For the moment it would be enough to locate her and cautiously observe her movements.

He left the motorway at the Edenburg junction, and turned again on to a narrow road that led north to Woodvale. A few hundred yards down it he stopped, backed into a driveway and waited for a couple of minutes, pretending to study his map. When he was satisfied that he wasn't being tailed, he drove on.

The clinic proved oddly difficult to find. Woodvale itself turned out to be a surprising little residential backwater in the valley of the Jukskei River. It was not quite country and not quite town, more like a patch of the English stockbroker belt transplanted unwillingly to Africa. Three or four narrow roads meandered across the hillside; none of them appeared to have a name, as though to discourage any casual visitors who might happen upon them. Split-pole fences and rows of fir trees sheltered the houses. Glimpses of stables and patches of dung on the road gave evidence of horsey pursuits.

There were no pedestrians in sight, and few cars. Marriner felt uneasily conspicuous, more especially since it was obvious he did not know where he was going. When he stopped to get his bearings an Alsatian barked at him furiously from behind a hedge. Turning back to where he thought he had come from, he found himself instead in a narrow cul-de-sac between two high fences. He had driven into the grounds of the hospital almost before he knew it.

He passed a discreet little pair of gateposts made of pale yellow brick, and only at the last moment caught sight of a brass plate that said WOODVALE CLINIC. PRIVATE PROPERTY. In spite of this warning the gate was open and unguarded. He paused in the opening, then edged the car through.

Inside, a tarred driveway curved around a wide expanse of lawn which dipped, near the centre, into a willow-shaded hollow where a small stream had been dammed to form a water garden. Beyond this, perhaps a hundred yards away, stood a group of single-storey buildings, pleasingly modern and functional in style, all made of the same yellow brick, many interconnected by glassed-in walkways. The only clue to their purpose was the tall brick smokestack of a hospital incinerator at the rear, and even that was not obtrusive. The buildings took up only a small portion of the land, which must have run to four or five acres and was tastefully landscaped and planted with clumps of shady trees. A few of the clinic's patients strolled about or sat on benches scattered around on the grass.

He drove cautiously on, guessing that no one was likely to query his presence unless he entered one of the buildings. He could see that like all hospitals this one must have a constant stream of people entering and leaving its grounds. Fifteen or twenty vehicles, including a private ambulance, stood in a car park to the left. Beside it, a direction board pointed the way to Reception, Admission, Wards and so on. Another sign, indicating the Substance Abuse Unit, gave his memory an unpleasant jolt. It was one of the euphemisms used for the various alcoholic wards where he'd visited his father, in the Home Counties equivalent of just such green and pleasant surroundings as these, during the two years before his death. Marriner had had an irrational dislike of such places ever since.

The clinic was impressive all the same. It had tranquillity and it had seclusion. The land sloped gently down from west to east, overlooking the narrow river and a landscape of small vegetable farms across from it. Beyond that was the wide slash of the Johannesburg–Pretoria motorway, but from this distance its traffic seemed to glide along in silence. Pine trees had been planted all around the perimeter to mask the less appealing sight of an eight-foot boundary fence of steel mesh. This, however, was more a deterrent to intruders than an actual barrier. When it came to safeguarding Kumalo here, the real security of the place would lie in its isolation, the ability to seal it off discreetly without many outsiders even needing to know.

He moved slowly along the driveway, past the gardens to the left and the main administrative block on the right with its glass-fronted reception lobby. The buildings had windows of smoked glass, making it impossible to see what was inside, apart from two structures that toned in with the rest but had no windows at all. One had a functional crudity suggesting it was an auxiliary power plant – a necessity for every hospital, vital for one where operations were performed. The other building, plumb in the centre of the complex, was undoubtedly the operating theatre itself, with a domed metal roof protruding above its flat brick sill.

The driveway meandered across the grounds and doubled back on itself near the southern perimeter. Marriner swung the car around, stopped for a minute and studied the view of the clinic from this new angle. Just beside him, the stream entered the grounds from an overgrown gully beyond the fence. From there it ran diagonally down the slope, feeding the roots of the big old willows that lined the banks, then filling the lily ponds of the water garden, finally tumbling out through a cleft beneath the eastern fence to join the river below. Calling it a river was being polite, in fact. Although its valley was deeply eroded, the Jukskei appeared to be a typical African seasonal watercourse, a mere trickle for most of the year which would turn to a briefly dangerous torrent after heavy rain.

'Are you visiting a patient, sir?'

The voice was startlingly close. It made him actually jump in his seat. It came from a young white man in a security guard's uniform, bent beside the car, his face barely a foot away from Marriner's.

'Sorry. Did I give you a turn?' The man was apologetic but slightly wary. 'It's just that you seemed to be waiting for someone.'

'No. . . . No. I took a wrong turning. I drove in here by mistake.'

'Oh. Yeah. That can happen,' the guard conceded. He was a lumpish young fellow with a Birmingham accent. A brass pin on his shirt identified him by the improbable name of Virgil. He must have approached the car on Marriner's blind side. 'Where was it you were looking for?'

By some miracle a name seen on a gatepost five minutes ago came back to him. 'Bracken,' he said. 'A house called Bracken.'

'Down the road a bit. On the right.' Virgil stepped back, inviting him to move off, but continued to regard him curiously. It was almost as though he were trying to prompt some further explanation out of him. Marriner realized that he'd stupidly left his new binoculars and map in full view on the seat beside him. Eventually Virgil said, 'You from the old country too, then?'

'Ireland, actually.'

'Never been to Ireland. I'm from Solihull myself.'

'I've never been to Solihull.'

That seemed to close the conversation. Marriner started the car and drove off the way he had come. In the mirror he saw the guard standing straddle-legged in the middle of the driveway, watching his departure, and he cursed his own foolishness. He had drawn attention to himself, and for no good reason at all. He found he was shaking slightly. He had almost been caught in his first real lie and, trivial though the incident had been, he felt almost fatefully compromised by it.

Distracted, he made a genuine wrong turning soon after leaving Woodvale. Heading south on the motorway, he was momentarily confused by a plethora of signboards at a junction; instead of staying on the main route he found himself after a minute bumping along a potholed side road across a patch of rubble-strewn veld. Ahead, to his surprise, he saw the unmistakable low smoky sprawl of a black township. Curiosity pushed him on a little further, until he could read a sign he had spotted by the side of the road. *Alexandra Township* it said, *No Unauthorized Entry*, and to reinforce the point a police and army roadblock had been set up a couple of hundred yards ahead, close to the edge of the settlement: a Hippo riot truck, a Land Rover, some indistinct helmeted figures.

He remembered the name. Alexandra was a famous ghetto and a romantic legend. It was the home of township jazz and an original racy style, and had always been the scene of much political agitation. It was the only one of Johannesburg's townships not neatly segregated off into the satellite city of

Soweto to the south-west. Close to white suburbia, it was about as different as it was possible to imagine from the tranquil affluence of Woodvale only a few minutes' drive away.

Mariner stopped the car well before the roadblock, turned around and headed back to the motorway. He could do without having to explain himself twice in one morning.

Virgil shambled back to his customary position beside the counter in reception. 'I think there was another one of them here,' he said to Yvonne.

'Another what?'

'One of them Security Police blokes.'

Judith, passing by the counter, stopped and looked at him sharply. 'Who was he?'

'I don't know. Claimed he'd lost his way. Said he was from Ireland. They've got a few overseas blokes among them, I dare say. I know the look of them. What is it they want here, anyway?'

The London office of the People's Congress occupied one of a row of drab three-storey Victorian houses just off the Chalk Farm Road. Like its counterpart in Lusaka, it had suffered its share of destructive attention. Three years ago, a bomb had blown out the windows of the information office on the ground floor. More recently, the offices had twice been broken into. On both occasions the burglars had done nothing to hide the evidence of their intrusion. They had broken the locks on filing cabinets and desks, ransacked the files, looted some records, and even torn up others in apparent frustration.

No one was ever arrested for these crimes, though it was not difficult to guess who had inspired them. If the intention of the bombing was clearly to intimidate the eight employees of the office, the motive of the burglars was harder to fathom. They could not have expected to learn much that was useful. Like all revolutionary organizations, the Congress maintained a strict division between its political and propaganda

189

branch, which functioned in the open, and its activist military wing whose operations were conducted in the strictest secrecy. Under its director, Moses Mohaila, a former schoolteacher, the London office performed thoroughly respectable functions. It publicized the movement, lobbied politicians and solicited openly for funds. Even the money it collected from private donors was insignificant when compared to the sums paid by sympathetic governments. These were rarely channelled through London in any case.

It had come to be taken for granted, therefore, that the burglaries had been carried out by agents of the South African National Intelligence Service desperate for information of any kind. The inference drawn from that was that they had no easier way of obtaining it.

Jasper Darries left the office at midday that Wednesday on his regular weekly errand to the Fulham Palace Road. It was one of those cold, dull, dry days of late autumn, with a vague threat of snow in the air, and he shivered in his threadbare overcoat on the walk to the Camden Town Tube station. Jasper had grown up in the balmy air of the Eastern Cape, and after four years in London he still dreaded the approach of winter.

He claimed, however, not to mind the weekly trek to the printer's shop to deliver copy and page layouts for the Congress's London newsletter, which he helped to edit. It wasn't a job that could be left to a courier, since the printer often had queries that needed sorting out on the spot. Given that and the time spent waiting for Tube trains and buses, it was usually three o'clock, sometimes later, before he got back to the office.

Half an hour could easily go unaccounted for in such a period.

Half an hour was all the time he ever gave them, and they had never pressed for more. From the beginning he had set out his own terms. He would meet them only during working hours, and only when he himself judged it to be safe. That way, he had held them at arm's length, had kept them from invading his private life.

Jasper transferred his battered attaché case from one hand to the other, giving each a turn to warm up in his pocket. He kept meaning to buy some gloves. What he would really like was to spend a whole day in Oxford Street fitting himself out with a complete winter wardrobe. He could afford it if he wanted, but he didn't need the Controller to tell him that that would be the silliest sort of mistake. He could wait. He had waited four years, and had only one more to go before he qualified for British citizenship. Then he would no longer need a work permit. Then, in turn, he would no longer be tied to this boring and ill-paid job, and could kiss both the Congress and the Controller goodbye. Although he had worked conscientiously for both of them, because that was in his nature, he had not the slightest interest either in promoting revolution or in fighting it. Jasper was interested only in making his own way in the world. For the moment he was content to be just as he appeared: a rather diffident young coloured man of modest attainments, the obedient servant of two conflicting causes.

He dived into the welcome warmth of the Tube station, and within a couple of minutes was travelling on the Northern Line to the Embankment. There he had a longish wait for a train to Putney Bridge, and as the crowd thickened around him on the platform he wondered, not for the first time, whether anyone had ever followed him on one of these journeys. He had been warned never to act as though the thought had even crossed his mind. He would be unlikely to spot a professional tail anyway, and looking out for one would seem like guilty behaviour. He could only follow the drill and take sensible precautions.

From Putney Bridge he walked up to Fulham High Street and caught a bus almost at once, reaching the printer's shop at a few minutes to one. There were no problems with the material he had brought, and Jasper had left the premises again by a quarter past. A little way down the Fulham Palace Road he bought a copy of the *Evening Standard* and entered the saloon bar of the King's Arms. He bought a half of Guinness and a pork pie and found a seat at the edge of a table. The place was as crowded as usual at this time of day, and Jasper didn't bother trying to spot the lookout man or watch for him leaving, immersing himself in his newspaper while he ate and drank. The *Standard* was the signal. If he was carrying one, the meeting would go ahead. If not, it would be cancelled.

Four and a half years ago Jasper Darries had been a penniless youth who had walked through the bush across the border into Botswana to claim the status of a political refugee. Luckily, when he applied to join the Congress, they were not able to check too closely into his story of harassment and arrest as a student protester in an obscure town of the Eastern Cape. Now he had a bank deposit account, known only to himself, with forty-five thousand pounds in it. In another year it would be close to sixty thousand. That was when he planned to take it and drop out of sight. Leave London altogether, settle down in some provincial city and start his own business. This was still a country of opportunity for immigrants. Look at the Asians and their corner shops. Start small and grow big. No chance of that in South Africa – at least, not for a *Boesman*, a coloured man. Live quietly, in a flat with central heating. He would leave no traces behind him in London, and there was no reason why he should ever be found. After exactly ten minutes, Jasper left the pub by a side entrance which gave on to a long deserted lane of mews, a short cut of sorts back towards Putney Bridge. Every move he had made so far was perfectly innocent, but all were part of an elaborate security procedure. No one could follow him down the lane without making himself obvious. By the time any such tail had waited and then hurried after him, he would find that his quarry, still with every appearance of innocence, had simply vanished. He would not see the closed Volkswagen van that was parked five yards around the next corner, which opened its sliding door as Jasper approached, and within a few seconds had swallowed him in from the pavement and was driving off towards Chelsea.

There was a hardboard partition, with only a small opening in it, between the front and rear of the van, so Jasper never got more than a glimpse of the driver or the lookout man who sat beside him. The rear was done out like a rather makeshift camping vehicle, with benches facing each other across a folding table. The interior was gloomy and unheated. The man Jasper knew only as the Controller sat huddled in a quilted anorak with a hood, like an Arctic explorer in his tent. Presumably he missed the heat too.

The Controller grinned at him. '*Alles reg*, Jasper?'

'Everything's OK.'

The van moved in fits and starts through the Fulham Road traffic. The Controller reached into a cupboard beside him and produced a bottle of Scotch and two plastic tumblers. 'For your nerves,' he had said the first few times, but the drink was by now a ritual.

'No trouble at the shop?'

'No trouble for me,' Jasper said. 'But still a general air of distrust after that air raid. It does not make life easier for me.'

The Controller poured whisky into the tumblers. 'We've been over this twice already. I told you it gave me a scare as well, when I heard about it.'

'It gave *you* a scare? What about me? The information I gave you was precise. If they had to act on it, why be so blatant about it?'

'I can't tell you, Jasper. I don't know. I am a sprocket and you are a cog in a great big machine.'

The van jerked, slopping some of the Scotch out of the tumblers. The Controller raised his and tipped it towards Jasper.

'*Gesondheid*,' he said. They drank. They were on friendly terms, as friendly as it was possible to be in the circumstances. They could get annoyed with each other without taking offence. 'If you want my opinion, Jasper, it was just too tempting a target not to hit. It was done to please the hard men in the military and the State Security Council. Still, no harm done. No fingers pointing at you.'

'No,' Jasper admitted. 'Not at anybody in the office. Not since the two burglaries.'

'I know you wondered whether they were necessary.

Maybe now you can see the sense of them. They were meant to make you look clean. If they achieved that, then I'm glad. OK, as usual we have no time to waste. Have you got any paperwork for me?'

'No. Nothing worth taking. Nothing I could risk copying. As I told you, the atmosphere is not relaxed.'

The Controller looked disappointed. He liked things on paper, presumably because they proved he was doing his job. From the pocket of his anorak he took a small cassette recorder with a built-in microphone. He placed it on the table and pressed the RECORD button. 'All right. Tell me your news.'

'Well, Harry Makibani is still around. Somewhere in Europe – I don't know where at the moment. As I told you, he came to London during the Algiers conference. Later he went to Switzerland. As you know, we – they – have their bank accounts there.'

'Dates, Jasper. Give me dates.'

'I was coming to the dates. He arrived in London on the twentieth, a Sunday. I didn't see him, but I know he met Mohaila a couple of times. On the twenty-second he went to Ireland for two days.'

'Why Ireland?'

'I have no idea. One thing I have since discovered is that he took a cheque for five thousand pounds with him.'

The Controller gave a low whistle. Before he could ask the obvious questions, Jasper said: 'I can't tell you who for or what for. It was a cash cheque, drawn on a small account that the Congress finance committee keeps in London. Not under its own name. A joint account, Mohaila's signature and one other required. The reason I know about the cheque is that there weren't actually the funds in the account to meet it. The money had to be telegraphed from Zurich. Makibani arranged that a couple of days later, when he flew there. The Swiss bank – the Handelsbank Bauer, it is – sent us a confirmation that it had been remitted, and I was sent hurrying round to the National Westminster with that piece of paper to make sure it had actually turned up. The messenger boy, that's me. They didn't want the cheque to bounce. Mohaila enclosed a letter explaining it all. Naturally, I read it on the way, and sealed it into a fresh envelope.'

The Controller looked impressed, but he said: 'You couldn't have made a copy? On the way?'

'There wasn't time. As it was, I got to the bank a minute before it closed.'

'So,' said the other man thoughtfully, 'we're talking about five thousand pounds from Switzerland that has been, in effect, laundered through a bank account in London and paid anonymously to someone in Ireland. Does that suggest anything to you, Jasper?'

'Nothing. The Congress has sympathizers in Ireland but, if anything, the money should come from them to us.'

'Have they ever had dealings with a terrorist organization over there? The IRA?'

'Not that I've ever heard. And I find it hard to imagine such a thing. The Congress is keen to win the support of Western governments, and it wouldn't help their case to have any truck with terrorists in their own back yards.'

'The IRA are terrorists and the Congress people are freedom fighters? That's rich, don't you think?'

'I have no views on the subject,' said Jasper a little pompously. Two could play at this game of cogs and sprockets.

'I would love to find out where that cheque went to, Jasper. Can you do that for me?'

'I doubt it. No. Wait a minute. Let me think.'

Jasper was interested in anything to do with money. He knew that most banks these days no longer enclosed paid and cancelled cheques with the statements they sent out to their customers, unless they were specially requested. There was nothing to stop him, over the phone, requesting that cheque back on behalf of Moses Mohaila. It would be posted to the Congress office, and as long as he knew when to expect it he could be sure of intercepting it before it reached Mohaila himself. It wouldn't necessarily tell the Controller very much, but it would satisfy his craving for paperwork. There was a risk, of course, but Jasper thought he could cover himself.

'I'll try,' he said. 'If I can get hold of it, I'll bring it next Wednesday.'

'Sooner. Use the dead-letter drop.'

'What's the hurry?'

The Controller didn't answer. Something else seemed to be bothering him. 'You mentioned the name of a Swiss bank. Bauer, was it? Spell that.' Jasper spelled it out for the tape recorder. 'But don't they keep their money in the Union Banque Suisse?'

'Not all of it, any longer. I know a little about that, too, but I hardly thought it was worth mentioning.'

Jasper explained that one reason for Harry Makibani's visit to London appeared to have been to get Mohaila, as a member of the finance committee, to agree to diversify the Congress's investments in Zurich. This had involved opening a new account with the Handelsbank Bauer in addition to those already held with the UBS. Jasper had learned of this by sneaking a look at a memorandum Mohaila had left lying on his desk. It was obviously nothing worth hiding. It mentioned no figures. It seemed to cover a mere technicality, and Jasper had attached no importance to it.

'It's not for you to decide what's important,' the Controller said. 'It's not for me, either.'

They talked on for another fifteen minutes while the van threaded its way from Chelsea to Knightsbridge, into Piccadilly and down the Haymarket to Trafalgar Square. At the bottom of Northumberland Avenue they turned along the Embankment and finally dropped Jasper a hundred yards from the station. It was a bit too close to South Africa House for his liking, but it allowed him to catch a Northern Line train straight back to Camden Town, just as though he had retraced the whole of his outward route. Today he was back in the office before three o'clock.

The Controller had reached his own office somewhat earlier. This was not in the embassy, as Jasper had always imagined it to be, but in the consulate-general across the square, a place

196

where comings and goings were far less noticeable. Within a few minutes he had discarded his anorak, put on the jacket of his suit and resumed his role as Hannes Koekemoer, deputy head of the consulate's commercial section. Only six other people in the embassy and the consulate knew of Koekemoer's true position as head of the London station of the South African National Intelligence Service. The commercial section's sandy-haired young junior officer was not among these six, though he did have his own thoughts about the lightness of Koekemoer's official workload and his frequent unexplained absences from the office.

Tonight Koekemoer would be transmitting a report to Pretoria, as he did after every meeting with Jasper Darries. There was much that was appetizing but little of any real substance in what his agent had told him. And, of course, it was always a devil of a job to get any documentation out of him. Jasper wouldn't be pushed. Jasper was loyal only to himself. He was also one of the most valuable assets the Service had.

Two things were especially tantalizing, although connected in only the most casual way. The fact that the Congress had opened a new account with a different bank in Zurich was, as Jasper himself had surmised, probably of no more then peripheral interest. But why had they immediately taken five thousand pounds from it for payment to someone in Ireland? Granted, it wasn't a lot of money. What was abnormal was its destination. The idea of establishing some link between the Congress and a subversive organization in Ireland had taken root in Koekemoer's mind. If such a thing could be proved, it would do much damage to the respectable image the Congress was seeking to cultivate with the British and other Western governments. The British might even close down Moses Mohaila's office and throw him out of the country, just as they had done to the Libyan People's Bureau a few years ago. It would be a convincing demonstration of what Pretoria had been saying all along: that the Congress was a communist-inspired terrorist movement with no claim to speak on behalf of the Black South African masses. It could be a diplomatic coup.

17

Houghton Drive: a long, tree-lined avenue bisecting a couple of square miles of the priciest residential land in the country. An address that spoke for itself. Close to the city and yet distanced from it in a way that the outer suburbs weren't, a little kingdom of large solid houses and vast mature gardens, tended by an army of servants. *Nouveau riche* territory fifty or sixty years ago, it now had the mellow look of old money about it.

By seven-thirty that Thursday morning Marriner was parked fifty yards down the road from the gates of the Roses' house. It was just ten hours since he'd given up an earlier vigil in the same spot, in the dark. By daylight he felt uncomfortably exposed, but he'd been gripped by a certain desperation when he realized that today was December the first. There were fifteen days to go, and he had yet to make any real progress in what he had been sent here to do. It was his fourth morning in Johannesburg: risk or no risk, he was going to have to make contact with Judith Rose.

The house itself was invisible from the road. All that could be seen through the bars of the iron gates was a gravelled driveway flanked by low hedges, a glimpse of well-tended lawns and flowering kaffirboom trees. Marriner had found the address on his way back from the clinic yesterday, and at first hadn't lingered outside it. Instead he had searched for a vantage point from which to overlook the house and found one a little way to the south, in a spot oddly known as the Wilds. It was an amenity area, a few acres of rocky hillside planted with indigenous shrubs and trees, with benches from which to take in the view to the north. With his binoculars he had located the house at once: an elegant burnt-brick building with a red-tiled roof, standing in what looked like the best part of two acres of gardens. There was an all-weather tennis court and a sizeable swimming pool, and terraced lawns dotted with flowerbeds and coloured umbrellas. At the front, the drive led up to a wide forecourt and a garage with spaces for three cars. Only one space was taken, by some kind of American station wagon, though they probably referred to it as a shooting brake.

There had been no point in hanging about here either. He had gone back to the hotel and returned to the Wilds just before five o'clock, in time to see two more cars arrive at the house within half an hour. One was a grey Daimler Jaguar, the other a sporty little red Opel Manta. Although they both drove into the garage and he could not see their drivers getting out, he was fairly confident he knew who they were. Cars tended to define their owners. The Jag would be the eminent surgeon's official vehicle, so to speak; the station wagon must be the wife's family runabout. That meant that the Opel belonged to the daughter.

A little later he had gone back down to Houghton Drive to park in the shade of a sycamore near the gates. There was a chance that the girl might go out again, in which case he would follow her; another chance that the parents would leave the house, making it safe for him to approach her. It was nine o'clock before he could be sure that neither of these things was going to happen. With that came the depressing realization that it could go on like this for the rest of the week, with Judith Rose commuting between the house and the clinic and giving him no chance to approach her.

There was one means of waylaying her, and that was to arrange a small car crash. Hardly the happiest way to make her acquaintance, but it would have the merit of seeming accidental.

At ten to eight the Jaguar nosed its way out of the gates, swung right and accelerated past him, heading north. Marriner got a glimpse of Dr Rose as he passed: a patrician profile, a head of wavy grey hair. It was another half an hour before he saw the Opel Manta appear at the entrance with its right flicker going. He started his engine. Obviously Judith kept more ladylike hours at the clinic than her father did. He watched in his mirror as she waited for a gap in the fast traffic heading into the city. Finally she turned. Again, he caught only a profile view of the driver as the car sped past, but it was her all right: the same strong serious face that was in the photograph, a pale complexion, a mop of rich dark curls. He waited a few seconds more, giving another car time to get between them, before turning into the traffic and beginning to follow her.

She drove fast and aggressively. She got so far ahead that he had to overtake the intervening car in order to keep her in sight. Where the road divided at the far end of Houghton Drive she was held up by a traffic light, and he coasted in slowly behind her. Now, before she bore right to head for the Pretoria motorway, was the time for a little accident. Just the slightest of bumps, hop out of the car, sorry, no harm done. . . . But as he crept the Orion up behind her the lights changed to green and she gunned the car and raced off.

She didn't take the right fork. Without a warning or a signal, she turned left. Marriner belatedly tried to switch lanes and got caught up in a snarl of traffic halfway across the junction. By the time he had disentangled himself, the Opel Manta was a distant red dot heading up Riviera Road, cutting across the city to the west. Wherever she was going, it wasn't to the Woodvale Clinic. Bewildered but determined not to lose her, he pushed the Orion as hard as it would go and tried to follow.

As soon as the young man from the Central Pharmaceutical Stores arrived at the prison dispensary that morning, the pharmacist sent Phineas Molefe to fetch coffee for them both. There was a bit of a fuss in the kitchen about providing it so early, and it was twenty minutes before he got back. The moment he entered the room, he knew things were about to go very badly for him.

He had known all along roughly what to expect, of course. Today was the first of the month: stocktaking day. Perhaps he had half-convinced himself over the weeks, however, that the disappearance of the Dexedrine tablets would not be noticed, or would be put down to some error in the records. When he saw the way the two men stood behind the counter, however, he understood that it was him they were waiting for. How had they found out so quickly? They both wore the kind of grim, empty-eyed, almost sorrowful expression that white men took on when you had outraged them beyond anger. He wished they would be angry. He wished they would knock the shit out of him and leave it at that, but common sense told him that wasn't going to happen either. All he could do was begin by protesting his innocence, then later tell them part of the truth. They believed things if you made it hard work for them.

For a minute neither of the men spoke. They watched him set down the tray and hand them their cups. Phineas's hands had begun to tremble, and he spilt some of the pharmacist's coffee in the saucer. He muttered an apology but his boss didn't even grumble, which was another bad sign. He knew that the pharmacist's anger would be tempered by embarrassment – at least, while the stores officer was around.

The pharmacist put sugar in his coffee and stirred it slowly. 'Phineas,' he said at last, '*kom hierso.*'

'*My baas?*'

Phineas went round the counter to where the dispensary records were spread out on the table: the stock sheets, the day book, the drugs register. The pharmacist hated these occasions at the best of times, especially since they'd been sending this pushy young storeman around – not the usual dim-witted clerk but a sharp accountant type who performed wizardry with a calculator.

'There's something missing, Phineas.'

'*My baas?*'

'Missing. Tablets. Amphetamines. *Verstaan?*'

Phineas gave the sort of dumb, uncomprehending look that was expected of him. But it was the storeman who spoke next.

'He understands well. Phineas, there are eighty-one Dexedrine tablets missing. They've been signed out on the drugs register, but there are no corresponding requisitions for them. No prescriptions from any of the hospital doctors. What happened to them, Phineas?'

He puckered his brow in thought. He had entered the

tablets in the register as a temporary safeguard, against the chance that the pharmacist himself might find they were missing. 'I don't know, *my baas*. The *baas* here, he signs for everything.'

'Of course he does,' the younger man said with quick contempt. 'He signs what you give him to sign. You know far more about the records in this place than anyone. And you know where those tablets went.'

'No, *my baas*.'

'I'm giving you the chance to come clean.'

'I know nothing.'

'Right. The security officer will have to take this over. There's another thing,' the storeman said, shooting a significant glance at the pharmacist. 'While I was cross-checking the prescriptions, I found one of the dockets missing.'

'One of the dockets?' Now the pharmacist seemed to be playing dumb. Nobody cared about the prescription dockets, but this smart-arse would have to poke his nose among them. 'Does it matter?'

'I think this one might. It was a prescription for Stilboestrol hormone tablets. They were for Prisoner 4008.'

The pharmacist's face suddenly seemed to have gone a shade whiter. He glanced at Phineas, then back at the stores officer. 'What are you saying? That the docket was stolen, too?'

'All I'm saying is that you've got two discrepancies in your records. Are you going to call the security officer, or shall I?'

The Opel Manta cut a zig-zagging trail across the northern suburbs of Johannesburg. After twenty minutes or so, however, it had set course along a fast dual carriageway that seemed to be taking it towards a high rocky hill surmounted by a big water-tower that was a landmark for miles around. *Northcliff*, it was signposted. The highway petered out soon, giving way to a two-lane road that rounded the base of the hill and then began to climb it. There was little other traffic here, and Marriner followed more cautiously, the red car disappearing from his view for a few seconds at a time as it took the bends at speed.

Northcliff was one of the exposed ridges of the gold-bearing reef that stretched east and west beneath the city. It was smothered in rocks and tough grass, except where the ground had been levelled to make room for stylish houses and low-rise apartment blocks. The road twisted up between them, with driveways branching off it to left and right. Somewhere near the top, Marriner realized that the Opel had been out of sight for almost a minute. Then, suddenly, he found himself back at a junction he'd already passed. The road went no higher, but simply made a loop around the summit of the hill. Somewhere along it Judith Rose had turned off, and he'd lost her.

Cursing mechanically, he stopped the car and thought for a minute. This was the only way back down the hill, so the logical thing to do was to wait here and pick her up again as she returned. That could be in a matter of minutes or hours, however. It could be all day. Maybe she had a day off from the clinic and was spending it with a friend or a boyfriend. He realized he knew nothing whatever about the life of this woman. He'd been told a few odds and ends by a relative who had last seen her as a little girl, and otherwise simply had no idea what sort of person she was. This put him at a severe disadvantage. He had come to see that an open straightforward approach was the only one left to him, but could not guess how she would react to it.

He was too impatient to wait. He decided to go searching for her. There was a chance that she would slip out from behind him, but a quite equal risk of his wasting yet another day awaiting a further opportunity. He turned left and began to traverse the hillside.

Although the ground was bare, it was also uneven, so that many of the houses spread out across it were hidden, either down in hollows or behind outcrops of rock. Starting from where he had last seen the Opel, he began methodically driving into each entrance he came to, backing out or turning around only once he had established that Judith Rose's red car wasn't present. Guard dogs ran out to bark at him. Mystified servants and housewives stared from verandas and windows. To each he gave a small wave and an embarrassed grin, indicating that he'd made a mistake. He was beginning to feel extremely foolish.

The hill was several hundred feet high. Its northern slopes overlooked undulating country almost as far as Pretoria. To the north-west, even through the steadily increasing heat haze, he could make out the Magaliesberg hills which he had visited on Tuesday. As the road curved gradually to the south, the spectacular skyline of Johannesburg became visible across a chasm of suburbs.

He was close to the summit again, entering perhaps his twentieth tortuous driveway – this one leading to a small block of flats – when he had to brake sharply for a car coming out. They stopped almost bumper to bumper, and Marriner reversed into the road to let the other vehicle past. The man at the wheel waved an acknowledgement as he cleared the entrance. Marriner was about to swing through the opening again when a second car emerged. It was the red Opel.

He had no time to consider what to do. He shot the Orion forward, blocking the entrance, and stopped it there. Judith Rose braked sharply, with a rasping of tyres on the gravel. Her car rocked to a halt with its nose inches from the side of his.

He leaped out of the Orion and trotted round behind it. Unexpectedly, she had got out of her car just as quickly and stood next to it, a slim, square-shouldered figure in blue jeans and a cotton shirt. Her hands were on her hips, her stance was aggressive.

'I'm sorry . . .,' he began.

'You fucking bastard!' she shouted.

He flinched. He realized she was very angry. Her features seemed gathered together, in the centre of her long pale face, in a knot of unspeakable rage. 'I'm sorry,' he repeated, but again the apology went unheeded.

'You sneaky fucking creep,' she said. 'Leave me alone!'

'I didn't mean to scare you. I have to talk to you.'

'You don't scare me, mister. If you've come here to intimidate me, embarrass me, then you might as well give up. I don't embarrass easily.'

Intimidate? Embarrass? What was she talking about? He saw her glance beyond him, towards the road. Turning his head for an instant, he saw that the man who'd preceded her down the drive had stopped his car a little way down and was waiting. They'd been leaving together, then. He said, 'I don't think you understand. . . .'

'I understand perfectly well. Do you think I didn't hear about your visit to the clinic yesterday? Do you think I didn't see you this morning, waiting to follow me? I thought I'd managed to lose you up here, but obviously you're determined to hound me. Well, I can't stop you people wasting your time, but I'd prefer it if you didn't waste mine. Will you please get that car out of my way and let me go about my business?'

Realization hit him between the eyes. He'd thought her anger was not just unwarranted but slightly artificial, and now he knew there was fear behind it. 'You think I'm a policeman?' he said.

'For Christ's sake, stop playing games!'

'I had a reason for following you. We have to talk. I'm not what you take me for.' But how did he prove it without scaring her further? 'Give me a moment,' he said.

She had no choice but to wait while he went to his car. He opened the door and took the photograph from the glove-box. As he turned away he heard the door of the car down the road being slammed: the other driver, coming to see what the hold-up was.

He went back to Judith Rose. He held the picture out to her, and she took it and stared at it uncomprehendingly.

'Turn it over,' he said. She did so, and he saw the shock start into her face. He explained quickly, 'Joshua Rosenblatt gave me that, just last week. It's to prove that I've come from him. He wanted me to contact you, about the letter you sent him. I've got to discuss it with you.'

She looked up at him, and she was no longer trying to disguise her fear. It shone out at him from her clear brown eyes. 'Who are you?' she said.

'Patrick Marriner. The name won't mean anything to you.'

He heard the crunching of footsteps on gravel behind him,

and then the voice of the man. 'Is anything wrong, Miss Rose?' Marriner turned with slight, belated alarm. He hadn't had time to consider who or what the man might be, but he looked innocuous enough: early thirties, glasses, business suit. He stopped at a polite distance.

'No, it's all right,' the girl said. 'Sorry. I won't be a minute.'

The man withdrew, but not all the way to his car, lingering instead on the road nearby. The interruption had given Judith time to marshal some defences. She said in a fierce stage whisper, 'What if I told you I don't know what you're talking about?'

'It's a bit late for that. I've seen the letter. I've come specially from Europe to talk to you about it.'

'You could still be from the Security Police.'

'With my accent?'

'Anything is possible. You could have stolen this picture.'

'I've got a phone number for Joshua, in Europe. I'd like you to talk to him yourself and verify who I am.'

'I told him not to . . .' She checked herself, still not willing to admit anything.

'You told him not to make contact with you,' Marriner supplied. 'You wrote to him in confidence, I know, but what you had to say was too important for him to keep to himself. More important than you realize. I'll explain everything, if you'll just agree to talk to me.'

'And if I don't?'

'Then I'll just have to keep following you around until you do. That might not be too safe for either of us. I'm sticking my neck out, too, if it makes you feel any better.'

'It doesn't.' She looked past him again, at where the other man waited. 'Listen, I've got to go. I can't stand here talking.'

'Who is he?' Marriner asked.

'Nobody who matters. Some personal business. Will you please move your car if I promise to think about it?'

'No,' he said bluntly. 'I haven't time to wait while you think.'

Judith bit her lip and took a decision. She looked at him

with a mixture of dread and resentment. 'You know Eloff Street Extension, on the south side of town?'

'I think so.'

'There's a café called Choy's, about halfway down on the left. Meet me there at seven tonight.'

'Right.' He turned away at once and went back to the Orion. When he'd reversed a few yards he watched her start her car with a jerk and race it out through the opening and down the hill. The other man had got into his car, and he pulled away and followed her at an easier pace. Marriner grunted with amusement and relief. He backed into the driveway, turned the car and headed back towards the city, this time making no attempt to tail her. He wondered vaguely what she had been doing out here.

At the Windsor Hotel there was a message asking him to phone Mr Labuschagne at the estate agency. He went at once to the public telephone off the lobby, having resolved from the start to make no outside calls from his room. Incoming calls and messages could obviously not be avoided but were easily forgotten about; outgoing calls would be logged and charged to his account, and were therefore traceable.

Labuschagne told him he had found four farmers who were willing to consider renting out their farms if the price was right. He'd made tentative arrangements to look them over on Saturday. Marriner told him that would be fine. Things were starting to move, he thought, and in a self-congratulatory mood he ordered a pre-lunch drink from room service, a gin and tonic brought by the ever-attentive Nimrod. Pondering on his progress over the past four days, however, he didn't seem to have got all that far. There were still several vital things missing from the equation, not least of which was the failure of the Congress to get in touch with him. Maybe it was time for a call to that number in Zurich, he thought, but he resisted the temptation. If they wanted him, they knew where to find him. Meanwhile, the less he did to jeopardize his cover, the better.

18

It was worse than Phineas had feared. Nobody had beaten him. Nobody had even shouted at him. Instead he had been surrounded by a kind of awestruck consideration, as though he had just been sentenced to death and no more harm could come to him. The security officer and two warders had marched him without a word down a maze of echoing corridors into a region of the prison unknown to him. There they had locked him into a windowless cell with a brightly burning light and left him alone for several hours. He felt as though he had truly been condemned and was waiting only while they sent for the hangman.

It was bad enough that the Dexedrine tablets had been missed, but that was something he had been more or less resigned to, something he was quite ready to admit and that could be explained as an ordinary theft. Out of character, perhaps, but not wholly unexpected. It had never entered his calculations, however, that the absence of the prescription docket would be noticed at the same time. It was too much of a coincidence – and now, naturally, it was that flimsy bit of paper that was going to interest them even more than the tablets did.

Phineas also had deep doubts that what he had done had made any sense, or done any good. He knew from Bobbejaan that his message had been delivered – if not to the Leader's daughter as he had planned, then at least to his lawyer – but had it been understood? Could it be acted upon, or had it merely been laughed at and thrown away? There was no possible way of telling. All he was sure about was that the Boers were taking the whole business very seriously, and that seemed to confirm everything he had feared.

There were fifteen more days to go. Fifteen more days for him to bluff his way out, or stand up to their questioning. After that nothing would matter. The third alternative did not bear thinking about; if he talked, if he told them what he knew, he was as good as dead.

They left him alone for so long that when he finally heard footsteps approaching the cell he was almost ready to believe it *was* the hangman. A summary execution, a secret burial – fantasies of this sort came readily to the mind of a *mugu*, for they controlled your life so completely in here that it was easy to believe they could casually snuff it out. And yet another part of his mind told him that it was precisely in order to frighten him that they had locked him away in here. While he retained an almost superstitious dread of what was to come, he felt mentally quite well prepared for it.

A key grated in the lock, the door swung open. A white man in civilian clothes came in, smiling as if he were greeting an old friend.

Most men seemed big to Phineas, but not all of them were threatening. This man was both. He had short grey-blond hair, evenly cropped, and a brutal face with a square and massive jaw and watery, slightly bulging blue eyes. Still smiling, he sat down on the bunk opposite the one where Phineas squatted, carefully adjusting his trouser creases over his massive thighs. He said nothing until the warder who had admitted him had relocked the door and tramped away down the corridor.

'Phineas Molefe?' he asked unnecessarily. 'I am Major Booysen.'

He surprised Phineas by speaking in English, a courtesy that Afrikaners rarely extended to blacks. Such politeness was dangerous. Major Booysen was without doubt a member of the Security Police, and ten times more to be feared than any dumb Boer of a warder.

'I think you know why I'm here, Phineas.'

'I stole some pills, sir.'

'You stole some pills, *ja*. What did you do with the pills, Phineas?'

'Took them, sir. Swallowed them.'

'You swallowed eighty-one amphetamines?'

'It was nearly a month ago. I took two, three, every day.'

'For three years you've worked in that dispensary, is it, Phineas? And never once stolen anything before?'

'You mean never got caught stealing, sir.'

Even this bit of cheek failed to arouse the major's anger, though his eyes seemed to bulge a little more. 'Yes, I'll grant that you're a smart thief – at least, to judge by your record. And that's why I don't believe you. You're too smart for a stunt like this. Why did you need those pills, Phineas? Who did you pass them on to?'

'Nobody, sir.'

'Did you need to buy a favour from somebody?'

'No. I swear to it.'

'I can easily question the others in your cell block, you know. Nobody is going to carry the can for you.'

There was a measure of bluff in this, Phineas knew. There were forty others in Cell Block C. To question them all thoroughly would take several days, and unless Bobbejaan's nerve cracked they would still learn nothing.

'You can ask them,' he said with a show of nonchalance. 'They cannot tell you what they don't know. I took the tablets. I used them myself. Nobody else knew.'

The major sighed and leaned back against the wall of the cell. The smile had gone now. He looked hard into Phineas's face. 'OK. Let's forget the tablets for now. If you want to know, I don't give a shit about the tablets. If you co-operate with me, I can maybe persuade the prison commandant that they don't matter to him either. I want the truth about that prescription docket, Phineas, and I want it quickly.'

Here was the purpose of the visit. The Security Police didn't concern themselves with petty thefts. Phineas summoned up a look of dumb helplessness. 'The other *baas* spoke of this docket. I don't know what he means. Sometimes there is no docket. Sometimes one goes missing. Those files are not important.'

'But this one was.'

'Which one?'

'Are you trying to tell me you don't know who Prisoner 4008 is?'

'Yes, sir. I don't know, sir.'

'You may be a clever thief, Phineas, but you're not much of a liar.' Booysen's latent anger was beginning to show. His eyes were swollen. 'You took that docket, and you took it because it referred to Lincoln Kumalo. What happened to it?'

'I don't know. I didn't take it.'

'Did you smuggle it out?'

'No!'

'What have you heard about Kumalo?'

'Nothing.'

'Are you a follower of his?'

'No.'

'You can tell me the truth now, Phineas, or we can do it the hard way.'

'God's truth, I know nothing.'

'OK.' Major Booysen stood up abruptly. He was smiling again, but now it was a grim little smirk with no pretence of friendliness. 'You're going to come with me, for a little drive to a place we've got downtown. Are you a religious man, Phineas? Do you go to confession in your church? That's what it will be like. It's a place people go into with sins on their souls, and they come out pure and shining. When it's over you'll wonder why you ever wanted to sin in the first place. They all wonder the same thing, Phineas. Believe me, I know.' He turned away and hammered on the door to be let out.

A dim neon sign identified Choy's Café as a pair of greasy shop windows set among factory buildings in a bleak industrial zone just south of the city. In the blunter language of Marriner's boyhood it was what had been known as a 'native eating-house', a place that sold plates of stew and mealie porridge and bottles of lemonade to black workmen, and probably doubled as the headquarters of a fah-fee game. With night falling and the workers packed into buses and trains on their way back to Soweto or Alexandra, it looked almost deserted. It seemed an odd place for Judith to have

211

chosen for a rendezvous, but he'd been aware since this morning that he was dealing with a rather odd lady.

He parked his car and went in, carrying the telephone scrambler in its little black case. The café was long and narrow, with a glass-topped counter down one side manned by an elderly Chinese in a grubby apron; across from that was a row of rickety tables at which half a dozen Africans were eating from enamel plates. Their conversation died as he entered, but the looks they gave him were curious rather than hostile. There was no sign of Judith. He glanced around uncertainly, and the Chinese, catching his eye, jerked his head slightly to a door in the rear.

When he opened it he found himself in another room, brightly lit, hardly smaller than the first, with eight or nine tables and an altogether livelier atmosphere. Township jazz blared from a big portable stereo on a kitchen dresser. There were four Chinese playing mah-jong and sharing a bottle of Scotch at one table; several of the others were occupied by Africans engaged in animated conversation. In a corner, Judith sat alone.

He went over to her. She pointed to the chair opposite her, and he sat down.

'What the hell is this place?'

'A shebeen, among other things. An illegal pub.'

Now he realized what it was that was familiar about the scene. It was as though someone had tried to recreate the set of an old gangster film, the back door from a quiet drugstore opening into a rowdy speakeasy. He had to raise his voice to be heard over the music. 'It's not exactly what I had in mind. It's hardly private.'

'It's safe enough. Choy greases the right palms and the police keep away. It's a hangout for musicians and actors. It was the place to come to when I was a student. Very radical chic, don't you think?'

Marriner looked dubiously about at the bare walls and floorboards, the harsh lights, the plastic tablecloths. A beautiful Chinese girl in a waitress's overall came and stood attentively by their table. 'I'm going to eat,' Judith said. 'Are

212

you hungry? You can have chicken with noodles, or chicken with fried rice, or just chicken. And whisky or beer to drink.'

'Whisky. And chicken with noodles.'

'The same for me.' When the girl had left, Judith rested her chin on her hands and looked at him without expression. She was on her home ground and, although her manner remained offhand, she seemed much more relaxed than he'd seen her that morning. Her serious look was a little betrayed by the profusion of rich black curls that framed her pale face, as though she had tried for a dramatic effect but failed. 'Well, Mr . . . Marriner? You want to talk, and I want you off my back. Go ahead.'

'I'd prefer you to start by speaking to Joshua, getting him to vouch for me. Is there a phone here we could use?'

'Do you really expect me to say yes to that? I have no idea who you are or what you want, and I'm not going to walk into some kind of set-up.'

'How else can I convince you to trust me?'

'It'll be uphill work. Virgil told me about you snooping around the clinic yesterday. He was sure you were a policeman.'

'Virgil.' He remembered the young security guard. 'Well, Virgil was wrong.'

'That's why I was so annoyed when you turned up at my flat.'

'Your flat?' He was puzzled, and she seemed taken aback. Then the penny dropped. 'You're moving house? To that place in Northcliff?'

'That was the owner I was with this morning. We were going off to sign the lease. It's all mine now. It was arranged before any of this happened, but I was trying to keep the address confidential. Well, now you know.'

'I gather you're afraid they may be watching you. I can't say I've seen any sign of it.'

'Neither have I. But that doesn't mean anything.'

'Look,' he said, 'I can only give you my word that I was sent to see you by Joshua Rosenblatt and certain other people. To ask for your help.'

213

'What other people?'

'I think you can guess.'

'You're asking me to trust you. I think you should lay your cards on the table.'

'And my head on a block?'

'If that's the way you see it.'

'I—' He was interrupted by the waitress, who placed on the table two large tumblers half-full of neat Scotch. That was all. The girl withdrew, and Marriner stared at his drink with misgiving. It was at least a treble.

'They cater for man-sized thirsts here,' Judith said, catching his look. 'Too much for you?'

'I try to be careful with this stuff.'

'It's more than I do. Cheers.'

Since he had first caught sight of her that morning he hadn't once seen a smile on her face. Now it was there, suddenly and surprisingly, a little ironic twist to her mouth that wiped away all the seriousness. But only for an instant. 'You were saying . . .,' she asked.

'All right, here it is. The substance of your letter to Joshua was that your father is going to operate on someone at the request of the Security Police. We have reason to believe that that someone is Lincoln Kumalo.'

Judith held her glass poised in front of her mouth, which opened in astonishment. She said nothing.

'That's the first half of the story. The second half is this. From a separate source, the Congress has received information suggesting that the authorities are going to use this as an opportunity to get rid of Kumalo. How, where and when, we have no clear idea. I'm here to find out if that's true, and if necessary to rescue him.'

That was too much for her. If her disbelief had been suspended for a moment, it now came crashing down to earth. She banged her glass on the table and gave a burst of nervous laughter, loud enough to make heads turn briefly from the neighbouring tables.

'*Rescue* him? You've been sent to—?'

'Shut up,' he said softly, with more menace than he'd

214

intended. Oddly enough, it seemed to work. She fell silent and stared at him uncertainly. At length she took a swallow of Scotch and gasped.

'I can't believe it!'

'I could hardly believe it myself, at first. But I've had time to think about it, and it's begun to make sense. There are rumours going around that he's soon to be released. If enough people start believing them, if the conviction grows, even among his supporters, that the Government has finally seen the light and is prepared to let him go, then anything that happens to him after that will seem like an unfortunate accident. Particularly if the authorities can show that their hands are completely clean. You suspected they were using your father to give respectability to what they were doing. They may be using him in a way that neither of you has guessed at.'

She leaned far back in her chair, as if to create a distance between them. 'Mr Marriner . . .'

'I'd rather you called me Patrick.'

'I'd prefer not to. Assuming there is some truth in this . . . fantastic notion, why are you trying to involve me in it?'

'You already are involved. You can't undo what you've told Joshua. You were willing enough to have this business exposed.'

'That was before Kumalo's name came into it. And provided it didn't bounce back at me.'

'It may not have to. But what I do need are more precise details about the arrangements for this operation: when Kumalo is due at the clinic, where he'll be kept, how long for, what sort of security there'll be. More particularly, the exact timing of the operation itself. He'll have to be snatched beforehand, otherwise he'll be immobilized.'

'You would still have a sick man on your hands.'

'I gather he has a prostate condition, which isn't acute. He could have the surgery once he was safely out of the country.'

The waitress arrived with a bowl of steaming noodles and another of chicken. She set out two smaller bowls and two pairs of chopsticks. They helped themselves to the food and ate for a minute in silence.

'What you're really suggesting I do,' said Judith finally, 'is betray my father.'

'Not really. You could be doing him a favour. Saving his reputation.'

She looked thoughtful. 'It strikes me that there's a much simpler way out of this. I have a lot of disagreements with my father. On balance, I don't think we really like each other much. I thought he was taking on this job for the wrong reasons, but I don't doubt his integrity as a doctor. If I saw to it that he found out about your suspicions, he would refuse to go ahead with the operation and that would be that.'

'No. If they really want to eliminate Kumalo, they'll find another way. At least we have some prior knowledge of this plan. It's the only chance we may ever have of saving him.'

'We? You're taking my complicity rather for granted, aren't you?'

'I was talking about Joshua Rosenblatt and the other people who want to see Kumalo safe.'

'You don't seem like one of them yourself. What's in it for you? Money?'

'Yes, money,' he said rather testily. 'But there's more to it than that. If they did kill Kumalo, I would know I'd failed at my job. How would you feel if you knew you'd turned down a chance to prevent it?'

'If, if, if,' she retorted. 'What evidence can you show me that this plot actually exists?'

'Not very much, at the moment,' he admitted. 'But I've got to plan as though it were definite. There are only fifteen days left.'

The look she was giving him now was half-amused, half-scornful. She was frightened of taking him seriously. She said: 'You're hardly drinking, Mr Marriner.'

He took a cautious sip from his glass. Her own was almost empty. 'Well,' he said, 'will you talk to Joshua?'

She nodded resignedly. 'For old times' sake, yes. I promise nothing more than that. Not from here, either; I know of a better place. And I want another drink first.'

* * *

It was after nine o'clock by the time they left. Judith had drunk three of Choy's large whiskies to his one, but she seemed to be driving quite competently as he followed her Opel through the city centre.

Johannesburg was divided by a great sweep of railway lines, crossed by many road bridges, the way other cities are divided by rivers. Judith led him over the Johann Rissik Bridge and into the car park beside the South African Airways terminal, and they went into the building. It was a good choice: a big circular concourse, not crowded but just busy enough for them to be inconspicuous in. The row of open telephone cubicles was deserted, and they chose one at the end. Judith stood just behind him, shielding him from view, as he took the scrambler out of its box and stood it on a small shelf beside the phone. With some misgivings he placed the receiver into the AX cradle, lifted the portable receiver and got a dialling tone from it, slightly muffled. He fed in several of the one-rand coins Choy had given him in change, dialled the international access number, the 41-1 code for Zurich and then the number Rosenblatt had given him. It rang only once before it was answered. Immediately he inserted the code-key plug with the number 1 marked on it and got a piercing howl of static in his ear. Within a few seconds it stopped as the matching key was inserted at the other end. He heard Rosenblatt's voice, tentative and slightly distorted.

'Patrick?'

'Yes, it's me.'

'How are you getting on?'

'Not bad.' He realized he was sweating in the evening heat. He tried to imagine Rosenblatt surrounded by snowy Alps and placid muffled burghers. 'I have nothing definite to tell you yet, but I do have Judith here. She'd like to talk to you.'

He turned to see a panicky look on her face. 'How do I know it's him?' she demanded.

'Of course it's him!'

'It could be anybody. I haven't spoken to him for fifteen years.'

217

'I'm sure you'll recognize each other.' He thrust the receiver at her and stepped out of the cubicle.

He heard her say hello and then he strolled away, watching from across the terminal for five minutes until he saw her put down the phone. When he returned he found her pale cheeks faintly flushed with excitement.

The same old Josh! Same voice, same expressions, everything!'

Marriner put a finger to his lips. 'Not so loud.'

'He was the one who could hardly believe it was me!'

'Well, did he give me the OK?' He began to pack away the scrambler.

'Oh, he confirmed who you were. And he asked me to give you whatever help I could.' She paused. 'I'm not sure how much that means.'

He fastened the clips on the vinyl case and looked up at her.

'All that information you want. I'm sure my father has it, but it's stored in a computer file to which only he has access. I barely know how to operate the thing, let alone extract anything like that from it.'

'I don't know much about computers myself,' he said, 'but I gather anything that's put into them can be got out by someone with the right knowledge. It's something I'll have to think about. But you do see that I'm going to need your co-operation?'

They began to walk towards the exit. 'Yes,' she said, 'but in spite of what you say I can also see that there's a good chance the information leak will be traced back to me. It's all very well for you, skipping the country with Kumalo, but I'll still be here. You're asking me to put my head on a block now, Mr Marriner, and I'm not sure I'm ready for it.'

'There may be a way of covering up for you, laying some false clues.'

She turned and faced him squarely in the doorway of the terminal. 'Look, I'm not unwilling to help. But I'd like to be sure it isn't all for nothing. I believe you and Joshua are quite sincere, but a lot of what you've told me seems to be

218

guesswork, frankly. Whether you're right or not, the result is going to be the same for me if I'm caught tampering with those computer files. If I knew for certain that I was helping Kumalo . . .'

'Then that would make a difference?' He knew this wasn't the moment to push her. 'All right. Let's think about that as well.'

They made arrangements for staying in touch. Then, out in the car park, they shook hands with a rather awkward formality and she zoomed off into the night.

By the time he had driven back to De Villiers Street, left the car in the parking garage and walked to the hotel, it was after ten o'clock. He was still thinking about something Judith had said as he retrieved his key from the desk and took the lift up to the third floor. Guesswork, she had called it, and maybe she was right. There was still not one bit of solid evidence to support all the conjecture about what might be in store for Kumalo. It had come to seem real to him, but it had taken someone with a fresh eye to see it in a less certain perspective. To that extent, their conversation had merely added one more element of uncertainty to the situation.

He walked to the end of the wide, deserted corridor. He put his key in the lock, turned it and opened the door.

He groped for the light switch on the wall to his left. Before he had found it he saw, by the shaft of dim light that fell through the doorway, that the bed was in disarray, the covers pulled back and the mattress dragged half off the frame.

For perhaps half a second it occurred to him that he had somehow unlocked the door to the wrong room. Instinctively he made to back out, but at once something was clamped hard over his left wrist, pinning it to the wall. He caught a pungent reek of sweat and gave a gasp of surprise. Another hand took hold of his arm, yanking him into the room, propelling him forward so that he lost his balance and fell, pitching head-first on to the displaced mattress. The telephone scrambler flew out of his grasp. The door was slammed behind him, and all light was blotted out.

219

19

Marriner rolled off the mattress. He heard his attacker come after him, lunging at the spot where he'd fallen and missing. Marriner swung himself into a crouch, reached out blindly and got hold of something, a handful of cloth that tore in his grasp as a limb was jerked away. It was like trying to wrestle in a blindfold. The other man's eyes were already adjusted to the dark and now, gauging Marriner's position, he dived at him, knocking him to the floor again, falling full-length on top of him and grasping at his throat.

On his back this time, Marriner was able to roll with his assailant's weight. He raised his knees, got them into something soft and then, using all his strength, heaved upwards with both legs and both arms, throwing the man off him in a kind of horizontal caber-toss. The man grunted and flew several feet across the room, crashing into something solid and dropping to the floor.

Marriner sprang to his feet, ready for another charge. But now, with his night vision improving, he could see that his attacker was staying crouched on the floor, a dim silhouette against the white paintwork of the built-in wardrobe opposite his bed.

'Stand up,' he commanded. The silhouette moved slightly, but did not rise. 'Come on. On your feet.'

Marriner stepped forward, and then heard the sharp imperative snap of a gun being cocked. He froze in disbelief.

'Up your arse, white boss. Stay where you are.'

The voice was light and tense and menacing. Marriner had had no time yet to be afraid, but now he felt his scalp prickle and move as though it had come alive.

'You go on standing there, white boss.' The man had spoken in slightly accented English, but now he threw out a phrase in some African language. Suddenly the overhead light came on, blinding Marriner as effectively as the darkness had. He shielded his eyes and blinked. When he lowered his hand he saw a young black man squatting by the wardrobe with his knees drawn up, grimacing against the light but watching him steadily. He was wearing the khaki drill uniform of a hotel floor boy, with one sleeve pulled loose at the shoulder where Marriner had torn it, and he had a heavy automatic pistol balanced on his knees. It was pointed straight at Marriner's middle.

'Put your hands on your head,' he said.

As he did so, his glance went involuntarily to the door. The floor boy, Nimrod, still had his hand on the light switch. He looked terrified, and he began at once to babble apologetically: 'I couldn't stop him, sir, this is no good, sir, sorry. . . .'

'*Tula!*' The younger man silenced him with a sharp word of command and began to lever himself to his feet, keeping the pistol trained on its target. Marriner saw now that it was not just his bed that had been disturbed. The whole room had been thoroughly ransacked, the drawers pulled out, the wardrobe emptied, his clothes and books scattered about on the floor.

'If it's money you were looking for . . .'

'I think you know very well it wasn't,' said the man with the gun. He glanced at Nimrod again. 'Empty his pockets.'

Fearful and hesitant, the floor boy came over. He stepped behind Marriner and went through his pockets gingerly, removing his wallet, passport, some traveller's cheques, his notebook and a few other scraps of paper. He took them in a bundle to the young man, who placed them on the dressing table beside him and flipped through them with his free hand, taking his eyes off Marriner for only a second at a time. He inspected the passport with care, studied the credit cards he found in the wallet but ignored the two or three hundred rands in cash that were also there. Finally he gave the white man his full attention. He had thick hair, prominent cheekbones and a narrow jaw. At a guess he was twenty-five, and his eyes seemed prematurely knowing and bitter.

'Your name is Patrick Marriner?' he demanded.

'That's what all that paperwork says, doesn't it?'

'I am asking the questions. Tell me your full home address and telephone number.'

Marriner recited them.

'You had a visitor from Africa there recently. What kind of car was he driving?'

Marriner hesitated. 'I think I ought to know who I'm telling this to,' he said, but the young man merely gave the pistol a threatening jerk.

'What kind of car?'

'A red Ford Fiesta.'

'You later met in Switzerland. Where?'

'A place called the Aurora Bar, in Zurich. Round the corner from the Meilenhof Hotel, where I was staying, if that answers another question. Would you like to know what we had for lunch?'

The young man ignored the sarcasm. Little Nimrod stared at them both as though they were mad.

'All right. I think we can take it that you are who you say you are. But that still leaves other questions to be answered.'

Marriner had felt anger building up inside him. 'Answer a question for me. You've known all along who I am and where I'm staying. I've been waiting for you to approach me. You could have done it days ago.' He glanced around the room again. 'Why was all this necessary? And why the gun?'

Emboldened by such plain talk, Nimrod spoke up again. 'I tried to stop him, sir. I said this is no good. I fixed it for him to meet you, only that . . .'

The other man interrupted him angrily in their own language. Nimrod answered back, and for half a minute they traded insults in harsh low whispers across the room. 'Go back to your work,' the gunman finally said in English. With a gesture of disgust and a last mute appeal for forgiveness from Marriner, the floor boy opened the door, poked his head around it and left, shutting them in.

Now the young man seemed to watch him uncertainly, as if he wasn't quite sure where to begin. 'I will explain,' he said grudgingly. 'We had better sit down.'

Marriner lowered his arms and sat in the chair indicated by the other man with a flick of his gun. He himself pulled a stool out from the dressing-table and perched on it, letting the pistol dangle between his knees. Marriner recognized it, irrelevantly, as a Soviet 9-millimetre Makarov.

'So Nimrod is a Congress informer,' he said.

'We have many of them. You were sent to this hotel so that he could keep an eye on you.'

'Why didn't you send a message through him? It isn't safe just to turn up here like this.'

'Please do not try to tell me what is safe and what is not, Major Marriner. I have still not decided whether to trust you.'

Marriner stiffened in his chair. How many more people did he have to convince of his credibility? 'Listen. I was chosen to do this job by Harry Makibani. If you have any doubts about me, refer them to him. I don't see that I have to prove anything to you.'

'I will introduce myself.' The young man's tone was calm but still far from amiable. He raised the gun again, weighing it in his hand, pointing it at nothing in particular. 'I am Comrade Duma. First name, Mzwandile, also known as Alex. I am the one who sent the message to Lusaka. As a result, Makibani has sent you here and asked me to give you all possible help. Now that is all very well, but those people in Lusaka cannot tell us how to fight our battles down here. We make our own decisions, because often our lives depend on them being the right decisions. Involving the right people.'

'You think I'm not right because I'm white?' said Marriner.

'I am not a racist, Major. I accept what Makibani says, that white men are needed for this task. But it is too important a task to risk letting anyone, white or black, make a mess of it. Makibani has been out of this country for a long time. I think perhaps he has come to believe some of those myths of the white man's superiority that they have created for themselves. The brave English officer who comes to show the peasants how to fight their oppressors? It's not like that here, Major. We are not your spear-carriers. It's you who need us.'

'I've always known I would have to have your help.'

'You need it more than you realize. What is going on here is a revolution – sometimes quiet, sometimes not so quiet. The success of a revolution depends on the support and sympathy of the masses, and that is not something that you, an outsider, can simply walk in and command.' He paused. 'Let me tell you something. I mentioned that we have many people working for us, some even inside the prisons. Ever since that message reached us from Pollsmoor we have done our best to trace it back to its source, so far without success. This evening, however, some information reached me from Cape Town. A prisoner named Phineas Molefe was taken out of Pollsmoor today for questioning by the Security Police. Why, what for, we have no idea. We have never heard of the man. The interesting thing is that he is employed in the prison dispensary.'

Once again Marriner had that strange sensation in his scalp, as though caterpillars were crawling over it. He said: 'The prescription? The message? You think he sent it, and that they've caught him?'

'Maybe. There is no way of knowing. If it's him, the Security Police will not be long in getting the truth out of him. It is three weeks since that message came out of there. It struck me as a strange coincidence that this should happen almost as soon as you arrived in the country.' Duma raised the gun a fraction and gestured with it around the room. 'It could have been that you were an impostor, someone they had planted on us. In that case, Major, I would have blown you away.'

The room was large and bare, perhaps twenty feet square. It had no windows, but strips of neon set in the ceiling gave an even spread of hard white light. The walls and ceiling were completely covered in a cladding of fibrous soundproofing material. This much Phineas had seen before they pulled the hood over his head and stood him on the bricks. That, he estimated, had been about six hours ago.

His two interrogators had paused in their questioning now, as they did once every hour or so. When that happened, coffee would be brought to them and he could smell it as well as the smoke of the fresh cigarettes they would light. Occasionally one or the other would leave the room briefly and his partner would pace restlessly about, presumably watching Phineas to see that he didn't fall or try to change his position. Once in a while Major Booysen would come in and there would be a brief discussion. Then they would start again, as abruptly as they had left off: the same questions all over again, sometimes in the same order, sometimes jumbled up or rephrased to make them more confusing.

One of the men, whose name was Captain Kriek, would ask his questions harshly, swearing and threatening under his breath at the answers he got. The other, Warrant Officer Willemse, was gentler, cajoling and at times almost pleading with the prisoner to see the sense of co-operating.

It had puzzled Phineas at first that they hadn't beaten or kicked him. All they had done was to put on the hood and made him stand in his bare feet on two bricks lying end-to-end on their sides. For the first thirty minutes or so this had seemed simple. Then the narrow sides of the bricks had begun to bite into the soft flesh of his insteps. As the pain gradually spread up his calves, then his thighs, he began feeling dizzy. The bricks seemed mysteriously to increase in height, and he had the sensation of teetering on a precarious platform several feet up in the air. He knew this was ridiculous, yet could do nothing about it. The pain grew relentlessly, the lower half of his body becoming leaden, immovable, fused to the ground, while with the upper half he seemed to sway on a terrifying height, fighting to keep his balance.

He was on the edge of a high cliff. He was hovering on the roof of a tall building. He had wanted to tear off the hood to reassure himself that these were hallucinations, but now he was too afraid to do that. He feared that he would see rocks hundreds of feet below him, or ant-like pedestrians down in the street, and looking down would bring the final loss of balance, the screaming descent to oblivion.

The questioning disorientated him further, coming at him from different parts of the room, distant or close. He sweated and shivered in turns; he constantly swayed. Once, after about four hours, he pissed himself, the warm liquid spreading through his shorts and running down his legs on to the bricks. They didn't even bother to taunt him with it, just pausing for a moment in their questioning and then starting again, as now.

'What did you do with the tablets, Phineas?'

'I swallowed them, sir.'

'And the docket, Phineas, where did the docket go?'

'I took no docket.'

'Did you steal them at the same time or separately, Phineas?'

'No, sir. There was no docket. I didn't take it.'

'That's not what the others say.' That was Willemse, gentle and insinuating. 'The others in your cell block are making shit dry for you, Phineas. They say you bottled the pills and the docket together.'

'Then they're lying, sir.'

'Why did you take Lincoln Kumalo's prescription docket? Is he a hero of yours?'

'No.'

Deny everything. He had told himself that from the start. It was easier to lie outright than to prevaricate: it gave you something to hold on to. He was lucid enough to know when they were trying to trap him, as well. Only he and Bobbejaan knew anything, and if they'd had Bobbejaan's name they would have thrown it at him by now. They hadn't questioned the others; they were hoping to get it all out of him.

'You're the one who's lying!' snarled Captain Kriek, suddenly close beside him. Kriek seemed not to enjoy this bland form of questioning, to be always on the verge of losing his temper. 'You think it's tough standing on those bricks, *kaffertjie*? I can make it a lot tougher. I can make you wish you were dead!'

The door opened and Phineas heard Major Booysen's voice.

'*Hoe lyk hy nou?*'

'*Nog steeds hardkoppig, majoor. Ek wens ek kon hom sommer stukkend slaan!*'

'*Pas op, Kriek. Dood is hy niks werd.*'

Suddenly the hood was ripped off over his head. The light of the room exploded at him. He raised his hands to his eyes and finally lost balance and toppled off the bricks. Pain shot through him from the feet upwards, and he blacked out.

When he came round he was sitting propped against the wall. Booysen was bending over him with his mad eyes bulging. He held a tin mug to Phineas's lips, and the prisoner gulped weakly at the water. His legs felt paralysed; when he glanced down at them he saw his feet and ankles swollen like fat brown balloons.

'Still sticking to your story, Phineas? All right, we're used to that. We're going to give you a little time in your cell to think it over now. Time for food and time for thought, but not for sleep. No sleep allowed here. And when you come back the questions are going to start all over again, understand?' He took away the mug and said to the others: '*Vat hom.*'

Kriek and Willemse lifted his hundred-pound weight easily between them, his arms over their shoulders, and carried him from the room. On the way to the cell, his dazed glance went to a full-length window at the end of the corridor and he saw a myriad lights twinkling in the darkness far below. He was in a tall building somewhere in the centre of Cape Town. After the closed van that had brought him from the prison, after the windowless cell and the interrogation room, the view of the city was like something in a dream, a place that had no reality whatever.

'It's quite simple,' Duma said. 'Tell me what you're planning to do and I'll tell you how I can help.'

'No, it isn't simple. I agree that we must pool our resources. I agree that we now begin seriously to prepare for an attempt to rescue Kumalo. But it still isn't safe for us to know too much about each other.'

227

'That sounds like a very one-sided arrangement to me, Major. What is it that the Congress has told you but not me? What is it that they trust you with, but not their own comrades?'

'It isn't a question of trust,' Marriner said. 'It's a matter of who needs to know what. Some information reached the Congress quite independently of yours. It allowed them to put two and two together. It persuaded them to put up the money for this project, and without it we'd get nowhere. You and I are on the same side – isn't that all that matters?'

The black man thought about that, still squatting on his stool, the gun dangling loosely in his hand. The matter of trust had been bandied about too much this evening, Marriner thought, though he seemed to have won a certain grudging amount of it from Duma. The young man needed delicate handling. He was jealous of his own position as one of the front-line troops of the Congress, but once given enough reassurance he was not unresponsive to reason. All the same, Marriner had no intention of telling him about Judith Rose or the Woodvale Clinic just yet. The need to know was a cardinal rule.

'If this Phineas did send the message,' Duma said, 'and if they are questioning him about it, then it's a sign that they are taking it seriously.'

'It's also a sign that the message is authentic. But if they make him talk . . .?'

'Oh, they will make him talk. Then the trail will lead to Kumalo's lawyer, and then to his daughter, and then perhaps to me. But that is where it will stop, because they won't find me.'

Marriner wondered how Duma could be so sure of this, but he kept the thought to himself. 'They will still know, or at least suspect, that there's been a leak of some kind,' he pointed out. 'They will be on their guard. Now I know where Kumalo is going to be, and roughly when, and I'm hoping for more specific information. When I've got that, when I know exactly how to proceed from there, I'll tell you everything. In the meantime I want to be kept informed about this Phineas man, and to be told anything else that you learn. Above all, I need to talk to these white soldiers you think may come in with us. Is that a deal?'

'Something else puzzles me,' Duma said. 'Harry Makibani said I was to report only to him in Lusaka, and nobody else. Why is he running this thing by himself?'

Marriner was saved from answering by a soft rap on the door. Duma swung round, startled, pointing his gun at it, but then he heard Nimrod's voice, low and urgent, from behind it. They spoke for half a minute. Nimrod went away and Duma faced Marriner again.

'He's going off duty. I must leave with him or I will be noticed here, and that could mean big trouble.' He gave an unexpected grin. 'I am a little bit notorious, you know.'

'You mustn't come here again. In future we'll communicate through Nimrod. How soon can you contact these soldiers?'

'Maybe tomorrow.'

'And what makes you believe they would help us?'

'Disenchantment is one motive. Money would be another.'

'Then tell them there's good money in it. Don't say anything specific about the job.'

Duma nodded and stood up. 'All right, Major, you've got your deal for now. Just don't hold out on me once you start making your arrangements. I have a personal interest in seeing that Kumalo gets through this safely.'

Duma lifted the jacket of his uniform and shoved the heavy pistol into the waistband of his trousers, covering it with the jacket flap. He went to the door, opened it carefully and peered out. Then he was gone, closing the door gently behind him, leaving Marriner to stare around at the wreckage of his room.

20

Because their working hours tended to vary, several employees of the People's Congress in London had their own keys to the front door. Whoever turned up first in the morning would unlock the office, then take the burglar-alarm key from its hiding place under the hall carpet and turn off the alarm. The most natural thing to do after that was to pick up the morning post that was usually lying on the doormat by eight o'clock.

Jasper Darries had his own key, and he was always among the first arrivals. For the past two mornings he had made a point of being ahead of everyone else. This Friday he was there even before the postman, whose delivery he heard clattering through the letterbox a few minutes after he had let himself in. He went quickly to the front door and found the letter he had been expecting on top of the pile: an envelope marked *National Westminster Bank* and addressed to Moses Mohaila. He placed the rest of the mail on the receptionist's desk and carried the letter up to the first-floor room which he shared during working hours with two other people.

He opened the envelope and took out the paid cheque he had requested on the telephone, using Mohaila's name. He merely glanced at it, confirming that it was the right one, before slipping it into a new, plain envelope and putting it in his jacket pocket along with the torn-open one from the bank.

He went to the phone, dialled a number, let it ring twice and cut it off. He dialled again, left it to ring twice more and then replaced the receiver. Jasper had rarely called this number, which was for use only outside office hours. He guessed it was the Controller's home number, but he didn't know and had never asked. After twenty seconds his own telephone rang twice in its turn and then stopped. That was confirmation that his message was received and understood; no conversation, hence no danger of its being intercepted.

Towards nine o'clock the rest of the staff began to drift into the office, among them Mohaila himself. It would take an extraordinary stroke of bad luck for Mohaila ever to find out that a single cancelled cheque, no longer of any value, had been spirited out of the possession of the bank; even then, confusion rather than suspicion was likely to follow. Over the years Jasper Darries had got very good at calculating such risks exactly.

Long ago he had also established a pattern of making brief departures from the office to visit the local library, where he would check facts or do research for articles in the Congress newsletter. Hence, nobody raised an eyebrow this morning when he announced where he was going.

The Camden Borough Council branch library was just a few minutes' walk away. When he got there it was all but deserted and he had the shelves of the reference section to himself. He took two books and carried them to a table. One was a volume of the *Encyclopaedia Britannica* which he had a genuine excuse to consult; the other he had calculated to be the least-used book in the library, an old leather-bound edition of Hain's one-volume Persian–English dictionary, published in 1953. Why it even remained there was a puzzle, but it had served Jasper and his controller well.

He looked up what he needed in the encyclopaedia. Then he opened the dictionary. At the back, the long narrow slit he had made with a razor blade down the edge of the binding was still there. It was barely noticeable, but when he prised its edges apart he opened up a pocket between the binding and the endpaper that was just big enough to conceal the envelope in.

He replaced the books in their correct positions on the shelves. Even in the most unlikely event of anyone's needing to consult the Persian dictionary in the next hour or so, there would be no indication that it was anything but a rather quaint old book with a slightly damaged binding.

Hannes Koekemoer collected the envelope from the dead-letter drop exactly forty minutes later. He did not open it until he was safely settled in his office in King Charles II Street.

231

The cheque was as Jasper had described it, payable to cash for five thousand pounds sterling, and carrying two signatures. One was certainly Moses Mohaila's, the other might have been Harry Makibani's. It was computer-numbered like all cheques nowadays, but not 'personalized' with the printed name of the drawers. Presumably that was by arrangement with the bank, making the holders of the account a little less readily identifiable.

Koekemoer gave a grunt of satisfaction. Jasper, he knew, doubted the usefulness of procuring bits of paper for him, but a cheque like this could tell you a hell of a lot. It had been written on the twenty-first of November; it carried a cashier's stamp dated the twenty-eighth and a final PAID stamp from the National Westminster when it had found its way back to them and been debited to the account. That had been just yesterday, the first of December.

The cheque had been cashed – or more likely deposited, given its size, at the Bank of Ireland, Bandon, County Cork.

He turned it over.

Now here was an unexpected bonus. Somebody had signed the back of the cheque. Not really necessary, since it was made out for cash, but something people tended to do out of habit.

The signature was bold but practically illegible. There was a capital *J*, a capital *S*, followed by a *w* or a *v*, then maybe an *a* or an *e*. The rest was squiggle. On a sheet of paper Koekemoer jotted down a few possibilities: *J. Swa—? J. Swe—? J. Sve—?* He studied them without inspiration. He was still staring at them when the commercial section's junior officer came in to retrieve a file.

'Can you make this out?' Koekemoer showed him the signature. He didn't need to know what it was about.

'Swa—' The young man was just as baffled. 'Swain? Swann? It seems longer, somehow. Svenson?'

'It could be Irish. Think of some Irish names.'

'Sweeney? But then there'd be a tail on the *y*. No. Sorry.'

Koekemoer sat back in his chair. 'Where would I find some Irish telephone directories?'

'Their embassy, I suppose. They also have a tourist office, just over in Bond Street. You'd have to go there and ask, I guess. . . . Unless I can help?'

It was instinctive for Koekemoer to refuse. He almost did so, but then thought: Why not? He didn't care to show his face too much around London, besides which he had a pile of work to catch up on. This young fellow was discreet enough, and he still needn't be told anything. 'Well, maybe you can,' he said.

'I could walk over there at lunchtime, if it will wait till then. What is it you want to know?'

'Yes, it'll wait. It's only an off-chance, anyway. I need to trace someone with a name like this in the area of Bandon, County Cork. If he's not listed in the phone-book . . . well, too bad; I'll have to think of another way.'

'Bandon?' The young man was looking puzzled. 'That rings a bell.'

'Yes?' Koekemoer was interested in things that rang bells.

'I can't place it.' The young man shook his sandy head. 'Someone I've met in the last week or two. Maybe it'll come back. I'll report to you right after lunch, then?'

'I'll be extremely grateful to you,' Koekemoer said.

West of Johannesburg, the old mine workings were spread across the veld like the aftermath of some geological disaster that had turned the earth inside out. It was a sterile post-industrial landscape of sand dumps and slime dumps, the crackled surfaces of dried-up dams, the concrete plinths of blocked shafts, their headgears long since dismantled and carried off. These had been among the earliest of the city's big gold mines, but they had been worked out years ago and their owners had followed that fabulous reef far to the east and west.

This was the debris they had left behind. Some of the spoil dumps were simply mountains of soft pale sand; others, the slime dumps, had been shaped from successive layers of liquid sludge that dried out to form steeply terraced, flat-topped artificial hills, creamy yellow in colour and looking like half-completed pyramids.

It was up the side of one of these that Marriner found

himself climbing in Duma's wake towards lunchtime. The message from Nimrod an hour ago had been unexpected, urgent, mysterious: Come at once. Under a motorway arch at the end of Market Street, Duma had slipped into the car like someone escaping from a crime.

'You must see them today,' he said. 'Otherwise it's next week. They have leave at the weekends.' He'd been tense and uncommunicative ever since, merely directing Marriner through grim factory landscapes and out among these eerie dead hills.

They had left the Orion at the edge of a bluegum plantation and walked through it to get here. A steep track ran up the side of the dump, along which the coco-pans full of sludge had once travelled, and it was marked by the tyres of a heavy vehicle. Near the top, Duma put a restraining hand on Marriner's arm and gave a low whistle. A moment later a bronzed young white man appeared from behind the ridge. He was bare-chested, but wore brown army trousers and boots, and was holding an R4 self-loading rifle loosely at his side. He grinned at Duma.

'My man,' he said.

'Peace, Mr Carver,' said Duma.

Carver was crop-haired and powerfully muscled. He studied Marriner curiously before turning and vanishing over the ridge. They followed.

A ledge fifteen or twenty feet wide ran around the top of the dump. Behind it the ground sloped down to a flat rectangular basin of powdery cyanide-stained earth. Invisible from anywhere but the air, it was almost a perfect refuge, just the sort of place where you might find a party of meths-drinkers or felons on the run.

The group that occupied it today seemed even odder.

A Saracen armoured personnel carrier was parked close to one side of the basin, painted in yellow-khaki camouflage. Close to it, seven more soldiers sat or lay in various idle postures. All had their shirts off; some were stripped to their underpants and were sunbathing. Something was cooking over a fire, and the area was littered with beer cans. All the men were watching the newcomers.

234

Marriner followed Carver and Duma down the slope, feeling like a visitor to a bandit encampment. Whatever he'd been expecting, it wasn't this: the studied silence, the looks of indolent hostility. He stopped in front of them. Duma made a nervous announcement.

'Well, white boys, did you think I was lying to you? This is the man. This is Major Marriner.'

None of them looked impressed. It was as though they had to outdo each other at being cool. Marriner matched their silence with his own. Finally it was Carver who was embarrassed into speaking up.

'Duma, ah, didn't tell us anything about you, sir. Like what kind of major are you?'

'Was. British Parachute Regiment. What outfit are you?'

'How about you explain what brings you here first, Major?' That was a dark, heavily built young man who was idly shuffling a pack of cards.

'Later. I'd like to know who I'm talking to.'

'Hey, man, you could be anybody,' said a scrawny youth in khaki underpants. 'You could be the Law.'

'I don't think Duma is too friendly with the Law.'

'Duma is full of shit.'

'Duma is always telling us stories,' someone else chimed in.

'Listen, white boys, cut the crap, will you?' The black man was growing angry. 'This is no way to treat a man who has come to offer you a deal.' He looked at Marriner and pointed to a man at the back of the group. 'Talk to him. Rendle. He's supposed to be in charge of them.'

This man hadn't yet spoken. He seemed to have been biding his time, drinking beer and poking at the *boerewors* cooking on a sheet of wire mesh over the fire. Now he stood up unhurriedly, strongly built in the rangy South African way, with oddly luminous pale blue eyes. He looked older than the others, and at once tougher and more intelligent. He shook hands with Marriner. He addressed him as an equal.

'Yeah, I'm Frank Rendle. We're Fourth Armoured Infantry, based at Lenz camp. That is to say, we go back there when we have to. At the moment we're taking a break. We take a lot

235

of breaks.' He gestured round at the sun-baked sand. 'It isn't the Riviera, but it's probably more peaceful.'

Marriner glanced at the Saracen. It had a 7.62-millimetre machine-gun mounted in front of its turret, and the crew's personal weapons were stacked against its side, a row of semi-automatic rifles and an Uzi gun. It also had a tall VHF radio aerial.

'Aren't you in contact with your base?'

'Not very often. Lightning bends the radio. He's our electrical wizard.' Rendle indicated a lanky youth grinning up at them from the sand. 'We arrange it so that most of the time nobody knows where we are. Our job is township patrols. We put in an appearance now and then, but we don't get involved in any aggro. That's not what we joined the army for.'

'Who joined the army?' said the scrawny one indignantly. 'We just fucking got put into it!'

'All right, Brakpan, we got put into it.'

'Well, hell, it makes a difference. Don't give this man the wrong impression. We didn't all used to be officers and hot-shot chopper pilots!'

'Shut up, Brakpan.' Rendle spoke without raising his voice, with a quiet, commanding menace. 'I don't have to go on making life easy for you arseholes. Go look after that fire.'

The man called Brakpan seemed about to answer back, but thought better of it and scuttled away. Rendle walked to where a couple of six-packs of beer were stacked in the shade of the Saracen. He tossed a can of Lion Lager each to Marriner and Duma. 'Well,' he said, 'that's our story. What's yours, Major?'

'You'll have to forgive me for asking, but did I hear that right? You were an officer? And you flew helicopters?'

'It's no secret,' said the corporal with a shrug. 'I'm just a bit touchy about it sometimes. I used to be a lieutenant in the air force. Could have been a major myself one of these days if they hadn't thrown me out. Used to fly Alouettes, Puma gunships, Super Frelons. Now all I do is ride herd on this wagonload of monkeys. Do you blame me for not being very interested?'

Marriner took a decision. 'Can I talk to you alone?' he asked.

Rendle considered for a second, then nodded. Duma said, 'Now, wait a minute. I'm not just the boy who carries messages between you two white bosses.'

'You'll get your look in, Duma. Just hold on.'

They strolled out together towards the centre of the sandy basin. From his own experience Marriner knew how troublesome soldiers would often turn their rejection of higher authority into a perverse loyalty towards one of their own. It was why insubordinate privates sometimes made the best NCOs. Rendle had given shape to this bunch of malcontents, and they looked up to him without perhaps knowing why. Rendle, he had quickly recognized, was the key to one whole part of this enterprise.

'What did Duma tell you about me?' he asked.

'Just that you were looking for some guys to do a job. That there was good money in it.'

'Do you know anything about Duma? Who his connections are?'

'I don't want to know, but I can guess.'

'Then maybe you've also guessed something about the general nature of this job. I'm talking about putting a big cat among a lot of fat pigeons, Corporal. Changing a lot of people's lives, including yours. Does that idea make you nervous?'

Rendle suddenly grinned, and Marriner knew the question had been unnecessary. 'All right. What about the rest of them?'

'Some of them hardly think beyond the next fight or the next fuck, but they're all fed up, if that's what you mean. As the trouble gets worse here they can see themselves pushing more and more time in the army until they're in it almost permanently.'

'I think this is going to mean that you're all in or all out. It also means that you'll have to skip the country, and possibly never set foot here again.'

Oddly, Rendle showed no surprise. He took a thoughtful sip of beer. 'There's politics involved, of course. Bound to be if Duma's mixed up in it. Well, I was planning to leave

237

anyway. I've had it with this country. It would be nice to have some money to go with. The others have probably never thought about leaving, but if the idea looked attractive enough they might buy it. Most of them have had bad bust-ups with their families. Lightning has no family at all. There's not a lot to keep them here.'

'And they all have combat experience?'

'Sure have. They may not look like much, but that's because they don't give a shit any longer. We were over in South-West Africa together – that's probably Namibia to you – mixing it with the SWAPO guerrillas. We got into Angola, too, against SWAPO and the government forces. Man, you wouldn't know a tenth of what goes on in that place. Russians and Cubans on their side, Bushmen and mercenaries on ours, civilians like sitting ducks in the middle. We came through some pretty sticky stuff. Night ambushes, pathfinder patrols, we even took part in some commando raids. Yeah, the boys are all good, and some of them have their own specialities. Brakpan drives anything on wheels like it was a Formula One racer. Lightning is radio and electrics. Blikkies Steyn is a natural bush fighter. Carver and Fish like it at close quarters, on the streets.' Rendle paused. 'Just tell me this. Does this job of yours involve wasting anybody?'

'Not if it can be helped. Quite the opposite, in fact. I want someone rescued and taken over the border.'

They stopped and stood facing each other under the searing sun, the pale sand shimmering around them. 'Quite a tall order,' Rendle said. 'I suppose this is the right time to ask about the money.'

Marriner had already thought about that. 'I think I can rustle up eight hundred thousand pounds sterling between you. That's a hundred thousand each, enough to give you a new start.'

Rendle looked impressed. 'That will get the boys interested. The next question is: When do we see it?'

'I haven't had time to work that out. At the moment it's in Switzerland.'

'Not much point in bringing it here, then, is there? We'd

never get it out again. On the other hand, you can't expect the guys to go into this just on the basis of a promise. We'd need some kind of guarantee.'

Marriner had not considered this either. 'Something in writing, you mean? I've been trying to avoid that. Still, perhaps we can work something out. There isn't a lot of time. The job has to take place two weeks from today, and I've barely begun to work on the details. It should be possible to accomplish the whole thing within a few hours, but it will take careful planning and training for. That means giving me quite a lot of your time. Can you manage that?' Rendle nodded. 'And on the day itself . . . well, I suppose you're just going to have to disappear the way you have today.'

'Should be no problem.' Rendle took a final mouthful of beer and lobbed the can away like a hand grenade. 'Who else is in on this?'

'In this country, just you and me and one other, so far. Even she is only on the sidelines.'

'A woman?'

'You'll probably never meet her, so there's no need for you to know who she is. And then there's Duma, of course.'

'Yes. Duma.' The corporal glanced back to where his squad were gathered by the armoured car with the black man now sitting among them. 'I don't like the idea of him being involved.'

'You don't trust him?'

'No, it's not that. He's just bad news. He's a kind of unknown quantity, just somebody we picked up on a township street. He plays his own little games.'

'I can't really do without him,' Marriner said. 'But nobody is going to find out any more until they need to – and I've told you about as much as I can for the moment.'

'That's all right. I get the picture.'

'There's something I'm curious about, though. Why were you busted out of the air force?'

Rendle gave him a long, penetrating stare. 'Were you ever given an order you knew you couldn't even pretend to obey, Major? Something you knew you'd never get off your conscience if you did?'

'Not really,' Marriner said.

'Well, it happened to me. But it's a long story. It'll keep. I'm just glad you didn't lay any speeches on me about the difficulty of betraying my country. I've gone beyond all that shit. As far as I'm concerned, my country betrayed me.'

Marriner nodded, feeling more reassured than ever by Rendle. The young man's chilly blue eyes were deceptive, masking a degree of aggression and even anger behind their suggestion of indifference. Some men would be disconcerted by this, he guessed, and many women would find it fascinating.

They turned and began to walk back across the burning sand. 'All right, Major,' Rendle said decisively. 'It's on. As far as I'm concerned, it's on. Just give me some time, maybe a couple of days, to convince the others.'

The young consular assistant had returned from the Irish Tourist Board and was back in Hannes Koekemoer's office by two o'clock. He had copied half a dozen sets of names and addresses from the 02 Irish telephone directory and had drawn a ring around one. It was: Mrs J. Swanson, Kilquade Farm, Bandon, County Cork. There was also a phone number.

'*Mrs?*' Koekemoer didn't know why he was surprised. He'd simply assumed the signature on the cheque was a man's. The name could well be Swanson, now that he looked at it again.

'It's certainly the most likely one,' said the young man. 'It's the only name remotely like that in the Bandon area itself. However, I borrowed a map and found a few nearby villages with names like Swann and Swanton listed against them, so I wrote those down as well.'

'Thank you. That is really excellent.'

A neat bit of detective work, Koekemoer thought, but where did he go from here? The puzzle was: why had the People's Congress transferred money from their account at the Handelsbank Bauer in Zurich through a bank in London for payment to Mrs J. Swanson of Kilquade Farm, et cetera? If, indeed, she was the person who had countersigned the cheque. There was no guarantee of that. There could be other Swansons not listed in the phone book. Still, it was a good start. Somewhere around this little place called Bandon, somebody was receiving money from the Congress. It could hardly be for a legitimate purpose. If even the most tenuous links could be found with another subversive organization, it could do great damage.

It was worth a trip to Ireland to try to find out. That would have to have clearance from Pretoria first, of course, and the weekend was coming up, but there was no vital urgency about it.

Koekemoer was so engrossed in the possibilities of all this that he had forgotten to ask the young assistant why the name of Bandon had rung a bell for him that morning.

21

In spite of his protests to the contrary, young Mr Labuschagne was showing signs of impatience. They had called at three farms in the course of that Saturday morning, and after each visit Marriner had made the sort of noncommittal noises that to any estate agent signified a transparent lack of interest. 'I'm not quite sure what you *are* looking for,' Labuschagne complained at one point, and Marriner couldn't enlighten him. He was supposed to be looking over the land, but his eye was really on the farmhouses. He needed a secluded one. Although the properties appeared well hidden from the road, the homesteads on the high ground above it had been well within view of others. The tendency in these hilly parts was to build close to the summit of the *koppies*, so that in spite of their love of privacy the farmers were more or less in sight of each other. But he could not tell Labuschagne that. He'd said the first place at fifteen hectares was too small, the second at seventy too large. The third, which the agent had specially recommended, was a perfect balance at forty-five hectares with a pleasant house to go with it, and he'd mumbled something about the grazing looking pretty poor. It wasn't much good anywhere, in fact, among these rock-littered hillsides, and Labuschagne had given him a look that seemed almost suspicious.

They had lunch on the terrace of a hotel overlooking the Hartbeespoort Dam, where the Crocodile River had been trapped to form a deep blue lake in a gorge of the Magaliesberg. Marriner paid, and also pressed a couple of vodkas on Labuschagne, which put him in a better frame of mind when they set off for their fourth and last appointment.

The farm was a couple of miles south of the dam, and Marriner could see even as they approached up the winding driveway that it wouldn't do either. The natural ground cover of scrub and bush had been cleared for a hundred yards or so around the house, a modest bungalow standing high above the valley. He had to express some interest all the same, and once the two visitors had introduced themselves to the farmer and been shown around, he dutifully asked about the size of the herd and the profitability of the land.

'Profitability!' This farmer spoke good English. He was a blunt, no-nonsense type, and now he gave an explosive laugh. 'Excuse me, but I assumed you were just another of these weekend farmers. I haven't made a living out of this place in years, man. I have two bigger farms further north. I've been building a house on one of them, and I've just been hanging on here till it's ready. You won't make any money out of this bit of land, sir.'

'If the bush were cleared . . .?'

'Too expensive. You'd never get your investment back.' He gave Marriner a curious look. 'I thought all you wanted was a short lease, anyway?'

'Perhaps with an option to buy. I'm open to suggestions.'

'Well, I'm not going to bullshit you. You'd be wasting your time and your money here.' He paused. 'If you wanted a place just for a few months, there is somewhere just near here.' He turned to Labuschagne. '*Ken jy daai plek van ou Meiring?*'

242

'*Nee?*' The two of them talked briefly in Afrikaans, then Labuschagne said reluctantly: 'There is another place, belongs to an old man who's a bit of a – what do you say? – recluse. The Government is buying him out, and he has to move by next September. In the meantime, it's possible that he would consider renting it.'

'He could use the money,' the farmer put in. 'He's had to sell off his herd over the years, and the land has been lying idle.'

Marriner was ready to grasp at any straw. 'Could it be worth seeing?' he asked Labuschagne, who looked dubious; he'd lost faith in the bonanza this client had seemed to promise. He glanced at his watch and muttered something about having to get back, but the farmer said: 'It's practically on your way. Shouldn't take you more than a few minutes.'

Again in Afrikaans, he gave directions to Labuschagne. They thanked him and drove off, the estate agent by now in a quiet temper. A little way down the road, as they rounded a bend, a vast and strange structure loomed suddenly ahead of them among the hills. It was about a mile long, a long, low, concrete building without windows, with a tall, tapering smokestack rising from it like a warning finger. It hadn't been visible when they'd been driving south, but from here it dominated the landscape, faintly sinister in its stark modern functionalism.

'What's that?' Marriner asked.

'Pelindaba,' said Labuschagne shortly. Marriner's silence forced him to elaborate. 'It's the Pelindaba nuclear reactor.'

Suddenly he took a turn to the left and they were driving straight towards the building. Before he could ask any more questions, Marriner saw with dismay a security gate ahead, a checkpoint with armed guards, a high barbed-wire fence snaking off into the bush. A notice said *South African Atomic Energy Board. No Unauthorized Entry.*

Just before the gate Labuschagne took another turn, this time down a bumpy unpaved track to the right. From behind the fence a couple of dark-uniformed guards watched them pass. Labuschagne grudgingly proffered some more information.

243

'This old fellow, Meiring, is having his land expropriated by the atomic energy people. They're expanding their facilities here, and they've already got him practically surrounded.'

Through the fence, Marriner could see that the area around the reactor had been cleared of bush. More guards patrolled the grounds, there were two or three army vehicles parked close to the building, and in the distance a helicopter dipped and hovered, orbiting the area. After a quarter of a mile or so the track veered away from the fence and began to descend a steep hillside. In a minute they came to a sagging fence and a rusted iron gate held closed by a loop of wire. A wooden sign with the paint peeling off it gave the name of the property: Rietvlei.

Marriner got out, opened the gate for the car and closed it once Labuschagne had bumped over the cattle grid just inside. Suddenly they were in a much less ordered world of thick virgin bush and tall savanna grass, hidden from the tidy parkland that surrounded the reactor. The only human imprint here was the track twisting its way down into deeper bush. It travelled for half a mile or so before levelling out, and now they could hear running water to their right. They were on the floor of a valley, with the Crocodile River churning over rapids beside them, a brown swirl that was only just visible through the reeds and bushes that lined its banks.

They came upon the house unexpectedly. It was a ramshackle wood and iron building at the end of the track, backing on to the hillside and looking out over a wide level clearing towards the river. It was shaded, in fact almost camouflaged, by mimosa trees and surrounded by a kind of miniature junkyard, a detritus of old artefacts that had collected here for perhaps half a century and never made it back up the hill. Two rusted Chevrolets from the 1950s stood on blocks on either side of the house like ornamental buttresses. Stacked around them were a collapsed brass bedstead, a collection of bald tyres, wooden cartwheels, oil drums, iron washtubs and a stack of rotting lumber. There was a kind of neatness within the disorder, however, as though all this stuff had been put on display rather than simply dumped. There was no squalor, no sign of festering rubbish; this was cherished junk, and its owner was happy in his surroundings.

The farm, if it could really be called that, lay somnolent in the damp heat of the valley. It was utterly isolated, a small world's end tucked into the folds of the hills and forgotten.

It was perfect.

No, it wasn't. The nuclear reactor and the security that surrounded it were alarmingly close by. In spite of that, Marriner knew he hadn't a hope of finding anywhere as suitable as this in the time he had left, which was now thirteen days.

They had got out of the car. The deep silence of the valley was broken by the squeak of an unoiled spring and the slamming of a screen door. The hermit had emerged and was watching them from the stoep of his house, shading his eyes against the glare.

'*Namiddag, meneer!*' Labuschagne called as they approached. The old man did not reply. He was tall and gaunt, possibly seventy years old, but still strong and fit-looking. He wore a colourless trilby hat, a checked cotton shirt and bib-fronted overalls. A jar of moonshine in one hand and a shotgun in the other might have completed the classic hillbilly picture, but he carried only a coiled sjambok, a tough little whip of rhinoceros hide. Whether he intended to use it was not a matter that Labuschagne seemed willing to put to the test; he stopped a dozen feet from the end of the stoep and explained their presence, gesturing round at Marriner and at the farm.

Old Meiring listened in silence. Eventually he nodded and spoke a few sentences. Labuschagne smirked and explained to Marriner: 'He thought we were officials of the *atoomkrag*, the Atomic Energy Board. He's had enough of them; he was all ready to chase us off.'

'Is he interested in renting the place?'

245

'He says the idea had never occurred to him. He needs time to think about it.'

'What's he going to do, once they make him leave?'

The two men spoke again, and Labuschagne translated: 'He's got a sister in Pretoria. She collects his pension for him and brings him supplies every couple of weeks. He supposes he'll go and stay with her, but he doesn't like the idea. He's lived here practically all his life. He'd like to buy another bit of land, just a smallholding, but he can't afford it. The Government is paying him only eight thousand rands for this land; they just named a price, and he hasn't got the money to contest it through the courts. The place is unsaleable, really; it has no market value.'

Marriner nodded. He was going to have to risk sounding pushy. 'What if I paid him in advance, a full ten months' rent up to next September? Would that make up what he needs to buy another place?'

The agent gave him a look. 'You mean you're actually interested in this land?'

'I could be. I'd like to look it over.'

Labuschagne translated, and Meiring studied Marriner curiously, rubbing the week's growth of beard that studded his chin like clippings of steel wire.

'He wants to know first how much you might offer.'

'How about a thousand a month?'

These words Meiring understood. He gave a slow grin, while Labuschagne stifled his surprise.

'He'd be getting a bargain, Mr Marriner. If you don't mind my asking, what has this place got that those others haven't?'

'Peace and quiet.' He waved around him. 'Charm.'

'The house looks rather dilapidated.'

That was true enough. Perhaps he was sounding a bit too eager. Before he could reply, however, old Meiring, getting the drift of the conversation, said angrily to the agent: 'Wil jy die man wegskrik, of hoe?' He clapped Marriner on the shoulder and said: 'Kom, ek wys jou rond. Ek ken 'n goeie Engelsman as ek hom sien.'

'What does he say?'

246

'He says he knows a good Englishman when he sees one,' said Labuschagne resignedly. 'He'll show you around.'

Twenty minutes later they were on their way back to the office at Muldersdrift with the deal agreed. Labuschagne had cheered up at the prospect of making two and a half thousand rands in commission and bonus, and Marriner was privately more excited than he could let on. One week from today, on December the tenth, he would hand Meiring a cheque for ten thousand rands and take over Rietvlei farm. That would leave him another six days to get everything and everyone else ready, and suddenly that seemed like no time at all.

He was back at the Windsor Hotel by half-past four. He went to his room, collected the security phone and went out again, to the railway station down the road and the row of telephone booths in the booking hall. Using the second of his twelve code-key plugs, he was through on the scrambled line to Joshua Rosenblatt's number in Zurich within a minute.

He told the Congress treasurer in brief outline of the progress he had made so far, and then explained his needs. He wanted the equivalent of fifteen thousand rands cabled to him at once in care of the Standard Bank. That was to cover the rental of the farm and Labuschagne's commission and bonus, plus a couple of thousand for further contingencies. He said he also wanted a new account opened at the Handelsbank Bauer, this time in the name of Frank Rendle, and he wanted eight hundred thousand pounds sterling deposited in it. Rather as he'd expected, Rosenblatt baulked at that.

'Patrick, that is eighty per cent of our entire contingency fund! I really never envisaged using it all up in one go!'

'It's what the money is there for, isn't it? And it's what I've agreed to pay out. Get Harry to OK it, if you insist. You can still keep control of it for the time being, on the same basis that you control my second account: you remain the signatory, but you make this man Rendle the nominee. There's no time anyway for providing signatures and means of identification. All I need is a piece of paper, a receipt from the bank, with his name on it. It's a token of my good faith.'

'Well, all right,' said Rosenblatt reluctantly. 'But I can't do any of this till Monday.'

'As long as you can arrange it first thing, the money ought to be here by Wednesday. There's also no time to airmail the receipt, so you'd better send it by courier. There's a slight risk involved in that, but there's no alternative. Send it care of a man called Jepson at the head office of the Standard Bank. I'll alert him that it's coming.'

The pips began to sound on the phone, and he put down the receiver. He disconnected the scrambler, packed it away and left the station. Back at the hotel, he found himself once again at a loose end. There was not much he could do now but wait.

He was tempted to phone the Widow Swanson. It was six days since she'd seen him off at Cork airport, and although she wasn't expecting to hear from him it would be nice to say hello. It would be three o'clock in the afternoon over there, though, and her weekends at this time of year were filled with a hectic round of hunting and point-to-points. Instead he went downstairs to the call box and dialled the number of Judith Rose's new flat.

For some reason they had allowed Phineas to sleep. Maybe it was because they were exhausted themselves, for it had not escaped what remained of his numb attention that all three of his interrogators – Booysen, Kriek and Willemse – had grown grey-faced and haggard as they continued with their questioning. Maybe it was because even when he did try to answer he was no longer making sense, his brain seething and his mouth burbling rubbish in a mixture of Sotho, English and Afrikaans.

Somehow, in spite of the hood over his head and the pain and the hallucinations, he had managed vaguely to measure time. The window at the end of the corridor, which he passed on each journey between his cell and the interrogation room, told him whether it was day or night, creating a rhythm from the passing hours. For something like forty hours he had stood on the bricks, six hours at a time with

248

half-hour breaks for food, water and the lavatory. Then he could no longer stand, and nothing they could do or threaten could stop his swollen legs from collapsing under him. So they had taken away the bricks, and fastened handcuffs around his wrists, and suspended him by the handcuffs from a frame of some sort, until it felt as though every muscle in his arms and shoulders was being slowly, very slowly, torn apart, and the bones seemed to be stretching and then separating, and he had screamed until he'd lost consciousness. From a period of what seemed intensely happy oblivion he had woken lying on the bunk in his cell, riven and shivering. Major Booysen had been there, looking down at him with something like concern in his crazy blue eyes, wondering perhaps whether they'd gone too far ever to get anything out of him.

Then they had let him sleep. Perhaps, he thought now, that was just part of the treatment too, giving him something to appreciate so that he'd miss it all the more when it stopped. He had no doubt that it would soon start again. They hadn't gone this far with him to give up now.

His arms and legs felt feeble and useless, and he could hardly move at all without some part of him shrieking in pain. Yet his mind was oddly clear and sharp, even analytical. Sleep had swept away his confusion. He knew now that he would never last out, certainly not for thirteen more days. Within a day, two at the most, he would be dead or utterly broken. He would have told them what they wanted to know by then, he would have begun the process that would lead them to the Leader's friends, and by then his own life would be worthless. There was only one way to stop the process, and there would be only one chance.

With difficulty, with his body protesting in a dozen places, he managed to swing himself into a sitting position on the bunk. He gave himself a minute there and then, inch by painful inch, using the wall as a support, he levered himself to his feet. Only the agony in his feet told him they were in contact with the ground, for there was no other sensation there but pain. He took a tentative step towards the door of the cell, and then another. In spite of what his body was screaming at him, he could walk. He tottered to the door, leaned against it, turned around and steered himself back to the bunk, where he sat down, exhausted. He tried again a minute later, more successfully, feeling foolishly elated when he made it back to the bunk. He could move around. He could do what he knew now, with the certainty of an old conviction, had to be done.

They came for him half an hour later, Willemse and Kriek, seeming surprised to find him awake and sitting up, with the blanket from the bunk wrapped around him. There was a strange glazed look to his eyes, as though their arrival had only half-aroused him from some reverie. They eased him to his feet, supporting him on either side, and took him in a stiff cramped walk out of the cell.

They turned into the corridor leading to the interrogation room. The full-length window at the end was a pale rectangle of light, showing it was still daytime, looking out over a patchwork of streets and greenery with the ever-present mountains in the background. The two policemen carried most of his weight, but when he was halfway down the passage he shrugged himself loose from their grip, indicating with a gesture that he found it easier to walk on his own. They stood aside, just holding his elbows lightly for balance, and he began to hobble forward on his horribly clumsy feet.

With ten yards to go, he halted for a rest. The white men waited tentatively on either side of him. No hurry to get to the soundproofed room, all the time in the world once they were in there.

With all the strength in his arms, Phineas thrust them both away from him, pushing them aside, knocking them slightly off balance. Free of their grasp, he ran forward, hearing their shouts of alarm, feeling himself lurch and stumble as he struggled to gather speed on his swollen floundering feet, needing all the momentum his slight frame could gather. He heard them come charging after him, leather soles slapping the floor over the thuddings of his bare feet, catching up with him as he covered the last couple of yards and then launched himself, head first, at the window.

It was made of toughened glass, but it did not resist the impact of his head. It exploded outwards. He went through it in a clean dive that took him several feet clear of the building, out into a blur of swirling sky and sea and mountain, before he dropped like a stone from the height of thirteen storeys. He crashed on to the roof of a moving car in Roeland Street, bursting his skull and breaking his spine. He dented the car deeply before falling off it, trailing a thin slime of blood and brain behind him as he rolled into the gutter at the feet of a horrified group of pedestrians.

Warrant Officer Willemse nearly went out after him, lurching to one side at the last moment after making a grab at the prisoner's collar, teetering on the edge of the abyss in the space where the window had been. Glass went on plinking down into the street for several seconds after the flat metallic crash of the body. Several screams began together and floated gently up to them, going on and on like sirens.

Kriek and Willemse stared at each other in horror. The door of the interrogation room burst open and Major Booysen took it all in at a glance.

'Julle konte! Julle kakvreters!' he screamed. He seized hold of them both, a big fist going into the scruff of each neck, almost lifting them off the ground and shaking them until their heads bobbed. 'You fucking cunts, do you know what you've done?' His eyes bulged maniacally. 'You've lost him! You've let him jump, in broad fucking daylight! He's gone, and he's taken what he knows with him!'

Still shouting, Booysen backed them up to the wall and banged their heads against it, stopping only when two other policemen ran up and pulled him away.

Tertius Van Straaten's office was on the first floor of the west wing of the Union Buildings. The view from the window was not quite as grand as it was from the Cabinet ministers' rooms on the floor above, but it was seductive all the same. Below the terraced gardens that fell away gently to the south, Pretoria with its thousands of jacaranda trees in bloom lay like a purple smudge in the valley of the Apies River. Beyond that, the Voortrekker Monument was distantly visible in the heat-haze.

Van Straaten turned away from the tall window and went back to his desk. He had no yearning to be anywhere else. He enjoyed spending his Saturdays in the office. Apart from the security guards and the Service's duty officer, he had the vast building practically to himself and could catch up on his paperwork with no fear of distractions. In half an hour he was due at Deputy Minister Hoeksma's house, together with Colonel Prinsloo, for a drink and an informal chat about the progress of the Induna project, and he was almost sorry to have to leave.

He had read carefully through the report from London first thing that morning, then put it aside and attended to other work. It had kept creeping back into his thoughts, however. He had thought of calling Koekemoer on the scrambled line, to ask for further clarification, but had decided against it. Koekemoer was a good operator, his stuff was always factual and well balanced, and he had set out his conclusions as plainly as possible. There was no sense in going over the same ground once more. The report would be circulated to the members of the Joint Intelligence Committee in the normal way and discussed at their weekly meeting on Tuesday.

It would be useful all the same, Van Straaten thought, if he could take some action of his own in the meantime. It would give him something positive to contribute to the meeting. Information equals power: it was the basic equation of all civil service politics.

It was time to claim his first favour from Hoeksma, he decided. He dialled the deputy minister's home number, and a houseboy answered. The master and madam were on the tennis court, he reported. Van Straaten didn't want to interrupt them; he would just have to arrive a few minutes early and hope for the best.

Next, he phoned the home of his brother-in-law, who also

252

happened to be his bank manager. Nothing official, he said; he had just a few casual questions to ask about the currency regulations. The information more or less confirmed what he already knew for himself. Satisfied, he locked away his files, closed up the office, checked out with the duty officer and left the buildings.

Although he was relatively new to professional intelligence work, it was a fascination with power and intrigue that had led Professor Doctor Van Straaten into his peculiar hybrid career as an academic specialist on the subject. Plenty of noses had been put out of joint when this obscure professor of strategic studies had suddenly been appointed number two in the National Intelligence Service, with the prospect of becoming number one well within his sights. Van Straaten had shrugged off the criticism, though he had tactfully ceased to use his academic titles. He had set out to prove to the hard-boiled veterans who were his subordinates that there was no great mystery to their trade, that mastering any job was only a matter of adaptability and intellect.

The house which the deputy minister maintained in Pretoria was not on the scale of the mansion in the Cape, but was discreetly impressive in its own way, a white clapboard affair complete with pool and tennis court in the fashionable suburb of Sunnyside. Hoeksma and his wife had only just come off the court when Van Straaten arrived, and were both red-faced and panting from their exertions. Hoeksma was put out to be found in white shorts and an aertex shirt in which, admittedly, he did cut a rather undignified figure. He was polite but somewhat stern. He led his visitor back into the garden, to some white-painted chairs in the shade of a mulberry tree.

'What's on your mind, Tertius?'

'I do apologize for turning up early, Minister. I wanted a word with you in private. This is something a little . . . outside Prinsloo's scope.'

'It's something you don't want him to hear,' said Hoeksma with unusual directness.

'Prinsloo is an excellent policeman, but he has his area of

duties and I have mine. This has nothing to do with the Induna project. At least, nothing that I am aware of.'

'Then why are you bothering me with it, Tertius?'

'Because I'd like your help, Minister, if you'll just bear with me. As you must be aware, my service keeps track as closely as possible of the activities of the People's Congress overseas. Their financial affairs are of particular interest, of course. Just last month they were promised something in the region of seven million dollars in aid by a number of the so-called Non-Aligned Nations. Now normally the bulk of their funds is kept in the Union Banque Suisse in Zurich. I learned this morning that within days of that money being pledged to them they had opened a new account with another, much smaller Swiss bank, the Handelsbank Bauer. How much went into the account I have no idea, but they must have opened it for a particular purpose—'

'For the purpose of making it more difficult to trace?'

'Exactly, Minister. And—'

'Tertius, I really wish you would call me Frans. We work closely together, and there's really not much difference in our ages or stations.'

'Very well . . . Frans. It's precisely my guess that they have set aside some of that money and want to ensure greater secrecy about the use to which it is put. Already a small sum has been filtered through a bank in London to someone in Ireland, but what concerns me much more is the possibility that some of it, possibly a lot of it, may find its way here.'

They were interrupted by the arrival of the houseboy wheeling a little white trolley of drinks across the lawn. When he had parked it at Hoeksma's elbow and departed, Van Straaten continued.

'The money might be earmarked for some subversive purpose in this country. I'm only saying it *might* be. There are many ways of bringing it in, but very few are safe. Smuggled currency can be seized, lost, stolen. The best method is to do it officially, through a bank. Now, the details of all foreign-currency transactions are passed on in due course to the South African Reserve Bank—'

'That's how they keep track of our foreign reserves.' Hoeksma gave a condescending smile. 'I am an economist, you know, Tertius.'

'The thing is, Minister – Frans – that there are tens of thousands of such transactions every week. It's quite possible to trace the source of any money that's imported, but usually only after the event. In other words, the funds can be slipped into the country and paid to some reliable intermediary, and both he and the money can disappear before we even know about it. It's happened before.'

Hoeksma stood up and busied himself with the drinks. 'I'm having whisky-soda. Same for you? I don't quite see what help you expect from me, Tertius.'

'I want to speed up the procedure a bit. Under the Internal Security Act I can demand to see the records of the Reserve Bank. But a lot of people would have to get involved, and we'd still have to sift through a mountain of paperwork. I would prefer an informal approach, from the top. All it would take is one key person in the right department, with instructions to tip us off the moment they were notified of any transfer of funds from the Handelsbank Bauer. There can't be many transfers from such a small bank. It should be easy to spot. I was wondering if you could have a word with the Minister of Finance.'

They heard a car door slam loudly in the street outside. It was a careless, to-hell-with-the-neighbours slam, not quite the thing in Sunnyside, and they both guessed that Colonel Prinsloo had arrived.

'All right, Tertius, I'll see what I can do. I hope you're not letting this little matter distract you from our other business.'

'It's because it *was* distracting me that I want it put in hand. Nothing may come of it, but at least I'll have taken precautions. Thank you, Frans.'

'Where did you come by this information anyway?'

'Oh, just a source.' Van Straaten gave him a tight little smile that told him that there were some things that couldn't be mentioned, even to friendly Frans.

They rose to greet Colonel Prinsloo as he came striding

across the lawn. He was right on time, but something in his bearing told them immediately that this was more than the planned semi-social call. There was a kind of grim satisfaction to his expression that suggested that he was bringing bad news.

22

Colonel Prinsloo hadn't been altogether surprised to find Hoeksma and Van Straaten cosily established in the garden, sipping whisky and first-naming each other like old college friends. Maybe that's what they were. More and more of these button-down academic types were leapfrogging their way to the top these days, over the heads of farm boys like himself with his Standard Eight schooling and his size-twelve feet. Still, there were things you learned on the streets that Stellenbosch could never teach you, and one of them was not to be squeamish. He'd spared them none of the dainty details of Phineas Molefe's death. He'd told them the story just as it had reached him from Cape Town, right down to the brains in the gutter and the eyeball found half a block away, and he'd watched them squirm.

Hoeksma, white-faced, had needed another drink. Invited to help himself from the dinky little trolley, Prinsloo poured an enormous neat brandy and downed it in a gulp.

'I'll have the balls off those stupid bastards,' he said with relish. 'I'll have to go down there and sort this out myself.'

Van Straaten had recovered some of his composure. 'This prisoner was taken from Pollsmoor on Thursday?' he said. 'Why weren't we told?'

'There was nothing to tell, sir. All Major Booysen knew at that stage was that the prescription docket was missing and that this little Phineas had probably taken it. The suspicion was that he'd used it to smuggle a message out, a warning. The point was to establish whether he ever succeeded. The longer he went on denying it, of course, the more obvious it was that he was lying.'

'Why was that?' Hoeksma asked. 'If he knew nothing, he'd have had nothing to tell.'

'It doesn't work that way, sir,' said Prinsloo confidently. 'After a while, a man who's got nothing to hide starts making up stories, telling you what he thinks you want to hear. Not this one. He took everything they could give him.'

'Which was what, exactly?' Van Straaten inquired, and Prinsloo looked at him with lightly veiled contempt.

'Well, you don't think they were hitting him with feather pillows, do you?'

The deputy minister and the intelligence officer exchanged a glance. They didn't like this line of talk, either. They wanted the truth presented to them in hygienic little dossiers, not red and raw and newly wrenched out, the way it often had to be.

Prinsloo poured himself more brandy. Hoeksma said: 'We're talking seriously about the possibility of a leakage of information on the Induna project, is that right?'

'That could be the case.'

'To the People's Congress?'

'I can't think who else would be worth telling.'

'And I can't think why you sound so pleased about it, Colonel. This is just the sort of thing that you are supposed to prevent.'

'Are you sure we're not exaggerating this?' Van Straaten said. 'What can one little hospital clerk really have found out, after all?'

'Well . . .' Prinsloo was going to enjoy this too. 'You may recall, sir, that on the day we met Dr Rose in the prison you and I talked afterwards in Dr Els's office. You insisted on telling me about an idea you had just had, the idea that got all this started.'

'What do you mean, I "insisted"?' Van Straaten said indignantly.

'I didn't think that was a very safe spot for that kind of conversation. But you were in charge; it wasn't my place to object. It turns out that this little Molefe used to work in the very next room, with a rather thin partition in between. It

257

could just be that you were sharing your idea with him as well as with me, Mr Van Straaten.'

There was a stunned silence. Van Straaten glanced instinctively at Hoeksma for reassurance, but got only a neutral ministerial stare. Finally he shrugged. 'All right. That was indiscreet of me. But what you're saying is only conjecture. Does all of this actually change anything?'

'Maybe not,' said Prinsloo. 'The first thing is to assess the damage. Luckily the newspapers are not allowed to report anything pertaining to a prisoner in custody, including his death. But Molefe's nose-dive was witnessed by at least fifty people, and it's certain to be on the bush telegraph by now. As for finding out whether a message ever got out of the prison, we are back where we started – except that we now have forty of the bastards to question instead of one. I think we need to let this cool off for a couple of days. Booysen and his team are wrecked anyway; they'll be no good for anything just yet.' He threw back his drink and smacked his lips. 'Well, gentlemen, unless there are any more questions, I'll be off.'

They watched the Colonel shamble away with an odd sense of relief. If they thought him crude, they also found him intimidating. He'd made it clear that he considered them a pair of dilettantes, and there was no real defence against this attitude.

'I don't like to give that man the satisfaction of being right,' said Van Straaten when he was safely out of the way. 'But if the Congress has somehow got wind of the Induna project, you do realize how serious the consequences could be?'

'Of course I do, Tertius, but it's all hypothetical. I see no reason to change our minds. Induna goes ahead in thirteen days' time. Meanwhile, I think it's time we cranked up the rumour machine.'

'Let me drive,' Marriner said.

'No, I'm fine.'

'You're not really. Let's go and pick up my car and I'll run you home.'

'Look, I am *fine*, God damn it!'

258

Judith was just tight enough to resent the suggestion that she was anything but absolutely sober. God knew how many of Choy's big slugs of whisky she had got through without any sign of ill-effect, but out on the pavement the fresh air had suddenly made her reel. Now she was fumbling the key into the ignition lock of the Opel Manta and Marriner was regretting that he hadn't brought his own car. It had seemed much simpler, since she'd had to drive into town anyway, to let her pick him up at the hotel.

She nudged the bumper of the car behind her as she manoeuvred out of the parking space. It was close to midnight, but the Saturday-night traffic was still heavy. Concentrating fiercely, she swung out into it. Almost immediately she shot through a red light without, apparently, noticing it.

'Watch it,' he cautioned nervously.

'Relax, Patrick. God is on my side tonight.'

Patrick. Well, that was an improvement on 'Mr Marriner', which she had persisted in calling him for the first half of the evening. It had been a strange sort of evening altogether. It had had the makings of a disaster, in fact, starting with an argument about where they should eat. He had chosen a pleasant little Italian place he had found near his hotel; she had insisted on going back to Choy's. It was safer, she said, without specifying why; there'd been no further hint that the Security Police were watching her or were even interested in her. More, he suspected, it was a question of feeling safer from *him*. Choy's was where they had conducted their official business, so to speak, and she felt she could keep him at arm's length there.

All the same, she questioned his motive for asking her out at all. She thought he wanted something from her, and that this entitled her to be offensive.

'I hope you don't think I'm going to change my mind about helping you. I still don't see how I can.'

'I wasn't going to say a word about it. In fact I've been too busy to give it any more thought.'

'Well, I did have my suspicions.'

259

'I just felt like some company, all right? It's Saturday night. I was free, and so were you.'

'Did you expect me to be free?'

'I didn't know. I took a chance.'

'I used to think I was missing out if nobody asked me anywhere on a Saturday. Not any more. All the nice men I knew have left the country. The others are creeps,' she said meaningfully.

This time they had eaten Choy's chicken with glutinous fried rice instead of noodles. It surprised him to see such a pale skinny woman eat with such gusto: three helpings, washed down with beer. Then, after a couple more Scotches, she'd become provocative and personal.

'Are you the sort of man who needs a quick lay as soon as he hits town?'

'No.'

'Feed them and fuck them – isn't that how most men see it? Actually I'm quite good at fucking, or so I'm told. It's about the only thing I am good at.'

He ignored this attempt to shock him. It was childish. He said: 'If you really want to know why I asked you out, it's because I thought we might have some civilized conversation.'

'I'm sorry.' She surprised him by sounding genuinely contrite. 'I'm afraid I haven't got the measure of you. You make me nervous, if you want to know.'

After that they managed to talk more easily, and now it was she who was making him nervous as she steered in fits and starts up the neon-lit canyon of Eloff Street.

Judith drove in silence, watching her co-ordination, conscious of Marriner's scrutiny. When he had phoned her she had paused on the brink of an excuse she had already concocted. Somehow she had known he was going to ask her out, had prepared herself to say no and had spent all evening denying what she really felt. The truth was that she'd found something disturbing and exciting about this mystery man who'd invaded her life talking about a plot to free Lincoln Kumalo. Her instinct was to back away; instead, she found herself becoming more intrigued. She'd never met anyone

260

like him before. He was years older than she was, but mature without being stuffy. He seemed to know exactly what he wanted; there was a controlled strength about him that was unnerving and yet fascinating.

Of course she had tried to tough it out. That was how she always stopped people getting close to her. It was what made her, in her father's word, abrasive. With Marriner it didn't seem to work, though; it simply made her feel foolish.

She brought the car to a jerky halt outside the Windsor Hotel. She turned to look at him. 'Well, thank you for dinner.'

'I really don't think you should drive all that way home, you know.'

'I'm perfectly all right,' she said with dignity.

'Why don't you come in and have some coffee, at least?'

'Ho ho ho.' Her sarcasm was automatic. 'That's a very old line, isn't it?'

'I won't be making any passes at you in a hotel lounge. I'm trying to sober you up, not seduce you.'

'How disappointing.'

She leaned over and kissed him on the mouth. He was so astonished that he jerked his head back as though he'd been stung, and she laughed.

'What's the matter? Scared of me?'

'Hardly. Just surprised.'

'I can be quite surprising, Mr Marriner.'

She kissed him again, this time forcing her tongue briefly between his lips. Her breath was spiced, not unpleasantly, with whisky. For a few moments a thin flicker of desire flared into something more powerful, but he did not return the kiss. A small note of warning struck deep inside him. She sat back and went on looking at him, her dark eyes faintly luminous under the street lighting. 'You're quite a sexy man, Patrick. Did you know that?'

'Only *quite*?' he said, making light of it.

'Quite.'

'Come and have coffee.'

'All right.'

He opened the car door quickly, like a safety exit, and got out. She followed him and they entered the hotel together.

The front door was open but the lobby was deserted, the lounge that led off it closed and in darkness. The receptionist had gone; an African was dozing behind the porter's desk. He woke up with a start when Marriner approached.

'Room number, sir?'

'We'd like some coffee.'

'Lounge is closed, sir. Coffee in your room.'

He turned to Judith in confusion. 'I'm sorry. I've never come in this late before. I didn't know everything stopped.'

'That's all right.' She was smiling at him sardonically. 'Coffee in our room,' she said to the porter.

'What number, ma'am?'

'Now hold on . . .,' Marriner began. But the man was waiting patiently, obviously assuming they were sharing a room, and there was nothing really to object to. 'Three-one-six,' he said lamely, and when the porter turned for the key Judith stood on tiptoe beside him and whispered: 'Fate!'

With an unreal feeling he rode up in the lift with her and led her to his room in silence. Common sense warned him to let this go no further; but something more basic than common sense was telling him that an attractive girl was practically throwing herself at him and it would be ungrateful, if not unnatural, to refuse her.

In the room, he positioned himself carefully in an armchair while she sat on the bed, bouncing once or twice as if to test the springs. She wore a smile that was open to almost any interpretation.

'I'm sorry for being so bratty.'

'You've said sorry once. It doesn't matter.'

'I'm actually quite shy, under all the bullshit. I felt I wasn't getting through to you. You're quite hard to get to know.'

'I don't like talking about myself. It's not that I have much to hide. I just find it boring.'

'So do I, actually. It's people who don't really know who they are who are always busy exploring themselves.'

There was a tap on the door. Marriner had been

262

half-expecting Nimrod, but it was the porter himself who came in with the coffee. Automatically he placed the tray on the bedside table, next to Judith, and took the bill to Marriner, who paid and tipped him. He left, saluting his thanks.

'Obviously he considers it your job to pour the coffee.' He wanted to keep her talking. 'I suppose sexual stereotyping doesn't appeal to you.'

'Oh, it does and it doesn't. Men are subject to it, too. There's never seemed much point to me in trying to be something that I'm not. Sugar? Milk?'

'No sugar. Black. I recommend the same for you.'

She passed him a cup. 'Women's Lib is a bit of a luxury in this country, anyway. It seems irrelevant in the face of much bigger problems. Like so many other things that people get worked up about in other places. You might as well belong to a sewing circle.'

'Politics gets in the way of everything, you mean?'

'It overshadows everything. Any conversation that doesn't become political is hollow, somehow. Look at us, now . . .'

Sipping their coffee, they were suddenly talking about anything except what seemed to have brought them up here. There was nothing odd or awkward about it. They were like people who had come through some brief intense experience together and now saw each other in a new way, more comfortably and intimately.

The coffee sobered Judith up, but the evening's drinking was making her yawn. Eventually she lay back on the bed, and when Marriner returned to the room after a pee he found her asleep. So much for passion, he thought, amused but a little regretful. There was no point in waking her. She shifted and muttered a little as he took off her shoes and pulled the bedspread over her, but remained sound asleep. Marriner switched off the light, undressed in the dark and lay down on the sofa. The night was still warm, and he needed only his dressing-gown for a cover.

*　　*　　*

He was dreaming, yet somehow he knew he was dreaming. He was back in his bunk in the aircraft-carrier *Hermes*, pitching her way through heavy South Atlantic seas. In a few hours' time a Sea King helicopter would be dumping him on a godforsaken mountain on East Falkland. This was the last decent sleep he was likely to get for weeks, and some bloody fool was ringing an electric bell. Long insistent rings. A head-up alert. It was an air raid.

He started awake. The telephone shrilled again on the bedside table. He rolled off the sofa, stumbled across the room and groped blindly for the receiver.

'Hello?'

'Major Marriner?'

'Yes.'

A pause. 'This is Duma. Listen. Phineas Molefe is dead. The man I told you about, in Cape Town. He jumped from the top floor of the Securitas Building, the headquarters of the Security Police. I only just heard.'

Marriner was still thick-headed with sleep. In the bed beside him Judith hadn't stirred. 'What does this mean?' he said.

'It means he killed himself to avoid talking. It means there is no doubt that he sent the message.'

'You're sure he jumped?'

'Wasn't pushed, you mean? No, of course I'm not sure. But if they had wanted to get rid of him they would have chosen a less messy way – and then only after they had got what they needed from him. If you wanted some final proof that the message was genuine, Major, this little Phineas has given it to you.'

'Yes. It seems so. Well, thanks for telling me.'

There seemed nothing more to say, but Duma didn't put down the phone. He said: 'This means the job is on for sure, Major. Doesn't it?'

'I suppose it does.'

'Then I'll be expecting to hear from you soon. Remember our agreement.'

'I'll contact you as soon as I'm ready.'

Marriner replaced the receiver and went dazedly back to

264

the sofa. His watch told him it was half-past three on Sunday morning, the fourth of December. Twelve days to go, and quite suddenly the whole thing had taken on a hideous reality that it hadn't had before. A man was dead because he'd been trying to keep a secret. The man was no more than a name to Marriner, and yet he felt strangely involved in his death, burdened by its consequences. Up to now, whatever the risks might have been, this had had the neat bloodless precision of a war game. Now he could not walk away from it.

His brain was churning, and he guessed he wasn't going to get back to sleep. After a few minutes he heard Judith shifting, then getting out of bed. The telephone must have disturbed her after all. He lay still on the sofa and watched her feeling her way through the dark to the bathroom, a dim silhouette against the pale glow from behind the curtains. He was sure she would leave for home now, and decided his best course was to pretend to have gone back to sleep.

He heard her emerge from the bathroom. He kept his eyes closed, heard her padding over the carpet and then sensed her pausing beside him. She was very close; he could smell that she had splashed herself with the cologne provided by the hotel management.

She whispered: 'Patrick?'

He didn't stir, but in the heavy silence of the room he could hear his heart pounding. He felt something press against his cheek and realized it was her palm, cool and cologne-scented. He guessed he couldn't go on faking complete inertia, and he gave a sleepy groan. Far from discouraged, Judith ran her hand slowly down his face, under the dressing-gown and halfway down his back, and he discovered something else: he could feel the whole of her arm lying along him now, from the fingertips to the edge of her shoulder. It was a naked arm. It hadn't been naked when she went to the bathroom.

Now it was difficult to keep his eyes closed. She shifted and stretched slightly, bending over him, and another part of her touched his face, something deliciously unmistakable, warm and globular with a pliancy within its firmness

265

and a harder point at its centre that nuzzled his cheek.

Something heaved and swelled within him. Without direction from his brain, his hand reached up and took hold of her breast, cupping it like a small warm offering to the lustful spirits that were taking hold of his senses.

'Patrick. Move over!'

There was nowhere to move to but she slipped on to the sofa all the same, throwing aside his dressing-gown, clinging to him to keep herself from falling. Then she was all over him, wrapping herself around him, small breasts and bony hips pressed down on his body, her mouth working frantically on his as if trying to burrow into him.

Suddenly he was electrified with desire. His earlier reluctance seemed a dim and dotty memory. He wanted her now, at once, the way she wanted him, without prelude or gentleness. Her thighs were already around his hips and she gave a little gasp, almost of shock, as he clasped the small of her back and thrust himself hard and urgently inside her. Her skin was hot under his hands, soapy to the touch, smelling of the cologne and a fragrant, underlying sweat. Her body hung over his, almost luminously pale in the darkness, her breasts quivering in little circular movements in time with his impatient thrusting. Her eyes were closed, her mouth open, panting, her black hair tumbled over his face. Too soon, he felt the surge of his approaching climax, but her response was even faster. Her back arched, thrusting out her breasts, and she gave a long shuddering cry of abandon. She fell moaning on top of him as he flooded ecstatically into her.

A little later they moved over to the bed and made love to a more languid and tender rhythm. Then they fell asleep. They woke up at seven o'clock and coupled again as ardently as before. Judith dozed off once more but Marriner lay awake, listening to the desultory sounds of Sunday-morning traffic. He felt as though he were floating, a ship becalmed on a tropic sea. Like every man of his age he had worried a little about the edge of his potency going, but Judith had filled him with heedless adolescent lust. It was like discovering some hidden psychic or healing power in himself; it was astonishing, flattering and a little confusing.

When she finally stirred again he said, 'Would you like some breakfast? I can have some sent up.'

'No. I really think I ought to go.'

He half-wanted her again now, looking at her lying in the crook of his arm, watching him with serious brown eyes. He wondered what she was thinking. That she had got something out of her system, or added something to it? She surprised him by saying, 'What was that phone call?'

He hesitated for only a moment, then told her about Duma and Phineas Molefe. It seemed ridiculous to hide anything from her now. Was that what it was really all about, some unspoken realization that Judith's involvement had been inevitable from the start? Had spending the night with him been part of a wider commitment? She listened with concern, with none of her former apprehension, then said, 'That makes it definite, then? They're going to do something to Kumalo?'

'I don't see how it can be otherwise. There's the evidence you were looking for.'

'And you still need my help?'

'It's going to be vital.' He paused. At least she couldn't accuse him of seducing her, of taking advantage. 'It always has been.'

'All right. Then you've got it.'

She hopped out of bed. On her way to the bathroom she shot him a look, suddenly mischievous. 'Why don't you come back to my place and we'll talk? I'll give you breakfast.'

They got dressed and left the room. On the way downstairs Marriner had a swift sensation of guilt over Jenny Swanson, no doubt lovingly restoring Ballygarron House for him.

He dropped his room key in the slot at the porter's desk and as they turned around he saw Frank Rendle walking through the door.

The corporal was dressed in civvies, pale blue slacks, white shoes and a tight navy shirt that emphasized his muscular arms and shoulders. Seeing Marriner and the girl together, he halted and stared.

'Hello, Major,' he said blankly.

'Well . . . hello.' The confusion was mutual. 'What are you doing here?'

'Sorry. I suppose I should have phoned.' Rendle's cool blue eyes flickered uncertainly over Judith. With one arm possessively around Marriner's waist, she was the only one who was not put out. 'It's just that I've got a message for you.'

An introduction seemed to be necessary, but Judith didn't wait, announcing her name and sticking out a hand. The corporal shook it. 'Frank Rendle,' he said without elaborating, and then rather pointedly to Marriner: 'It won't take a minute.'

'I get it. Men's talk.' She gave the newcomer a lazy, slightly sardonic look and detached herself from Marriner. 'I'll go on ahead, Patrick.'

She left the hotel, throwing her sling bag over her shoulder, swinging her hips jauntily. Rendle watched her with some suspicion until she'd disappeared.

'You're right,' Marriner said. 'You shouldn't have just turned up.'

'I stay at a friend's place quite close to here when I've got leave. It seemed safer than phoning.'

'Come and sit down.'

They sat in a couple of armchairs in a corner of the lobby. 'Was that the woman you told me about?' Rendle asked immediately. 'The one who is in this with us?'

'I didn't actually expect you to meet.'

'You also didn't mention that you were involved with her. That isn't too cool, Major. I hope it doesn't complicate things.'

God damn it, Marriner thought. He'd never met a woman yet who could resist showing off her conquests, and with that smug look on her face Judith could hardly have made it any plainer that they'd just been to bed together. Still, it wasn't all her fault, and he could understand Rendle's misgivings. He would have to speak plainly. Men's talk.

'I wasn't involved with her until last night. It's something that just happened. I also need her help. Now, what's your news?'

'Well, I've talked the boys around. Nicky Flynn was the only difficult one, rather the way I expected. I had to promise him something in writing.'

'I'm taking care of that. It should be here in a couple of days.'

'OK. Then, if it's still on, we're with you.'

'It's on all right. But before we go any further I need your help across a couple of hurdles. Are there any computer freaks among that crowd of yours?'

'Lightning knows quite a lot about them. At least, he's always boasting that a computer is nothing but a glorified bunch of light switches.'

'Then maybe we can give him a chance to prove it. Another thing: speed and surprise are absolutely vital to this operation. The way I saw it originally was to recruit a pilot to get us out in a charter plane. Then I realized we already had a pilot.' He watched Rendle steadily. 'All we need is to find something for you to fly.'

'Bed or breakfast?' said Judith an hour later.

'How about both? Or is that being gluttonous?'

'Oh, I'm all for a bit of gluttony now and then.'

The main bedroom of her flat commanded an amazing view over the city to the south. The building was perched almost at the very summit of Northcliff, and the balcony on which they later took a belated breakfast had an equally spectacular outlook to the north.

'What's the name of that hunk again?'

'Rendle. Frank Rendle.'

'Do you like him?'

He caught a note of deliberate casualness in her tone. 'Sure I do. Why?'

'I didn't think he liked me.'

'He didn't want to talk in front of you. That's understandable. He's risking even more than you and I are. That hunk is going to steal a helicopter for us.'

269

PART THREE

THE JOB

23

December in the south of Ireland had started out cold and sunny, but within a few days had reverted to its more usual conditions, which were mild and wet. Jenny Swanson had taken advantage of the brief fine spell to get the decorators going on the outside walls of Ballygarron House, but when the rain arrived they had abandoned that and moved indoors. The stripping and repainting of the woodwork was well under way; this morning they would start repapering the drawing-room. She hoped Patrick would appreciate all the trouble she was going to. Actually, she was enjoying herself immensely and was only mildly put out that the ungrateful bugger still hadn't been in touch with her. He had warned her that his movements would be uncertain, but surely Africa wasn't so primitive a place that he wasn't occasionally within reach of a telephone?

This Wednesday morning had dawned leaden and damp, and it was starting to rain again as she nosed the Range Rover down the avenue from Kilquade House. Just outside the gates a small white car was parked with its bonnet open. A man stood beside it, staring despondently at the engine.

Jenny stopped and turned down her window. 'Do you want any help?'

He came gratefully over. He was wearing a long black trenchcoat of Continental cut and had an earnest, vaguely foreign look about him.

'Are you perhaps going to Bandon? I don't know what it is with this car.'

'Wet points? That's often the trouble in this weather.'

'I think something more serious. It is a damned nuisance. It is a rented car and I must telephone to Avis at Cork airport. But better to get back to my hotel first, I think, out of this rain. I am a tourist, you see,' he added somewhat unnecessarily.

'Get in. I have an errand to run on the way, but I'll only be a few minutes.'

'You are very kind,' the man said. He returned to his car, slammed down the bonnet and locked the door, then climbed into the passenger-seat of the Range Rover. He was still groping for his seatbelt as Jenny swung out on to the road.

'Very kind. A damned nuisance,' he repeated.

'Not the best weather for a breakdown. Or a holiday,' she said conversationally. She had identified his accent now. 'You're Dutch?'

'From Amsterdam, yes.'

'I know it well. What part do you live in?'

'Originally I am from Ransdorp, just outside? Now I am living in Nieuwe-Zuid. You know Beethoven-straat?'

They chatted easily about Amsterdam. The man was in his forties and obviously respectable. He told her he was an accountant in an industrial diamond firm. He had found himself with a week's leave and had indulged in a long-held whim to look around Ireland. He was travelling alone and had spent the past two nights in Bandon. He asked her only one question: 'That is your farm, back there?'

'Yes, that's mine.'

They fell briefly into silence. Jenny switched on the radio, and her passenger sat staring ahead, past the slashing windscreen-wipers at the steady, monotonous rain.

Something wasn't right about all this, Hannes Koekemoer thought. He had sensed it as soon as he arrived in this quiet farming district on Monday evening and he was even more sure of it now, sitting beside Mrs Jennifer Swanson of

272

Kilquade Farm. He knew now that it was she who had the bank account. He had ascertained this by the simple means of paying ten pounds into it. A helpful cashier, in response to his enquiry, had assured him the money would go into the right account: she was the only Swanson on their books. Other, more casual conversations – with a gossipy waitress and some of the bar customers at his hotel – had elicited other bits of information. Mrs Swanson had lived in this area all her life. She was the widow of a respectable farmer and was quite rich, one of the local gentry in fact. It was hard to imagine anyone less likely to be connected with an Irish terrorist organization, let alone with the South African People's Congress. Yet the inescapable fact remained that she had paid five thousand pounds of their money into her bank account.

The thought had struck him that Mrs Swanson might not know the true source of the funds; perhaps she was being used by someone else as a further means of disguising their origin. In the end there had seemed only one hope of finding out more, and that was to contrive to meet the lady herself. What he saw of her now gave him more reason for his doubts. She was attractive in the casual, unselfconscious way of the upper-class countrywoman. She wore a cashmere sweater, a Husky jacket, tailored cavalry-twill trousers and expensive leather boots. She behaved as though she had nothing whatever to hide, and she was taking him completely at face value.

Koekemoer himself was quite confident in the part he was playing. His Dutch ancestry, unlike that of most Afrikaners, was comparatively recent, his father having been a merchant seaman from Rotterdam who had settled in Cape Town after the Second World War. This ambiguous background had always been a valuable asset in Koekemoer's work. He had studied at the Free University of Amsterdam, he spoke the language fluently and could easily pass himself off as a native Hollander. The tourist act was also not difficult to sustain, though there was a limit to how long it could last. There were few if any other foreign visitors to the area at this time of year, and there was not enough to keep even a dedicated sightseer busy for more than a couple of days. He needed to learn more, and quickly.

They had been driving for ten minutes or so when Mrs Swanson turned through the gates of another farm. Bally-garron, it was called: the name was painted on the gateposts. At the end of a tree-lined avenue they came to a substantial old house where she parked the Range Rover beside a couple of battered vans. Cans of paint, ladders and building materials were visible through their open rear doors.

'Please, what is this place?' he enquired politely.

'It belongs to a friend. I'm having it fixed up for him while he's abroad. You may as well come inside.'

She got out of the car, opened the back and began hauling out rolls of wallpaper. Koekemoer offered to help carry them, and they entered the house together. Half a dozen workmen were busy in the rooms off the hall: a carpenter mending an architrave, painters up on scaffolding at work on the ceilings. Mrs Swanson greeted them, whisked a couple of them off into one room and left Koekemoer standing, rather at a loose end, in the hall.

The carpenter working on the door frame gave him a friendly smile. Koekemoer muttered something trite about the facelift the house was being given.

'Oh, it'll be grand when we're finished with it. It was badly let go. There was an old man living here for a long time and, well . . .' The carpenter gave him a sidelong glance. 'He was a bit too fond of the whiskey, between you and me.'

'So now there is a new owner?'

'Well, not quite new.' The carpenter was measuring the door frame with a steel tape. 'The Major is here a good few years now. He's the old man's nephew.'

'And this lady is his friend?'

'Yes. His friend.' The man gave him an odd look, as though wondering whether he was implying something. 'They're friends and neighbours, you might say. You're not from these parts yourself, then?'

'No, I'm just visiting.' Koekemoer's interest had been stirred. 'Where is he now, this . . . Major?'

'Away in Africa, I believe.'

At that moment Mrs Swanson reappeared in the hall. 'We can go now,' she said brightly. 'Sorry for keeping you.'

When they resumed their journey Koekemoer found himself suppressing a peculiar feeling of excitement. He was sure he had stumbled on something significant without being very clear what it was. By seeking to strengthen one suspicion he might be in danger of rousing another. He chose his words carefully.

'That is a lovely old house. In Holland one would have to be quite rich to own such a house.'

'Holland is a richer country.'

'But to make such big repairs is expensive anywhere, I think.'

'Oh, one just has to be careful not to let it get out of hand. Especially when one is spending someone else's money.'

'He is like you a farmer, this Major . . .?'

'Major Marriner. Yes, he has beef cattle.'

'Marriner.' He tried out the name. 'But now he is in Africa, that man was telling me. He is on holiday?'

'He has some kind of business to do there.'

'I have been to South Africa,' Koekemoer said. The name evoked no apparent response from her. He decided to test the water a little further. 'Also to do with my work. Diamonds, you know. That is a very rich and beautiful country, but they are treating the black people very badly.'

'So we're always hearing,' Mrs Swanson said neutrally.

'Is that where your friend is?'

'I don't really know.' She shrugged. 'That sounds silly, now that you ask, but I don't believe he actually mentioned which country. Perhaps because he knows I can hardly tell one from another.'

She dropped him in the centre of Bandon five minutes later. Once again he would have to revise his thinking, he told himself as he entered his hotel. Though he was reluctant to let go of the idea, it was perhaps not an involvement with

275

Irish terrorists that he should now be searching for, but some more direct connection with the People's Congress. He was more than ever convinced that Mrs Swanson was an innocent party to whatever transaction had taken place. That made it seem all the more logical to transfer his suspicions to this Major Marriner, who had skipped off to Africa without saying where or why at just about the time his lady friend was banking that cheque. And spending it on mending his house? That seemed almost too banal to believe, but then stranger things had happened.

Well, Koekemoer thought, he would have to find out more about Marriner, and that meant staying here on his doorstep. He guessed his tourist façade would stand up for one more day, especially since his car had broken down. The Avis people would make him seem a bit of a fool when they told him the problem was only a loose battery lead, but there was much to be said for looking stupid at times.

'You've found yourself a farm, then?' said Mr Jepson cheerily.

'Just a place I'm renting for a few months, while I go on looking around.'

'Whereabouts? Did you try the Magaliesberg, as I suggested?'

'Out that way,' said Marriner vaguely. He thought he had been open enough about his intentions up to now; the time had come to start covering his tracks. It wasn't that he had any reason to mistrust Jepson; the man simply had the guileless curiosity of a child, and that made Marriner uneasy.

'Do you want me to have your account transferred? We have a couple of branches in that area.'

'No, thank you. I'll leave it here for now. What concerns me more is what's happened to that letter.'

The money from the Handelsbank Bauer had reached the Standard Bank that morning, and Jepson had phoned to say it had been credited to his account. The receipt from Switzerland confirming the transfer of eight hundred thousand pounds to an account in the name of Frank Rendle had still not turned up, however. It was supposed to have come by courier and should certainly have been here by now. Its non-appearance had confirmed what Marriner had always feared about committing any of these arrangements to paper: there was too big a chance of something going astray, or even falling into the wrong hands.

'Can't help you there, old boy,' said Jepson. 'All I can suggest is you chase them up from the other end. Never had much faith in these courier chappies myself. Anyway, be assured that I'll be on the blower to you the minute it arrives.'

Outside the bank, Rendle and the man he called Lightning were waiting in his car. He had picked them up, dressed in civilian clothes, at the slime dump that morning. He explained about the letter from Zurich, and Rendle said: 'No sweat. We've still got another nine days.'

Marriner drove to the city centre, parking close to a big radio and television store called Polliack's to which Lightning directed him. They entered the shop and went straight up to the first floor, into a showroom where two-way radios, Citizen's Band systems and car telephones were displayed. Lightning mooched about among them, checking the specifications of various bits of equipment. He examined a walkie-talkie transceiver and shoved it contemptuously back on the counter.

'Crap,' he said. 'All crap. Toytown Radio stuff.'

'Can I help you, gentlemen?' A young salesman had sidled up beside them.

'Show us something professional,' Lightning demanded. 'Show us the best FM two-way you've got.'

The man gave him a dubious look. 'Everything is on display. Apart from the specialist models we sell to security firms and suchlike.'

'That's us,' said Lightning, unabashed. 'We're thinking of going into the security business.'

'Well. . . .' The salesman led them to a stockroom at the rear. He opened a cardboard crate and pulled the polystyrene packing off a heavy solid base-station unit. It was finished in black and had an impressive array of dials and knobs. From another box he picked out one of the hand-held transceivers that went with it, bigger and more cumbersome than the ones in the showroom, a full eighteen inches long with its rubberized aerial extended.

'This is American. It's a Johnson 541 with a built-in scrambler. The police over there use them for surveillance and crowd control. It'll work equally well in or out of a vehicle.'

Lightning was studying the set and nodding with approval. 'Two-fifty to two-eighty megahertz. Two hundred kilohertz bandwidth. That looks good.'

'Of course, you need a licence to operate this, and a frequency allocation.'

'We'll sort all that out.'

'How much?' Marriner asked.

'I'll have to check. We don't sell one of these every day.'

The salesman left the room. Lightning said: 'You know how the range is determined on these things? From the point of transmission to the horizon. Have you got some nice high spot on that farm where we could site the base safely? With a power supply, of course.'

'Hell, no,' Marriner said, remembering Rietvlei Farm in its deep valley. 'It doesn't even have electricity.'

'We'll need somewhere else, then. Somewhere pretty high up. We need a range of thirty, maybe forty kilometres.'

Marriner thought for a moment. 'What about Northcliff?'

'Perfect. It's the highest point for a long way around here, and nicely at the centre of the whole operation. You've got somewhere we could stow this safely up there?'

'I think I might have.'

The salesman returned to tell them that the price of the base unit was fifteen hundred rands. Four portable transceivers would add six hundred to that, but he was willing to round the total down to two thousand rands for a cash sale. Marriner gave him a deposit of five hundred, with a promise to pay the balance when they picked up the equipment on Friday.

As they left the shop, Rendle gave him a significant

glance. 'You're asking her for some pretty heavy involvement, aren't you? You expect her to co-operate?'

'I hope she will.' He didn't know why he felt defensive about Judith when Rendle was around. 'I don't want to ask too much of her at once. It's enough for now that she's agreed to let us have a go at that computer.'

Colonel Prinsloo's plane arrived in Cape Town at a quarter to two that afternoon, and he reached the Securitas Building just after three. The phoney Latin names they gave these places always amused him: more evidence of earnest academic minds at work. He took the special lift that carried him straight up to the Security Police headquarters on the thirteenth floor, and in Major Booysen's office found a small apprehensive group awaiting him: Booysen himself, Willemse and Kriek.

It was four days now since Phineas Molefe had flung himself from the window, and the attitude of his interrogators still wavered between contrition and defensiveness. Booysen accepted the responsibility, but his line was that no one could have expected a timid little bugger like Molefe to do anything so drastic. Kriek complained that there ought to have been bars put up on these windows years ago, while Warrant Officer Willemse – who struck Prinsloo as by far the most intelligent of the three – merely shook his head and said it had been a fucking mess.

'Yes,' said Prinsloo with feeling, 'it was a terrible fucking mess. But it's behind you now, and what I want to know is what you're doing to make up for it.'

Booysen explained that the forty men who had shared Phineas Molefe's cell block had all been removed from the prison for questioning. There was nowhere near enough room for them in the holding cells in this building, so they were being kept at Roeland Street police station across the road. It was important to maintain their isolation from others, but not possible to keep them apart from each other, which made the business of interrogating them that much more difficult. All of them had made brief preliminary

279

statements; all had denied any knowledge of the Dexedrine tablets, the prescription docket or a message that Phineas might have wanted smuggled out.

'So now we must start bringing them over here one by one and squeezing them. It's a hell of a job, Colonel. If we could just have some more men . . .'

'More men, more wagging tongues, more people getting in each other's way. No. You're the ones I chose for this job, and I want you to carry it through. There has got to be some way of narrowing down the field of suspects. Was Molefe specially friendly with any of these forty, for instance?'

'We've tried checking that,' said Kriek. 'No one will admit to knowing him well, and he does seem to have been a bit of a loner.'

'I wonder whether we shouldn't think of approaching it from another direction', Willemse ventured. 'We are trying to find out whether a message was smuggled out of the prison. If we started by assuming it *did* get out, maybe we could work backwards to the source. It had to be given to someone, after all at a particular time and place.'

'It could have happened any time in the course of one whole month,' Kriek objected. 'And all these *mugus* were doing outside work. They were all over the place.'

'All the same, it seems to me we shouldn't be questioning only them. We should be talking to the warders as well, seeing if they remember anything.'

'And involving more and more people?' Prinsloo said dubiously.

'They only need to be told so much.'

'All right, Willemse. Take charge of it yourself,' said Prinsloo. 'But keep the questions casual, you understand? Now, let's go over to Roeland Street. I'd like to get a look at this lot for myself.'

They left the building and crossed the road to the police station. The place had the smells and sounds Prinsloo had known as a rookie cop thirty years ago. This was the raw stuff of the basic police work that he still relished, and he walked with a new spring in his stride.

280

24

At twenty to six on Thursday evening Dr Rose stuck his head round the door of the Woodvale Clinic's administrative office and was surprised to find Judith still at her desk. She was typing some account entries into the computer.

'Not going home yet?'

'Not for an hour or two. I want to get these out of the way.'

'Well. Good. Don't overdo it.'

There seemed little more to say, but he lingered in the doorway as though reluctant to end the conversation there. Things had gone better between them for the past week, he thought, ever since she had moved out of the house. She was co-operative at work and had an unusual air of serenity, almost of fulfilment, about her. He'd been tempted to remark on it, but their relationship was still a little too edgy for that.

He nodded towards the computer screen. 'Got the hang of that now, have you?'

'Well, I'm a lot better than I was. Some of it will always be a mystery to me.'

'Don't hesitate to ask me. Oh, and if you ever feel like popping home for a drink or a meal. . . . Your mother would be glad to see you. Only if it suits you, of course,' he added hastily.

She gave him a neutral look. 'Thank you. I will.'

'Well, I'll be off, then. Good night.'

From the window she watched her father heading for the car park. As soon as his car had pulled out of the gates she went to the phone and dialled the number of a call box down the road. When Marriner answered she said simply, 'He's gone. You can come now,' and put down the receiver. Then she left the office and went nervously in search of Virgil, the security man.

After working hours the atmosphere of the clinic became even more relaxed. Patients confined to bed had their dinner served at seven o'clock; the others were free to turn up in the dining room any time before eight, and were not required to return to their wards until ten. Visitors came and went. All the same, it would be best to deflect Virgil's curiosity; a good way of doing that was to appeal to his taste for conspiracy.

She found him strolling – 'patrolling' he would probably have said – along the path from the Substance Abuse Unit.

'Did my father see you before he left?' she asked.

'No.'

'Well, there's a message. Two men are coming to do some work in the office this evening, and they'd like to be left alone.'

'Who are they?'

'Men from the Government, Virgil, like before. Just let them in without any fuss and bother, will you?'

'Ah, them,' he said knowingly. 'What do they want here, anyway?'

'I know as little as you do. I suggest we both just keep clear of them.'

She returned to the office in time to see Marriner's car arrive and draw up in the car park. Virgil was watching from a distance as Marriner and another man approached the building, and she went out to reception to meet them.

'In here,' she said without preamble. She led them to her own office and locked the door behind them. Marriner's companion was a gawky young man in a suit, obviously borrowed, that had trousers two inches too short for him. He grinned at her amiably. Marriner introduced him as Lightning.

'How long is this going to take?' she asked.

'All depends. Let's get a look at the system.'

Judith led him to her own terminal and switched it on. She began to explain what she knew of the computer's operations, but Lightning cut her short. 'I know. It's basically like a row of lockers, and you all have keys to your own. But there's got to be a master key that will open them all, right? And it's your old man who keeps that?' She nodded. 'Plus he's got a private locker all to himself, and it's the key to that we're looking for. OK. Show me how you get into the system.'

She sat at her desk and typed out her initials, JRO, and her six-letter password. They appeared on the status line at the foot of the screen, beneath the general directory.

'G-E-R-A-L-D.' Lightning read out the password. 'Why Gerald?'

'It's the name of one of my brothers,' she said neutrally.

'That's what most people do: choose a password that means something to them. Not such a hot idea, though, because it's open to being guessed at by anyone who knows them. Any clues to what your old man might choose? What's your mother's name, for instance?'

'Martha.'

'Six letters. Let's try it.'

Lightning replaced her in front of the terminal. She told him her father's initials, LRO, and he typed them out and followed them with MARTHA. A notice immediately flashed on the screen: BAD PASSWORD.

'Too obvious, huh? What about your name? Six letters as well?'

'Even less likely,' said Judith with a sardonic smile, but he typed out JUDITH. The result was the same: BAD PASSWORD.

'Better pull up a chair,' Lightning said. 'We could be some time.'

For ten minutes or so they sat together, with Judith offering him the names of every member of her family she could think of, the names of her father's parents and friends and colleagues, half-forgotten names that she dredged up from stories he had told of his young days. She even suggested JOSHUA. The result was the same: the computer accepted none of them.

'OK. One thing we know is he's not sentimental,' said Lightning. 'What about numbers? Your home phone number, for instance. The number of his car?' They tried them without effect. Lightning seemed not at all dismayed.

'I was hoping for a short cut, but it isn't going to work. No sense in fiddling around any more. With six numbers you've got a choice of a hundred thousand possible combinations; with six letters you've got something like eighty million. But the right combination is in there somewhere. We'll have to find a bypass.'

'What's that?' said Marriner.

'A way of bypassing the security has got to be built into a system like this. Somebody has to be able to override the program in case the person with the master password gets run over by a bus. In an emergency, somebody from the company that made the software will be able to find a way in.'

'And you think you can do that?'

'If I can get a look at the CPU – the Central Processing Unit,' Lightning explained. 'Where is it?'

'Through here, I think,' said Judith.

She led them out of the office to what had been a storeroom near the end of the corridor. A steel cabinet, the size of a refrigerator, had been set up against the back wall. It hummed gently with electric power supplied by a thick cable. Red and orange lights blinked on and off beside tiers of what looked like metal drawers. None of it meant a thing to Judith or Marriner, but Lightning stood gazing at it knowledgeably.

'This is the thing's brain,' he said. 'These are the circuits, those are the discs. It's really only a big pinball machine. It can't think for itself, and it can be fooled. Nobody's going to notice if I put it out of action for an hour or two, are they?'

'I suppose not,' said Judith dubiously. 'As long as you don't lose anything that's stored on it.'

'No, I won't touch the discs. All I'm going to do is isolate the program with the codes on it and work my way into it through the hardware. A process of elimination, that's all; but it will take a while. No point in you hanging over my shoulder.'

They took the hint, returned to the office and sat facing each other across Judith's desk. 'Where did you find him?' she said.

'He's one of Rendle's chaps. He's got a pass for the evening, but I have to have him back at the barracks by eleven.'

She was too tense to make any small talk, much less discuss anything serious. Every few minutes she stood up, either to move restlessly around the room or to go out and check on the whereabouts of Virgil. Once in a while Lightning would come back, work briefly at the terminal, grunt with satisfaction or annoyance and then return to the processing unit. An hour passed. Judith went to the kitchen and returned with three cups of coffee on a tray. Marriner carried one to the storeroom, where the sight of the processing unit alarmed him. Lightning had practically disembowelled it. All the drawers were pulled open; trays of silicon chips lay exposed within them and bunches of wire trailed out of them.

'Are you sure you know what you're doing?'

'Just about.' The young man slurped his coffee. 'Just about ready to give it a try.'

They returned to the office together. Lightning sat at the computer terminal and began to tap a series of instructions into it, pausing between each one and staring with brows furrowed in concentration at the screen. Night had almost fallen, and Judith had switched on the overhead fluorescent lighting. Now she glanced at her watch.

'Got it!' Lightning shouted.

He sat back and gazed triumphantly at the screen. The others hurried across the room and peered over his shoulder. The screen was blank, but for a single line of meaningless digits at the centre.

'That's *it!*' Lightning said. Obviously he thought they weren't impressed enough. 'That's the override code that's built into the system. I found it by stripping everything else out of it. I fooled this damned machine into revealing its biggest secret!'

'And now?' asked Judith.

Lightning was scribbling the numbers down on a sheet of paper. 'Now all I have to do is restore the programs, and we're into them all – as deep as you want to go.'

He vanished down the hall towards the storeroom again. An agony of time seemed to go by, but it was actually only twenty minutes later, just after eight o'clock, when he returned. The three of them formed a tense little bunch around the terminal as the soldier typed the code into the system. Immediately the screen was filled with more incomprehensible figures and letters.

'All technical data,' Lightning said. 'Kind of a maintenance manual provided with the software. Ah, here we are.' He had found a line that said MASTER CONTROL.. He blocked up to it and pressed the READ button, and a list began rolling up the left of the screen. When it stopped they saw what it was. The employees of the clinic were named in alphabetical order, and against each name was a set of three initials and a six-letter password. Opposite Dr Louis Rose's name they read: LRO-CLINIC.

'Dead simple, huh?' said Lightning, flushed by his achievement. 'Your old man's password is CLINIC. Why didn't we think of it?'

'Let's see what's in his file,' Marriner said anxiously.

The soldier keyed in the letters and the password. He got another list on the screen, this time the headings of all the items Dr Rose had chosen to keep for his private scrutiny. The one at the top bore the title INDUNA. Lightning selected it, pressed some more keys and a page appeared headed *Induna Project, Page One of Fifteen*. It was the beginning of a carefully plotted schedule: dates, times, places, names. . . . Marriner stared at it in fascination, almost in disbelief, as Lightning slowly scrolled it up. It was far more than he had been counting on, a complete breakdown of the arrangements. 'Let's see some more,' he said, suddenly hoarse with excitement, and Lightning scrolled faster, up through pages 2, 3 and 4, until Judith, very agitated, said: 'You've got what you wanted. Don't waste more time. Just take it, please, and go!'

Lightning rolled the schedule back to the start and pressed the SEND button. The printer in the corner began to chatter. 'Don't forget to erase the print record,' Judith said. She was extremely nervous now, and for that matter so was Marriner. His hands shook as he tore the pages off the printer one by one. Before half of them had come through the machine Lightning was already using the KILL button to destroy the evidence. Finally he switched off the terminal and trotted back to the storeroom to check that he had left nothing amiss with the processing unit.

Marriner stacked the fifteen pages of printout, handling them as carefully as though they were rare manuscripts. He folded them and put them in his jacket pocket. Then he faced Judith.

'I hope you know how much I appreciate this. You've been marvellous.'

She was not susceptible to praise tonight. She said: 'I hope you appreciate the risk I'm taking.'

'I do. Believe me.' He kissed her cheek. 'This stuff is going to make a real difference, you know.'

A minute later they were ready to leave. Judith would hang about for another half an hour to avoid the appearance of any connection with them. As they walked towards the car park Marriner saw Virgil loitering beside the path and decided to brazen it out with him. He halted in front of the security man, who gave him a nervous grin.

'Listen. You haven't seen anything, all right? We weren't even here.'

'OK, Chief.'

When they were in the car the tension broke and they dissolved into laughter. 'He thinks I'm from the Security Police,' Marriner said. 'I'm afraid he's in for a shock.'

He got Lightning back to his barracks by ten o'clock, and was home in his room at the Windsor by eleven. He changed into comfortable clothes and sent for a pot of coffee. When the porter had brought it and left, Marriner spread the computer printouts across his bed and read carefully through them, half a dozen times. He had given up any idea of sleep. He took a pen and a thick pad of paper, pulled a chair up to the bed and began making notes. Referring in turn to his maps and to the details of the Induna Project, he began to plot a critical path analysis: a flowchart of lines and circles that drew every element and phase of the operation into a coherent whole. It was a relief at last to have an exact goal and a clear vision of how to attain it; on the other hand, its complexity was frightening to contemplate. Planning was something he had always enjoyed. Deploying men and resources to the best possible advantage was an intellectual challenge. The difference was that in the army you could call on all the men and materials you needed. You could pass your requirements to someone whose job was to provide them. Here it was all down to him, and his resources would be spread so pitifully thinly that there was no room for a single mistake.

The sun was well up before he had finished. His notes filled forty pages of the pad, and there were still many details to be filled in. There were also more things to do before he could consider sleep. He needed to phone Rosenblatt in Zurich again; there would have to be several calls back and forth, in fact, far too long and complicated to make from a public callbox.

At seven-thirty he sent for breakfast and more coffee. Then he went downstairs and phoned Judith, in time to catch her in the flat before she left for work. He found her mood just as brittle as it had been last night, but she agreed without difficulty to let him use her flat and her phone. The key would be on the lintel above the door.

Marriner showered, shaved and dressed. Then he collected his car once again and set off, bleary-eyed and wincing at the strength of the morning sun, for Northcliff.

Hannes Koekemoer had got back to his London flat on Thursday night. He had caught a bad cold in Ireland, and it was not until after lunch on Friday that he made a groggy appearance in his office. The amount of work that had piled up in his absence was enough to dispirit him further, and almost enough to make him regret that he had gone away at all. Having set out to establish what he'd imagined was a connection between African revolutionaries and Irish terrorists, he had been left instead holding one end of a tenuous thread leading from the People's Congress to the minor gentry of County Cork. It was true that his enquiries into Major Marriner had revealed glimpses of an intriguing past: he was a former British Army paratroop officer and he was rumoured also to have served in the SAS. Yet everything pointed to a man who had left his background behind him, who had settled for the past several years into a fairly comfortable farmer's life with no hint of mystery to it. It was also true that he had dashed off to Africa at short notice, but Africa was a big place and apparently he knew it well. If there had been something that tied him in with South Africa itself, that might have been a different matter; it seemed far more likely that some old contact of his further north had come up with the offer of a job or a business opportunity, and he had gone out there without feeling he needed to explain himself.

Koekemoer would file a report on the trip, but he would hesitate to draw any conclusions from what he had learned.

He swallowed some aspirins and immersed himself in other work. By the time five o'clock came he had pushed his researches in Ireland well to the back of his mind. Lights were being switched off and other consulate employees were locking their offices and getting ready to leave. The young commercial assistant, whom he had seen only briefly earlier in the afternoon, popped his head through the door on his way out.

'By the way. You remember me telling you last week that the name of that place you were going to was familiar? Bandon?'

'What about it?' said Koekemoer without much interest.

'I've just remembered. About a week before that we had a visitor who came from there. Bandon: the address was on the card he filled in. He was inquiring about buying some farmland. Pestered me for a letter of introduction to someone, in fact. It just seemed an odd coincidence.'

The intelligence officer leaned back in his chair. 'What was this man's name?'

'I don't remember offhand. It will be on the file. Seaman? Sailor? Something to do with the sea.'

'Marriner,' said Koekemoer flatly.

'That's it, Marriner. You know him, then. Well, I just thought I'd mention—'

'Come in here, son.' Koekemoer flattened his palms on

289

the desk and gave the young man an intimidating stare. 'Come in. Take off your overcoat. Sit down. I think you rather fancy yourself doing a job like mine, don't you? Well, you can start right now. You can tell me everything you remember about this man Marriner.'

Judith seemed to have exhausted all her emotions in the course of half an hour. First she had exploded with anger, then she had cried, then she had let Marriner take her briefly, sobbing, in his arms. At last she had moved to sit on the sofa across the room, and he felt there was something calculated and final about that withdrawal. Something had snapped between them. It was as though she had suddenly become aware that whatever it was she had been searching for in him wasn't there to be found.

Now she sat and stared dully at the immediate cause of all this grief, the Johnson radio transceiver which she had come home to find installed on her sideboard. It was the uncompromising physical proof of her involvement, and she was in no mood to believe that Marriner felt as badly about it as she did.

Again he tried to speak soothingly to her. 'I'm sorry, Judith. Believe me, I didn't intend to present you with a *fait accompli* like this. I was going to ask you. Too much else got in the way. I suddenly realized this thing had to be picked up today, and I have nowhere else to keep it.'

'You've taken advantage of me,' she said tonelessly. 'I feel that you've been using me right from the start.'

'No, Judith, I think you knew what you were taking on. You just went on hoping it wouldn't have to touch you. What would you have said if I'd asked you to keep this set here for me? Yes or no?'

She shrugged. He felt he was moralizing, and the memory of their brief weekend of intimacy made the feeling much worse, but he had to go on.

'Listen, Judith. Everything has changed. You're going to have to leave the country. You'll have to come with us.' He paused. 'I knew that the minute I saw those computer documents. There is no longer any way of keeping your role

290

in this hidden. I think you know it, too, and that's what got you so uptight last night. You can't just sit around afterwards pretending to be innocent. I've worked out a way of getting you out, a way that will make it safer for all of us, and I've already told Joshua that you're coming.'

'Oh, thank you. That really gives me a warm feeling all over.'

'You know it has to be done. What's left for you here, anyway? Hadn't you thought about leaving yourself?'

'That would have been my own choice,' she said with a little more spirit. 'Now you're forcing it on me, and there's a big fucking difference!'

'You were the one who sent that letter. That's how it all got started.'

'I also still hate the idea of betraying my father.'

'If he has the integrity you claim he has, then he'll come to understand why. You've done the right thing by helping Kumalo, and I know how hard it was for you. This country has a way of paralysing people's moral courage. You've done him a favour and you've done me one. Now do one for yourself. Think about it positively. Get out and make a new beginning.'

She gave him a long look then, with a kind of new understanding in it. He knew she was adjusting her responses to him, wondering whether she had lost a lover but discovered a friend. Maybe even a fatherly friend, he thought in a wry moment, and perhaps that was the way it should have been all along. She said: 'All right. But just don't expect me to jump for joy about it.'

'No. But I'm going to ask you to do two other things for me. Small things.'

She gave a weary sigh. 'What are they?'

'Tomorrow we're all going to meet out at the farm. In the afternoon Frank Rendle has arranged to pay a visit to his old air base near Pretoria. I'd like you to drive him there and spend some time with him.'

'The other thing is this. I'm going to have to become a patient at the Woodvale Clinic. I want you to help me arrange it.'

291

25

'**B**obbejaan!'
The prisoner's eyes flickered in recognition as the warder from Pollsmoor called his name. The prisoner was a squat, heavy brute of a man, sitting at the edge of a group in the last of the row of cells at Roeland Street police station. They'd been eating breakfast, scooping brown malt porridge with their fingers from metal dixies, and all had paused to stare at the arrival of the white men outside the barred door.

'Bobbejaan! *Kom hierso!*

For a few seconds more the man went on watching them with a dull, animal tranquillity. Then, as though he knew exactly what was happening, he got resignedly to his feet, wiped the remains of porridge from his hands on his prison shorts and stood waiting.

'You're quite certain this is the one?' demanded Colonel Prinsloo.

'Absolutely, sir. There aren't two like him in the whole place. Strong as an ox. Quiet, but dangerous.'

'Well done,' said Prinsloo with a sigh, not to the warder but to Warrant-officer Willemse. It was Willemse's patient leg-work, and not the snarling inquisitions of Booysen and Kriek, that had finally yielded results. For two and a half days he had practically lived at the prison, checking back through old duty rosters and work records, jogging the memories of warders, at length prising out of this young idiot the hazy recollection of an incident that had occurred early in November. It was the kind of thing that could happen once or twice a week, some *mugu* working in the fields spotting somebody outside the fence and trying to cadge something off him. The warder had given him a good *klop* with his truncheon and that had been the end of it. They were all low-security prisoners, not political, not subversive. What could it matter? the idiot had protested, resentful at being dragged out of bed and down here at five o'clock on a Saturday morning. Prinsloo had told him to shut his face and keep it shut.

They stood watching Bobbejaan with a certain awe as he was led out of the cell. Booysen snapped a handcuff to each of his wrists and fastened them to his own and to Kriek's: there would be no more mistakes of the sort they had made with Phineas. The man was built like a tank, the turret of his head turning slowly on his mighty shoulders as he studied his captors. His face was heavy and without expression and yet his eyes seemed to contemplate them hungrily, one by one, almost as though he relished whatever challenge they were offering.

'You won't frighten this one,' Prinsloo said thoughtfully. 'You won't tire him out. There's only one way to handle him, and this time I want no mistakes.'

Koekemoer's report from London had been relayed to Van Straaten at his home just before midnight. He had at once put a request through the Service duty officer to the Immigration Department, and when he reached his office in the Union Buildings first thing that Saturday morning a telex message lay on his desk with the details he had asked for. Patrick Marriner, British citizen. Occupation given as farmer, but described in his passport as an army officer. Arrived Jan Smuts Airport 28 November, which was twelve days ago. No record of departure. Address in South Africa, c/o The Windsor Hotel, Johannesburg.

Superficially, at least, there was nothing to get excited about. Marriner's motive for visiting the country seemed legitimate and he had presented himself quite openly at the consulate-general in search of information, which was hardly the action of a man with something to hide.

Unless, of course, that was precisely what he wanted them to think.

There remained his connection with the Swanson woman, and the unexplained payment of Congress money into her bank account. There remained the coincidence that he had flown to South Africa at just about the time the money was being paid. And, in Van Straaten's mind at least, a niggling worry was still lodged about the new Congress bank account in Zurich and what they intended to use it for.

Strictly speaking, this end of the business should now be a matter for the Security Police to look into. Van Straaten distrusted their ham-fisted approach, however, so clearly personified by Colonel Prinsloo. It wouldn't be beyond them to barge straight in on Marriner and take him off for questioning, thus scaring off whoever he might be dealing with as well as drawing a lot of flak from the British Embassy. A subtler strategy was called for. Van Straaten buzzed the duty officer, gave him the names of two of his own most trusted younger subordinates and asked him to call them in.

'Pelindaba!' Corporal Rendle spoke the name like an African curse. 'Are you serious, Major?'

They had just turned off the road south of Hartbeespoort, and the pale ominous shape of the nuclear reactor lay straight ahead. In the back seat of the car Lightning, Carver and Fish had suddenly stopped horsing around and had fallen silent.

'Of course I'm serious. The farm is just behind it, but it's well out of sight.' Marriner glanced at Rendle beside him. 'Anything wrong with that?'

'Major. . . .' Rendle seemed to be groping for words. 'I don't think you understand. Pelindaba is one of the most sensitive places in the country. They say it's where we make our nuclear weapons.'

Marriner's hands went rigid on the steering wheel. He knew of the rumours that South Africa had its own nuclear arsenal, but he had never thought to connect them to this place.

'It's never been officially admitted,' Rendle explained, 'but that's what they say. The point is, the place will be lousy with security. They're sure to take an interest in a stranger moving into the area, bringing carloads of people in.'

'Jesus Christ!' Marriner breathed. He glanced in the mirror at the Opel Manta a hundred yards behind, wondering whether the same thought was going through the minds of Judith and the rest of Rendle's squad. Of all the stupid strokes of bad luck he could imagine, this was possibly the worst. No, not bad luck:

carelessness. The extent of the security surrounding the place should have alerted him. He hadn't mentioned the exact location of Rietvlei Farm to anyone, merely as a routine precaution, and that was probably just as well. It would have been too late to start looking for somewhere else.

The security fence and the entrance to the plant lay just ahead. It was time to put a bold face on it, he thought. It was time to produce the letter from the consulate-general in London.

He stopped the car beside the gate. Judith drew up behind him and he signalled to her to stay where she was. Two men in dark blue uniforms, one of them cradling a machine-pistol, emerged from the gatehouse and stared at him suspiciously through the mesh as he approached.

'Good morning,' he said breezily. 'I thought I'd introduce myself, just in case you wondered. I'm the new tenant of the farm down there.'

He handed over the letter, which the men read in silence. It didn't mean much, but its heading was impressive and served as a stamp of official approval which seemed to reassure them. He explained that some friends were helping him move in. In fact they were going to have a bit of a housewarming party. 'If you feel like a beer when you come off duty, you're welcome to join us,' he added as a final sweetener. The men thanked him non-committally, but by the time he turned back to the car he was sure he had won their grudging confidence. Quite likely they, or others, would come down to check up on him, but he had several more days in which to establish an innocuous presence on the farm. A good few comings and goings were also to be expected of a new arrival.

'You think that was wise?' Rendle asked as he nosed the Orion down the track towards the farm.

'Better than leaving them to wonder. They're employed by the Atomic Energy Board, aren't they? I have some confidence in the notion that the left hand of government very rarely knows what the right hand is doing. Besides, there could be certain advantages in this place. Who expects a criminal to hide in a police station?'

He didn't know whether he was fooling even himself, but he

had no more time to dwell on the subject. When the little convoy reached the farmhouse they found old Meiring ready to leave, his possessions heaped on the back of a pickup truck in which his sister had driven out from Pretoria. Labuschagne from the estate agency was there as well. If any of them wondered about Marriner's arriving in the company of a woman and eight able-bodied young men, none of them remarked on it. There was a bit of impromptu party atmosphere anyway, with Rendle passing beer cans around and the old couple joining Marriner in a toast to their respective futures. The formalities took only a minute: Marriner and Meiring both signed two copies of the lease, and the new tenant handed over a bank draft to the old man and another to Labuschagne. Eventually the pickup rattled away, followed by Labuschagne's car, and Marriner and his guests had the place to themselves.

They helped him carry his supplies and equipment into the rickety farmhouse. He had checked out of the hotel without any notice first thing that morning, pausing only to give Nimrod a message for Duma. Besides his luggage there were gas lamps, a camp bed and a sleeping-bag purchased from a camping supply shop and a box of basic provisions picked up on the way out from Johannesburg. Other, less innocent items would be brought here over the next few days. Meanwhile this would be Marriner's home until he could get himself admitted to the clinic, and he was resigned to its spartan comforts.

When everything was stowed away he led them out of the house and they sat in a circle around him in the shade of a mimosa – all except Judith, who leaned against one of the battered Chevrolets some distance away. The river gurgled from beyond the reeds. The perpetual humming of insects seemed muffled by the dense, moist air of the valley.

Marriner began to address them.

'We haven't got a lot of time. Frank and Judith have to leave after lunch, so I want everything to be as clear as possible in everyone's mind before then. I'm going to tell you my plan, and then we're going to discuss it, and after that we're going to start rehearsing it. Each of you will have a special job to do, and I don't want you just to listen to me. I want to hear your ideas as well.

'Phase One. We are going to take Lincoln Kumalo out of that clinic, and we are going to make him disappear. We're going to bring him here by road, and for a short distance on foot, and nobody is going to know where he is – at least, not until it's too late to matter. Maximum time allowed: one hour. I will be in charge of Phase One.

'Phase Two. We will transfer Kumalo to a helicopter waiting here for him. We will fly him due east, to the closest possible point on the border, overflying Swaziland and landing at a designated point in southern Mozambique. Maximum time allowed: two hours. Frank Rendle will be in charge of Phase Two.

'Phase Three. At our landing point in Mozambique we will be met by representatives of the People's Congress, who will escort us to a safe hiding-place and in due course make arrangements for us to leave the country. Phase Three will be in the hands of the Congress and the Mozambique government, and I don't expect to have any specific details until our arrival.' Marriner paused, looking around at their tense faces. 'Are there any questions at this stage?'

The manager of the Windsor Hotel was trying to be co-operative, but could scarcely disguise his impatience. He had an unusually busy Saturday afternoon ahead: a wedding reception in the ballroom and a coachload of German tourists arriving at any minute. He supposed he ought to be grateful for the circumspect way in which these two young men had approached him but he didn't like their manner. When they'd learned that the guest they were interested in had checked out that morning they had become almost accusatory, as though the manager himself were somehow to blame.

Facing him across his office desk, they were now asking him a lot of fool questions that he couldn't possibly answer. Obviously they had no idea how a hotel was run.

'So he left no forwarding address? Isn't that unusual?'

'By no means. As you see, we have the home address in

Ireland that he wrote in the register. Any mail that arrived for him would be sent on to him there.'

'And you say you never saw him yourself?'

'I may have. I may not have. Look, I've had a hundred and twenty guests in here on any one night in the past two weeks. I never meet more than a handful of them personally. As far as I'm concerned this Mr Marriner was just a name and a room number. He caused me no trouble and he paid his bill.'

'He paid in cash, I notice.' One of the men was studying a duplicate of the itemized and receipted bill. 'A businessman would be more inclined to use a credit card, surely? I also see that he made not one telephone call from his room in twelve days.'

'You expect me to account for a thing like that?'

'No, sir. I'm really just thinking aloud. It seems to me that Mr Marriner was very careful to keep himself to himself. He had quite a lot of meals served in his room, for instance. Who would have brought them to him?'

'His floor boy, usually.'

'Then, we'll need to ask him some questions. We want to keep this discreet, sir. We don't want to start a lot of talk among your staff. First of all we would like to look over Mr Marriner's room.'

'Certainly. I'll get the housekeeper to arrange it.'

'We'd prefer you to show us it yourself, sir.'

The manager helplessly rolled his eyes. 'What is it you want this man for, anyway?'

'I'm afraid that's a matter of state security.'

From time to time, once an hour perhaps, Colonel Prinsloo had strolled into the interrogation room to see how they were getting on. He didn't like to stay long, partly because he knew his presence was inhibiting, partly because even he couldn't stomach watching what was going on in there. Certainly the three security policemen didn't want him around; maybe even Bobbejaan didn't want him. Something intensely personal was being acted out between the four of them, a struggle of wills so powerful that it excluded everything and everyone else. To enter that room was to intrude on a private mystery, a shameful secret that seemed to involve and defile them all.

This time, five hours after the interrogation had begun, the sight of Bobbejaan had given Prinsloo a fright. He was naked, and his great black body gleamed from head to foot with sweat. He was fastened in a cruciform position, his ankles and wrists bound by thick leather straps fixed to ring-bolts on the wall, and his head was lolling on his chest. Warrant Officer Willemse had just fetched a bucket of water, and when it was thrown over him the prisoner seemed to revive, raising his head, shaking it like a dog and staring wild-eyed at his tormentors. Prinsloo knew that his earlier prediction had been right: there was no fear in Bobbejaan's eyes, there was nothing but anger and pain. Several of his front teeth had been knocked out, and his mouth was a shapeless red gash, dribbling blood and saliva, adding to his ferocious appearance. His testicles were swollen to the size of tennis balls and the skin of his scrotum was darkened by livid bruises.

In their own way his interrogators were also close to the end of their endurance. They were heavy-limbed with exhaustion. Booysen and Kriek had stripped off their sodden shirts; Willemse was so drawn and pale he looked in danger of being sick, and his hands shook as he lit a cigarette.

Once again Captain Kriek knelt in front of the prisoner and the nutcrackers gleamed in his hand, an ordinary pair of nutcrackers that he wielded with the precision of a dentist's forceps. Prinsloo turned away, unable to watch, feeling his stomach turn over, and saw Willemse doing the same. A second later Bobbejaan's roar of pain shook the room, a deep and mighty animal bellow rebounding from the soundproofed walls, echoing through their heads long after it had died away to a moan.

'The man is made of iron,' Booysen muttered, coming over to the Colonel. 'Twice, three times with the nutcrackers – I've never known it not to work. This one has had it a dozen times, and still he says nothing. It's as if he was trying to break *us*.'

'It looks almost as if he's succeeding,' Prinsloo said curtly. 'You need a rest, all four of you. Time to unscramble your brains. Two hours.'

He left the room and found that Willemse had followed him

out. Instinctively Prinsloo knew why, and he stopped and rounded sharply on him.

'Well?'

'I've had enough of this, sir. It's not what I joined the police for.'

'I've got news for you, Willemse. It's not what *I* joined for, either. This is work invented for us by little men with their heads so far up in the clouds that they've never seen the colour of their own shit. But I'm stuck with it and I'm seeing it through. Not to please them but to spite them. To show them that in the end it's people like us who make their system work for them.'

'Then, perhaps you'll understand,' said the other man, 'if I ask to be excused from any more of this. I'm thinking of resigning, in fact.'

'You can do whatever you like when all this is over. Send your resignation direct to Hoeksma, for all I care. Stuff it down Professor Doctor Van Straaten's throat. But you try backing out on me now, Willemse, and I'll have you in that bloody room yourself!'

It was only mid-afternoon when Nandi Kumalo was startled by Duma's familar knock on the back door of her house. With a puzzled frown she put aside the copy of the *British Journal of Guidance and Counselling* she had just begun reading. It was one of a batch of professional publications that had arrived that morning, the envelope ripped open for inspection and resealed with deliberate clumsiness by the Security Police. It wasn't that they seriously suspected her of receiving subversive literature; it was just one of their little ways of letting her know they hadn't forgotten her.

As soon as Duma had slithered through the door she was certain that something was wrong. He was tense and fidgety, a nocturnal animal exposed to the daylight. He refused her offer of a chair and began his familiar routine of pacing about the kitchen.

'Nandi, they've found something out. I thought I'd better tell you at once. Major Marriner left his hotel this morning and a few hours later they turned up looking for him.'

300

He repeated what Nimrod had hastened to tell him as soon as he'd come off duty after lunch. Marriner's hotel room had been searched, and Nimrod had been questioned by two men who called themselves government officials. Since they were dealing with a mere floor boy they had not felt obliged to be any more explicit about their identities. He had been present when they searched the room, poking about in cupboards and drawers without, apparently, finding anything to interest them. Then the questions had begun. Had Marriner had any visitors? Had he sent Nimrod on any errands? Had he said where he was going when he left the hotel? What did he look like? By his own account Nimrod had answered as vaguely as possible while trying not to seem evasive. The men had lacked the hard edge and the probing manner of policemen, he had thought, but obviously they were connected in some way with the security services. They had spoken to two or three other employees who were hardly more helpful than Nimrod, but what they might have found out was of much less significance than the fact that they had turned up at all.

'They have learned something about Marriner, God knows how. And now he has dropped out of sight. I have no way of reaching him, nothing but a message from Nimrod to meet him on Monday. Perhaps they will have picked him up by then. The damned man has been keeping me in the dark.'

Nandi had pulled a chair out from the kitchen table and sat down. She felt faint and slightly nauseous. Over the past month, while she continued to work at her usual strenuous pace, her moods had gone through bewildering swings. It had been equally impossible to ignore the increasing rumours of her father's impending release and her own growing conviction that he was in mortal danger, so that eventually she hardly knew what to feel, let alone what to believe. Even when Duma had told her of the arrival of this man Marriner, her responses had been contradictory; on the one hand the news raised a new hope, on the other it made the threat to Lincoln Kumalo seem that much more serious. Now both these feelings were overtaken by a kind of numb despair.

'Duma, what are you going to do?'

'What can I do? I've sent a message to Makibani. Maybe he will know what's gone wrong. Perhaps Marriner has done something stupid.'

'Duma, listen to me.' She grabbed his arm and steered him round the table, forcing him to sit down and face her. 'I am tired of this uncertainty. I am tired of hearing you tell me how other people are playing around with my father's life. Now I'm not blaming you for that; if anything it's my fault, because I was the one who really started all this. And I feel responsible for it. Just what is it that they are going to do?'

'Marriner knows where Lincoln is going to be. Marriner and these white boys are going to get him out. At least, that is their plan. They've still told me nothing more. They seem to think they don't need much help from me. Maybe now they will call the whole thing off.'

'You must find out exactly what is going on, Duma. And you must tell me. Promise you'll tell me.'

'I'd quite like to know what's going on myself, Nandi. But there is some sense in what this Marriner says, about everybody needing to know only so much.'

'Ha! I am only his daughter, and so I need to know nothing, is that right? And what about him? Do you realize that the one person who is totally unaware of any of this is my father himself? I can't stand the idea that he is facing all this alone and in ignorance. I can't let it happen that way!'

He looked at her sharply. 'You're not thinking of getting involved yourself, I hope.'

'I don't know what I'm thinking.'

'The best thing you can do is just sit tight and pray that this scheme works.'

'I wouldn't do anything to jeopardize it. Just learn what you can and let me make up my own mind about it.'

Duma sighed. He would still do almost anything to please Nandi or, perhaps more important, not to upset her. 'Maybe I will find out more on Monday,' he said. 'That is, if they haven't already caught Marriner by then.'

26

Frank Rendle had suddenly become talkative.

'It was in Angola. I was with Nineteen Squadron, flying one of those Puma gunships you saw back there, giving close support to one of our armoured columns. Well, one morning my crew and I got new orders. They wanted us to zap a village about forty kilometres behind the Angolan lines. They said it was a SWAPO guerrilla base-camp, and we were supposed to give it the works: rockets, napalm, the lot. The funny thing was, I'd overflown that village the day before on my way back from another patrol, and it was full of women and kids. Forty, maybe fifty kids: once they saw we weren't going to hurt them they came out of the bush and started waving up at us, for Christ's sake!

'Well, that's what I told them back at base, but they insisted there were gooks there, that they kept the women and kids there as a cover. I said: So what? They were still women and kids, weren't they? Did they want me to zap the lot of them for the sake of burning a few guerrillas? That wasn't an argument that appealed to them, so I just refused to go. Just point-blank said no. Hey, is all this boring you?'

'Not at all,' said Judith.

She was driving him past the perimeter fence of the Zwartkop Air Station, and it was the sight of the parked helicopters that had got him going, row after row of Pumas and Alouettes painted in green and brown camouflage lined up in front of the service hangars. These machines of war held no interest for her, but they had shaken Rendle out of a long silence.

'In the air force you just don't say no to an order. There was a quick court martial and a dishonourable discharge. They wanted it kept quiet: no morale problems in our patriotic defence force. Oh, no. Getting kicked out didn't freak me as much as the fact that all I'd ever wanted to do was fly, and now it was all over. As well as that, my record didn't exempt me from regular national service, so it was back to square-bashing and

303

rifle drill, and then back to Angola. You've seen it from the air, now see it from the goddam thorn bushes. Not to mention the tripwires and the landmines, which you don't see unless you're careful. I learned a new way of surviving, and I pulled my squad through without losing any of them. Ever since then we've stayed out of trouble.'

Zwartkop was only one part of a very large military complex set among the bush-speckled hills just south of Pretoria. Within its general perimeter lay the Voortrekkerhoogte army camp, the army and air-force gymnasiums, the Waterkloof air station with the Buccaneers and Mirage fighter-bombers of Strike Command and the bases of any number of other ancillary, supply and service detachments. The complex itself was crossed by public roads; getting into any one of the bases, however, required either official permission or the pulling of strings.

Rendle's friend was waiting to meet them in the carpark of the big army hospital. His name was Captain Cross, his nickname was Jumper and he was a pilot with 19 Squadron. He greeted Rendle enthusiastically, but once he'd been introduced to Judith he said in some embarrassment: 'My girl isn't off duty for another hour. As I explained, Frank, I'd like to take you both for a drink at the mess in the meantime, but . . . well, you know the circumstances. Do you mind coming back to my room? We can be alone and hoist a couple of beers.'

'That would be great.'

They got into Jumper's car and he drove them back to the air station. At the gate, guarded by military police, he presented his ID and formally vouched for his guests, who were made to sign a visitor's book and given passes. Then they were on a road skirting the airfield and Rendle was again gazing nostalgically at the helicopters as they talked.

'I'm really sorry about not taking you to the mess,' Jumper repeated, 'but I'll make it up to you. Dinner and a disco on me, is that all right? Or what passes for a disco in Pretoria anyway.'

Judith was secretly amused at her role as Rendle's girlfriend, and at the rather juvenile idea of going on a double date with his old air force pal and his girl. It would seem far more natural, he had explained, than for him to turn up on his own and pump the information he needed out of Jumper Cross. Jumper was a decent guy, she gathered, who shared Rendle's dislike of the gung-ho, super-patriotic types in the squadron and had privately sympathized with him over the stand he had taken in Angola. If they had gone to the mess, they would probably have been thrown out.

At the single quarters, which resembled a smart modern block of flats, they went straight up to Jumper's room and sat drinking beer on the balcony. The building overlooked the airfield from a distance, and Judith could sense Rendle mentally storing everything he observed, comparing the layout of the station and the disposition of its units with what he remembered.

'So you're still driving the Pumas, Jumper?'

'Yeah, *driving* is right. Excursion trips, tactical exercises, that sort of thing. We've converted to this new model, you know, the XTP, with a computer-controlled gun, mapping and surveillance radar. And you? Still cruising the townships? It's a bloody shame, Frank. What the hell is this country coming to?'

Rendle steered the talk back to helicopters, and Jumper needed little encouragement. Flying was his main passion. Although he apologized to Judith once in a while and tried to include her in more general conversation, within a minute or two he was always back to shop-talk. She sensed that he found some relief in conversing with Rendle, to whom he could confide his complaints and misgivings about the super-patriots. This made it easier to coax other things out of him in an almost incidental way: information about the flying routines of the squadron, its operational readiness, its strengths and weaknesses. Jumper seemed quite unaware that he was being indiscreet. When darkness had begun to fall over the airfield and the perimeter lights suddenly came on, he leaped to his feet.

'Jesus! My girl will be waiting. She'll be mad at me as it is when I have to tell her about next weekend.'

'What about it?' Rendle asked casually.

'The long weekend, you know? We were going to take off early on Friday and head for one of those resorts in the Drakensberg, but now I've been told I'm on duty. The Day of the

305

Covenant: big military parade in Pretoria, big gathering of the faithful at the Voortrekker Monument, aerial flypasts and all that stuff. It's just a fairground occasion, but they want all hands on deck and all our hardware up in the sky. You haven't heard about it?'

'No,' said Rendle numbly.

'Oh, well, it's strictly an occasion for Boer drum-banging as far as I'm concerned. Reliving the Battle of Blood River and impressing our black citizens with how tough we are. I'd be surprised if your crowd weren't involved, Frank – unless they need you to keep down any riots, of course.'

Rendle gave a hollow laugh. 'I'm only a corporal now, Jumper. Nobody tells me these things.'

Colonel Prinsloo was dozing uncomfortably behind the desk of his makeshift office in the Securitas Building when the telephone rang late that night. A bleary glance at his watch told him the time was ten to eleven.

The caller was Major Booysen. There was no triumph in his voice as he said what he had to, barely even a sense of relief. 'You'd better come upstairs,' he concluded.

In the interrogation room Prinsloo found Bobbejaan as he'd been before, naked and strapped to the wall with his head sagging on his chest. There was still anger in his eyes but now it seemed directed inwards, the irises like opaque brown pebbles as his gaze flicked dully around the room.

'What made him talk?'

'Nothing in particular,' Booysen said. 'It sometimes happens that way. He just suddenly decided he'd had enough. Actually, I thought he still had some fight in him.'

Prinsloo as yet had not heard one word from the prisoner, had heard nothing but that animal roar of pain, and there seemed little point now in speaking to him directly. He said to Booysen: 'So he gave the messsage to Ibrahim Khan.'

'That two-faced *koelie* lawyer, yes. But it was meant for Kumalo's daughter. He says he doesn't know what was in the message, and I'm inclined to believe that. There was no reaon for him to know. Phineas Molefe merely paid him for his

306

services, and he used the Dexedrine tablets to buy himself some nice tender arsehole.' Booysen turned to Bobbejaan. 'The boys are not going to think you're so pretty any longer, hey?'

Nobody laughed. All of them felt tainted in some way by this experience. Prinsloo glanced at Bobbejaan again, hanging in his leather harness, and at the wall behind him speckled with blood and the floor awash with water.

'Get him out. Lock him in solitary while I decide what to do with him. And have this place cleaned up.'

While Captain Kriek went to organize this, Prinsloo spoke to the others. 'So at last we know where we stand. There was a leak, and we know where it went to. We don't know what the message said, but presumably little Phineas found out enough to justify the risk of sending it out. It reached Ibrahim Khan, and we must assume it was passed on to Nandi Kumalo. Next question: how much further did it get?'

'Next step: pick them both up and ask them,' said Booysen.

'Don't be dumb,' Prinsloo said irritably. 'You might as well send a telegram to the Congress telling them what we know.'

Kriek came back, together with two armed and uniformed police constables, one of them carrying a clean pair of shorts and a prison blouse for Bobbejaan. Still fascinated by this implacable brute, the security men watched as his ankles were unstrapped from the wall and his legs eased into the shorts. The blouse was more of a problem. The policemen pulled it over his head, but to get his arms into the sleeves they had to unshackle each wrist in turn. While they wrestled with his heavy limbs Prinsloo went on musing, half to himself, 'It's time to look at this from a different angle. Khan would not take any risks, and Nandi Kumalo has always kept her nose clean, but I don't doubt that if she thought her father was in danger she would do something about it. We must assume she has been in contact with the Congress, and ask ourselves how they would act on this information. Nandi is worth watching, but she's only the next link in the chain. They would listen to her, but they would probably not let her know their intentions.'

Willemse seemed to be the only one paying attention to this. He said: 'What do you think they might do? Expose it?'

'They have had plenty of time to do that before now. Man, I only know what my bones are telling me, and that is that they're not going to sit idly by—'

At the edge of his eye Prinsloo caught a sudden sharp movement, a violent thrashing of limbs. He turned, incredulous, to see one of the two uniformed policemen locked in a struggle with Bobbejaan.

The prisoner's right wrist was still fastened by handcuffs to one of the ring-bolts on the wall. Somehow he had managed to get his left arm around the throat of the constable and was holding him in a head lock, crushing him close to his great chest while the captive flailed and punched and gave out half-strangled groans. Before anyone else could move, Bobbejaan swung himself in a wide pivoting movement to the right, using the bolt as a fulcrum. He lifted the man clean off his feet and rammed his head with sickening force against the wall.

He dropped the victim at his feet, senseless if not dead, and stood glaring wildly at the rest of them like an animal defending its prey, challenging them to approach. For a moment none of them did, mesmerized by this terrifying display of strength, beginning to understand that Bobbejaan had gone quite berserk. Then the other uniformed man was cursing and reaching for his revolver and Prinsloo was stepping forward to restrain him. In those seconds of confusion Bobbejaan turned to face the wall, bracing himself against it with knees and forearms, gripping with both huge hands the iron ring that held him, and pulling.

The bolt came straight out of the wall with a screech and a shower of cement dust. Bobbejaan was free. He staggered back a pace, then righted himself and turned, and flung himself at the white men with a roar.

The nearest was the second uniformed constable, backing away with a look of wild panic on his face and again trying to drag out his gun. Bobbejaan swung at him with the heavy ring still fastened to his wrist, and it cracked him on the jaw and flung him into a corner. The rest of them were already scrambling for the door.

Against any other threat they might have put up some united

resistance; but there was no coherence in their thought, only a separate awareness in each of them that an enraged beast had broken loose among them, and there was something primeval in their fear. In the confinement of the windowless room there was no space to dodge, no means of defence. They ran in a bunch to the door, and Bobbejaan went after them.

He caught up first with Captain Kriek. He seized his tormentor from behind, under the armpits, and lifted him kicking and wriggling from the floor, propelling him into the other three and jamming them against the door. His hands went around Kriek's throat as he held him aloft, thick fingers contracting like a band of steel around his neck, compressing the muscles and the windpipe, crushing the larynx and the cervical vertebrae. Bobbejaan's demented strength was superhuman. Kriek's spine went into a rigid arc, and the next moment he was limp and sagging in the black man's grasp. Bobbejaan tossed his body aside and went for Booysen.

The major ducked and managed to slither away from the door. Bobbejaan darted after him and trapped him in a corner of the room. Booysen was a tougher proposition than Kriek, and he lashed out in terror with his feet and his fists. The blows bounced harmlessly off the prisoner, who seized Booysen around the neck with one hand, pinning him like a struggling insect against the wall and choking him until his tongue protruded and his mad horrified eyes seemed about to pop out. With the other hand, Bobbejaan began to hit him with the iron ring.

The exit was clear now, and Willemse yanked the door open and ran out, yelling for help. Prinsloo, about to follow, was halted by a sudden sense of his own responsibility for this horror. He had a nightmarish vision of Bobbejaan running amok through the entire building, even out into the streets. He turned back, scuttling for the far side of the room and crouching beside the policeman who had tried to draw his gun. As he scrabbled at the man's holster he heard Bobbejaan bringing the ring-bolt down with repeated crunching blows on the top of Booysen's head.

Prinsloo got a grip on the butt of the .38 and dragged it free.

309

Across the room, the black man released his hold on Booysen, who slid with his skull crushed to the floor. Bobbejaan turned, his face distorted by rage and bloodlust, in time to see the gun being levelled at him. With another wild bellow, he charged.

The revolver was attached by a lanyard to the policeman's shoulder-strap, and Prinsloo couldn't move from where he was crouched. He remembered just in time to slip off the safety catch before firing, point-blank, at the black man bearing down on him.

The shot crashed and roared in the soundproofed room. Prinsloo heard it thwack home as he fired again. The first bullet had taken Bobbejaan in the midriff, the second hit him in the chest, but still he came on, lurching, looming over Prinsloo with his arms raised, his broken teeth bared in a kind of hideous deathly grin. Prinsloo got in one more shot as Bobbejaan fell on him, and saw it blow out the underside of his jaw in a spray of blood and bone. Prinsloo collapsed under his weight, and still there was some blind convulsive strength in Bobbejaan that sent his hands groping for the colonel's throat, contracting and squeezing. Prinsloo let go of the gun, seized the wrists and tried to tear them away. Then, slowly, he felt the grip of the hands slacken, the strength ebbing from Bobbejaan as palpably as air from a balloon until, suddenly, he gave a gurgling sigh and his shattered head sank on to Prinsloo's chest.

Somebody heaved the body off him, somebody else helped him to his feet. The room rocked and quaked about him, filled with excited voices and smoke and the stink of cordite. Prinsloo turned aside and vomited, adding his own measure to the mess of blood and bodies that littered the floor. He looked up through bloodshot eyes and saw cops, armed to the teeth, milling about the room. Willemse was standing beside him, and their eyes met in a long moment of shocked understanding.

'Was anything worth this?' Willemse demanded. 'Is anything in the whole world worth it?'

Jumper Cross had warned them that the disco would be pretty dire. Actually it wasn't all that bad, Judith considered. It was noisy and crowded, it had good music and lighting, and all it lacked was a genuine sense of spontaneity. Seated at their corner table, the four of them shared a certain condescending amusement at the young Afrikaners who bopped self-consciously on the dance floor, as though caught between a yearning for fun and a fear of its consequences.

In other respects it had been a passable evening. It might have been more enjoyable if she and Rendle hadn't been there under false pretences. Jumper's girlfriend, who was a nurse at the army hospital, turned out to be good company and she and Judith had talked a lot, leaving Rendle to continue quietly prising information out of his friend. They had danced a bit, and had a couple of drinks, and now at a quarter to twelve were getting ready to leave.

Jumper's girl had just gone to powder her nose when Rendle leaned across to him and said: 'You know, I would love to see how one of those new machines handles. The modified Pumas you're flying now? How about taking me up in one?'

'Not much chance, Frank. No tourists allowed.'

'I wasn't thinking of doing it officially, just hitching a ride. Next Friday, say, during this flying-circus act you were telling me about. It wouldn't be like going on a real operation. Nobody would need to know.'

'Hell, Frank, I'd be grounded if I got caught. I'd be risking a serious charge. You know the rules.'

'Well enough to know when they can be broken. I've already worked out how it can be done. It's just a bit of a lark, Jumper, but it would mean a lot to me.'

'Well, I don't know . . .' Judith could see that Jumper was in a quandary. He'd enjoyed his reunion with Rendle, he'd even talked about their meeting again next weekend, and now he didn't want to disappoint him. 'Others would have to see you. The ground crew, my own gunner—'

'I'd be logged in as extra crew, properly kitted out and everything. I know the drill, after all.'

'I suppose it might work,' Jumper conceded reluctantly. 'Just as long as none of my true-blue brother officers gets to hear about it. Uh-oh, here come some of them now.'

Two men in civilian clothes had approached their table.

311

They were both in their mid-twenties and they had a similar look about them: short fair hair and neat moustaches. They greeted Jumper noisily in Afrikaans, and Judith realized they were both rather drunk.

Jumper muttered an uncomfortable reply. The two pilots caught something odd in his manner and turned to look at his guests. Judith saw one of them stiffen in recognition at the sight of Rendle.

'*Magtig, kyk wie is die!* Rendle, isn't it?' He broke into English, shouting over the music. 'Aren't you Rendle? The bloke who got DD'd in Angola? Chickened out of a mission and lost your pips and wings?'

Rendle said nothing. He sat and watched the man with a flat empty look in his eyes. This annoyed the pilot, who taunted him further.

'Chickenshit Rendle, we called you after that. You've got a bit of cheek showing your face in this town, you know.'

'Leave it out,' Jumper said.

'Hey, I remember him now,' said the other man. 'Not really suitable company for you, Jumper, is he? I think you should tell him to leave.'

'Who I drink with is my business,' Jumper said angrily. 'Just piss off and leave us, will you?'

'It's all right.' Rendle had finally spoken. He stood up calmly and took Judith's arm. 'We were leaving anyway.'

'That's good, Chickenshit.'

The first man smiled triumphantly, but it seemed this victory had been too easy for him. He picked up Rendle's half-full glass and tossed beer in his face.

Judith held her breath. Rendle let go of her arm, but only to reach into his pocket for a handkerchief, with which he mopped his brow and his eyes. There was no expression whatever on his face. The music had stopped for a moment, and she was aware of a pocket of complete silence around them. The pilot was still wearing a mocking grin when Rendle kicked him hard on the shin.

It was a perfectly judged kick, and very hard. It caught the man just under the kneecap and his leg collapsed under him.

312

He gave a brief scream of pain. Beside him his friend had already moved, grabbing a beer bottle off the table and smashing it against the edge. Rendle spun on his heel, caught his wrist and twisted it sharply, sending the jagged neck of the bottle flying out of his grasp. Rendle let go of the wrist, seized him by the scruff of the neck with one hand and slammed the heel of the other under his jaw. The man staggered backwards, crashed into a table and sat down in a heap.

It was all over in five seconds. The first man was down on one knee, nursing the other with both hands, immobilized by pain and staring up in disbelief at Rendle. The other sat slumped against the wall beside an overturned table, glassy-eyed and barely conscious.

People had risen from their chairs and scattered in a circle around the scene. Now some moved forward to help the victims while the rest went on staring at Rendle. The thumping rhythm of disco music started up again, seeming to diminish the incident and restore a kind of normality. Judith was still standing open-mouthed when Rendle seized her arm and marched her to the door.

'I'll be in touch,' he called back to Jumper.

27

Marriner drove back to Johannesburg on Monday morning. His first stop was at an isolated callbox in the northern suburbs, where he put through a call on the scrambler to Zurich. Joshua Rosenblatt had been in regular contact with Harry Makibani in Lusaka over the weekend, and he reported that the plans for their reception in Mozambique were well in hand.

Rosenblatt told him another thing. The much-proclaimed efficiency of the Handelsbank Bauer had broken down over one small detail. The letter confirming the transfer of funds into Frank Rendle's account had not been sent by courier after all, but had been accidentally airmailed to Marriner care of the Standard Bank.

God damn it, he thought. It was just the kind of trivial mishap that would cost him more time that he couldn't afford and more worry that he could do without. The letter was unimportant in itself, since Rendle was willing to take his word for it that the money was there. What bothered him about the letter was that it was dangerous. He unhooked the scrambler, dialled the number of the Standard Bank and told Jepson what had happened. Jepson said nothing had yet arrived, but of course he would continue to keep an eye out. 'Surely there's somewhere I can phone you, old boy?' he said.

'No. I don't have a telephone now. I'll ring you again.'

Resuming his journey into the city, he had plenty of other things to mull over. The arrangements for the three phases of the job were all, theoretically at least, now in place, but there were imponderables attached to each of them. If Rendle's squad and their Saracen were pulled off their township duty on Friday and sent to take part in the parade in Pretoria, it would be that much more difficult for them to disappear. Not impossible, they had assured him; it was just that their absence was likely to be noticed more quickly, making Phase One somewhat more hazardous than it already promised to be. Phase Two, in the hands of Rendle himself, he was less concerned about. Rendle would not promise what he could not deliver, and what he had undertaken to deliver was an Aerospatiale SA330 Puma helicopter gunship, capable of carrying as many as fifteen people and flying more than three hundred miles on one tank of fuel at a maximum speed of one hundred and sixty-eight miles an hour. That should get them to the border of Swaziland in approximately seventy minutes and into Mozambique thirty minutes later, when Phase Three would begin. Pursuit was inevitable; speed and surprise were the only advantages they would have, and if these were thrown away they were lost.

This left open the question of creating a diversion, something that would be vital to the success of Phase One. It would have to be a large and serious diversion, something to give scope to the talents of Comrade Duma.

When he reached the city centre the first thing he did was go to the car-hire firm in Main Street and pay a third week's rental for the Ford Orion. It was exactly a fortnight since he had arrived, and he had the strange sensation of having been here for ever, of having no past that did not involve this project. He got back into the car and drove westwards for his meeting with Duma.

It was six hundred miles from the South African border at Beitbridge to the frontier between Zimbabwe and Zambia, and normally the young Congress courier reckoned to cover it in twelve hours. The rainy season had now well and truly set in, however, forcing him to reduce his speed as he drove through successive downpours and adding another hour to the journey. As usual, he spent the night in a guesthouse on the Zimbabwe side, setting off early the next morning on the final leg of eighty miles to Lusaka.

He reached the Congress headquarters at the appointed time of ten o'clock. The offices occupied a rambling collection of single-storey buildings in an alley off Cairo Road, with a protective presence of Zambian policemen at either end, and he had to be frisked for weapons or explosives before he was allowed in.

Almost always it was Harry Makibani who received him here, so he was surprised this morning to be met by a leaner and dourer man who did not bother to introduce himself but whom he knew as Lawrence Gumbi, the head of the Congress military wing. There was the menace of a bandit chieftain about Gumbi; he had the reputation of instilling fear as well as respect in the young guerrillas he trained and commanded, and the courier was nervous of him. Gumbi showed his face in here even less often than the other members of the executive, preferring the safety of hideouts in the bush.

Usually Harry would spare the time for a chat, and possibly dig a couple of beers out of the fridge, when the courier arrived. It was a way of thanking him for his modest efforts on behalf of the Congress. Gumbi had no such flair for diplomacy, however. He merely took the parcel of dispatches and thanked the courier perfunctorily before dismissing him.

Gumbi walked from the outer office to an empty one at the back, where he sat down, unsealed the package and began to

315

examine the two or three dozen letters it contained. Many were addressed to him: they contained routine reports from agents and military cadres in the townships. One envelope had Harry Makibani's name on it, however, and was undoubtedly from his young protégé Comrade Duma. Without hesitation Gumbi tore the envelope open. Harry had been playing games with the rest of the executive for far too long now. He was always receiving these private messages from Duma and he was forever on the phone to Rosenblatt, who himself should have been back from Zurich at least a week ago. Between them they were up to something, and Gumbi had no doubt that it concerned the conflicting rumours over Lincoln Kumalo. It was high time Harry was put back in his place.

'You're telling me you've known this since Saturday?'

'What could I do about it? I didn't know where the hell you were.'

'If I'd left the hotel a few hours later . . . if I'd gone back there today, they'd have pulled me in! How did they know, Duma?'

The young man shrugged. Studied indifference was his pose this morning, though he hadn't been able to disguise his relief when Marriner had turned up for their meeting at the slime dump. Probably he was also getting some satisfaction out of the white man's dismay. 'Maybe you have done something careless, Major. How can I tell? I haven't seen you for the past week. I told you from the start that you were making a mistake, thinking you could do this on your own. I told Harry Makibani the same. So now you must consider yourself a wanted man. Where does that leave the rest of us?'

'But wanted for what?' Marriner stared out over the wilderness of the old mine workings. There was a tight little knot of fear in his stomach, but his thinking seemed all the sharper for it. 'To judge by the questions they asked, they didn't know much about me except my name. I'm bloody sure I've done nothing since I arrived here to attract their attention, and that leaves only one other possibility. There's got to be a leak from inside your organization. Who have you been talking to?'

'Nobody. Well, Nandi Kumalo had to be told, but I swear

316

that she's the last person on earth who would have said any-thing. She knows her father's life depends on you.' Duma paused. 'If you'd been around, I could have told you something else. I heard from Cape Town yesterday that a few days after Phineas Molefe died the Security Police took away everyone in his cell block for questioning.'

'So they're still chasing the source of that message. That's even more of an indication that there's a limit to what they know.' Marriner wondered whether he was clutching at straws, but he turned to face the black man resolutely. 'If the leak didn't happen at this end, it must have come from outside the country. Obviously they have found out something to interest them in me, but that doesn't necessarily mean they've connected me with Kumalo. As long as I can stay out of sight, there's a chance that the damage can still be contained. Harry and Rosenblatt will have to do their best to trace the source of whatever has got out. In the meantime we've got to carry on as though this hadn't happened. Sweat it out for four more days. I'm ready to tell you more now, Duma. I'm ready to tell you how you can help.'

The young man was looking at him strangely. 'You mean that, Major?'

'Of course I mean it,' he said, puzzled. 'Isn't that what you wanted?'

'It's not that. I was half-expecting you to say you were pulling out. Running away.'

Marriner gave a grim little laugh. 'There doesn't seem any-where for me to run now, does there?'

An hour later, driving back to the city, he wondered why the thought of running hadn't occurred to him. It was what good sense would normally have suggested he ought to be doing. In spite of his Falklands decoration he considered himself neither a brave nor a cowardly man, merely one with an instinct for weighing up risks. What that instinct was telling him now was that the scales had tipped badly against him, and yet it was the threat to the project rather than a sense of personal danger that seemed oddly uppermost in his mind. Maybe it was the fact that too many people had come to depend on him, or maybe he had simply invested so much of himself in the thing that the idea of abandoning it was intolerable. At any rate, as he headed for the address Judith had given him he was aware of a comforting sense of anonymity in the vast city that surrounded him. One serious possibility of exposure remained: it was still vital that he get himself admitted as a patient to the Woodvale Clinic. That, he now realized, would mean backing his own hunch that all they knew about him was his name. Having officially disappeared, as it were, the logical next step was to become somebody else.

Besides being in charge of the Substance Abuse Unit at Woodvale, Dr Clooney was also in private practice as a consultant psychiatrist. In this capacity he was in attendance at his rooms in Jenner Chambers, in Jeppe Street, three mornings a week.

Twenty years of specializing in the treatment of alcoholics had given Dr Clooney much insight into their patterns of behaviour. While he was always sympathetic to their problems he had learned to be wary of their motives. Sometimes they did volunteer themselves for treatment, but more often in the wake of trouble than in anticipation of it. Almost always there was a fretful spouse or a concerned employer in the background. None of these circumstances seemed to apply to this Mr Davis, who had walked in on him without an appointment and seemed to know exactly what he was about. Perhaps it was this mechanical approach, this lack of selfconsciousness, that made Clooney wonder about him. Still, one had to give patients the benefit of the doubt. One should be grateful for those who were responsible and honest with themselves. Superficially Mr Davis seemed extremely fit and healthy, clear of eye and steady of hand. He had not been referred to the psychiatrist by his GP, which would have been the normal practice, for the simple reason that he didn't have one. He had come as a contract engineer to South Africa a couple of years ago and had never needed to consult a doctor in that time.

'But you say you had treatment in England? Where was that?'

Mr Davis rattled off the names of several hospitals in and around London.

'And it's five years since you had a drink?'

'Until three days ago. There was no particular reason: it just seemed more important to have a drink than not to have one. Once I started I could feel the old pattern reasserting itself: it became very difficult to stop.'

'Well, those five years should be a great encouragement to you. Time is the true healer, and you obviously have a good understanding of your problem. I'm going to start by giving you a prescription for Antabuse tablets—'

'Oh, I've always got a supply of those. The problem is persuading myself to take them. Look, I've been through all this before, Doctor, and I know the score. I'm frightened of going on a prolonged bout, and what I need is a week or two of medical supervision. I understand you're connected with the Woodvale Clinic.'

'It would certainly do you no harm to go in there.' Dr Clooney raised an eyebrow. 'You do have some idea of their fees, though?'

'I think so.'

'Well, I do know there are beds available. I can arrange for you to be admitted tomorrow, if that's what you really want. Who recommended you to me, by the way?'

Mr Davis smiled for the first time. 'I think it was someone I met in a bar,' he said.

Twenty minutes later Marriner was on his way back to Reitvlei Farm, as satisfied as he could afford to be with his morning's work. He was due to check into the clinic tomorrow, where a private room would await him and he would submit to a prescribed routine of rest, abstention and psychotherapy. After observing his father's long, losing battle against alcoholism, it had been a distasteful but hardly a difficult task to invent a similar history for himself. The illness defied any true clinical definition, and in the case of someone who claimed not to have been drinking for five years there would be no physical symptoms. Diagnosis depended largely on the patient's own account of his drinking habits – and since there was no way of checking on those there seemed no reason why he should not be accepted for what he claimed to be: Mr John Davis, a reformed addict worried that he was about to suffer a relapse.

319

He also knew from Judith that the Woodvale regime was a liberal one which encouraged patients to take responsibility for themselves. He would not be confined to bed and would be free, within certain limits, to come and go as he pleased.

On the way he stopped at a hardware store and bought a tubular-steel woodsaw with a couple of spare blades, a claw hammer and two large bags of six-inch nails. When he reached the farmhouse he ate a hasty lunch and then went out with these new tools to the stack of old lumber that Meiring had left behind.

Marriner had examined it the day before. It consisted of a hundred or so lengths of rough deal planking, two inches by four in section, obviously intended for some reconstruction job that Meiring had never got round to. It had rested on a base of concrete blocks which had gradually subsided into the spongy earth, so that the timber had been rotting from the bottom up for a number of years. There were enough sound planks near the top to suit Marriner's purpose, however, and he hauled a dozen of them off the stack. Using a pair of oil drums for support, he sawed them into three-foot lengths. He took one of these and began driving nails diagonally through it. Twenty-four nails, placed in pairs at opposing angles and from alternate sides, turned the plank into a spikeboard that would be lethal to any moving vehicle. Thrown on to a road, it would always land with its spikes up and would rip open the tyres of a speeding car in an instant.

Satisfied with his prototype, he started on another one.

There was little traffic on the long, monotonous road through the sodden forest and scrub east of Lusaka, and soon it became obvious to Harry Makibani that the beaten-up Ford Cortina was following him. Once he pulled off the road to let it pass, but it simply stopped a few yards behind him and waited. Through the steamed-up rear window of his Toyota he could see that the car contained four young black men. He was tempted to get out and give them a tongue-lashing, but it was raining hard again now and it seemed hardly worth getting himself soaked in order to make his point. He knew who they were, or at least who had sent them, and he knew why. Gumbi was trying to scare him. Gumbi had been angry when he'd confronted him with Duma's letter this morning, and Harry had been angry right back. Attack was always the best form of defence against someone like him.

It was another thirty miles to the camp, and dusk was falling by the time he reached the turn-off, an unpaved and unmarked road that twisted through the bush to the south. The Cortina followed him down it. Several times his wheels spun and the Toyota slid sideways on patches of mud. At the end of the track he came to a fence and a gate of barbed wire, where two sentries in gleaming ponchos and armed with Kalashnikovs took a good look at him before waving him through. They let the Cortina in as well, locking the gate behind them before scuttling for the shelter of a hut beside it.

It was Gumbi who had called the emergency meeting of the executive, and Gumbi who had chosen his own ground for its venue. Until five years ago the camp had been a mission school and its inoffensive look had been preserved as far as possible, particularly from the air. It was a collection of long one-storey buildings, some of brick and iron but mostly of mud and thatch, scattered around a clearing and shaded by acacias and fever trees. The parade-ground was still carefully marked out as a soccer pitch, for which it was also used. The buildings, too, served functions similar to their original ones, as classrooms, offices and dormitories. The essential difference was that instead of accommodating three hundred secondary-school students, they now housed nearly five hundred guerrilla recruits of the People's Congress.

They were at their evening meal when Harry arrived, gathered at the long tables under a shelter beside the cookhouse, their conversation making a steady dull roar over the clashing of cutlery. The rest of the camp was correspondingly quiet, apart from the hissing of rain. He parked his car beside the main office and, ignoring the Cortina which pulled up behind him, climbed the steps on to the porch.

This was one of the brick bungalows, with a row of interlinking offices in which the camp's administrative staff worked. At

321

the far end was a conference room, and it was here that he found Gumbi, Godfrey Pahlani and J. K. Govender awaiting him.

Harry's arrival was punctual, but it was clear that the others had arranged to get here before him. From the way the single vacant chair was placed, across the table from the others, it was equally clear that this was to be more in the nature of an inquisition than a meeting. Harry was ready for it.

'Good evening,' he said.

Only Pahlani acknowledged the greeting, with a slight nod. The others watched him as he pulled the empty chair up to the table, sat on it and leaned forward on his elbows, deliberately diminishing the formality they were trying to create.

'Anybody got a beer?' he asked.

'This isn't a party,' Pahlani said.

'Then I'll have to make do with this.' Harry pulled a hip flask from the pocket of his safari suit, uncapped it and took a mouthful of whisky. He sighed and put the flask down on the table. He sat back, crossing his arms over his chest, and smiled at them expectantly.

The rain pounded steadily on the iron roof. Pahlani had a heap of papers in front of him, with the letter that Gumbi had intercepted that morning on top of them. He slapped it with the back of his hand and said: 'We want to know what the hell has been going on, Harry.'

'I think you know almost as much as I do now. We're getting Lincoln out. By this time on Friday we should all be reunited. Doesn't that please any of you? You don't look very pleased.'

'Just try not to be facetious, will you? Why was this kept from us?'

'I was intending to tell you tomorrow. You would have had to know by then anyway, since the formal request for help from the Mozambique government must come from the full executive. Everything else is already in place. All the preparatory work is done. Now you've gone and spoiled the surprise,' Harry said to Gumbi. 'Shows what happens when you go opening other people's mail.'

'Harry, I don't think you realize the seriousness of your position,' Pahlani said sternly. 'You've committed a breach of

Congress discipline. You've undertaken this adventure, you and Rosenblatt and Mohaila, without any authorization from the executive. You've committed a million pounds of our money to it, again without any authority. You expect us just to accept this? Congratulate you on it, or what?'

'Frankly, Godfrey, I'm not terribly fussed what you think of it. The bottom line is that Lincoln is coming back to us, and if it had been left to you it wouldn't be happening.'

'You talk as though it were already accomplished. It could still go wrong.'

'Nothing will stop Marriner going ahead now. Nothing except treachery, that is. I was just coming to that.'

Harry picked up his flask again and took a slow, deliberate drink from it. He put it down and looked at them, no longer smiling. 'We had another reason, Joshua and I, for keeping this to ourselves. After the air raid on the motel, we weren't sure who else we could trust. There had to be an informer somewhere in the movement. And, as you can see from what Comrade Duma has to say, there still is one.' He gestured at the letter. 'Someone has fingered our friend Major Marriner. It can't have been anyone here in Zambia, because none of you knew about him until today. Keeping you in the dark has therefore been doubly useful. You're all in the clear, my friends.'

'It's very kind of you to say so, I'm sure,' said Pahlani, 'but—'

'The leak can only have come from London. I have asked Mohaila to investigate it, to see how bad the damage is. I don't believe it can be too serious, because even Mohaila knows none of the details. As long as Marriner keeps his head down—'

'Harry, all this is beside the point,' snapped J. K. Govender. 'Who are you to set yourself up as a one-man investigating committee? Who are you to make free with the Congress funds in this way?'

'I venture to point out, J.K., that a majority of the finance committee voted in favour of allocating funds to this project.'

'By that you mean a clique led by yourself, Harry. You don't make Congress policy. We do. We have a constitution, a book of rules, and we abide by them. It's called collective responsibility.'

'This is hardly an issue of procedure, is it? There's only one question to answer, and that is: do you want Lincoln Kumalo back or don't you?'

He met their eyes, each in turn, challenging them. Gumbi held his gaze, while Pahlani and Govender glanced uneasily at each other. He had them cornered with this argument, he knew, but he didn't care for Gumbi's ominous silence.

'Of course we are not saying no,' Pahlani muttered. 'What we do not like is having a gun held to our heads. We're not going to put up with that, Harry. We've decided that you are going to face a disciplinary tribunal. It will be convened next week, once this business is over for better or worse. In the meantime we are placing you under arrest.'

Harry could not believe his ears. He felt his heartbeat quicken, but his mind refused to comprehend. His only response was to laugh – not his usual big-bellied chuckle but an incongruous nervous titter. 'Arrest me?' he said when he had found his real voice. 'What sort of joke is this, Godfrey? You can't arrest me.'

'I'm afraid we can, Harry. You're going to have to stay here, in the camp, under guard. Heaven knows where you might get to otherwise.'

He heard the door open and glanced around. As if at some secret signal, four men came lumbering into the room. He recognized the young men from the Cortina, now changed into the combat fatigues of the camp, and saw that two of them were carrying Russian machine-pistols. They stood in a row against the rear wall, awaiting orders. He had regained some of his composure, however, and he picked up his hip flask and drank from it again, defiantly.

'Lincoln won't put up with this,' he said. 'Lincoln will laugh at you.'

'That all depends on whether Lincoln makes it, doesn't it?'

It was still Pahlani who spoke, but somehow Harry recognized Gumbi's thoughts behind the words. He stared hard at Gumbi, as though to provoke a reaction out of him.

'I think I see what's behind this now. You don't want Lincoln back, do you? You're scared of him, even if you won't admit it to yourselves. You're scared of having him take over. You're jealous enough to actually sabotage this operation, or at least to allow it to fail, just as long as none of you has to take the blame.'

Harry was still holding his hip flask close to his mouth. Suddenly Lawrence Gumbi stood up, leaned across the table and slapped it out of his hand. It clattered into the corner of the room, spilling whisky as it went. Gumbi pressed his fists down on the table, putting his weight on them and bringing his face threateningly close to Harry's.

'Listen to me, Harry. I speak for myself now. I am not scared of Lincoln Kumalo. He will come back, and he will take his place among us as an equal. The question of the leadership can then be democratically decided, not simply imposed on us. I am the one who has built up the forces of our armed struggle, and I intend to remain in charge of them. In that capacity, it is I who will be in control of the third phase of this project. It is I who will receive Kumalo when he crosses the border, not you. That's what all this is about, Harry: not sabotaging the project but keeping it in perspective. It will be a homecoming for Kumalo; we're not letting it turn into a coronation.'

Harry went on staring at him like a rabbit mesmerized by a snake. Then Gumbi broke his trance by standing back and signalling to the young guerrillas. They came forward, two of them seizing Harry by the arms and pulling him to his feet. He mustered his dignity.

'I can only repeat what I said. Lincoln won't stand for this. Lincoln is too big for you, Gumbi. He's too big for any of you. You'll see.'

'Yes, we'll see,' said Gumbi, and he gestured at the men to take Harry away.

28

Colonel Prinsloo seemed to have brought a new kind of anger back with him from Cape Town.

It hadn't helped, of course, that he had turned up early for the meeting, hot and sweaty after driving straight from the airport that Wednesday afternoon, but that was his own tactless fault. What made it worse, somehow, was that he'd been just in time to meet Hoeksma and Van Straaten returning chummily to the Union Buildings from lunch at the Pretoria Club, surprising them like a pair of guilty lovers. It seemed to confirm all his own plebeian prejudices about these two, as well as reinforcing the impression that he was the only one who had real work to do.

In the quietly elegant surroundings of Hoeksma's office, when they got down to exchanging information, the anger went on radiating out of him. Now, after reading the newly opened file Van Straaten had sent for, he stood up and tossed it contemptuously on the desk.

The others waited for him to speak. Hoeksma sat behind the desk, but it was to the intelligence officer that he turned, seated in a leather armchair across the room.

'You're telling me you've been sitting on this for four days?'

'Hardly sitting on it. We took action at once and we've drawn a blank. That's why I'm passing it on to you.'

'Can you tell me why you didn't do that right away, sir?'

'Because I wanted it handled delicately. More delicately than your people seem capable of managing.'

'At least we get results Mr Van Straaten. Who made these enquiries for you? A couple of philosophy graduates with their heads up their arses, to judge by the way they went about it.'

'This was information procured by my service, I should remind you, and we have our sources to protect. You were in

Cape Town anyway. Your hands were full. Your job is to oversee the security aspects of the Induna Project, and there is still nothing to connect this man Marriner to it.'

'Nothing?' Prinsloo gave a derisive snort. 'Haven't you heard of circumstantial evidence? Here you've got a former British Army special operations man with an African background and a strong likelihood that he's been taking money from the People's Congress. He turns up here soon after a leakage of information on this project, and then he mysteriously disappears. You call that nothing?'

'I call it suspicious, but not conclusive,' said Van Straaten. 'There's a danger of letting it distract us too much, of dissipating our resources. Now my men have carried out all the obvious checks: the registers of other hotels, airlines and railway reservations—'

'Yes, yes, I've read the file,' Prinsloo said impatiently. 'It's not just a matter of asking questions, it's who does the asking. It's how they are asked.'

'Ah. But it's your methods I wanted to avoid. A lot of blood was spilt in Cape Town during your interrogations, Prinsloo. How much did it actually achieve?'

'I'll tell you how much. We've established that there was a leakage of information, and we've established that it reached at least as far as Nandi Kumalo . . .'

'That surely is a long day's work from knowing what the Congress intends doing about it. You haven't considered interrogating her?'

'No.'

'You do surprise me.'

Prinsloo gave him a condescending look. If Van Straaten thought he was incapable of subtlety, he had another surprise coming. 'Pulling in Kumalo's daughter is quite a different proposition from questioning a couple of dumb *mugus*, sir. That's not to say we are overlooking her. It will take only one move on her part to establish the link. If these people are planning something, then I want them flushed out, not scared off. That's why I wish I had known earlier about this man Marriner.'

'The connection is still not there. There's nothing to justify turning the country upside down to find him. But if you think your men can do a better job than mine, then go ahead.'

'Gentlemen . . .,' Hoeksma intervened a trifle nervously. 'I think you are both getting slightly sidetracked. We have less than two days to go, and important things still to discuss. I suggest you sort out this difficulty later. Meanwhile, let it be clearly understood that nothing is going to stop this project going ahead.'

To Hoeksma's relief Prinsloo sat down again, and they both gave him their attention. This was to be their final meeting before the events of Friday and he had allowed himself to hope it might pass off without the usual antagonism between these two. At first their latent hostility had seemed no more than a sign of healthy professional rivalry. It had been fuelled, however, by a conflict between their personalities and by a mistrust that led to their keeping things from each other. Instead of listening to their views, Hoeksma found himself too often with the perplexing task of refereeing their squabbles.

'We now have our final timetables,' he said, 'and I would like us to run through them together, compare notes and check for any discrepancies. Tertius, will you begin?'

'Certainly.' It was Van Straaten's office which had supplied the master schedules, neatly bound into thin folders and marked *Geheim/Secret*. Each of them had one in front of him, and no other copies existed. 'We have of course received Dr Rose's timetable for the medical procedures, and have integrated these into our own. We start at six o'clock tomorrow evening, when Kumalo will be first informed that his operation is to go ahead. An hour later he will be transported by helicopter direct from Pollsmoor to Ysterplaat air station. A Merlin jet transport plane fitted as an ambulance will fly him up here to Waterkloof air base. Expected time of arrival: ten p.m. Dr Els will be accompanying him all the way.'

'Are you happy with your end of things so far?' Hoeksma said tactfully to Prinsloo.

'Most of this stage is in the hands of the air force, whose crews have been told only as much as they need to know. There will be armed guards on board the aircraft, of course.'

'For the next stage, he will be transferred to a joint police–military road convey for transfer to the clinic,' Van Straaten continued. 'Slower than a helicopter, but less conspicuous. Time of arrival: eleven p.m.'

'By then our ground security forces will have established themselves at the clinic by arrangement with Dr Rose,' said Prinsloo. 'This will be done under cover of darkness, again so as to attract less attention.'

'What about the other patients?' Hoeksma asked. 'And the staff at the clinic? How much are they going to know?'

'As little as possible. There are few night nurses on duty at that time, and the patients will be confined to their wards until morning. As you know, no new patients are being admitted as from tomorrow, and a whole ward is being cleared to accommodate Kumalo and some of the guards. The existing patients will be discharged in the normal way over the next week or so, so they don't really matter. The whole thing – the official story, at least – will be public knowledge by Friday afternoon anyway.'

'All right. Let's go back to Kumalo's arrival, then. Once he's settled in, Dr Rose goes home for the night. Dr Els is being quartered in the clinic, and you and your men are effectively in control of the place for the next six hours or so, correct?'

'Until Rose and his team arrive to conduct the operation. Six hours is about right.'

'Very well.' Hoeksma leaned back in his chair. He looked almost too boyish for these patrician surroundings of teak-panelled walls and shelves laden with leather-bound books. 'Exactly what happens during those six hours is something that only the three of us and Dr Els will ever know about. It's something we should never discuss again, even among ourselves. It's our chance to manipulate history a little, gentlemen, without the reward of going down in the history books.'

329

Van Straaten gave a thin smile. Prinsloo remained expressionless. Suddenly the intercom on Hoeksma's desk buzzed and his secretary spoke his name.

He snapped down the reply switch, his plump face reddening with annoyance. 'I told you I wasn't to be disturbed!'

'I'm sorry, sir. It's a call for Mr Van Straaten. They say it's urgent.'

Hoeksma gestured resignedly at Van Straaten, who rose from his chair and picked up the telephone. He listened for a minute, giving monosyllabic replies, while the other two waited uneasily, pretending to study the contents of their folders. When Van Straaten finally put down the receiver he gave them both a very odd look. It was the policeman he chose to address.

'You talked about getting results, Prinsloo. Well, I've got a lead to the Handelsbank Bauer. Follow it up yourself, if you really think you're more efficient at that kind of thing. Ah, but you didn't know about that, did you?' he said, seeing with satisfaction the puzzled look on Prinsloo's face. He explained quickly the connection between the Congress and the Zurich bank, and then turned to Hoeksma. 'You remember the man in the Reserve Bank? The one you helped me arrange to keep us posted on foreign-exchange returns? Well, he's just found one from the Handelsbank Bauer. A transfer made on the seventh of this month – when was that, just a week ago? – for fifteen thousand rands, to the Standard Bank in Johannesburg. It's the only one there's been from that source since we alerted him. It's got to mean something.'

'Who was it payable to?' Prinsloo asked.

'They don't get that information, but of course the Standard Bank will know.' Van Straaten reached for the phone again, then remembered something. 'Wednesday. The banks will have closed at one o'clock.'

'Closed to the public, maybe. Never closed to us.' Prinsloo's grin was sardonic – they'd been playing games behind his back again – and he shrugged as if to trivialize the news. 'Fifteen thousand isn't much to get excited about.'

'It's not the amount, man, it's who it might lead us to. Now, are your people going to check this out, or mine?'

'Oh, I don't think I should turn down the opportunity.' Prinsloo was already standing up, and still grinning. 'I like to stick to what I'm good at, Mr Van Straaten.'

It was Judith who had checked Marriner in at the clinic the previous afternoon, and it was she who stood behind the reception desk now, giving him a politely brittle smile. Yvonne was hovering in the background.

'Going out, Mr Davis?'

'Just for a couple of hours. That's all right, isn't it?'

'Of course. We just like it if you let us know. Oh, I think there's a message for you.'

She reached into the rack behind her and handed him an envelope. 'Will you be here for dinner?'

'I'm not sure yet.'

'It doesn't matter. We do like you to make sure of being back by ten o'clock, though. Thank you, Mr Davis.'

He tucked the envelope into his pocket, left the office and headed for the car park, wondering how much of her play-acting was strictly necessary. They could hardly be seen to be on personal terms, of course, but she seemed to have seized the opportunity to create a defensive barrier against him. There was still some resentment in her at the choice he had forced her into; that and sheer fright had got her very uptight indeed over the past few days, and she avoided confiding in him. One thought only reassured him that her nerve wasn't going to crack: like him, she was too far in to back out.

The inside of the Ford Orion was like an oven, and he rolled down all the windows before setting off. The sense of freedom enjoyed by all the patients in the Substance Abuse Unit was scarcely an illusion. He had never stayed at a health farm, but he imagined its atmosphere to be something like this: without rules as such, merely a set of expectations to which everyone seemed quite willing to conform. Apart from receiving a visit from Dr Clooney first thing each morning, and attending a group therapy session before lunch, they could do what they pleased with their time. Some would go home for a few hours if they lived nearby; others found the clinic's atmosphere so restful that they had no wish to leave it. The only thing on which there was gentle insistence was that they be present at ten o'clock at night to be given their various medications before retiring.

All of which suited Marriner just fine. He had spent most of yesterday with Rendle's squad at the top of the slime dump, staking out a model of the clinic with lengths of tape on its flat surface and practising the tactics to be used in the attack. He had also found time to buy some special clothing and equipment. Today he would give them their final briefing, and then all of them would lie low for the next twenty-four hours.

On the quiet road that led south from Woodvale he stopped the car, checked his watch, then took the walkie-talkie from the glove box, switched it on and spoke into it.

'Unit one to two. Receiving?'

'Unit two receiving.' Rendle's voice came loud and sharp, amplified and unscrambled through the base unit that Judith had left switched on in her flat.

'Good. Three, do you hear me?'

'Three here. Got you.' That was Brakpan, also somewhere in the vicinity of the Saracen.

'Unit four?'

'Unit four speaking, *my baas*.' Duma, the cheeky bastard, was holed up somewhere in Soweto, his voice clear enough but distorted by static.

'Don't bugger around, number four. I'll call you again at plus-twelve hours. Two and three, see you in a few minutes.'

'Roger.'

'Roger.'

He snapped off the set. To save the batteries of the walkie-talkies and avoid detection they had arranged to communicate only briefly, and at prearranged and coded times, until Friday morning when they would be permanently patched through to each other. Meanwhile it was

332

reassuring to know the system was working perfectly over a wide area.

He drove on. He joined the Pretoria motorway at the Edenburg junction, then cut off it again a couple of miles north, on to the old and almost disused two-lane road that had once linked the two cities and now served only to connect a number of small farming centres. A few hundred yards along it stood an abandoned petrol station, its custom and its pumps long ago dried up, its tarred forecourt cracked by the sun and infested with weeds. He turned off and drove around to the rear of the building. It was Rendle who had picked this place as the final staging point for the Saracen's crew, and Marriner could see that it was ideally positioned. Invisible from the road, it looked out over the Jukskei valley to the west. Immediately behind the petrol station was a steep and barren slope, but across the river the rise of the land was gentler, leading up to the wooded and secluded terrain south of the Woodvale Clinic.

At the back of the building was a wide opening into what had once been a service bay. The Saracen was backed in there, its great protruding armoured snout making it look like a pig confined to a dog-kennel. Rendle and his squad were sprawled about it in their usual indolent way, but they stood up and gathered around Marriner when he stepped out of the car.

'All OK?'

'OK,' said Rendle. 'But we've got to be quick. We're way out of our usual territory here.'

'I'll only be a few minutes. I like the view from here.'

They turned and stared out over the valley. Here they were some distance south of the farms and smallholdings that faced the clinic across the river, and it was only just visible a mile and a half to the north-west. Its perimeter was blurred by the heat-haze but was still distinctive, a rectangle of pine trees with the cluster of yellow brick buildings at its centre and the smokestack rising like a beacon from among them.

'Have you checked out the best approach?' It was Brakpan to whom Marriner spoke now. Shielding his eyes against the mid-afternoon sun, in a peaked forage-cap and with oversized field-glasses slung around his neck, the Saracen's driver looked like a diminutive Rommel surveying the Western Desert.

'Yeah, Major. There's a shallow spot where the river widens out a couple of hundred metres to the south. We can cross it there, no problem, then head straight uphill. No cover on the eastern side, so we go for the fence on the south.'

'Right.' Marriner turned to the others. 'It's the south fence I'll be concentrating on from the inside, then. Just as soon as I know how the guards are positioned, I'll tell you the best time and place to take them out. That and cutting the fence will have to be done in the dark. I wish we could do the whole thing by night, but since we won't have the chopper until nine o'clock there'd be too much of a time-lag.'

'It's going to look a bit strange, isn't it?' said Nicky Flynn. 'I mean, this monster trundling around the veld in broad daylight? Several hours after it's gone missing?'

'Not necessarily.' There was always one worrier in every squad, and Marriner had long ago detected that the lance-corporal filled the role here. 'There's going to be a heavy security presence at the clinic, and to any ordinary soldier you're going to look like just part of it – at least, for as long as it matters. Don't forget that Duma is going to be making trouble for us just a couple of miles east of here. Vehicles like this are part of the scenery wherever there's trouble – and by then yours will have different markings. You got the right paint?' he said to Rendle.

'Yep. And new army numberplates. Nicked them from an old ambulance that's headed for the scrapyard. Nobody will miss them.'

'Good. Then, let's just run briefly through your schedules again. Starting at six-thirty tomorrow evening, when Blikkies Steyn goes AWOL from the barracks. You're sure that will work out all right?'

'No roll-call until we're formed up to move out,' said the young Afrikaner. 'All they can do then is notify the military police, and by then I'll be hiding out on the farm.'

'Just make certain you get in there without any of those

Pelindaba guards seeing you. And the rest of you are still pulling out of the barracks at two in the morning, is that right?'

Confirmation had come through yesterday that Rendle's squad and their vehicle were among the detachment from the 4th Armoured Infantry Battalion being sent to Pretoria to take part in the ceremonies. This would cost them the freedom they normally enjoyed of roaming about at will, and it was certain that their absence would soon be discovered. On the other hand, providing they could slip out of the convoy *en route*, they would have the advantage of being able to hide up here within a short distance of the clinic.

'We leave at two and we're scheduled to arrive at Voortrek-kerhoogte camp at three-thirty,' said Rendle. 'You know what armies are like: the parade doesn't begin till nine, but they always want you in place hours before they need you. It does mean the wagon will be missing for five whole hours.'

'They'll have a lot on their minds. We'll just have to hope they won't look for you too hard. By then you'll have other things to worry about, Corporal. Around three o'clock you'll pick up Judith's car at the place you've agreed on. Here is her spare set of keys.' He handed Rendle the envelope Judith had given him. 'I gather you've made your own arrangements with her about the gear you'll be needing.'

Rendle gave him a look. 'That's right. It seemed simpler to fix it between us. Now, how about the equipment you promised?'

Marriner went to his car and opened the boot. Beside the twenty spikeboards that had been in there since Monday there were torches, two gas-lamps, two pairs of powerful wire-cutters, several lengths of quarter-inch nylon rope and half a dozen rolls of plastic insulating tape. They carried the lot into the petrol station and dumped them in a corner. In exchange, Rendle produced an airline bag and handed it to Marriner. It contained a Very pistol and six tear-gas grenades from the Saracen's own inventory, as well as four cylindrical smoke grenades that he had managed to draw from the stores on some pretext. Marriner inspected them, then zipped up the bag and put it in the boot. They stood and looked at each other.

'It doesn't seem like much, does it?' Rendle said. 'Not for what you have to do.'

'Let me worry about that. You just deliver that helicopter on time.'

'There's one other thing . . .,' Nicky Flynn said tentatively. 'That letter from the bank in Zurich, confirming that the money is in Frank's name. It still hasn't turned up?'

'No. It hasn't.' Nicky had asked the same question yesterday. He was the only one still bothered about the letter. 'I'll give it one last try tomorrow, but I think you'll just have to take my word that it's there.'

'We'd better go,' said Rendle.

Brakpan had already returned to the Saracen, and now its huge 160-horsepower engine grumbled into life and he eased it out of the service bay. The place needed to be kept secure from thieves and nosy-parkers, and with a liberal application of lubricating oil Rendle had managed to get the rusted roller door working. With some difficulty and a lot of shrieking from the metal they hauled it down. Rendle fastened it with a padlock and handed the key to Nicky Flynn.

'All yours now, baby.'

With an odd anticlimactic feeling, Marriner shook hands with each of the soldiers in turn. He felt as though something in the nature of a speech was called for, but knew there was never anything to say at times like these.

'Good luck,' was all he could manage. 'See you all on Friday.'

'Good luck, Major.'

They climbed into the vehicle, the rear doors were slammed, and with a single wave from Rendle in the turret it disappeared round the corner. Marriner checked his watch again. He would give them a five-minute start before heading for the city and his final rendezvous with Duma.

When he heard his name called over the public address system at the Wanderers cricket ground, Mr Jepson of the

Standard Bank felt disbelief and guilt in equal measure. He disbelieved because he was certain no one knew he was here, yet he was conscience-stricken because somebody obviously did. Now it was as though everyone in the grandstand was watching him, waiting for him to leave his seat, while the Natal team captain rearranged his field and the pause between overs seemed to go on interminably.

Could it be his wife? Or the office? No, surely not them. He'd been certain he would never be missed on a Wednesday afternoon, what with the bank being closed to the public. On the other hand, he surely wasn't the only man here taking an illicit afternoon off work. What with Christmas approaching and the Currie Cup season in full swing . . .

Indecisiveness kept him glued to his seat until the next eight-ball over began, and he sat through it without taking in a thing. Then the announcement was made again and he knew he could not pretend to ignore it: 'Will Mr Jepson of the Standard Bank report urgently to the information office behind the main stand?'

He stood up and threaded his way along the row of seats, his apprehension growing. At the top of the aisle he pulled up his tie and put on his jacket, feeling he would need as much dignity as he could summon up. He cast a wistful glance back at the oval of green, the white figures with their lengthened shadows scattered around it, and the scoreboard. Transvaal were putting up a dismal performance against Natal, but with a new ball the last half-hour of play had promised to be exciting.

The two men who waited by the information desk seemed instantly out of place. Both were dressed in suits and ties in spite of the sticky heat. They looked like people who had had a tiring day's work and were quite ready to resent anyone who hadn't.

'Mr Jepson?' said the taller one. 'You took your time getting here.' His tone was accusatory, almost startlingly so for a complete stranger. He gave Jepson a momentary view of a plastic card encased in a leather folder. 'I am Colonel

337

Prinsloo of the Security Police. This is Warrant Officer Willemse. We have some questions to ask you. We've had quite some trouble finding you, Mr Jepson.'

'Security Police?' Jepson realized he was gaping at them ignorantly. 'What on earth do you want with me?'

'Nothing to do with you personally, sir,' said the man called Willemse, with rather more grace than his superior. He took Jepson's arm and led him away from the desk. 'Your general manager put us on to you. It's about a sum of money that was transferred from the Handelsbank Bauer in Switzerland just a week ago, and converted to South African currency by your department. We need to know urgently where it went from there.'

'Handelsbank Bauer? I don't. . . .' Jepson was still dazed; his mind was a blank. A roar went up from the stand behind him, and he recollected himself. Dignity was required; dignity and discretion. 'Look here, old boy, there's the question of confidentiality involved. I can't just go telling you our customers' business.'

'We do have certain statutory powers in these matters. Your general manager said to check with him if you were in doubt.'

'He didn't tell you to look for me here, surely?'

'He seemed to think it was the most likely place.'

Jepson shook his head in sorry wonder. 'All right. As far as I know we have only one customer who receives money from that source. His name is Mr Patrick Marriner.'

'Mr Patrick Marriner.' Colonel Prinsloo did not sound surprised, but he gave Willemse a long, significant glance. 'And where can we find this Mr Marriner?'

'Well, that I don't know exactly. He's moved out to the Magaliesberg somewhere, but I don't have an address. On the blower to me every couple of days.' Jepson had relaxed somewhat; he had done his duty by discretion, and now he was openly curious. 'What's he been up to, some currency fiddle?'

'I think we'll go back to your office,' said Prinsloo, steering him away, 'and have a good long talk.'

29

There was just the faintest tinge of grey in the sky when Duma started awake. Not even a cock had yet crowed anywhere in Soweto that Thursday morning, but some instinct of the nocturnal animal had him instantly conscious and sitting up in bed, tense and alert. Nandi, who had been awake for the past hour, stroked his bare shoulder reassuringly.

'It's all right, Duma. Relax.'

'What time is it?'

'Half-past four.'

'I have to go.'

He swung himself out of the bed, groped for his clothes and began to get dressed. Halfway through, he seemed to sense some crassness in his behaviour and he kneeled beside her and kissed her tenderly.

'I'm sorry. That was wonderful, Nandi.'

'After all that time, I hope you weren't disappointed.'

'Of course not. I didn't disappoint you?'

'No.'

'Are you sure?'

'I'm sure.'

She could say that truthfully enough. She was even touched that he should seek such reassurance from her. All African men considered themselves studs, but there was a soft centre to Duma that made her feelings towards him almost motherly. She hadn't actually planned to take him to bed. In the knowledge of what would happen tomorrow there had been a kind of fearful finality to his visit last night; words had no longer seemed an adequate bond between them, and trust and comradeship had turned to desire. Other thoughts and feelings, crystallizing over the past few days, had reinforced her need to make a passionate commitment. She knew now exactly what she had to do, and she was grateful to Duma for understanding this.

339

He stood up and finished dressing, and she left the bed and pulled on a bathrobe.

'Do you want some food? Some tea?'

'No, there isn't time. They'll give me food at the safe house. Tonight I have to leave as soon as it's dark, so I won't see you again until . . . well, until I see you. You promise you'll think about me, Nandi?'

'Yes.'

'And you'll wait for me? Give me a chance to prove that I love you?'

'I think I know you do,' she said, and heard him give a soft chuckle of pleasure in the dark.

In the kitchen he found the big Russian pistol he had left in the dresser drawer and tucked it into his waistband, concealing its butt with the flap of his jacket. For perhaps the twentieth time he said: 'You're certain about what to do tomorrow? Where to go?'

'Yes, Duma.'

They went to the back door together, and he unlocked it and opened it just a fraction. In the dim light of approaching dawn a few sparrows had begun to chirp. The only other sound was the clank of a passing bicycle, one of the first of the great army of workers who began setting off at this hideous hour for the white man's city a dozen miles away. He turned and held her, feeling her warmly pliant body against him, kissing her goodbye with a spasm of longing and regret.

'Take care, Nandi. *Amandla.*'

'*Amandla!*'

She watched him cross the backyard, leave by the rickety gate and lope away. Up the road, where they had almost finished rebuilding the policeman's house that had been burned down in the last riots six months ago, she heard him call a jaunty Zulu greeting to the watchman who dozed in his corrugated iron hut, supposedly guarding the stacks of bricks and timber.

'*Kunjane!*'

'*Longile,*' the man replied drowsily.

340

This time she didn't close the door until Duma had disappeared from view. She was as close to him now as she'd ever been to anyone, she supposed, and she only wished she could disentangle her feelings for him from what she felt about her father. As long as Lincoln Kumalo's fate hung in the balance, nothing else could matter; she had come to see now that for all these years she had only been running away from her own destiny. Last night she had told Duma she loved him; she regretted that she hadn't been able to speak the words with the same conviction as he'd said it to her.

At the next street corner Duma stopped and glanced behind him, almost as though he'd got a sudden suspicion about the half-completed house he had just walked past. It was only a momentary pause, however, and it gave the photographer a chance to snatch four more shots with the motorized Pentax before his subject turned and vanished into the grey township dawn.

The photographer lifted his telephoto lens and swung it back across the gap below the roof to where it had first been pointed, at Nandi Kumalo's house. The man beside him, however, went on staring through his heavy image-intensifying binoculars for half a minute at where Duma had been. Finally he swore softly and pressed the switch that activated the lip microphone attached to his radio headset.

'Hey, that was him.' He spoke in a whisper. The lip mike was designed to pick up sounds from only an inch away. 'Just leaving the house. That was Duma, for sure. Like we said last night. Over.'

There was a pause before a reply from base crackled through the earphones. 'Very good. Did you get pictures? Over.'

'Of course we got pictures. What do you think we've been lying here all night waiting to do?'

'Very good. Thank you. Out.'

The man turned in disbelief to his companion. 'How do you like that?' he said in the same undertone. The photographer could barely see him in the darkness of the half-built

341

house, but he could guess at the expression on his face. Ten hours they had been here together, suffering cramps, aches and unalleviated boredom, and that was the thanks they got for it. Even the excitement of observing the arrival of a man they'd been sure was Comrade Alex Duma, the much-wanted terrorist, had soon waned when it became obvious that base wasn't going to do a thing about him.

They lay on a platform of planks set on top of a scaffold that rose to just beneath the corrugated-iron roof. A gap of three inches had been made below the bottom layer of iron by sawing through the wooden board that supported the beams – a gap just narrow enough to be hidden by the overhang of the roof and just wide enough to afford a complete view of Kumalo's daughter's house and its sur-roundings. Three nights in a row they had spent in here, creeping in after dark when the workmen had left, sneaking out again before they arrived, not even the dopy old watch-man aware of their presence. The watchman was a wonderful decoy. Anything worth seeing down there would happen at night, Colonel Prinsloo had said, and he'd been right. Duma had been the only thing worth seeing; he'd been six hours in the house, a sitting duck, and now it looked as though they were just going to let him walk away.

The photographer was phlegmatically unloading infra-red film from his camera. The man with the radio impulsively jabbed at the transmitter button again. 'Well, have you got what you wanted? Can we leave now?'

'Negative,' said the voice at base. 'Don't you worry about Duma. Your business is with her. Just go on watching the house. Over and out.'

Mr Jepson was far from happy. If yesterday's experience had made him feel like a schoolboy caught playing truant, this morning he had more the sensation of being a suspect in a major crime. Two policemen had been waiting for him when he arrived at work and now, parked in his office, they seemed set to remain there for the day. Warrant Officer Willemse lounged in the chair across from his desk, reading *Die*

Transvaler, while the technician still fiddled about with the equipment he had set up on a table in the corner: a tape recorder plugged into Jepson's phone, two extension lines taken from a junction box on the wall and a radio-telephone with an open link to the main Johannesburg exchange just down the street.

They had urged him to carry on working, to take no notice of them – a thing much easier said than done. He was accustomed to privacy in his office and he found it impossible to concentrate. He stared at the day's printouts of foreign exchange rates without absorbing them; he rearranged the things on his desk; he studied his own morning paper with a purposeful air, turning covertly to the cricket scores.

When his secretary came in with tea she also brought the morning's mail, and he was glad of the few minutes' distraction that would provide. He glanced through it while he stirred his tea: some news bulletins from the finance houses, the monthly report of the Reserve Bank, an invitation to a Christmas party at Anglo-American – all routine stuff except for a grey airmail letter which, for one idiotic moment, he thought had been brought to him by mistake. It wasn't addressed to him; it was— he started and dropped his teaspoon with a clatter in the saucer. Willemse looked up.

'What is it?'

Jepson held up the letter. It had been franked in Zurich and was addressed to Mr Patrick Marriner, c/o Mr Jepson. When he turned it over he saw the sender's address printed on the back: Handelsbank Bauer, Talstrasse 562, 8022 Zurich. 'It's the one he's been expecting. The one he's been phoning me about.' He glanced at the date on the envelope. 'December the sixth. Held up by the Christmas rush.'

Willemse had his hand out for the letter, but Jepson hesitated. 'I don't know, old chap. It's addressed to him, and he is still our customer. It's not really—'

'Not really cricket, Mr Jepson?' Willemse gave a slight smile. 'I'm afraid Mr Marriner has been breaking the rules, and so must we.'

343

Jepson surrendered the envelope and the policeman tore it open without ceremony, extracting a single flimsy piece of paper. It was a printed form of some kind with details handwritten into it. Willemse studied it for some time, frowning, before suddenly making sense of what he saw. He sucked in his breath and looked up at Jepson.

'Ever heard of someone called Frank Rendle?'

'No.'

Warrant Officer Willemse nodded grimly, as though that was no more than he had expected. 'I need to make a phone call, Mr Jepson. In a hurry. And in private.'

'Frank Rendle.' Tertius Van Straaten was repeating the name blankly five minutes later. 'Who the devil can he be?'

'Well, if the People's Congress are paying him eight hundred thousand pounds, I'm ready to bet it's not for supplying them with paper-clips,' said Colonel Prinsloo. 'No, I've no idea who he is, but he's got to be in this job with Marriner.'

'What makes you so certain it involves Kumalo?'

'What else can you imagine them paying money like that for? And just at this time? Taken in conjunction with the leak from Pollsmoor, and with Marriner's arrival here . . . I'm telling you, Mr Van Straaten, this is the business. They're going to try something on us while Kumalo is out of that prison. And if they have some idea of our real intentions they're going to have to do it before the operation tomorrow morning. That gives us just twenty-two hours to find them and stop them. Or, of course,' he said after a pause, 'to call the whole thing off.'

Van Straaten shook his head. 'Hoeksma won't hear of it. The thing has acquired a life of its own. The rumours are like an epidemic now, and the fact that the Government deliberately hasn't denied them has only increased the speculation. Everyone is waiting for an announcement that Kumalo is going to be freed. The Government is losing support on its right wing. Something has to happen, Prinsloo. The country is expecting something.'

344

Prinsloo grunted. 'What you mean is you've painted your-selves into a bloody corner. Well, we can still make it work, provided we can get a grip on this other business and deal with it quietly. The important thing is to catch these people, not scare them off: that way there's a chance that nobody will be any wiser about our plans. Come over here and let me show you what we're doing.'

They had had to find the policeman a temporary office that morning within the headquarters of the National Intelligence Service, and with that a curious thing had happened to his relationship with Van Straaten. Prinsloo had taken over. Prinsloo had become the focus of authority in a crisis, and somehow this seemed a more natural arrangement. It allowed for an easier exchange of views and it even gave Van Straaten some relief to have decisions taken for him.

'Here is the Magaliesberg region.' Prinsloo was pointing at a large-scale map that had been pinned to a table across from his desk. 'You're looking at about three thousand square kilo-metres of pretty rough country. Pretty wild as well, considering it's so close to two major cities. There are still leopards in those hills. There are also hundreds and hundreds of little farms, some of them so hidden away that even the locals couldn't direct you to them or tell you who owns them. Now we're only going on what Marriner told this man at the bank – Jepson – about moving out there, and Marriner sounds smart enough to have been deliberately misleading him. On the other hand, somewhere like this could be ideal for his purposes. There are only three or four little rural police stations out there, with nothing like the manpower to swamp the area. That could be counter-productive anyway. What I've done is sent thirty of my men to move quietly round the villages and farms, to look around and ask questions. If we can locate Marriner's place, we'll mount surveillance on it before deciding on the next step. No sense in having a couple of country coppers walk in there and get their heads shot off.'

'Jepson said he thought Marriner had rented a farm,' said Van Straaten. 'Would he have done that through an estate agent?'

'We're checking on that as well. It's all humming along.' The Colonel turned away from the map. 'Now, what do we do about this character Rendle? Another foreign mercenary? Rendle doesn't have to be his real name, of course, but since it's all we've got to go on I'd suggest you get your fellows to check the immigration records for the past couple of months. If he's South African, his ID should be on the Population Registrar's file. Takes hours to dig anything out of those people, but the surname isn't common and we might just get lucky. Now—'

He was interrupted by a knock on the door. '*Kom!*' he called sharply, and a nervous young messenger entered and handed him a large manila envelope. Prinsloo dismissed the man, shook a set of photographs out on the desk and grinned at Van Straaten. 'Another branch of my inquiries that may just bear fruit,' he said.

The intelligence officer looked at the pictures. They were dark and grainy, with the artificial grey luminosity of infra-red exposures taken at night. They showed a young black man entering and leaving the door of a nondescript little house, unmistakably a township house.

'Nandi Kumalo's place?'

'That's right. And the visiting Romeo is a shit-stirrer called Alex Duma, a Congress cadre supposed to be very well in with some of the leadership in Lusaka.' There were a few other pictures of Duma, Afro-haired and with a furtive expression, glancing round towards the camera. 'Interesting that little Nandi, who's always made such a point of keeping clear of involvement, should be consorting with such a fellow right now. But I have a feeling that her heart still belongs to Daddy. If they have let her know anything – and I admit that's a big if – then with one move she could confirm everything we suspect. She could take us right where we need to go, and without us harming one frizzy hair of her head. Even if that doesn't happen, we'll always know where to catch Duma when we want him.' Colonel Prinsloo was full of vitality and in high good humour, but he couldn't resist a little sarcasm. 'All this is very mundane stuff to you, of course, sir. Simple policeman's work – but I don't mind telling you that I'm very good at it.'

Marriner did not venture out until nearly four o'clock that afternoon, and then only to find a telephone box a healthy distance from the clinic. The one he finally chose was in the suburb of Rosebank, about five miles away. He fitted the last of his twelve code-plugs into the phone before dialling the Zurich number, and Rosenblatt answered as promptly as usual.

'Patrick, I have your final instructions from Lusaka, and they're very simple. Once you reach Mozambique you simply keep flying due east until you reach the coast. You use the Ponto do Ouro lighthouse as your marker, turn north for one kilometre and land in a clearing where you'll see a group of white rondavels. It's apparently an abandoned holiday resort of some kind. You'll be met there and escorted north.'

'Ponto do Ouro?' Marriner remembered the place, a godforsaken outpost on the southernmost tip of the Mozambique coast. 'That's pretty close to South African territory, isn't it? Why not further north? Further inland? Every extra mile we fly increases the risk.'

'I don't know, Patrick. It's got something to do with the condition of the roads at this time of year.'

'Well, the route down to there was pretty bad last time I saw it.' Suddenly it seemed insane to be talking to someone in Switzerland about the state of the roads in Mozambique. 'All right. Ponto do Ouro it is. I hope Harry knows what he's doing.'

'I didn't speak to Harry. Lawrence Gumbi has made the arrangements.'

'Why him?'

'Well, he had to be brought into it some time, to provide the men and equipment.' Rosenblatt paused. 'I've had a message from Harry, Patrick. He's been put under restraint of some kind. Gumbi has taken charge.'

'Restraint? In God's name, what's going on among you people?'

'I wasn't going to mention it. You've got enough to think about. But . . . well, we did railroad the rest of the executive into this, and I never expected them to like it. It needn't change any of your plans. I'm sure it will be all right. Just be careful. Good luck.'

Marriner put down the phone with a feeling of utter unreality. As though delivering Kumalo and nine other people to Mozambique wasn't going to be difficult enough, the idea that they might not be welcome when they arrived was too grotesque to contemplate. He would have to confront the problem when he came to it, he decided; if he thought about it now it would only distract him further.

He had one more call to make. It was a mere chore, another minor distraction. He disconnected the scrambler and dialled the number of the Standard Bank.

Mr Jepson sounded oddly flustered, like someone disturbed at another task but determined to give him his full attention.

'Mr Marriner! Ah, good. Very good to hear from you. I do believe I've got something for you here at last.'

'Is it a letter?'

'It is. Now, what have I done with it? Could you hold on a moment?'

Marriner waited. Some indistinct clunking and shuffling noises went on as though drawers were being searched. It must have been a good minute before Jepson said, 'Sorry about this, old boy. Got it here somewhere. You settled down out in the hills now? You never did tell me exactly where you were living.'

Marriner was growing impatient. 'Just tell me if the letter was from Switzerland. That's all I need to know.'

'Ah, here it is. Yes, Zurich. The Handelsbank Bauer. Got here this morning. Do you want to come and collect it now?'

'Isn't the bank closed at this hour?'

'Closed to the public, but we can always let you in by the staff entrance.'

'I don't think—'

'It's no problem, old boy. Do come in. I'll take you out for a drink. Be nice to hear how you're getting on.'

Now Marriner knew something was definitely wrong. He didn't speak for several seconds, and there was a heavy unnatural silence from the other end.

'I'm in no hurry,' he said with deliberate calm. 'Keep the letter for me. I'll call you in the next day or two.'

'I can always have it delivered, if you'll tell me where you are.'

'There's no hurry,' Marriner repeated.

'Where are you speaking from?'

He put down the receiver. He snatched up the box with the scrambler unit in it and pushed open the door of the phone booth. It was all he could do to prevent himself running to his car. He started the engine shakily and made a wild U-turn into the northbound traffic. What could have gone wrong now? It wasn't Jepson's probing questions that had alerted him so much as the intensity of his voice and the strained cajolery of his manner. The man wasn't much of an actor. Somebody had been using Jepson to try to lure him into a trap, and the delaying tactics could only mean they'd put a trace on the call. Somebody? Who else but the Security Police or whoever those people were who had been asking questions at his hotel? How the hell had they traced him to the bank? No answer, except the old one that there was an informer somewhere in the People's Congress. Had the letter from Zurich really arrived, or was that merely a ploy to get him to the bank? If it had, it would have Frank Rendle's name on it. How long would it take them to trace Rendle? The questions crowded in on him as he drove back towards the clinic, a whole besieging army of questions, and all he could do was thrust them out to the boundaries of his mind. It was too late to get a warning to Rendle. No Rendle, no helicopter, no escape: it was that simple.

He found a strange sort of fatalism had possessed him. What he had started now was unstoppable, but somewhere in the process its objective had changed. Rescuing Kumalo was no longer an end in itself, but the means to his own survival.

In Jepson's office the police technician still had his earphones on, but he was shaking his head at Warrant Officer Willemse and drawing figures in the air with one finger.

'Thirty seconds,' Willemse said. 'If you'd kept him talking for another thirty seconds. . . . I'm afraid he caught on, Mr Jepson, and we lost the trace. I think you overdid it a bit.'

'Sorry.' Jepson was secretly relieved. He had been a reluctant participant in this, and probably it had showed. Gentlemen didn't read each other's mail, after all, or listen to each other's phone calls.

'Can't be helped,' said Willemse. 'Thanks for your co-operation. If he should call again, please let us know, but I think it's extremely unlikely.'

The technician took the headset off. He said: 'All they can tell us is it was a local call, made from the four-four-two exchange area. That covers quite a big chunk of the northern suburbs.'

'So he was calling from Johannesburg? Well, that's some-thing. In fact it has a certain logic to it.'

'You still haven't told me what you want him for,' said Jepson, feeling he had earned at least this much.

'I don't think you'd believe it if I did. In fact I'm having some trouble believing it myself.'

30

When he got back to the clinic at twenty to five, the first thing Marriner noticed was that a big motor caravan was standing in the car park, close to the administrative building. At least, it looked at a glance like a caravan. Almost neurotically on the lookout for anything untoward now, he recognized it for what it was: a military command vehicle thinly disguised with a new coat of dark blue paint. Built on a truck chassis and bristling with radio and radio-telephone antennae, it was in effect a mobile communications centre that would also house a miniature operations room and sleeping quarters. It was unattended at the moment and looked rather out of place among a dozen or so smart private cars, among them Judith's Opel Manta and her father's Jaguar.

He opened the boot of his own car and took out two small pieces of luggage: the airline bag Rendle had given him yesterday and a holdall he had picked up from Duma last evening. The car had been the safest place to store them up to now. As he closed the lid he saw Virgil, the security man, sidling over.

'Help you with those, Mr Davis?'

'No, thanks, I'm fine.' He shouldered the bags and jerked his head towards the caravan. 'What's that, then?'

'Oh, a couple of visitors. Government health inspectors, you know?' Virgil winked at him. 'I thought you'd have a better idea than me. Is it all about to happen, d'you reckon, Mr Davis?'

Marriner grunted noncomittally. The security man strolled beside him. Marriner had come to recognize Virgil as a lonely young man who lived in something of a fantasy world. Since his arrival as a patient in the clinic, Virgil had been more convinced than ever that this mysterious Mr Davis was acting in some undercover capacity. It suited Marriner to play along with this game, feeding Virgil with hints and suggesting that he ought to keep his conclusions to himself.

At the entrance to the Substance Abuse Unit, Marriner turned to face him. 'Are you on duty all night?'

'Sure am.'

'Well, I think you may be seeing a few things happen. No doubt you'll be told something official later. Just between us, everything is not going to be quite the way it looks. I may be needing your help.'

'You've got it, Mr Davis!'

Marriner entered the building. It stood towards the north-east corner of the grounds, and like the rest of the clinic it had its functional features tastefully disguised. Thick, coffee-coloured Wilton carpeting covered the floors. The nurse on duty in the lobby wore a tailored tawny-yellow uniform and sat at a simple walnut desk surrounded by brilliantly flowering plants and by chairs and settees with tweed cushions.

Behind the lobby were a television lounge and a reading room with a small but up-to-date library, and off to the right were the eight private rooms for patients, each with its own bathroom.

Marriner's room was at the end of the corridor on the right. It had windows facing east and south, which gave him a view over the valley in one direction and the lawns sloping down to the water garden in the other, with the main building of the clinic only just visible off to one side. It might have been a comfortable hotel room anywhere, with the single giveaway exception that its door could not be locked. Alcoholic patients could be trusted only so far, which was why he had kept the two bags in his car until now.

He placed the airline bag containing the Very pistol and the tear-gas and smoke grenades on the top shelf of the wardrobe among his other luggage. Then he unzipped the holdall Duma had given him, and took out the gun.

It was a Czech-made 7.65-millimetre Skorpion machine-pistol. In the bag with it were a clip-on silencer, a short leather sling and four loaded twenty-round box magazines. It was a versatile weapon and as accurate as any of its kind, as he had discovered when he had fired a few practice rounds at the slime dump. He fitted the sling and one of the magazines, but left off the silencer and kept the metal stock folded forward over the barrel. This way, the gun was only slightly longer and heavier than an ordinary pistol, and almost as easy to conceal. With the stock extended it would become as useful as a submachine-gun; the nine-inch silencer, nearly as long as the gun itself, made it particularly efficient as a stealthy killer. Perhaps it was superstition that made him leave it off.

He slid the gun, the silencer and the spare magazines deep under his mattress, where his radio transceiver was already concealed. The shadows were lengthening on the grass and he set off for a stroll around the grounds, killing some of the time that now seemed to yawn ahead of him, an eternity of waiting.

In Dr Rose's office, Colonel Prinsloo quickly scanned the list of names that had been handed to him.

'Are all these people known to you personally?'

'Either to me or to Dr Clooney.'

'And their backgrounds are . . . how shall I say? Straightforward? Respectable?'

Louis Rose sighed. 'What I know about them is their medical histories, Colonel. But if you're looking for an average profile of my patients, I would describe them as white, middle-aged to elderly, and wealthy. Also quick to complain, as rich people usually are in my experience. They're paying upwards of four hundred rands a day to be here, and they're not paying to be treated like inmates of some internment camp.'

'Yes. All right. I get the picture.'

Prinsloo irritably folded up the list and put it in his pocket. These remaining patients were a source of annoyance to him. There were sixteen of them left now that one ward had been cleared for Kumalo, and Dr Rose had insisted that they were not to be inconvenienced. This, however, had been easier to promise than to put into practice. The possibility that the Congress had managed to infiltrate the clinic had not escaped Prinsloo, and for that reason he had arranged for the vetting of its staff. The patients were a different matter. He could not, in all conscience, see where any danger might lurk among a group of well-heeled alcoholics and recuperating invalids, but it was the principle that mattered. They constituted a gap in the security net he was tightening about the place. They had a nuisance value that far outweighed their numbers.

Well, he would have to rely on Rose's assurances. He said, 'Just as long as they understand that there will be certain restrictions . . .'

'Colonel, with people like these it's much easier to ask for their co-operation than to start making rules. I'll have a little chat to them later.'

'Very well, sir.'

Prinsloo left the office. On the way out he caught Rose's daughter avoiding his eye as she stood with the little coloured girl behind the reception desk. A hostile one, he had always felt, but too scared actually to make any trouble.

353

Just outside the building he met the earnest army major who had completed his inspection of the perimeter and who fell into step with him on the way back to the caravan. They talked about their arrangements. The major would be in charge of the company-sized detachment of troops appointed to guard the place, a hundred and fifty men in all. They would be quartered under canvas in a field half a mile down the road. Half of these men would be on sentry duty at any one time, together with a Security Police detachment and a special squad of élite anti-terrorist commandos. A hundred and ten men, in all, would surround Kumalo day and night. In addition, barriers would be set up on all roads approaching the clinic and outlying pickets would be posted in the veld surrounding it. It all sounded very good. It was a textbook operation. Maybe that was the niggling worry at the back of his mind, Prinsloo thought as he listened to the major enthusing. This man Marriner, to judge by what they knew of him, had probably read the textbooks too.

Among the task force of Security Police detectives who had spread out into the Magaliesberg, two had been detailed to make enquiries at the offices of estate agents. They had called at Labuschagne & Son in Muldersdrift shortly after lunch and found that young Mr Labuschagne was out showing a property to a client. When they returned just before five o'clock they were confronted by a locked door and a notice announcing that the office had closed early for the holiday weekend.

'Shit!' muttered Sergeant Brink.

'Do we forget about it?' asked Constable Smit.

'I don't think Colonel Prinsloo would like us to forget about it. I think Colonel Prinsloo would dump on us from a dizzy height if we even suggested forgetting about it.'

'Hell, it's not even a lead. We've been running around since seven this morning.'

'And come up with nothing, right?' said Brink. 'Colonel Prinsloo does not like negative information like that, my son. This Labuschagne has got to live somewhere. Let's go and find him.'

There was nothing to stop Rifleman Blikkies Steyn applying for an evening pass and strolling out of the front gates of the Lenz army camp any time after supper, but he didn't want the time of his departure to be remembered afterwards. Instead, he walked to the northern boundary fence, to a point hidden behind a technical stores building that was closed after office hours. He tossed his kitbag over the wire and then rapidly followed it, scaling the eight feet of barbed wire with a natural agility reinforced by his tough training. He dropped to the ground, retrieved the kitbag and moved quickly into the cover of an adjacent field of ripe mealies. In a small clearing among them he stripped off his uniform and changed into the clothes he had brought in the bag: safari tunic, shorts, long socks and polished shoes, the conventional rig of the young rural Afrikaner that he was. Dressed like that, he knew, he would have no difficulty hitching lifts all the way to Pelindaba. There was a path through these fields that would bring him out on the northbound road connecting with the motorway ring that skirted Johannesburg.

He stuffed his army boots, shirt and trousers into the kitbag, being careful not to cut himself on the twin edges of the panga that it concealed. The panga was the only weapon Blikkies carried, a fifteen-inch length of car spring honed to razor sharpness, a lump of industrial scrap fashioned into a perfect primitive tool, as useful for carving a path through the bush as it was for lopping the head off a snake. Or a man, for that matter. Blikkies was going back to the bush, and the thought brought a kind of primeval excitement to him.

They had brought a wheelchair to his cell, but Kumalo had refused it. The way he strode down the long corridors of the prison you might almost imagine he owned the place, Dr Els thought, his escort of warders and medical orderlies having to hurry along on either side of him like so many attendant flunkeys. He had shown no surprise when Els had given him an hour's notice of their departure; he had merely asked what he needed to bring, and now he was dressed for the journey in the plain white shirt and fawn slacks they had given him, and he carried his own small suitcase: a man quite unselfconsciously in charge of himself and presumably looking forward to the trip. The furthest he had travelled in twenty-five years had been when they brought him the few miles from Robben Island to Pollsmoor.

They had planned a tortuous route through the prison so that no other inmate would get a glimpse of him. They moved without stopping, doors and gates being hastily unlocked ahead of them. Only when the small western gate was finally swung open and he stepped outside did Kumalo pause, halting everyone else, breathing deeply in the warm fresh air and gazing out at a view that was entirely new to him. The sun had sunk behind the sharp spine of the Cape mountains, leaving a soft iridescent light over farmlands rich with summer greenery. To the south lay False Bay: curling white breakers close inshore giving way to a deep, violent blue further out and finally merging with the sky in a grey twilight haze. Obviously Kumalo's senses were assailed by all this; he looked almost giddy.

'Are you all right?' Dr Els asked.

'I'm all right.'

They set off again. It was round a corner of the building and two hundred yards to the helicopter pad where the huge Super Frelon stood with its rotors idly turning, looking like some ugly great bird with its belly too full to let it fly. A steep mobile stairway had been wheeled up to the cabin door just aft of the cockpit. Kumalo shrugged off Dr Els's offer to help him up.

'Take it easy,' Els cautioned him. 'You're supposed to get all the rest you can. They want you good and fresh for the morning.'

'I've been taking it easy for a long time, Doctor. I want to enjoy this!'

They were met by a flight-sergeant in helmet and flying

suit who pointed them silently to two seats facing the door. Twenty soldiers and policemen were harnessed into their own seats down either side of the narrow gloomy cabin, craning their necks for a look at Kumalo as he sat down and the flight-sergeant strapped him in. Their curiosity amused him, and he gave his big Zulu grin, white teeth gleaming in the half-light.

'Well, where are we off to? It can hardly be a secret any longer.'

'Ysterplaat air station,' said Els. 'And from there to Johannesburg.'

'Ah. Igoli. The big city. I suppose I might have guessed. I believe it's changed a lot. I would feel lost there nowadays.'

The airman slid the cabin door shut and fastened it, then scrambled forward into the cockpit. A moment later the pilot throttled up his three turbojet engines and the main rotor began spinning faster, its dull churning sound rising to a high-pitched whine, obliterating all conversation. Dr Els was glad of the silence thus forced upon them. He had never flown in a helicopter before, or for that matter in anything smaller than an airliner, but the nervous knot in his stomach seemed to have little or nothing to do with any fear of flying. He dreaded the thought of what was to happen tomorrow, and he didn't know who to resent the most for forcing it on him: Hoeksma, Van Straaten or Prinsloo. It wasn't that Els couldn't accept the necessity of the thing, at least on an intellectual plane: he was an Afrikaner, and the survival of his tribe could almost be said to be at stake here. He simply wished he did not have to be a part of it. To those other three Kumalo was a symbol and a cipher; to Els he was a man, a patient, someone he'd come to know and guardedly to admire. When he'd been reminded of the death of the prisoner called Matthew Mthembu, what Els remembered most vividly of all was the sudden discovery that he hated himself. He wondered if anything he did now could make any difference.

The engine noise grew. The helicopter strained, wobbled

357

and began to rise. Its nose dipped and it made a steep banking turn over the prison. They were on their way.

Seven o'clock was the most popular time for dinner at the clinic. When Dr Rose entered the dining room at ten minutes past the hour he found ten or eleven of the remaining sixteen patients present, the others being either confined to bed or out for the evening.

Heads turned at his arrival. Louis Rose rarely put in an appearance at the residential areas, preferring to keep himself at a professional distance and guessing that the patients liked it that way. Now, however, he smiled proprietorial greetings at them as he passed the dozen small tables and turned to face them from one end of the room.

'Good evening, ladies and gentlemen. Please don't let me interrupt your meal. I just have a brief announcement to make. We're expecting a rather important new patient later tonight. Important enough to need a substantial number of bodyguards. Now there's no reason why this should affect you in any way whatever; I simply want to set your minds at rest, because you'll notice a certain amount of security force activity about the place and I don't want you thinking the Third World War has broken out.' A dutiful ripple of laughter went around the room. 'There will be absolutely no change to your normal routines. I would simply like you to remain in your own wards from ten o'clock onwards, which is what we normally ask you to do in any case.

'Tomorrow you may use the facilities of the clinic as usual, and you may come and go as you please. However, you will find that there are guards on the gate who may want to confirm your identity and to have you vouch for any visitors who turn up. I apologize for any inconvenience this may entail. These people are under orders to treat you with all due courtesy and respect, and I ask you in your turn to co-operate with them. If you have any complaints at all, please do not hesitate to bring them to my attention. Do you have any questions?'

'Only one,' said Mr Ahlers, who was sharing a table with Marriner. 'Who's the big news?'

'Ah, that's something I'm afraid I can't disclose at the moment.'

'Give us a clue? Mr Ahlers was an incorrigible old cove, forever in and out of the Substance Abuse Unit, and had a mischievous twinkle in his eye. 'We don't get much excitement in this place, Doctor.'

'I dare say you'll know all about him tomorrow, Mr Ahlers. Any other questions?'

There were none. Louis Rose apologized again for the interruption and departed, leaving a subdued murmur of speculation behind him. Marriner attended to his dinner. He had no appetite but he forced himself to eat: Tournedos Rossini, baked potatoes, green beans and a cheesecake dessert. He had no idea when his next meal would be and he needed all the energy he could get. He drank three cups of strong coffee, listening the while to some risqué stories from Mr Ahlers, and then left. He felt unpleasantly bloated. He strolled back to his own building, took a copy of the *New Yorker* from the reading room out into the lobby and sat paging through it without absorbing a thing. When he spotted Judith through the window, walking over from the admin block, he went to his room. She joined him there a minute later.

'Here.' She produced a key from her handbag, a big Chubb deadlock key on an iron ring. 'That's a master key that will open the outer doors to all the buildings, including the back entrance to the operating theatre.' She was all brisk and impersonal again, now handing him a small phial of tablets. 'These are Benzedrine. Take a couple if you feel sleepy. They'll keep you alert. I have to leave now, I'll drop my car in town. I'll switch on the transmitter at midnight. Is there anything else I should do?'

'Yes, Judith. You could talk to me as though you weren't leaving messages on an answering machine. How are you feeling?'

'All right.' She looked anything but all right, her face paler than ever, dark rings under her eyes and her mouth drawn into a colourless little line. Her nerves were strung out as tight as piano wire.

'It might help if you tried talking to me. We aren't exactly strangers to each other.'

'I'm sorry, Patrick.' She softened a little. 'I'm afraid of losing my nerve. I feel sick all the time. Yvonne has been giving me strange looks.'

'That's natural enough. Try to eat all the same. Get whatever rest you can. Tomorrow all you have to do is be in the right place at the right time. You still have a very important part in this. You haven't picked up any more clues about what they really intend to do?'

She shook her head. 'It's not just the mechanical details. I can handle those. To you this is a job, but to me it's still a kind of . . . treachery, I suppose.' She seemed to want to say something more, but couldn't find the words. She leaned forward and gave him a swift peck on the cheek. 'Good night, Patrick. Good luck.'

Immigration Control had been quick to respond to the request from the National Intelligence Service. By lunchtime that day they had been able to report that no one by the name of Rendle had entered or left the country during the past six months. This news did not surprise Colonel Prinsloo when it was relayed to him. He had better hopes of the Office of the Population Registrar in the Department of the Interior, even though getting information out of them was a famously cumbersome business. Formerly they had been responsible for issuing identity documents only to the white, coloured and Asian members of the population. Since the separate passes issued to blacks had been abolished a couple of years ago another fifteen million names had had to be added to their files, and they were still catching up on this workload.

It had been just before five o'clock that afternoon, therefore, before they came up with a likely prospect: a Francis James Rendle, in his mid-twenties, with an address at the holiday resort of Port Shepstone on the Natal South Coast, a hundred and twenty kilometres from Durban. It seemed an odd spot for the man they were seeking, but Prinsloo had immediately ordered two officers dispatched from Security

Police headquarters in Durban to follow up the lead. It wasn't the kind of thing that could be left to a local copper.

Finally, at eight o'clock, the men put in their report, speaking to Prinsloo directly on the radio-telephone in his caravan behind the clinic. They apologized for the delay; there had been heavy holiday traffic on the roads—

'Just get on with it!' the Colonel snapped.

They had found the address, they told him, but they had not found Francis James Rendle. They had been directed instead to a small tourist hotel that was run by his father. Rendle senior, a choleric colonial type from Kenya, had been at first suspiciously reluctant to talk about his son. Gradually it emerged that they were estranged from each other, that they hadn't been in touch for several years. The last thing the father had heard of him was a story about his being kicked out of the air force and being made to do his national service in the army. A wilful young bugger, the older Rendle had called him. He had, of course, no idea where or with what unit his son might be serving.

'What do you make of that?' Prinsloo demanded when he had put down the phone. 'In the frigging army! For all we know he could be one of the guards coming into this place in a couple of hours from now.'

'Not too likely,' said Warrant Officer Willemse. 'They're a company that just got back from South-West Africa. They knew nothing about this assignment until this morning.'

'OK, then, he's somewhere else, and that could be even more worrying. Now, I suppose, we have to get the Defence Department to check *their* records. More bloody red tape!'

'Do you want me to try them?'

'Yes, you make a start on it.' That was what he had brought Willemse up from Cape Town for. He was a good leg-man, and he was smart. While Willemse got on to the phone, Prinsloo opened the door and stepped outside. The seating in the caravan was comfortable but too cramped for his long frame. The two technicians who manned its communications equipment were standing smoking in the car park. He ignored them and stood on his own, gazing out over the grounds of the clinic and the undulating veld beyond. Night had only just fully fallen, one of those luminous starry Highveld nights that made the shadows move if you looked at them for too long. He still had no substantial reason to believe that anything could go wrong. Experience had taught him to put faith in the feelings in his bones, however, and what they were telling him tonight was that someone out there was planning to outwit him.

31

With some difficulty Dr Els had persuaded his patient to rest on his bunk for the first half of the journey, but after that he had insisted on getting up and sitting in the cabin among his escort of armed security policemen, chatting to them as amiably as though they were all on a jolly outing together. By the time the Merlin air ambulance touched down at Waterkloof air station at three minutes past ten, he had them all eating out of his hand.

There was something quite magical about the man, Els thought, watching him step down from the plane and cracking jokes with his guards as they flanked him for the few yards across the floodlit apron to the waiting motor convoy. By the time they had all climbed into the armoured van in the centre there was hardly any room left for Els, so he took up an offer to ride in the car with Warrant Officer Willemse who had been sent to meet him. He was surprised not to find Colonel Prinsloo there.

'He's in contact with us by radio,' Willemse said. 'He decided to wait at the clinic. He's got a few other things on his mind.'

They were on their way within five minutes, a Panhard armoured car at either end of the convoy and four police cars and a truckload of soldiers sandwiching the van. Motorcycle outriders staged them through the military complex, halting other traffic at the junctions, but they'd been ordered not to make too much of a circus out of it and they kept their sirens silent. Soon they were moving smoothly along the south-bound motorway, the floodlit bulk of the Voortrekker Monument looming up on their left, the centrepiece of tomorrow's ceremonies. Many people would be camping overnight in the grounds, ensuring themselves a good place to listen to the speeches, and the beams of headlights were already ranging about on the hillside and converging on the huge adjoining carparks.

'Quite a pilgrimage,' Els remarked.

'Yes. Not my kind of thing, I'm afraid.'

'Nor mine. Cigarette?'

'Thanks.'

Els gratefully drew smoke into his lungs, thankful as well to share a tacit distaste for the more excessive kind of patriotism. It wasn't just their history that the *volk* would be celebrating tomorrow, but their survival, and although Els had his own feelings about this, the rhetoric that justified them had come to seem increasingly empty. His people needed their history because they could not really see any future except the kind that Hoeksma and Van Straaten were hoping to buy for them. How much did they think tomorrow would buy? Ten years? Twenty? And after that – what? He idly wondered what Lincoln Kumalo would make of it all if he could look out from the armoured van, and he imagined the slight, knowing, ironic smile he had sometimes seen on his face.

Marriner heard the convoy arrive at a couple of minutes to eleven, bang on schedule. They entered the clinic without fanfare, with only a low growling of powerful engines from the direction of the car park and then a quiet opening and shutting of vehicle doors. From his room he had no view of the car park, but by leaning as far as he dared out of the south-facing window he could soon see activity among the main buildings of the clinic a hundred yards away: a flurry of dark moving figures against the outdoor lights, concentrated around ward A, the one they had cleared for Kumalo. Shufflings, footfalls and indistinct bursts of talk reached him through the still air. Once he heard the clear tones of Dr Rose calling out something about a blood-pressure gauge. Presumably the patient was being examined before being settled down for the night.

After a few minutes he left the window and sat down on his bed in the dark. He could hear old Mr Ahlers moving about in his room next door, but most of the patients preferred early nights and Marriner did not want to be the only one still obviously awake. Luckily there had been several people still up and about half an hour ago when the first shift of guards had arrived to seal in the clinic, so he'd been able to observe them innocently through the window of the reading room. Forming up at a staging point behind the car park, they had been dispersed with a minimum of fuss and noise around the perimeter. He estimated their numbers at between seventy and eighty, and he knew there would also be a substantial guard in and around Kumalo's ward.

Reassuringly, he had not heard the sound of any dogs. There were difficulties about employing dogs in unfamiliar territory, where everyone was a stranger and every scent was new, but presumably if the question had ever been raised Dr Rose would have vetoed it. There were only so many things his patients could be asked to tolerate, and the atmosphere of a prisoner-of-war camp was certainly not one of them.

He lay back on the bed. He knew he was in no danger whatever of falling asleep, and he was keeping the Benzedrine tablets until he needed them. The luminous dial of his watch told him, unbelievably, that it was still only a quarter past eleven.

When Judith parked her car in Gold Street she saw that the taxi she had ordered was already waiting twenty yards ahead, across from the Village Main Hotel. She got out, locked the door, stepped away and then turned to give the Opel Manta a last affectionate look. It was a bit like abandoning a much-loved pet, and even more disagreeable for having to do it here, on the grim industrial edge of Johannesburg in the shadow of an elevated motorway. She shook off her nostalgia and walked to the hotel entrance. She paused in the light there for a few moments, making it look as though she'd just come out of the hotel, then crossed the street to the taxi.

When she reached her flat she went straight to the kitchen and checked her watch against the electric clock on the oven. It was ten to twelve. She prepared a pot of strong coffee, then went through to the living room and phoned the same taxi firm, ordering a car to collect her at six-thirty in the morning. All her actions seemed mechanical now, a sequence for which she had programmed herself to shut out thought. She felt that if she left one out she would jam up completely the way that damned computer sometimes did. She was sure that Yvonne suspected something. She went to her bedroom and dithered over what clothes she would wear tomorrow. Still undecided, she returned to the living room.

She stood and stared at the radio base unit on the sideboard. She checked her watch again. At exactly half a minute to twelve she walked over and switched it on.

It made a brief buzzing sound as it warmed up, then it settled down to a low hum. At a few moments after midnight it crackled into life, and suddenly Marriner's voice filled the room.

'Unit one to base,' he said. 'Are you there? Over.'

She hastily turned down the volume knob. She pressed the transmitter button and said breathlessly into the microphone, 'Here!'

'Very good. Thank you.' His voice was as impersonal as an airport announcer's. 'Unit two, come in, please.'

'Unit two. We're OK.'

Rendle stood in the shadow of the squad's own eight-bed bungalow hut, speaking down into the walkie-talkie concealed beneath his combat jacket. Across the road in the vehicle park, the armoured convoy that would leave for Pretoria in two hours' time stood freshly painted and gleaming under the floodlights. The camp was alive with unaccustomed night-time activity so nobody was taking any notice of him.

'That's good. Unit three?'

'Yeah. Three here.'

The squad were supposed to be snatching a few hours' sleep before they set off, but each driver was responsible for seeing that his vehicle was spick and span, which had given Brakpan the excuse to lurk in the rear of the Saracen. The reception was badly broken up by the armour plating that surrounded him, but once they got moving Nicky Flynn would be able to use the walkie-talkie from the turret.

'Right. Unit four, can you hear me?'

'Unit four. I hear you.'

In a corrugated-iron shanty in Alexandra township, Duma sat at a table surrounded by half a dozen young black men. They were very serious young men, and they all stared intently at the transceiver Duma held in his hand, as though willing it to offer them something more than its cryptic coded messages. He wished he could offer them more himself. All of them were soldiers of the People's Congress; all of them were wanted, as he was, and would be putting their lives on the line tomorrow on the say-so of that anonymous voice. Marriner should be grateful for such unquestioning trust.

'Unit four, OK. Stand by.'

They looked questioningly at Duma. 'White man's magic,' he said, gesturing with the instrument, and his grin broke the tension. 'I think he can make this thing work, brothers. He had the chance to run away from it, and he didn't take it. I think we owe him our help.'

'Unit five?'

'Unit five, yes.'

'Are you in place?'

'Yes.'

Blikkies Steyn's place was lying flat on his stomach beneath the thorn bushes at Rietvlei Farm, on a slight rise close to the river and fifty yards from the house. He had made it here before eleven o'clock, creeping through the bush along the riverbank, keeping well clear of the guards who prowled the perimeter of the nuclear reactor. He was not tempted to enter the house, preferring the cover of the bush and the mobility it would give him in case of danger. From this spot he could observe all the likely approaches to the farm, especially the track leading down from the reactor.

He did not anticipate any danger. The worst he thought might happen was for one or two of those Pelindaba guards to come strolling by. But even for what promised to be only a dreary night of waiting, Blikkies liked to be well prepared.

'All right,' said Marriner quietly into his radio. 'Everybody's in place. Now, everybody listen. We switch off now and we keep radio silence until minus five hours. In case of emergency, but only emergency, I will try to switch on for one minute only every half-hour, on the half-hour. If you don't get me, try half an hour later. All clear, I hope. Over and out.'

He turned off his set and breathed a grateful sigh. He was glad above all that Blikkies Steyn had made it to the farm. Everything there was evidently normal. Ever since he'd spoken to Jepson he had been worried that they might trace him to the farm. The Magaliesberg was a big area, but if they were seriously interested in him they would sooner or later track him down there. Blikkies of course was ignorant of these possibilities, which was probably just as well. At least, Marriner guessed, the young Afrikaner was the most capable of them all when it came to looking after himself.

A few minutes earlier he had heard the night nurse moving down the corridor, quietly opening the doors to check on her patients. When she'd looked in at him he had been under the bedcovers in the dark, apparently asleep. She had been on duty for the past two nights as well, and he knew that she carried out this routine only once. Provided she was satisifed that everyone was settled down, she would stay at her post in the lobby for the rest of the night, presumably seeing no reason to risk disturbing them again.

Outside, after the brief activity surrounding Kumalo's arrival, the rest of the clinic had quietened down too. The guards would be well established in their routines by now. From time to time he could hear one of them cough, or rattle a piece of equipment, or exchange a few quiet words with another as they patrolled the perimeter. Soldiers could rarely be persuaded into absolute silence unless there was some actual physical danger. The nearest of them he estimated to be sixty yards away, beside the eastern fence.

It was time for Marriner to go on the prowl.

He had already changed into a dark sweatshirt, black lightweight corduroy trousers and plain grey running-shoes. Now he pulled on black cotton gloves and a knitted balaclava that covered the whole of his head except the eyes and nose, not to hide his identity but to leave the smallest possible area of skin exposed to reflect the starlight. He had no use for the machine-pistol or the walkie-talkie at present, so he left them under his mattress. He went to the east-facing window, already half-open, and carefully eased it wider. Then he stood beside it, waiting for Virgil's arrival.

He had kept track of the security man's patrolling patterns and knew that he passed by this end of the building every twenty minutes or so. This time he was right on cue, his tubby silhouette unmistakable with its American-style policeman's cap and the truncheon and flashlight dangling from his belt. Earlier this evening Virgil had had a brisk sense of purpose about him, anticipating some important role for himself in these goings-on; now he moved in a disconsolate slouch, entirely excluded from the arrangements, not even a pretend policeman any longer but a shambling night watchman. Marriner would have a use for Virgil later, but for now even he was best avoided.

The young man paused at the corner of the building and then passed out of sight. Marriner waited only a few seconds more before swinging his legs over the window-sill and dropping swiftly to the ground.

He fell without a sound on to the lawn of dense kikuyu grass and stayed beside the wall in a crouch, perfectly still, for a minute. He was at the base of a deep triangle of shadow thrown from the building by the main outdoor lights. Beyond

368

it he could just make out the two nearest sentries, pale colourless shapes in the starlight, wafting towards each other like ghosts against the background of pine trunks that disrupted the view of the fence. They met, they turned, they sauntered apart, while Marriner counted. Thirty seconds until they both reached the end of their beat and turned again. Thirty seconds with their backs to each other but say twenty to be safe, in which to flit silently from the edge of the shadow to the deep cover of the pines. They seemed alert enough, but their alertness was for what might approach from outside the fence, not inside it.

Like a stalking animal he plotted his route from one patch of cover to the next: from here along the wall to the far corner of the building, from there to the outer limit of the shadow, then into the trees that would hide him while he crept round to the south. He stood up slowly, took a deep breath and began to edge his way along the wall.

Prinsloo and Els had been waiting for Dr Rose in the reception area. When he turned up he was obviously in a hurry to leave, and he showed them out and locked the front door of the building behind him. He turned to face them in the half-light of the overhead lamps.

'Well, that's it for now. The patient is settled and in good shape for the operation. From what I've seen of your latest X-rays the hormones have considerably reduced the tumour, so I see no reason to expect any complications. My surgical team and I will be here at seven-thirty in the morning. Are your quarters comfortable, Els?'

'Yes, they're fine, thank you.' Els had been given a room at the end of the ward that accommodated Kumalo and the guards posted around him. Prinsloo would be sleeping in his caravan, if he slept at all.

'I'll say goodnight, then. Just try to remember that I want the routine of the clinic disrupted as little as possible.'

'We're doing everything we can to ensure that, Doctor,' said Prinsloo. 'Good night.'

Rose walked off towards the car park. The other two

watched him leave, then exchanged a glance. Prinsloo said: 'The stuff you need is waiting. You can have it any time you want.'

'Not yet. I want to be certain everything is quiet.'

'Just let me know. I'll leave it all to you.'

They parted and went their separate ways across the grounds. When he reached the caravan Prinsloo found Willemse just ending a conversation on the radio phone.

'Got something out of the army at last, Colonel.'

'They took their bloody time.'

'Holiday weekend. Offices closed, records locked up, like everybody else's. Plus they're in a flap over arranging this parade in Pretoria in the morning. Anyway, I finally got somebody in the Director of Personnel's office to go through their files, and what he's come up with is this. There's a Corporal F. J. Rendle with the Fourth Armoured Infantry Battalion, based out at Lenz, about forty kilometres from here. He sounds like the one we want.'

'Just a corporal?' It was hard to connect the idea of some lowly national serviceman with the People's Congress and a payout approaching a million pounds.

'He used to be an air force pilot. Got discharged, just as his father said. It had something to do with refusing a combat mission against a terrorist base in Angola.'

'Ah, now that makes more sense. A bad apple, Willemse, and maybe carrying a grudge? You'd better get your arse out there, boy. Check first of all that he's actually in the barracks, and ask the Military Police to detain him till you arrive.'

Willemse looked dubious. 'I doubt if they'd do that on the basis of a phone call from me. You know what they're like about us. They'll want some authorization from higher up.'

'OK, OK, leave that to me. You just get yourself going.'

As Willemse manoeuvred himself out from behind the small table and left the caravan, Prinsloo grabbed the telephone. He would enjoy getting a few of those pompous brasshats out of their beds, but behind his enthusiasm there was also some frustration. Those lazy bastards who were supposed to be searching the Magaliesberg had still come up with absolutely nothing. He checked his watch: twenty to one. It was the best part of thirty-six hours since he had first heard the name of this man Marriner, and after all that time he remained no more than that: a name, a shadow, an elusive but somehow deepening source of worry.

In their teams of two and three the detectives had drifted back during the late evening to the headquarters that had been set up for them in the police station in the small town of Brits. They had put their best endeavours into the search for Marriner, whatever Colonel Prinsloo might think, and they knew there was a limit to what they could accomplish after dark in the rugged and mostly unfamiliar territory around them. They had traversed the hills by car and on foot, they had visited a couple of hundred farms, they had questioned the owners of little wayside shops and garages. They had found no one who remembered seeing a foreigner of Marriner's description.

Towards the end of the evening a crowd of them drifted over to the Brits Hotel to catch the bar before it closed and line up some drinks for after it closed, and at one o'clock there were still half a dozen of them sitting in the lounge, slightly smashed. A group of safari-suited farmers sat at another table, talking in that loud, confident way that told the world they had no secrets from it, complaining about the price of land.

Constable Smit sat nursing his fifth glass of brandy. As the youngest and most junior of the security policemen he felt slightly left out of the boozy reminiscences of the older men and had tuned himself in idly to the conversation across the room. This was of no real interest to him either, so it was only the random mention of a name that made him sit up and pay attention.

'Nou die dag is daai kêreltjie Labuschagne na my plek. . . .'

Smit nudged the arm of Sergeant Brink beside him.

'. . . en hy bring die Engelsman saam met hom wat 'n plaas soek. . . .'

371

Brink and Smit stood up together. Twice this evening they had called at the bachelor cottage where the estate agent Labuschagne lived, both times getting no answer at the door. It hadn't seemed to matter much, it was one more dead end among many, but here now was someone talking about him. Talking, moreover, about an Englishman he'd brought along looking for a farm.

'Excuse me.' Sergeant Brink reduced the farmers to silence. 'Did you say something about Labuschagne? The estate agent? From Muldersdrift?'

'Fanie Labuschagne, that's right.' The man who'd been doing the talking looked blankly at the ID card that Brink flashed at him. 'What about him?'

'You said something about an Englishman being with him. Who was he?'

'No idea. Some bloke who wanted to rent a farm . . . oh, a week or two ago. Wasn't interested in mine.'

'Describe him.'

'Forty or so. Tallish, fair hair, slim.'

'Do you know whether he did find a farm?'

'No.' The man paused. 'Why don't you ask Labuschagne?'

'Because we can't find Labuschagne. He's not at home. He's probably away for the weekend.'

The farmers looked at each other incredulously. 'Of course he's away,' said one of them. 'Away from that cottage near the city, I mean. I thought you knew. We all know him around here. He spends most of his weekends camped down at the dam, fishing.'

32

When the roll-call was taken at one-thirty, prior to the departure of the armoured-vehicle convoy from Lenz, the absence of Blikkies Steyn was treated only as mildly puzzling. He was considered a conscientious soldier; he had never gone absent before; there had to be some other explanation. Corporal Rendle, in an unusually helpful mood, suggested to the lieutenant who commanded their troop that Blikkies might have taken an evening pass at the last minute. He might have had an accident or been delayed outside the camp. Hadn't they better check with the police and the hospitals? The lieutenant thought that sounded a bit drastic and went off muttering vague threats and even vaguer promises. Rifleman Steyn would be logged as AWOL until he turned up with some account of himself, and in the mean time there were other things to think about. The lieutenant dismissed the men to return to their bungalow huts and collect what they needed before leaving.

Five minutes later the squad were taken slightly off guard when two red-capped Military Police staff sergeants appeared in the doorway of their hut. They glanced round at the other six men before settling their gaze on Rendle.

'Corporal, come with us.'

Rendle straightened up from where he'd been bending at the foot of his bed, ramming a loaded magazine back into the butt of his Uzi gun after cleaning it.

'I think you're mistaken. If you're looking for Rifleman Steyn, he still isn't here.'

'No, Corporal. We want you. You're under arrest.'

Rendle stood and watched them from the end of the short aisle between the beds, the gun hanging by his side. His face was blank, and there was nothing in his demeanour to suggest anything but puzzlement. The other men seemed equally numbed. Confident of their authority, the two MPs moved forward.

It was only when they came fully into the room that they sensed the threat that surrounded them. Rendle signalled swiftly to the others with his eyes and at the same moment raised and cocked the submachine-gun. Younis the Greek slammed the door shut, and Carver and Fish took the MPs from behind, clamping their hands over their mouths and ramming bayonets against their ribs.

'I still think you're making a mistake,' said Rendle.

He gestured with the gun. Carver and Fish propelled the staff sergeants forward, forcing them face-down on to two of the beds, their eyes wild with fear. Younis and Brakpan had hold of their rifles now and they jammed the muzzles into the back of the captives' necks, pushing their faces into the pillows while the others hastily hunted for gags and bindings. Within a couple of minutes they had stuffed some cotton underwear into the two men's mouths and fastened their wrists and ankles to the bed frame with an assortment of kitbag cords, rifle slings and webbing straps. Carver and Fish had also taken their revolvers, jamming them in buccaneer fashion into their own belts.

Rendle ordered them all outside.

'Now what the hell?' demanded Nicky Flynn in a panicky whisper.

'Now we wait. I guess these guys won't be missed for twenty minutes or so. By then we're gone.'

'No, I mean, what the hell has gone wrong? Why did they come looking for you, Frank?'

'No way of knowing.' Rendle glanced at his watch. 'No way of finding out, either, not until the next commercial break. Meanwhile we just sit tight.'

Just before two o'clock Marriner got back to his position beneath the window of his room. Instead of climbing back in he waited for Virgil to appear, and when the security man came round the corner he gave a low hiss.

'Hey!' Virgil started. 'Who's that?'

'Me. Keep your voice down.'

Virgil came uncertainly towards him. Marriner saw him fumbling for the torch on his belt and whispered urgently, 'Leave that! It's me.'

'Mr Davis! What are you doing out here?'

'What do you suppose, Virgil? Keeping an eye on things. "Quis custodiet custodes?"'

'What?'

'Who is to guard the guards? With your name I'd have thought you would know that.'

'Ah.' Virgil spoke in a knowledgeable undertone. 'So that's your game, is it?'

'It's called counter-intelligence, Virgil. It means making sure that everyone around here is reliable. Nobody knows what I'm here for except the top brass. And now you, of course.'

Virgil gave a satisfied sigh. Everything he had ever thought about Marriner was justified. 'What do you want me to do?'

'Just carry on as you are. I may have other instructions later.'

'Right you are, Mr Davis.'

Virgil shuffled away, and Marriner hoisted himself up through the window.

Outside the gate of the Lenz military camp, Warrant Officer Willemse had to pull off the road to let a convoy of armoured vehicles by, great ugly shapes looming at him out of the dark behind their blazing headlights. The boom of the gate came down behind them, and Willemse had to get out of his car and show his ID to the sentries. He explained that the duty officer of 15 Provost Company of the Military Police was expecting him. When the corporal in charge had telephoned ahead and got no reply, he escorted the visitor to their office himself.

It wasn't until twenty past two that they found the two staff sergeants strapped down to a pair of barrack-room beds in the dark, with their mouths stuffed full of army-issue khaki under-pants.

It had taken an hour to drive from Brits and then hunt along the shores of the lake for the spot where Fanie Labuschagne had pitched his tent. It took another few minutes to rouse him from sleep and talk him into abandoning his little campsite and the night lines he had set for barbel and yellowfish. It was two-thirty when they drove him up to the gates of the Pelindaba nuclear reactor in the first of three cars packed with detectives.

'Jesus Christ,' said Sergeant Brink softly as the headlights picked out the barbed-wire fence, the gate and the guardhouse beside it. 'This is about the last fucking place on earth we would have come looking.'

'Cute, hey? I told you he was cute.' Colonel Prinsloo could

not disguise the triumph in his voice, patched through from his caravan via the Brits headquarters to the sergeant's walkie-talkie. 'Now, just go carefully, my friends. Take it one step at a time, and don't barge in like a herd of elephants.'

Their arrival had caused some alarm on the reactor site, the guards calling in to their command post as soon as they'd seen the cars approaching, and now there were a dozen of them gathered around the gate, competing for the attention of the Security Police with contradictory stories. What emerged was confirmation that Marriner had taken up residence on the farm in the valley: he had even shown some of them a letter from the Embassy in London to identify himself. He had spent last weekend there with a crowd of younger people and had been to and fro a good deal after that, but nobody had seen him since Tuesday. Which didn't mean, of course, that he wasn't holed up there now.

Sergeant Brink got some idea of the layout of the farm from the guards. To surround the place completely would take many more men than he had with him, but it seemed imperative to look it over at once. He ordered one carload of men back to the road to check out the approach up the river, and another group to fan out along the fence dividing the farm from the reactor. When they had all moved off he pulled the snub-nosed Smith & Wesson revolver from his armpit holster and said to Constable Smit: 'Come. You and I are going for a walk.'

They left young Mr Labuschagne drinking coffee in the guardhouse and they set off down the track to Rietvlei Farm.

For tonight's purposes Lightning had fixed the Saracen's radio so that for once it could both receive and transmit. At around two-thirty the routine hubbub of traffic between the convoy and the base at Lenz had suddenly died down. When he reported in he was told abruptly to maintain position at the rear of the convoy.

'Something's up!' he yelled back to Rendle in the turret. 'I guess they're going to stop us.'

'Who's going to stop us?' said Brakpan at the wheel. 'They

got any Centurion tanks out there? That's about the only thing that'll dent this lady's hide.'

'Just handle it as it comes,' Rendle called down to him. 'Whatever you do, don't let anyone follow you to the staging point.'

They were moving around the southern fringe of Johannesburg now, nearing the place where he would have to leave them, crossing a dark and desolate wasteland of old mine workings and run-down factories. Nicky Flynn would be nominally in charge from now on, but Rendle knew that without his own leadership there was nothing to hold them together except fear and a regard for their own survival.

'Here you go, Frank!'

He saw the motorway exit just ahead, a swath of fluorescent lighting curving down to street level. The vehicle was beginning to slow, Brakpan gradually easing off the accelerator, not wanting to fall too far behind the rest of the convoy. Rendle scrambled out of the turret, clutching the duffel bag that contained his Uzi gun and his walkie-talkie, balancing on the roof and bracing himself for the eight-foot leap to the ground.

They had seen no need to rehearse this move. It was the merest detail in the context of everything they had to accomplish, and he realized now that it was a detail they should not have overlooked. Brakpan couldn't see or hear him from the cab, and as they drew level with the exit ramp he accelerated at just the wrong moment, presumably thinking Rendle had already jumped. The vehicle jerked, knocking him off balance. Instead of jumping he went over the side in an uncoordinated sprawl, sliding off the edge of the roof, his arms and legs flailing, letting go of the bag. He managed to land on his feet and roll with the impact but felt his right ankle twist beneath him as he fell only inches from the moving wheels of the Saracen. He heard a single quick crunching sound as the vehicle passed by – a sound he couldn't identify, more concerned with trying to get to his feet and off the road. He scrambled to his knees, but when he tried to stand the ankle gave under him. Car headlights were bearing down on him now, and he crawled on all fours, like a drunken man in a panic, for the edge of the motorway. There wasn't much traffic at this hour, but it was moving fast. The headlights picked him out as he reached up to cling to the metal crash barrier, and then the car was roaring by, its horn blaring, swinging out into the centre lane to avoid him. He saw its wheels pass either side of a dark flat object lying in the middle of the road.

It was the duffel bag. The Saracen had driven over it.

Hugging the crash barrier, Rendle knelt there watching in disbelief and despair as the vehicle's rear lights dwindled away from him at the tail of the convoy, trying to will Brakpan into stopping and coming back, until finally the lights disappeared around a distant bend and he said to himself: This can't be happening. This simply can't be happening.

He hauled himself to his feet, using the barrier for support. His right foot was a solid mass of pain, but he guessed that the ankle was no more than badly sprained and he gritted his teeth and forced himself to put some weight on it. The ankle was a handicap, but not an immoblilizing one. The duffel bag was a different matter.

Another car went by, its horn sounding a warning and its lights pinning him to the barrier again. Christ, he had to get off this road!

He let go of his support and hobbled painfully to the centre of the motorway. He seized the bag by its drawstring and stumbled back with it just in time to avoid another car. Then, holding with one hand to the barrier, he began limping along the edge of the road towards the exit ramp.

In a couple of minutes he had made it down to the darkened streets of the Village Main area and found Judith's car. Rendle wasn't sure he trusted anything to have gone right any longer, so he opened the boot and checked that the suitcase and flying bag were there with his two changes of clothes, his helmet tucked separately into one corner. He shut the lid, unlocked the driver's door and slid behind the wheel. He opened the duffel bag.

It was every bit as bad as he had feared. The Saracen's huge wheels had crushed the radio beyond any hope of repair. They had left the body of the submachine-gun intact but had squashed the metal pistol grip and the loaded magazine it held, rendering the weapon all but completely useless. Most of the thirty-two 9-millimetre cartridges were bent out of shape; it was surprising that none of them had exploded.

He found three or four shells that remained undamaged and slipped them into the pocket of his combat jacket. He shoved the bag, the gun and the ruined walkie-talkie under the passenger seat and drove off, trying to think some coherent thoughts through the fog of near-panic, trying to assess the damage. His ankle was now painfully swollen inside his boot, making it clumsy to operate the car pedals. He might be able to bluff his way through the few minutes in which he would need the gun, but without the radio he would be quite out of contact with Marriner and the rest of them until the very moment of the rendezvous at the farm. At least there was still time to warn them of this, with a phone call to Judith, but it left no room whatever for any change of plan. In one stupid careless move, the tiny margin for error they had allowed themselves had been reduced to zero.

Blikkies heard the men approaching long before he caught sight of them. The first thing that alerted him was the faint but quite distinctive sound of a thorn twig caught in somebody's clothes and whipping back as it was freed. It came from a long way behind him, back along the riverbed. A minute later he could hear them quite clearly, three or four men moving with the strained attempt at silence that made them oblivious to noises they were never aware of: their own laboured breathing and the rustle of their clothing. These were city men who had never stalked game in the bush or hunted by night for a guerrilla band.

Soon he heard others, too, coming stealthily down the track towards the farmhouse, and after a while he spotted them, two dark figures outlined against the reflected starlight behind them. Blikkies felt his heartbeat quicken but he knew he was safe where he lay, perfectly still in the dark and screened by an impenetrable thicket of thorns. He heard the men from behind passing by him now, just a few yards away, and then saw them gather at the edge of the clearing, looking towards the darkened house.

They moved around the open space to join up with the other two. More men had emerged from the bush on the hillside to make about a dozen in all, spreading out now to surround the old shack at close range. Four of them sneaked up to the porch, and a few seconds later there was a sudden barrage of noise: the splintering of wood as the flimsy door was smashed down, threatening shouts, feet pounding on the floorboards, the whole Hill Street Blues routine. Torches were turned on, their beams chasing each other around in confusion behind the smudged window panes, and the men began chattering excitedly in Afrikaans as the tension ebbed. Blikkies might have found the whole thing amusing if it hadn't been for the terrible knowledge it contained: somehow they had found out about the farm. Somehow they knew what was up, or at least a part of it. He was sure Marriner had left no clues behind him to the purpose for which the place was being used. They also hadn't found Marriner, but having discovered his hideout they were unlikely to go away and leave it.

Blikkies allowed himself a glance at his watch. It was a quarter to three. One of the men was reporting in on a hand-held radio now, and the volume of its talkback crackling across the clearing discouraged him from any temptation to use his own. He had time in hand. He could only wait and see what happened.

The convoy had just passed the twenty-kilometre mark north of Johannesburg when Nicky Flynn in the turret spotted the string of headlights behind them. They were moving at well over the speed limit, much too fast for regular traffic.

'Behind us!' he yelled down into the cab. 'Cops, I think.'

Brakpan glanced in his wing-mirror. Beside him Lightning said nervously, 'What you going to do, man?'

'We'll wait and see. Play it by ear.'

The radio from Lenz had been ominously silent for the past ten minutes. They'd known that the column would be stopped – it was only a matter of where and when – but perhaps they had all secretly allowed themselves to believe that it wouldn't happen yet. Their hideout was only three miles ahead, off the next exit but one from the motorway.

Nicky Flynn gripped the coaming of the turret and felt panic rising in him as he watched the lights approaching. There were three cars led by two motorbikes, he could see now, closing in rapidly on the lumbering armoured vehicles. Within a minute they had him pinioned with their head-lights, and now the cars reduced their speed and kept themselves a hundred yards behind while the two motor-cyclists overtook the Saracen and roared past to the head of the convoy. They were military policemen, he saw, their white gauntlets flapping as they signalled to the leading vehicle.

The convoy began to slow. At the same time two of the cars crept up behind the Saracen, the other swinging out into the centre lane, drawing slowly level with it.

'They're going to box us in, boy,' said Lightning.

'The shit they are!' Brakpan muttered, shifting down through the gears. He'd been sticking close to another Saracen just in front of them, but now he applied the power-assisted brakes and dropped back a little. He glanced in the mirror again. Although their roof lights were switched off, the cars were close enough to be identifiable as police Chevrolets.

'Huh! Tin fucking cans!' he said contemptuously.

The rest of the column had halted, and now he brought the Saracen to a stop, its huge engine grumbling, leaving a ten-yard gap between it and the next vehicle. In the rear of the wagon, in the dark, Carver, Fish and Younis could only wait in a tense silence.

The MAG machine-gun mounted forward of the turret was loaded and cocked, but it hadn't even occurred to Nicky to use it. He was scared into immobility. He watched as though hypnotized as two of the police cars pulled in just behind them, the other drawing up alongside.

It was all down to Brakpan now. He gave Lightning a grin, then shouted to Nicky: 'Better get your head down if you don't want to lose it! We're going to burn these fuckers!'

Nicky recollected himself and ducked into his seat beneath the turret. Just as the doors of the cars burst open and cops with guns in their hands came swarming out, Brakpan engaged first gear and drove forward. He jammed on the brakes almost at once, halting the wagon just a few inches short of the Saracen in front. In one fluid movement he had double-declutched and changed gear again, reversing now, gathering speed over the ten-yard gap as the police scattered in sudden alarm across the road.

The flat armoured rear of the Saracen smashed into the front of the leading Chevrolet, crushing its light bodywork like so much tinfoil and collapsing its front suspension before it ploughed into the car behind it. With terrible shrieks from tearing metal, Brakpan went on bulldozing them backwards for several yards before rocking the wagon to a halt. In an instant he was in forward gear again, swinging out into the centre lane, clipping the other car aside like a toy and charging past the rest of the convoy.

There were a couple of bursts of wild gunfire from behind them, and they heard the thud of bullets flattening against the armoured rear doors. Inside the vehicle, the two collisions had been felt as no more than sharp jolts. Brakpan gave his manic laugh as they raced past the astonished MPs at the front of the column, pushing the Saracen up to its top speed of forty-five miles an hour.

'Hey, man, you don't know there isn't a roadblock up ahead!' Carver shouted from the rear.

'No time to set one up. At least, not one tough enough to stop us.'

'They can still follow us,' Nicky said.

'Not where we're going, friends. We're going to take the scenic route!'

At that moment they heard the overlapping wails of a pair of sirens starting up as the MPs began to give chase on their motorbikes. Soon Brakpan could see their lights in his mirror, but he was unperturbed. They reached the next motorway exit in a couple of minutes, and he flung the Saracen down the ramp, slowing it marginally on the secondary westbound road, looking for a suitable point to leave it. They were in a pocket of sleeping suburbia just here, but soon it gave on to a tract of open veld leading northwards, Highveld terrain, grassy and rocky, shining palely under the starlight. Brakpan swung off the road and through a shallow ditch, and then they were bumping up a slope over broken ground where no ordinary vehicle could possibly follow, leaving the blue side-lamps of the motorbikes winking impotently behind them.

Brakpan switched off the Saracen's lights and guided it without difficulty by the glow of the stars. The vehicle was at home out here, camouflaged by the colourless veld, capable of roaming safely and even stealthily through the night.

33

Marriner finally took two of the Benzedrine tablets at twenty-five past three, having caught himself falling into a doze when he least expected it. He had thought he was too worried for sleep. Neither Rendle nor Blikkies had responded to his scheduled radio call at three o'clock, and from the squad he had got an excitable account of an attempt to arrest Rendle and a close encounter with the police. At least the squad were all right. They'd been approaching their hideout at the petrol station at the time of the call, and he guessed they were safely tucked away there now. It meant, however, that instead of being merely missed they were now being actively hunted, and the search for them would be concentrated within a short distance of the clinic. It meant the police were one step closer to tracking them all down before Phase One had even begun. All in all, only Duma's plans and his own seemed to have proceeded without mishap.

Of the two who had failed to report, he wasn't sure which concerned him more. Probably Blikkies. It was clear that Rendle had been traced through the letter that had been sent to the bank, but luckily he had got away with his squad from the camp, and by their account he had left the Saracen in good time to collect Judith's car. It was of course possible that he'd been picked up since through some unlucky chance, but then the police had no reason to think he wasn't still with the Saracen. If Rendle didn't call in at four, that would be the time to start worrying. As for Blikkies . . . well, he'd come through good and clear at midnight, and the only reason Marriner could think of for his not responding at three was that something had gone wrong at the farm.

Something? A euphemism. People said something had happened to a man and they meant he had died. Only one thing could have gone wrong at the farm, and that was that the police had found it. Well, that would be very bad, but it didn't have to be disastrous. They could abandon the rendezvous at the farm and arrange it for somewhere else, just as long as they had some warning. A helicopter could land anywhere that had flat ground and enough room for it to manoeuvre . . .

He ceased his musing with a start and looked at his watch. It was within a few seconds of three-thirty, time to switch on for any emergency calls there might be. He groped under the mattress for his walkie-talkie, clicked it on and almost immediately heard the crackle that signified a transmission beginning.

'Patrick?'

It was the one voice he had not expected to hear. He pressed the transmitter button.

'Not my name. Please,' he whispered urgently. 'Over.'

'Sorry,' she said. 'Listen. I've had a call from Fr— from Unit Two. He's had an accident. His radio was smashed, and his gun. He's going ahead as planned, but you won't be able to contact each other. He'll try to phone me later in case there are any changes, but he can't promise. Did you get all that? Over.'

His mouth had gone quite dry. He tried to swallow. 'Judith . . .,' he began. God damn it, now *he* was doing it! He had to keep the panic out of his voice. 'Listen to me. It's possible, just possible, that we may have to change the rendezvous. I can't make a decision until I know more. Did he say when he would try to call?'

'No. Just if and when he can get to a phone. Over.'

'OK.' There seemed nothing else to say. 'Keep in touch with me. You'd better not go back to sleep.'

'*Back* to sleep?' Her laugh rattled drily through the speaker, and she switched off.

He waited for another minute in case there were any more calls, then turned his own set off and tucked it back in its hiding place. He lay down. The darkness appeared to swirl around him, enclose him, trap him. The tablets were taking effect; not only would he not fall asleep again, he even had trouble closing his eyes. It seemed as though all the under-pinnings of his careful plan were being knocked away, one by one, like the wedges beneath some great ship designed with a fatal flaw and now groaning on the slipway. How many more would have to go before it slid down to the water to turn turtle and sink?

Like a fierce dog that had been lying in wait for the first passer-by, Colonel Prinsloo turned his anger on Willemse the moment he returned to the caravan.

'Oh, this is fucking wonderful, isn't it? We've lost Mar-riner, we've lost Rendle, and now we've got a maverick armoured car roaming the fucking countryside! Tell me something, Willemse: are they smart or are we just stupid? Why is it that they've got us running round in circles when it should be the other way round? Why am I sitting here surrounded by a hundred armed men and *worrying*?'

None of these questions seemed to require an answer. Prinsloo wasn't sitting, in fact, but was moving about the tiny ops room in clumsy agitation, his head almost brushing the ceiling. The two radio technicians cowered in their alcove at the rear of the vehicle, and now one of them said tentatively, 'I've got Sergeant Brink for you again.'

Prinsloo seized the headset he was offered and clamped one can to his ear. 'Yes, Brink! Yes, you bloody well stay where you are. I don't want the place crawling with coppers, you hear? I want you and Smit to keep to the house and the rest of your men to stay right back, at a discreet distance. You understand the word *discreet*? Good. I want Marriner to walk in there suspecting nothing, and I want him picked up, together with anyone else who's with him. Alive, got it? Yes, I'm well aware he may never go back there. Yes, I'm also well aware that you've been on duty for twenty-two hours and you'll stay on duty for another twenty-two if necessary. Out!'

There was a tap on the door and the army major entered, giving Prinsloo a new focus for his displeasure.

'Well, are your people going to give me the extra men I want?'

'I'm afraid they're making difficulties, sir. A lot of units have been drafted over to Pretoria for this show in a few hours' time—'

'What are you lot, soldiers or parade-ground puppets?' Prinsloo sneered.

'As it is, they're having to bring men out from Lenz to look for this missing Saracen—'

'Can't they get it into their heads that the two things are connected, for Christ's sake? I think you're wasting your time looking for it, in any case. If this thing has been as well planned as I think, then they'll have it in a safe hiding place. All right. I'm not so sure now that extra men are the answer anyway. What I want are some anti-tank weapons around this perimeter.'

The major blinked. 'Anti-tank weapons? Isn't that a bit extreme?'

'I'm feeling a bit extreme, Major. And before you tell me that Dr Rose isn't going to like it I'll tell you that Dr Rose can bloody well lump it!'

Four o'clock. No word came from Blikkies, and there was no more news from Judith. Duma reported that he was OK, and the Saracen crew were safe and awaiting their orders.

'Right,' Marriner whispered into his radio. 'The guards are being changed now. We let them settle in, and we make our move at four-twenty. There's one stationary picket at the south-east corner, about forty yards out from the fence. You'll have to take him first, then move along the southern fence to where we've agreed to meet. Got all that? Over.'

'Got it. Out.' It was Carver who spoke, Carver who would be in charge of the little patrol about to set off from the petrol station. Marriner switched off his walkie-talkie and pulled on his gloves and balaclava. He hid the radio under his mattress again, but this time took out the machine-pistol, slung it nose-down by the leather strap across his chest and tucked its muzzle into the waistband of his trousers. He slipped the silencer into his pocket, went to the open window and waited. When he was sure there was nobody near the building he lifted his legs over the sill and dropped once again to the ground.

Rendle had driven by a roundabout route towards Pretoria, avoiding the major roads wherever possible and approaching it from the south-east rather than from the Johannesburg direction. He had a good deal of time to kill before he turned up at the air base. As he drew near the city he noticed an unusual amount of traffic heading towards it for this hour of the morning, and soon he understood the reason. Crowds of pilgrims had been flocking all through the night to the Voortrekker Monument for the Day of the Covenant celebrations. Happy enough to be taken for just one more of them, he joined the stream of traffic and turned off with it on to the spur road leading to the shrine itself. Cars were backed up along it for half a mile or more; it looked as though the car parks were already full, but there was plenty of parking space by the side of the road.

He pulled in behind a station wagon from which a vast squabbling family laden with camping equipment were extricating themselves and, after locking the car, tagged on to the crowds moving towards the monument and the vast amphitheatre where the *volk* were gathering. The pain in his ankle had died down to a throb, though he still walked with a limp. The air was as cool as it ever got at this time of year, and he shivered slightly in the casual slacks and sports shirt that Judith had packed for him, his discarded army fatigues stuffed with the rest of his gear in the boot of the Opel.

He could mingle quite anonymously among these thousands for a couple of hours, he considered. He'd been planning simply to park his car somewhere in the suburbs and wait, but this way was far less noticeable. It meant he wouldn't be anywhere near a telephone for a while, though he guessed that was less important than ensuring that he stayed free. He still had no idea how the MPs had got on to him, or how much they knew, and Judith hadn't been able to enlighten him. All he could be certain about was that they weren't going to stop looking.

The sentry on the hillside had settled himself comfortably on a flat rock overlooking the valley. His gaze was naturally drawn to the moving lights of cars on the distant motorway, so that when he looked back over the empty grey-black terrain in between he had to blink once or twice to get it into focus. This was also his first shift of guard duty, and he'd been out here only twenty minutes, so he wasn't yet used to the small night noises of the veld around him. The scurrying of field-rats had made him start once or twice, and the swooshing wings of a hunting owl had suddenly passed close over his head.

When he heard another sound from just down the slope he didn't know quite what to make of it. It was a brief crunching noise, as though a few pebbles had been dislodged from the ground. He stood up, clutching his rifle across his chest, and peered into the darkness. Nothing moved. A jumble of boulders lay just below his perch and beyond them stretched the empty expanse of valley.

Carver rose from a yard behind him. He jammed one

hand over the sentry's mouth. The other went under his armpit and seized his right hand and the rifle stock, pinning them to his chest. Carver pulled the man against him in a tight bear-hug, containing his struggling limbs, as Fish stood up from among the boulders and came at a light run up the slope. He punched the soldier in the stomach with his knuckle-dustered fist, and the man doubled over in Carver's grasp, making a faint choking noise behind his hand. Fish hit him again, this time with the butt of the military policeman's revolver, at the base of the skull just below the edge of his beret, and he sagged forward in Carver's arms.

Younis and Nicky Flynn rose from among the rocks and picked their way forward while Fish rapidly checked the man's gear and insignia. He was a private in the Natal Carbineers. He had no radio, and his only signalling equipment was a whistle on a lanyard and a Very pistol with a couple of flares.

The four men gestured in silence to each other. Younis and Nicky took the unconscious soldier between them, under the arms and by the ankles, and began to carry him carefully down the hillside.

It took five minutes to reach the little staging area they had chosen beside the Jukskei River, hidden in the deep shadow of its high bushy banks. Lightning was waiting for them here. The man was beginning to groan as they laid him down on a patch of sand, so they quickly gagged him with insulating tape and then tied him hand and foot with lengths of nylon rope already cut to size. They propped him against the riverbank with his head lolling. Younis took off the knitted fisherman's cap he wore and replaced it with the carbineer's black beret with its distinctive regimental badge. Otherwise they were identically dressed. Lightning stayed to guard the prisoner while Younis and Nicky set off in different directions up the slope.

When Younis got back to the soldier's perch, Carver and Fish had already moved off on their next job. Younis picked up the carbineer's rifle and took over his position on picket duty. Nicky, meanwhile, was making his way along the hillside to the south, taking care to keep well back from the fence. He couldn't move with the slithering silence of the others, and his job was to clear up after them.

Time spent on reconnaissance is never wasted.

Thus went one of the little maxims that had been drummed into Marriner as a cadet at Sandhurst, and he had since had more opportunities than most to prove its validity. During the hour and a half in which he'd sneaked about the grounds earlier in the night, he had absorbed a good deal of information. He knew the position of all the guards who surrounded the clinic. He knew they were working four-hour shifts because he'd overheard two of them complaining about it – complaining, in fact, because the first shift had had to put in an extra hour between eleven and twelve. He had also detected what slight weaknesses there were in these arrangements.

The ward which had been cleared for Kumalo was, like the Substance Abuse Unit, a self-contained building except for its being connected indirectly by an enclosed walkway to the operating theatre. It was where all pre- and post-operative patients were normally kept. The ward was heavily guarded, inside and out, by professional troops and police, and quite impenetrable. He had never seriously considered trying to get in there in the first place.

The one place in which no guards would be in Kumalo's immediate vicinity was the operating theatre to which, according to Dr Rose's schedule, he would be wheeled at precisely eight o'clock in the morning. Guards would of course surround the building, but the only people within it would be the patient, Dr Rose, his anaesthetist and pathologist, a government doctor named Els, a theatre sister and two nurses. The operating theatre was a soft target. In fact it was the only soft target.

On average, there was one sentry every twenty yards around the perimeter, each pair patrolling an overlapping beat of forty yards or so. None was therefore out of sight of any other for more than a few seconds at a time. There was one beat along the southern fence, however, that was cut off by more or less natural barriers from those on either side of it. At one end a thick clump of ornamental bamboo had been eccentrically placed, part of the decorative landscaping. At the other end lay the gully, about twelve feet wide and eight deep, by which the little stream entered the grounds. The sentries on the far side of the bamboo could not see those on this side of it, and those to the east of the gully did not overlap with those to its west. The two soldiers who patrolled this stretch were, therefore, more vulnerable than any of the others along this side of the property.

Marriner was squatting in the gully, beside the fence and under the shadow of the pines, when Carver and Fish arrived. Half in and half out of the stream, they came belly-crawling up to the fence from the patch of woodland that adjoined it and gave him a thumbs-up sign. He returned it. Carver took out his wire-cutters and raised a questioning eyebrow at Marriner. He shook his head, pointing to show they weren't necessary. The fencing did not provide a real barrier down here, since there was nothing to secure it to the sides of the gully. It was a mere flap of loose mesh, easily bent backwards and upwards, and it would be just as easy to replace later.

Carver wriggled through the gap, and then Fish, and together the three of them crawled the eight or ten yards downstream until they were in line with the guards, the nearest of them throwing a shadow across them as he reached the end of his beat and turned.

Marriner worked his way a little further on, to where the bank wasn't so high and he had a view of both the sentries, while the other two scrambled up to position themselves just below the rim of the gully. He was depending now on the supposition that two men will never walk at exactly the same speed, that some time in the next few minutes one of them would reach this end of the beat before the other arrived at the far end, that for a few vital seconds they would both have their backs to him.

They met halfway and crossed, exchanging some murmured remark. Marriner unslung the machine-pistol from his shoulder and clipped on the silencer, ready to use it but praying he wouldn't have to. He waited.

The man approaching the gully stopped and turned. Then he stopped again, looking back along the perimeter towards his companion. Marriner's gaze followed his. The other sentry was facing away from him but he wasn't moving. He was standing straddle-legged facing the thicket of bamboo. He was taking a pee.

Marriner glanced over his shoulder. The two guards on the other side of the gully had met in the middle of their stretch of fence and were looking through it, casually discussing something. He raised his hand and signalled frantically to Carver and Fish.

They sprang out of the gully together, two lithe and silent shadows merging into one as they took the guard from behind. All three shapes seemed to merge, then, into a multi-legged monster that tottered and struggled for a moment on the edge of the bank before plunging down it with only a faint scraping sound and a slight splash.

At once Marriner was on his feet and stepping into the open. He stood on the very spot from which the sentry had vanished. He pulled the balaclava up off his face and held the machine-pistol with its long silencer pointed upwards from his shoulder, so that at least from a distance it would look like a rifle. Then he began to stroll towards the other guard.

The man had finished peeing and was still zipping up his trousers as he swung round and ambled forward. Marriner kept as far as he could to the left, hoping he was only dimly visible in the shadow of the pines, as they approached each other.

The gap closed, from twenty yards to ten, and still the man gave no sign of seeing anything amiss about his fellow-sentry. He hardly seemed to look Marriner's way at all.

Five yards. Marriner quaked. The man spat casually off to his left. And then, incredibly, they were walking by each other with only five feet between them, the man muttering something barely audible but obscene, Marriner grunting in reply.

He stopped walking. He turned swiftly, gripping the gun by its barrel and swinging it with all his strength. At the last instant the guard sensed something and began to turn his head, but then the heavy stock of the gun cracked him behind the neck and he dropped like a stone.

His rifle made a ghastly clatter as it fell beside him. Now, though, there was no one to hear within fifty yards, and in a few moments Fish had arrived and they were dragging the sentry in among the pines and back to the gully. While Carver remained on guard above the stream, Marriner and Fish lugged the sentry with some difficulty through the hole in the fence.

They took him fifty yards into the woods, where Nicky Flynn waited to take charge of him. It was only when they came back that Marriner got a closer look at the other man. He lay on his back beside the stream, and when Marriner knelt beside him he saw that his mouth and eyes were open and he stared with a ghastly expression of bewilderment at the sky.

Marriner looked up in horror at Fish, who drew a finger across his throat. In rapid sign language he indicated that the man had fought them so hard that they'd had to force his head under the water to keep him quiet. By the time he gave up struggling he had also stopped breathing.

Marriner shuddered. He forced himself to take the body under the arms, and with Fish's help he dragged it backwards through the gap and into the trees.

Nicky Flynn had gagged their live captive and tied his wrists behind his back. He was stirring into consciousness now, and he and Nicky looked equally terrified as the dead man was laid down beside them. Marriner brusquely made signs to show that Nicky should hide the body somewhere deeper in the woods, and then he and Fish scrambled back through the fence, restoring the bent mesh behind them to its original position.

They separated, Marriner leaving the gully to circle back towards his room. He wished the soldier's death had been avoidable, but otherwise he could congratulate himself on a successful half-hour's work. He had two men inside the grounds now, and had neutralized the most important lookout position. The preparations around the clinic were well in hand, but what the hell was going on everywhere else?

In the woods, Nicky Flynn pulled the boots and socks off his prisoner and signalled to him to stand up. The man rose uncertainly, still staring at his dead companion, eyes wide with fear above the wrappings of insulating tape that covered the lower half of his face. Nicky prodded him with a bayonet fixed to his rifle, forcing him to walk. They would head well south of the woods before cutting down to the river and moving upstream to the staging area. Even if he tried to run for it, the barefoot man was unlikely to get far over the sharp shale of the hillside. There was, of course, no great hurry about getting rid of the other one.

Fish and Carver, wearing the Natal Carbineers berets of the sentries and carrying their rifles, had resumed patrolling in their place. Once Marriner was on his way, Fish stayed on guard midway between the two ends of their beat while Carver slipped over the fence and took out his wire-cutters. He chose a spot between two of the iron fenceposts and in line with a gap in the pine trees, and paced out a distance of ten feet. At either end of this he reached up and snipped through the tough supporting wire at the top. Then he worked his way down the mesh, cutting two strands out of every three on each side, leaving the fence strong enough to remain standing but weak enough for the Saracen to smash through with ease.

Dr Els had been putting off what he had to do for as long as possible, but now he knew he could delay no further. He hadn't slept, in spite of the several stiff brandies he'd drunk from the bottle he'd brought with him. All they had done was left him with a headache and a foul taste in his mouth.

He got out of bed and went to the bathroom. He cleaned his teeth, took a couple of aspirins and splashed water on his face. He returned to the bedroom and pulled on a tracksuit and trainers, remembering to clip to his collar the identity tag that would be needed from now on for everyone permitted within the inner security ring that surrounded Kumalo. He felt foolish and fraudulent in the tracksuit, since he never took any exercise, but it was a self-explanatory disguise for anyone moving about at an odd hour of the morning.

He left his room. It stood at the end of the building, and two men in the combat uniforms of the police anti-terrorist squad sat lolling back in chairs, cradling submachine-guns, just outside his door. Another two sat at the other end of the corridor and one was stationed halfway down, right opposite the room in which Kumalo slept, presumably peacefully.

The air was filled with the stale smell of their cigarettes. They gave him jocular greetings.

'Jogging, Doctor? Man, you are keen!'

'If they let me out of this place.'

'Rather you than me.'

More guards were seated around the lobby, the night nurse at her desk doing her best to ignore them, and when Els stepped out through the glass doors he saw another dozen slouching shadows against the lighted walls of the building.

The air was cool and bracing. Above the open veld to the east there was just the faintest tinge of grey in the sky as he set off at a brisk walk up the drive, past the reception area and towards the clinic gates. Once he was past the dining room he was out of sight of the main buildings, and here he turned right towards the car park and headed for Prinsloo's caravan.

34

Five o'clock.

For the first time in two and a half hours, Blikkies Steyn considered it safe to use his radio.

After the detectives had broken into the farmhouse they had spent nearly three-quarters of an hour milling about the place without, apparently, any clear idea of what to do next.

They had carried out a cursory search of the surroundings by torchlight, but hadn't come remotely close to his hiding place across the clearing. Finally, after receiving orders on the radio, most of them had scattered in different directions – back up the track, down the river and into the bush – leaving just two of them inside the house.

Blikkies could have left at that point, sneaked a safe distance back down the river, put in a call to Marriner and warned him to forget about the rendezvous at the farm. There seemed at least a chance, however, that the police would give up their vigil at daybreak, in which case the panic and the extra risk would have been unnecessary. He had decided to wait. There was still time to change their plans, even if it meant leaving Marriner to worry.

He had backed his way out of the thorn bushes and set off on a wide circular journey around the farm, moving with infinite patience, establishing how many of the cops there were and the exact position of each. He had crept through the bush behind the house, getting close to its thin wooden walls and listening for half an hour to the desultory conversation of the two inside, and the radio messages that went back and forth. Finally, satisfied that he understood their intentions, he had returned to his hiding place, collected the kitbag containing his walkie-talkie and his panga, and moved a quarter of a mile down the river to be certain he was out of earshot.

He turned the volume down low before switching on the set.

'Unit Five,' he whispered.

'Five! Where've you been, for Christ's sake?'

Blikkies told Marriner tersely what had happened. He told him there were twelve policemen stationed around the farmhouse at distances from two to three hundred yards, that they had orders to stay put indefinitely and to close their net around Marriner or anyone else who showed up. Even more ominously, there seemed to be reinforcements waiting nearby and capable of reaching the farm within ten minutes. It would be madness, he concluded, to bring Kumalo or the helicopter here.

There was a tense silence before Marriner spoke. 'We may have no alternative,' he said. 'Unless I can get a message to Frank, he'll be heading straight there.' He explained that Rendle was unreachable on the radio, and paused again. 'Is there anything you can do at your end? Anything to distract them, or buy us some time?'

Blikkies thumbed the edge of his panga. He glanced up at where the sky was beginning to lighten against the broken outline of the hills. 'Maybe there is something,' he said. 'I'll come back to you.'

'Unit Three?'

This time it was Unit Three that wasn't answering. Maybe he should start being more philosophical about these silences, Marriner told himself. He tried Unit Four instead.

'Yes, Four here,' said Duma rather perfunctorily. He was preoccupied with his final arrangements and could do without these anxious hourly check-ups. All night the comrades had been back and forth among the houses of Alexandra, exhorting the people to turn out early on the streets, distributing pamphlets, supervising the making of placards and banners. Others, less conspicuously, had stockpiled petrol bombs at strategic locations around the township. Now they were keen to be off before daylight came, to scatter to their own safe houses and hide until they could mingle safely with the crowds.

'Listen,' Duma said into the walkie-talkie, 'you can take it that everything is OK unless you hear otherwise, all right? Everything will go ahead as we have planned it.'

'Fine. I'll try not to bother you again. Good luck.'

Unit Three still did not respond.

Perhaps Brakpan had fallen asleep in the Saracen. Marriner went to the east-facing window of his room and stared hard across the valley, as though with an effort of will he might transmit some telepathic message to the petrol station. In half an hour or so, the way the light was gathering on the horizon, he might almost be able to see the place. He had reason to be grateful for the late sunrise in these latitudes, but from now on there could be no more sneaking about in the dark. Luckily most South Africans were early risers, so it would not seem too unusual if he left the ward soon after six o'clock to stroll in the grounds. Worried as he had been about Rendle and Blikkies, concerned to be in his room every hour to receive transmissions, he had had to leave out one important item of reconnaissance. That would now have to be carried out in the open, and Virgil would be able to prove his usefulness at last.

Brakpan had not fallen asleep in the Saracen.

Brakpan sat rigid with fear behind the steering wheel, ready if necessary to start the engine and roar out of the service bay, listening to the dogs that snuffled and whimpered on the other side of the steel roller door and to the sharp commands of their handlers. Brakpan knew nothing about dogs. He could only rely on the assurances of Carver and Fish that the couple of gallons of petrol, siphoned from the Saracen's tank and splashed liberally about the ground outside, would deaden their sense of smell. It was a trick they had learned from guerrillas captured in South-West. Although the petrol had long since evaporated and its fumes would no longer be noticeable to humans, enough of them lingered close to the ground to cover any human scent.

Thus the theory. In practice he had no way of even guessing what the dogs and the men might have discovered, but he heard them circle the building once and then return to the steel door. One of them gave it a kick, and then the padlock was rattled in its staples.

The dogs keened intermittently. There were three or four men with them, to judge by the voices he could hear. He couldn't catch any of their words, but at a guess they were debating the merits of breaking into the building. There were no windows, apart from a fanlight high in the iron roof, accessible only by ladder, so they would be left with the alternative of breaking the staples or cutting the lock.

The horrible thought occurred to Brakpan that the door

was old and rusted but the padlock was conspicuously brand new. It was something the squad had overlooked. They had overlooked nothing else, God damn it, not even after their flight off the motorway. They had driven well to the north of here, deliberately leaving tyre marks in the veld, before turning on to the tarred surface of the old Pretoria road and doubling back. They had given up any idea of using the gas-lamps, waiting in the dark until it was time for the others to leave, locking Brakpan in with the wagon. And, of course, splashing the petrol around. It would be ridiculous if the whole thing came unstuck because of a shiny padlock.

He realized the voices had stopped. He heard footfalls on the tarred surface outside, and it took him a few moments to realize they were moving away. When he next heard a dog yap it was some distance from the building. After a minute there was no noise at all, and he sagged forward over the wheel in relief. The men had departed as suddenly as they had arrived.

There was a chance that they had merely gone to fetch a ladder or some cutting equipment, of course, but he decided not to dwell on this possibility. There was work for him to do now that dawn was starting to filter through the fanlight. There was a new serial number to be painted on the side of the Saracen, there were new numberplates to be fitted, there were the spikeboards to load into it. It was only when he had climbed out of the wagon and reached for a spikeboard that he had realized how badly his hands were trembling.

The two observers on the rooftop were about to pack it in for the night when the one with the binoculars nudged the photographer and pointed. On this holiday morning few of the township jalopies that constituted Soweto's early commuter traffic were moving about, so the sight of a car drawing up outside Nandi Kumalo's house was of more than passing curiosity.

'Kaffir taxi,' said the photographer, refocusing the long lens of the Pentax.

'Can you see the number? Oh, OK, I've got it now.'

The taxi sign on the car's roof wasn't lit but was visible enough through the grey haze. The driver got out and began to walk up the short pathway to the house but was met halfway by a hurrying unmistakable figure in a dark blazer and skirt.

The photographer's camera motor was whirring away. The other man pressed his transmitter button.

'Can you copy this, base? Nandi Kumalo is leaving her house in a Plymouth taxi, looks like black or dark green, registration number TJ 183-986. Message timed at oh-five-three-two.'

They saw Nandi climb into the seat beside the driver, clutching a handbag and what looked like a shopping bag. The doors slammed and the taxi drove past the half-built house and vanished round the next corner.

'Thank you,' said the man at base. 'Which way is she going?'

'Eastwards. Towards town, roughly. Not in the direction of her office anyway.'

'Very good. I'll pass that on.'

Six o'clock.

Brakpan had checked in. Blikkies hadn't, but that didn't worry him. Rendle hadn't, and that still did.

Marriner had used the hour to enjoy a bath and a shave. He had dressed carefully in a pair of light denim slacks and a matching casual jacket, and had put his running-shoes back on. Now he strolled out of the ward, stood on the steps and inhaled the clear sharp air of the morning. A blazing sun was already making its heat felt through the cool, and it promised to be another searing, cloudless day.

He'd been right about the early risers. Mr Ahlers was out taking the air and even appeared to have been on a tour of inspection. He came grinning up to Marriner.

'Well, I see what Dr Rose meant. They've got the place closed in like Fort Knox. They won't tell me who they've got in that ward, but it's got to be the State President at least. Or maybe the Pope.'

Actually the security presence was not obtrusive, except in the immediate vicinity of Kumalo's ward. The influx of armed men had been absorbed by the tranquil surroundings, and the guards on the perimeter were tiny distant figures. Marriner went in search of Virgil. He found him drinking tea and eating toast on a little patio behind the dining-room. Apparently some of the kitchen staff had already come in, and they gave him breakfast before he went off duty.

'There's something I need to check out over at the main buildings, Virgil. I don't want those guards giving me a hard time. Will you come with me and help make it official-looking?'

They set off together, walking past the reception area and skirting round Ward A, where the slouching police observed their progress idly but did not challenge them. Virgil's uniform had done the trick. The operating theatre lay just to the south-west. Its main entrance was via a glassed-in walkway from the administrative block, which also branched off to connect it with the ward itself. At the rear of the building there was another entrance, a pair of large double doors which Marriner knew opened into a corridor leading round three sides of the theatre itself. He stopped outside these doors and looked around. Apart from the nearest of the guards, fifty or sixty yards away, the only person visible was an army officer moving briskly across the lawn. He glanced in their direction but didn't stop.

Marriner brought out the master key Judith had given him. 'I'm going in for a look round, Virgil. I want you to stay on the lookout here.'

For the first time a look of misgiving crossed the young man's plump, innocent features. 'What d'you want in there?'

'I can only tell you this much. That VIP who came in last night is having an operation this morning. With all these strange people running about it's important to guard against interference, sabotage.'

This argument appealed to Virgil. He said: 'OK. You know you can't go into the theatre itself? It's what they call super-sterile.'

'I'll just poke about the adjacent areas.'

He turned the key and swung one of the doors open. He stepped into a small, white-tiled vestibule with corridors leading off to either side, echoing faintly to the hum of air-conditioning machinery. No one was due here until seven-thirty, according to Dr Rose's schedule, and they wouldn't use this entrance, which was only for service and maintenance purposes. Marriner closed the door and relocked it. He moved to the left and turned down a short passageway with a door to either side. There were no external windows; the corridor was in darkness, but some dim light filtered down it from the vestibule.

Neither of the rooms was locked, and he peered into them in turn. The one against the outer wall contained the theatre's air-conditioning plant, a compact, electrically powered system at the centre of a labyrinth of air ducts and water pipes. The one across the corridor had sealed windows that looked into the darkened theatre itself. It was packed with monitoring equipment. It had interconnecting airtight doors opening inwards only, through which used materials and equipment would be passed during and after operations.

He went back to the vestibule and down the other passage. This whole area was, in effect, the back stage to the operating theatre, supplying all its ancillary services. The place that interested him here was a sterile supply room, where everything that entered the theatre was first rendered aseptic in autoclaves fed with high-pressure steam. Here, too, there was a window looking into the theatre and a pair of self-sealing doors. Anyone and anything entering from here had to leave by the other exit, as one further precaution against infection.

The geography of the place was all just as Judith had described it. Further along this corridor there was access to the main entrance, but he knew he need look no further. It was time to get back, to pick up what he needed, to make ready.

He was about to leave the supply room when a movement caught his eye behind the window, and he froze.

Someone was inside the operating theatre.

402

The room was a dim cavern surmounted by a dome with a small glassed-in viewing gallery around it. Some natural light entered the dome through narrow horizontal windows at its base, but all that could be seen in the well of the theatre was a faint sheen of pale walls and the dark regular shapes of the equipment around the operating-table. A darker shadow had crossed them for a moment and now it moved again, a blurred figure wearing some billowing garment, bending beside the equipment for a minute, then straightening up and crossing the room. It moved to the airtight door and paused there, as though listening.

Marriner stood in the dark and waited for this mysterious being to leave. He was no longer alarmed; instead he had a deep, compelling sense of disquiet. This person had obviously entered the building before he had. He supposed he or she might just be a nurse or technician preparing equipment for the operation, but why go about it so furtively, and in near-total darkness?

An answer came to him then, or at least part of an answer, and he realized he had lost sight of a much larger question, one that had always been so patently unanswerable that it had been pushed far to the back of his mind, almost forgotten among the details of preparation and planning. He had undertaken to save Kumalo but he had never known – none of them had known – what exactly it was they were saving him *from*.

Cursed be he that smiteth his neighbour secretly.

Could it be here that it was to happen, right under the gaze of the irreproachable Dr Rose and his surgical team? Had Marriner unwittingly got it right when he'd spoken to Virgil about interference and sabotage?

He watched the figure in its loose garment finally open the doors and leave. Through the window of the room across the theatre he caught sight of it again as the outer door was opened and it hesitated against the slightly stronger light in the far corridor. It was a man, a smallish man, dressed correctly for the sterile surroundings in a dark surgical gown, cap and face-mask. He closed the door behind him and left.

403

A sudden strange feeling of inadequacy took hold of Marriner. For the first time he was forced to consider the consequences of failing in his task, the consequences not for himself but for Kumalo. Anything could still go wrong, and if it did they would kill Kumalo, and somehow they would see to it that nobody knew they had killed him, and they would reap whatever dubious benefits they expected to get from his death. It seemed imperative to Marriner now that he should do something to prevent that happening, yet what could he do without putting everything else in jeopardy? *Who shall deliver me from the body of this death?* Wasn't that the ultimate justification for his being here?

He needed time to think about this. He had to get out of here anyway: get out, get back in and settle down before anyone else arrived. He opened the door of the supply room and stepped out into the corridor, just as the other man came round the corner.

They saw each other at the same moment. Somehow Marriner had assumed that this other intruder would also be using the back entrance. Perhaps he had tried to get out that way but had seen Virgil loitering there. Now he jerked back instinctively, as though to run away, before realizing there was nowhere to run to and stopping.

Marriner walked forward. The other man stepped back a pace, staring at him, and the light that fell on him from the vestibule showed him to be short and gingery, in his fifties, dressed in a dark tracksuit and carrying the green surgical gown wrapped up in one hand. Belatedly he decided to challenge Marriner.

'What are you doing here?'

'I was about to ask you the same question.'

'I'm a doctor.'

'What a coincidence. I'm a patient.'

'Look, I don't know how you got in here, but it's strictly forbidden. . . .'

'I suppose that's why you were sneaking around in the dark.'

Marriner stood close to him now and saw he was wearing a name-tag on the collar of his tracksuit. It said: DR J. H. ELS.

'I couldn't find the light switches. I had some equipment to check. I'm not on the staff here, I'm seconded. . . .' Els sounded very anxious. He was protesting too much, and even he seemed to sense it. He tried to assert some professional authority. 'I don't need to explain myself to you, whoever you are. Now, if you'll excuse me. . . .'

He tried to push past, but Marriner put a hand out against the wall and stopped him. He remembered Els's name and he knew now that the doctor was more than anxious. He was frightened.

'I want to know exactly what you were doing in that operating theatre.'

'It's none of your business. Now let me out, please, or I'll call for those police out there.'

'I don't think you ought to do that, Doctor.'

'Are you threatening me?' Els demanded.

'Not in the way you imagine. What if I told Dr Rose you'd been tampering with the equipment in there?' He watched the reaction on Els's face for a moment. 'What if I told him you were trying to kill his patient?'

'You must be insane . . .,' Els began, but Marriner thrust his dagger home.

'What if I told him you were going to kill Lincoln Kumalo?'

The doctor's jaw worked convulsively, as though he were trying to speak but couldn't get his mouth around any words. This time there was no indignant denial, no more bluster. He couldn't hold Marriner's look and he glanced away. Finally he said: 'Who are you?'

'We'll get to that in a minute.'

'How do you know about Kumalo?'

'I'm afraid the word got out.'

'And what else do you think you know?'

'Just about as much as I've told you. You've been sent to kill Kumalo, and I've been sent to stop you.'

'It's too late to stop anything now.'

'I don't know about that, Doctor. All I've got to do is keep you here till Rose arrives and tell him what I saw.'

405

Els sighed heavily, like someone reconciling himself to bad news. 'Well, your theory is wrong, as it happens.'

'Are you denying it?'

'I meant wrong in a technical sense. But I suppose that's neither here nor there.' Els turned to face him again, and his expression now was not at all what Marriner might have expected. It was still scared and strained, but there was also something like relief in it. 'Are you saying other people know about this? Kumalo's people?'

'Not the details. But, yes, they know.'

'Then, it can't possibly work. They wouldn't want me to go ahead now . . .' Els spoke in a rush. 'Everything depended on secrecy. I never wanted any part of it. They threatened to ruin me, but even so I'd begun to think I couldn't go through with it. Even there, in the theatre . . .'

'Who are *they*, Doctor?'

'No, no, I can't tell you that.' Els brought himself up short. 'Look, I still don't know who you are, what you want.'

Marriner pulled away from him and leaned back against the wall. 'Let's tell each other exactly what we're both doing in a place like this, Doctor. Let's start with you.' He looked at his watch. 'And let's make it quick.'

In his caravan, Colonel Prinsloo was mystified.

Two surveillance teams had been ordered to pick up Nandi Kumalo's taxi as soon as it left Soweto, and the reports they were sending in made no kind of sense.

'First of all she goes to that coloured township, Coronationville,' he told Willemse, 'and picks up a young unidentified female waiting for her on a street corner. Then they drive into a white area, the northern suburbs, and now they're heading for . . . it looks like Northcliff. What the hell takes her to a place like Northcliff?'

'I suppose it could all be quite innocuous?' Willemse ventured. It was his private opinion that Prinsloo was slightly obsessed with Nandi Kumalo, unable to believe that her father's revolutionary blood didn't run in her veins, unwilling to accept that she was not the final connection he had been seeking between the Pollsmoor message and the elusive Major Marriner. A lot of time and manpower had been spent in pursuit of this theory.

'Innocuous? Yes, maybe, Willemse, maybe,' he conceded. 'The only thing is, I've known her for twenty years, off and on, and I've somehow always had the feeling that she was too good to be true, that one day she would revert to type.'

Ever since daybreak the people had been drifting from the ramshackle houses of Alexandra, along its rutted streets towards a wide rectangle of baked earth near the centre of the township that was known as Freedom Square. They didn't know quite what to expect; they were tentative and edgy, though some seemed to sense a festive quality to the occasion and had brought parcels of food, sunshades and portable radios. Sellers of roasted mealies and fried chicken, quick to scent business, had set out their wares around the edges of the square.

They had been told that this was to be a kind of counter-demonstration, a rejoinder to the celebrations in which the Boers indulged themselves on this anniversary, but many were attracted also by curiosity. Hints had been dropped by the comrades who had visited them during the night that an announcement would be made about Lincoln Kumalo. All of them by now had heard the rumours of his impending release. A wilder rumour, originating with a prophet of one sect of the Church of Zion, had it that Kumalo had died three days ago and would be miraculously reincarnated in Freedom Square.

From the fortified police station at Wynberg, just outside the township, a van escorted by a truckload of troops set out to investigate. At the edge of Alexandra they found the road blocked by a crude barricade of timber and old tyres, and as they approached it was set alight. When they stopped short of it, young men emerged from among the shanties to pelt the vehicles with stones. A petrol bomb, falling short, smashed in front of the van and spread its viscous burning mixture of petrol, diesel fuel and gelatine across the roadway, a column of oily black smoke rising from it through the still air.

A hundred yards behind the barrier, Duma sat in the sidecar of a motorbike, watching the vehicles back off and hearing the loud squawking of their radios. They were sending for reinforcements. They would find out soon what Alexandra was like when it was angry. He clapped the rider of the bike on the shoulder and they drove off.

Judith knew she had drunk one Scotch too many.

She should never have bought the bottle, of course. It was tempting fate, as that priggish bastard Patrick would no doubt have pointed out, but she hadn't been able to face the long night without something to loosen the strain on her nerves. Fortunately she had also eaten, fear making her suddenly hungry around five o'clock, forcing her to devour everything that was left in the fridge. At six she had taken a grip on herself, had a cold shower, dressed in the pale yellow cotton jumpsuit and sensible flat shoes she had finally chosen, and prepared herself to leave.

She wasn't drunk; the whisky seemed merely to have spread a faint layer of confusion over her anxiety, so that when she heard the taxi draw up she thought in a panic that her watch had stopped. A glance at the kitchen clock told her it was only six-twenty, so the taxi was early. Well, it would have to wait. She couldn't leave for the clinic too soon. She went out on the balcony of the flat to call down to the driver and was further muddled when she saw a black face behind the wheel. It wasn't the cab she had ordered, but a township taxi designated for the use of blacks, and now two women were getting out of it and standing in the forecourt, looking up at her.

One was an African woman she didn't know, wearing a businesslike tailored maroon blazer and white blouse. The other was Yvonne from the clinic.

Yvonne smiled at her, morning-fresh in a loose sleeveless dress. 'Sorry to disturb you, Judith,' she called. 'Can we come in for a minute?'

'What. . . ?'

'We'll explain. It won't take long. Can we come up?'

'No, no, wait there!' Judith said, remembering with alarm the radio transceiver that glared from the sideboard. 'I'll come down.'

She went back in the living room, searched hopelessly for her keys and found them in her handbag. Her thoughts were so snarled up that it struck her as inconvenient rather than outlandish for Yvonne to turn up here at this hour. She left the flat, locking the door behind her, and hurried downstairs.

In her empty hallway, the telephone began to ring.

Rendle tried the number again, in case he had dialled it wrongly the first time, but once more it rang and rang. After a minute he slammed down the receiver in frustration and left the phone booth.

He sat in the Opel for a minute, thinking. Judith must have left early for the clinic: it was the only possible explanation. Admittedly he had cut things a bit fine. He'd had trouble getting his car out of its parking place near the monument, and then he'd been held up by the military traffic flowing towards Pretoria. It was twenty-five past six before he'd found the telephone, but she had been quite definite about not leaving the flat until half-past.

He was parked in a long jacaranda-lined road, with the early sun slanting through the rich summer greenery of suburban gardens. It was quite deserted apart from a couple of enthusiasts getting their lawn-sprinklers going before the sun grew too hot. They were casting him looks and he guessed he had better get moving.

He set off on an aimless crawl around the suburbs, with an hour still to kill and anxiety gnawing at him. He would have to try phoning her later, at the clinic, but if he couldn't make contact he would just have to carry on as arranged. He felt far, far out on a limb now, moving forward only because he could not go back.

35

Seven o'clock.

Blikkies called in. Brakpan called in. Marriner told Blikkies he had given up any hope of hearing from Rendle now, and that he'd better go ahead and do what he had to do at the farm. For Brakpan he had disturbing news as well: on his way back to the operating theatre he had seen objects being unloaded and assembled in the carpark which he'd identified as Entac anti-tank missile launchers. There was nothing either of them could do about this; Carver and Fish would have to be relied upon to deal with them. Marriner switched off his radio, left his hiding place in the air-conditioning room and returned to where Dr Els waited in the sterile supply area.

Els looked both saddened and unburdened, like someone who had just signed a confession after lengthy questioning. 'I don't suppose you've got a cigarette?' he said.

'Afraid not. But it's safe for you to leave now. Won't you be missed?'

'Not yet. They left me to handle this on my own. I was the only one who could do it, and they'll be taking my word that it's been done.'

Marriner nodded. He, too, had to take Els's word for it that he'd undone the damage in the operating theatre. He had no way of checking. The small gas cylinder that lay on the counter beside him looked identical to the one Els had replaced in its clamp on the anaesthesia machine. The pressure gauges next to it were outwardly just the same as the ones he'd put back. He thought he knew enough now, however, to trust Dr Els. He was a man who had kept some moral courage alive beneath layers of guilt and frustration. He had the gritty Afrikaner stubbornness that his own people had failed to recognize, and once he'd made up his mind to talk he had held back nothing of importance. He was wrapping up the cylinder and the gauges in his discarded theatre gown now; he had his own plans for disposing of them.

'Who supplied you with that stuff?' Marriner asked.

'I've said: I won't tell you any names.'

'But several people must have been involved.'

'Nobody needed to know very much. The gauges are standard, and I suppose they were doctored by technicians employed by the security people. I gather the carbon monoxide mixture was supplied by some state-owned company that had been experimenting with different combinations of gases. A lot of carbon monoxide is used in our synthetic-fuel industry, for instance.'

'The same gas that comes from car exhausts? That people use to commit suicide?'

'Oh, but this is pure, enriched. And of course extremely toxic.' Els patted the cylinder. 'It's a sneaky killer. Colourless, odourless, and absorbed very rapidly by the bloodstream. The funny thing is, the blood actually prefers carbon monoxide to oxygen. It combines with the haemoglobin something like two hundred times more readily than oxygen does. It prevents oxygen reaching the organs that need it, and the brain is particularly vulnerable. Oxygen starvation will cause global cerebral damage within two minutes.'

The plan, as Els had outlined it, had had a horrible simplicity. Under the normal pre-operative procedure, the anaesthetist would give Kumalo his pre-medication injection about half an hour before surgery began, a mixture of atrophine and morphine to make him drowsy and relaxed. Then, in the anaesthetic room, he would be injected with the short-acting barbiturate sodium pentothal to produce general anaesthesia. On the operating table this in turn would be controlled through a respirator supplying him with a carefully balanced mixture of oxygen, halothane and nitrous dioxide, all drawn from separate cylinders attached to the machine.

It was the third cylinder that Els had switched. Instead of pure nitrous dioxide, the new container held just enough of it to produce its characteristic sweetish smell, but was otherwise filled with poisonous, odourless carbon monoxide. At the same time he had replaced both the gauges of the oxygen supply – the one fitted to the cylinder valve and the one at the head of the tube leading into the patient's windpipe – with gauges that gave false readings. Instead of the standard thirty per cent of oxygen in the mixture, Kumalo would actually be receiving less than half of that: enough in itself, Els had explained, to cause similar damage.

'Then, why bother with the carbon monoxide?' Marriner had asked. 'Why not just deprive him of oxygen?'

'Because that would be noticed too quickly. Remember, he would have been cut open by this time. A straightforward lack of oxygen shows itself in the blood, which becomes bluer and darker. Carbon monoxide, on the other hand, turns it a very bright red. Between the two, it would balance out to roughly its normal colour. There are other safeguards, of course: the heart rate would increase and the blood pressure would start to fall, but by then he would already be beyond help. The diminished oxygen supply would be greatly aggravated by the carbon monoxide preventing its transport to the brain. Before any remedial action could be taken he would almost certainly be in a coma.'

That had been the intention, baldly stated: not to kill Kumalo, but to damage his brain beyond repair, to turn him into a vegetable. The carbon monoxide would disappear from his system within an hour or two, and there would be no autopsy to discover its presence.

'And you really believed you would get away with that?'

'I was quite certain of it. The point is, it would look like a simple case of anoxia. An accident of this sort does happen once in a while, and it's always due to negligence in monitoring the oxygen supply. I would have replaced the real nitrous dioxide cylinder, either in the immediate confusion or later in the morning, but probably it would have been overlooked anyway. There would be an inquiry, naturally, and Dr Rose and his colleagues would be hauled before the Medical Association, but they would be looking for a malfunction in the oxygen and the answer would be right there, in the faulty gauges. Why look any further? It would go down as an extremely careless accident, most unfortunate, on the part of a medical team quite above any sort of suspicion . . .'

'And the Government could throw up their hands in horror? And say how awful, particularly since we were just about to release him? That's what all the rumour-mongering was about, I suppose?'

'I don't know how much the Government as a whole knows about it.'

'But they'd be winning at both ends, wouldn't they? They'd be able to let Kumalo go, to live whatever sort of life was left to him, knowing he was no longer a danger to them. Above all, they'd be able to say with their hands on their hearts that it wasn't their fault. Look at this wonderful liberal Dr Rose to whose care we entrusted him. Is that about the size of it?'

Els shrugged. 'I suppose so. Look, I'd better go. You think you can cover for me? Keep what I've told you between us?'

'I'll do my best. If this thing comes off, then what happens or doesn't happen in here is going to be the least of anyone's worries.'

'I suppose I should wish you good luck.'

Marriner saw him to the back door, where Els let himself out with his own key. Virgil was no longer about. Virgil had finally gone home, rather reluctantly, after performing one more escort duty to and from Marriner's room. Now Marriner was alone in the theatre buildings, with his radio and his gun and his smoke and gas grenades, all packed into the airline bag. He had chosen the air-conditioning plant as the place where he was least likely to be disturbed before eight o'clock, and now he settled down there to wait.

'Well, well, well,' said Prinsloo. 'Now what did I tell you?'

His moods had become alarmingly variable, and after coming off the radio phone again he was on a sudden upswing.

413

'Little Miss Kumalo is now heading in this direction, and who has she got in that kaffir taxi with her but little Miss Rose?'

'The doctor's daughter?' Willemse said incredulously.

'The same. I must have underestimated that little bitch. But now do you see what this means, Willemse? This is the clincher. This connects Nandi directly with the clinic. Something is going to happen, and they're both in on it. The two of them, Marriner, Rendle . . . we don't need to chase them any longer, man. They're all going to come to us!'

The warrant officer looked thoughtful. 'If they're not already here,' he said.

'What do you mean?'

'I'm not exactly sure. Tell me how you see the connection between these two women.'

'Nothing direct. Not at first anyway. It all began with Nandi, or at least with the message from the prison. She passed it on to the Congress, and they roped Dr Rose's daughter in to help them. Not difficult, considering her relationship to Joshua Rosenblatt.'

'There's only one reason why they could have wanted her help, Colonel: to find out more about the set-up here. It means they may have detailed knowledge, and they may have had it for some time. Imagine you're a burglar. You know the layout of a house, you know the habits of its occupants, you even know where the valuables are kept. How do you go about stealing them? Smash down the front door? No. Look for a back window. Wait for the best time and opportunity. Better still, make friends with a servant girl and get her to open the door to you.'

'All right, infiltration; we've been through all that,' Prinsloo said. 'We've vetted the staff, we're checking the visitors. The patients are lushes or geriatrics, sometimes both. Dr Rose has okayed them all.'

'But you haven't seen them yourself?'

'Rose is sensitive about keeping them undisturbed. I didn't force the issue.'

'Things may be different now. Would you mind if I wandered around, had a look at them?'

'If it makes you feel any better. I've got a list of their names here somewhere.' Prinsloo scrabbled among the papers on his table. 'Just go about it quietly, you hear?'

At the northern end of the nameless road that ran through Woodvale stood a post office and a small grocery store – the nearest thing there was to a village centre. Here the Plymouth taxi stopped and the two women got out. Nandi paid the driver and they waited until he moved off before facing each other.

Judith had cancelled her own taxi and travelled with Nandi. There hadn't been much they'd been able to say in the presence of the driver, however, and now she asked the question that had been nagging her all the way from Northcliff.

'Why do you feel you have to do this?'

'I want to be with my father,' Nandi said simply. 'Whatever happens. I've decided that's where I belong. I want to be part of his struggle. Wouldn't you feel the same about your own father?'

Judith shrugged. There was a certain innocent but bitter irony in the question. 'You could leave later, join him abroad. They wouldn't stop you.'

'There's a chance he may not make it. In which case I would never see him alive again. I've never held my father in my arms, Judith. I've never touched him since I was a baby. Have you any idea how badly I want to touch him? I hope your friend Marriner will understand.'

'I won't see him until . . . well, until it happens. I'll do what I can. You wait here. If they're forced to take a different route or something, there'll be nothing I can do about it.'

'I know. I'm sorry to impose on you. Thank you.'

Judith left her and began trudging up the road towards the clinic. If anybody had imposed on her it had been Yvonne, she thought, and yet she couldn't be angry with her either. She, too, had done what she considered her duty. She had made the introductions and then set off for home, intending to call in sick, stay clear of the clinic, avoid any hint of involvement. 'I'm a comrade,' she had said unselfconsciously, standing there in the forecourt at Northcliff. 'Coloured people are, too, you know. No, I wouldn't have expected you to guess. As Duma says, we have people everywhere.'

Duma was only a name to Judith. Duma was the one that Frank said liked to play games, the one who had phoned Marriner in the middle of that mad lustful night. It transpired that he had approached Yvonne on Monday night, in her parents' home in Coronationville, one comrade to another. He had just learned where Kumalo would be, and he had asked her to see to it that Nandi was taken along when her father was brought out. Yvonne had apologized to Judith for the lack of a warning: 'I thought it would scare you off, frankly. You've been very screwed up lately. I suspected something was going on, long before I knew.'

Judith had about a quarter of a mile to walk to the clinic, and just ahead she could see the roadblock that had been set up on this side of it, a striped boom flanked by police vans and guarded by soldiers. Yes, she'd been very screwed up, she thought, and for more reasons than she could fully comprehend for herself. Fear had lived in her like an illness for the past two weeks, a fear of the future as well as of the present, of new beginnings as well as of old loyalties. It had blocked out some of her feelings and heightened others, distorting her judgements. That was why she hadn't quite allowed herself to believe in the ludicrous discovery she had made in the middle of all this, that she was in love. Deeply and passionately, and for the first time *really*, in love.

Duma was exhilarated. Bumped about in the sidecar of the motorbike, touring the outskirts of Alexandra like a general inspecting his troops, he'd felt as though the raucous, hedonistic spirit of the place had become his own. He'd skulked and hidden among streets like these for too long, he thought, and it was not in his nature to be so self-effacing. As the bike rocked him around the edge of Freedom Square he had a great sense of oneness with the thousands of people who had gathered there, a crowd in a volatile mood, waiting to have their feelings crystallized and made clear to them.

He hopped out of the sidecar as the bike came to a halt and strode to the makeshift platform set up on the west side of the square. Several of the comrades waited nervously on and around it, not quite sharing his enthusiasm, looking beyond the shanty roofs to where dark smoke marked the burning barricades at the edges of the township. Soon the Hippos and armoured cars woud come in; it was important to get the people moving before they were surrounded and immobilized.

He stepped on the platform and faced them. An expectant hush fell. Few in the crowd knew who this young man was, but they recognized something in his bearing that told them he would speak with authority.

'Comrades!' There was no loudspeaker, and he had to bellow a little. 'I wish there could be a gathering like this in every township today! I wish we could show the white people that we have a history, too. I would like to tell them that they have hijacked our history and ridden on its back for a hundred and fifty years!'

There was some applause. Congress banners had begun to appear among the crowd and, inevitably, the blown-up pictures of Kumalo. Encouraged by the sight of them, he went on.

'Today is the anniversary of the Battle of Blood River. Every time the Boers commemorate it, in Pretoria and elsewhere, what they are celebrating is not their victory but our humiliation. They think they killed our pride as well then, but that is one thing that will never die!'

A low murmur of assent came from the crowd. Behind him the comrades stirred restlessly, and in the far distance he saw the first vehicles of a police convoy nosing their way cautiously around a barricade.

'Listen! I am not here just to repeat what you already know. I have an important message from the People's Congress. At this moment Lincoln Kumalo is less than six kilometres from here. He has been brought out of prison, but

417

not so that he can be freed as the Government would like you to believe. They have brought him out to kill him!'

A collective gasp of disbelief turned within seconds to an angry roar. The banners and placards shook. Duma quietened the crowd with a wave. 'We of the Congress know this. Lincoln Kumalo has been brought to a hospital where there is a conspiracy to dispose of him. Can we let that happen?'

'No, no!' they shouted, and they were pressing around the platform now, eager to know more, sticks and clenched fists held aloft. 'Then let's go and show them that we know what they're trying to do!' he yelled. 'Let's go and stop them! *Mayibuye!*'

'*Afrika!*' they roared.

Duma stepped off the platform. The crowd made way for him and then closed in around him, letting him lead them, tumbling along in his wake as he strode out of the square. They began to chant in unison, 'Kumalo, Kumalo!' as they headed in a wide ragged column along the road, making for the edge of the township and the rolling bare veld that lay between it and the Woodvale Clinic.

Rendle reached the gates of the Zwartkop air station precisely at seven-thirty and found Jumper Cross already waiting for him. Jumper was nervy and agitated. He had come to see less and less point in this prank, and he said brusquely: 'Let's get a move on.'

'You have fixed it, Jumper?'

'Yes, yes. But as far as anyone here is concerned you're just a visitor. We're wanted out there at eight.'

They went into the guardhouse to arrange a pass for Rendle. He had been going to write a false name and address in the book, but he saw that the same MP was on duty who had been here last Saturday and thought the man might remember him. He signed his own name and waited while it was copied out on a visitor's tag. The MP gave them an odd look as it was. Who the hell had visitors at this time of the morning?

He followed Jumper's car and parked beside it outside the single quarters. He collected his flight bag and helmet from the boot, as well as the duffel bag, and on his way through the lobby he said: 'I've got to make a phone call.'

'Later. I don't want anyone recognizing you. Let's get kitted up first.'

Prinsloo left his caravan to meet Judith Rose as she approached the gates. Ten minutes ago the surveillance teams had reported that the Plymouth taxi had dropped both its passengers down the road. Nandi Kumalo had stayed hanging about there and he'd told them to keep watching her; she could be dealt with later. Judith had headed for the clinic. Now Prinsloo's hunting instinct had the adrenalin pumping fast into his veins. He could sense a threat approaching as surely as a summer rainstorm. He could see it, smell it, almost predict the time of its arrival. He stood at the entrance to the car park and stopped Judith with a look.

'Miss Rose. You're going to tell me exactly what's going on here.'

She stared at him. She seemed deliberately to compose herself. 'I'm afraid I don't understand,' she said.

'I have no time to play games. What is going to happen?' He got no answer. He said: 'Where are Marriner and Rendle? I want to know now.'

The two names seemed to strike her like blows. She watched him through dark-ringed eyes and her mouth opened and closed again. He had an almost irresistible urge to slap her face. She seemed about to say something but then a car swung in behind her and stopped, and a voice said angrily: 'Colonel Prinsloo!'

He turned to see Dr Rose climbing out of his Jaguar, stepping over to him, immaculately suited, stern and commanding. 'Colonel Prinsloo, just what do you suppose you're up to?'

'I'm afraid I have some questions to ask your daughter.'

'I don't mean that! I'm talking about these rocket-launchers or whatever they are that you've got spread about the place.'

'They're anti-tank weapons, and they're a necessary precaution.'

'Against what? An attack by a Panzer division? No sooner is my back turned than you've transformed my clinic into a war zone. I insist you remove them at once.'

'You don't understand, sir,' said Prinsloo, having to keep a tight grip on his patience. 'There's been a serious security leak and your daughter here is involved in it. I was about to ask her—' But he was interrupted again, this time by one of the technicians from the caravan, running up and halting breathlessly.

'Colonel, you're needed at once!'

'Nowhere more than I'm needed here.'

'No, no, this is different.'

His tone was so insistent that Prinsloo let himself be drawn aside. The man whispered urgently in Afrikaans.

'They say there's a huge crowd of blacks coming this way from Alexandra. Their mood is pretty ugly. They seem to know Kumalo is here, and they're going to march on the clinic.'

'Is *that* what it's all about?' Prinsloo breathed. He turned back to Judith, shooting her a look full of malevolence. 'I'll sort you out later,' he said, and then sprinted away across the car park.

Louis Rose was staring at his daughter. She was shaky, speechless. 'What have you been up to now, Judith? What on earth is going on here?'

'It's a complicated story,' she said after a moment. 'And it's twenty to eight. Aren't you running late?'

'I suppose I am.' He paused and considered. 'I never did think that chap had any sense of proportion.' He set off at his cracking pace towards the reception area, with Judith hurrying gratefully behind.

Willemse had nosed his way unobtrusively through the remaining occupied ward and through the Substance Abuse Unit. He had wandered into the dining room, where half a dozen patients were awaiting breakfast, and he had walked

420

about the grounds, counting and checking off against his list those who were not in their rooms or in the public areas of the clinic.

He had accounted for fifteen of the sixteen patients in residence. Only a man called Davis seemed to be missing.

Willemse returned to the Substance Abuse Unit, walked down the corridor to Davis's room at the end and knocked on the door. When he got no reply he went in. He looked around the room, glanced into the bathroom and then quickly began opening drawers and cupboards.

He found a set of car keys, but otherwise no personal effects whatever. No wallet, no chequebook, no means of identification. In the wardrobe were summerweight clothes, all with the labels of European manufacturers. A recent immigrant? One that said *Alan Best Menswear, Cork*.

Cork? Ireland.

He spotted a small heap of soiled clothes at the foot of the hanging-space and picked through them. He pulled out a pair of black cotton gloves and a black woollen balaclava cap. He stared at them, holding his breath.

'Davis?' said a voice at the doorway, and he whirled around. 'Oh, I thought you were Davis.'

It was old Ahlers, the sprightly little fellow from the next room, now looking at Willemse a bit askance. The policeman pulled out his warrant card. 'Security Police,' he said. 'I'm looking for Davis. He doesn't seem to be around.'

'Oh, he's around. He was up early.'

'When did you last see him?'

'About an hour ago? On his way over to the main buildings. With that fat little security man. Why don't you ask him? What do you want Davis for?' he asked, but too late. Willemse had already pushed past him and was striding down the corridor.

The crowd surged across the Pretoria motorway, climbing the crash barriers, halting the traffic and frustrating the efforts of the police in their armoured vehicles to head them off. They moved in a solid phalanx, walking fast with their banners held high, chanting as they went, flanked by lines of young men ready with petrol bombs for any vehicles that came close. Their tactics had taken the police by surprise, Duma thought with satisfaction, stepping out at the head of the column. This was no static crowd or passive funeral procession, more like an army on the march. Even the few tear-gas shells that had been fired had failed to scatter them. Short of risking a wholesale massacre the Boers could only try to block their path – not an easy matter over the open veld, impossible now that the motorway lay between them. The Hippos and Saracens roared off to either side in search of a way across, and now the Jukskei Valley lay ahead of the marchers, the clinic just visible on the horizon as a patchwork of yellow buildings with the smokestack rising among them.

'It's too late, Frank. I can't reach him now. The police have found the farm, but we have no choice but to go there. Frank?'

'Yes?'

'Look after yourself.'

'You too.'

Judith replaced the phone in its cradle and stood staring numbly out of the office window. She wished she could be anywhere but here. She wished she could even be just twenty miles away, protected by Frank Rendle's certainty and his tough young arrogance.

Rendle put down the phone in the crew room and strapped on his flying helmet while Jumper Cross fretted beside him. In their one-piece suits they hurried out, the last ones to leave, across the apron towards where the big Puma helicopters were parked, some of them with their rotor blades already turning. Rendle's transformation from civilian visitor to crewman had been easy to make, a little bullshit always going a long way to explain discrepancies in the flight-log. He was so obviously a part of the scene here that no one had even wondered why he was still carrying his duffel bag.

* * *

It had taken Willemse several minutes to find the new security man who had come on duty, and as they crossed the car park together they saw four army trucks pull up, troops leaping over their tailboards and hurrying towards the eastern perimeter. Some kind of flap was on, and the off-duty soldiers had been pulled in from their encampment up the road. Willemse ignored them and led the guard to the rear doors of the operating theatre. He glanced at his watch as he got there: eight minutes to eight. The man turned the key in the lock and swung one of the doors open. Willemse gestured to him to close it behind him.

He entered the little vestibule, removing his Browning pistol from its shoulder holster, slipping off the safety, cocking it and holding it close to his side. No one was in sight, and the building was now garishly lit and he could hear women's voices echoing down the corridor to his right. The theatre was being prepared for the operation.

Marriner had to be in here somewhere. It was the only place he had not already checked, and the only logical place. He entered the corridor to the left, rounded a corner and saw a closed door on each side, the passageway reaching a dead end beyond them. There was nothing to indicate what lay behind the doors, except the steady hum of an electric motor coming from the one on the left.

Willemse chose the door opposite this, on the side adjacent to the theatre itself. With extreme care he turned the handle and nudged the door open a few inches. Through the gap he saw an array of monitoring equipment on a counter facing him, a technician seated in front of it and looking through a window into the theatre. Three or four figures in green gowns and masks moved about in the glare of bright lamps focused on the operating table. He closed the door; the technician had been quite unaware of his intrusion. Suddenly he heard a voice from his rear, muffled behind the opposite door but raised above the whine of the electric motor.

It was a voice that he recognized.

It was the voice he had heard on the phone in Jepson's

423

office yesterday. It was Marriner. The hair prickled on the back of his neck as he stepped across the corridor and stood by the door, listening.

'Watch out for those Entacs, Brakpan. They'll be positioned some way back from the fence. I'm hoping Carver and Fish will take them out, but they may need some help from you. OK, now go!'

Brakpan laid the walkie-talkie on the seat beside him. The Saracen's engine was already warmed up and rumbling, filling the service bay with choking fumes, and now he eased his foot off the clutch and moved the wagon forward. Its front bumper pushed against the roller door, stretching it, buckling it, tearing it from its mountings. With a groan and then a crash, the door collapsed in folds over the front of the Saracen, which rolled over it as it nosed through the doorway. A few yards outside it, Brakpan paused. Diagonally ahead of him he could see the crowd from Alexandra moving over the veld like a great swarm of black ants; beyond them a couple of other Saracens and two or three Hippos had managed to cross the motorway and were churning dust as they raced to catch up. Brakpan gunned his engine and swung to the left, heading down the slope.

'*Jou ma se moer!*'

Prinsloo shouted his final and most horrible curse at Van Straaten, then slammed the radio-telephone receiver down so hard that it cracked the cradle neatly in two. He glared at the army major.

'Get one of your trucks round the front. I'm going to get Kumalo out of here.'

'My men can hold off that crowd, Colonel . . .'

'You may care to bet on that, but I don't. I'm acting on my own authority and I'm telling you to get it done!'

The Major backed hastily away and hurried off. Prinsloo followed him down the steps of the caravan and strode towards the main buildings. So this was how it would end, he thought, in even more of a fucking shambles than he could have conceived in his most cynical moments. For this Kriek and Booysen had died, not to mention Phineas and Bobbejaan. And what of that fine pair of minds that had created all this, Hoeksma and Van Straaten? Hoeksma was unobtainable, on his way to the ceremonies at the Monument, lovely patriotic alibi, and Van Straaten had simply copped out, a quivering bundle of professorial nerves, refusing to make a decision, passing the buck right back. So much for those clowns. So much for the fancy house of cards they had built around their empty intellectual posturing. Well, Kumalo dead was better than Kumalo free. Shot while trying to escape: the time-worn exculpation, the one definitive solution those mincing little bastards couldn't face.

Willemse had made a mistake.

He knew it in the instant between flinging the door open and going into the room in a crouch, but by then he was too late to stop himself. He was ready for anything but the darkness.

After the glare of fluorescent lighting everywhere else in the building, it somehow hadn't crossed his mind that there wouldn't be a light on in the windowless air-conditioning room. Now the dark sucked him in and he was surrounded by half-seen objects, swinging his pistol in an arc, glimpsing machinery, metal cabinets, a confusion of pipes, before he made out the paler, less definite shape of a human figure standing against the far wall. He levelled his gun.

'Marriner!' he said.

Marriner had had two or three seconds to prepare himself. He fired twice with the machine-pistol, the silenced shots making two quick coughing noises, not even as loud as the smack of the bullets striking home. From ten feet away, with the policeman outlined against the light from the doorway, he could hardly have missed. One shot caught Willemse on the right side of the chest, the next hit him in the shoulder, spinning him around, throwing him backwards. As he fell, his finger tightened convulsively on his pistol trigger and the shot crashed deafeningly in the confined space, the bullet thudding harmlessly into the ceiling.

Marriner stepped over to the man. He was clutching his chest, breathing in ragged gasps. The pistol had fallen out of his hand, and Marriner kicked it across the floor. He heard noises from outside, a shout and then the sound of running feet. It was three minutes to eight, three minutes too early, but now he couldn't wait. He picked up his bagful of grenades and stepped out of the room, closing the door behind him.

A man in a white laboratory coat stood in the opposite doorway. A nurse was hurrying towards him from the vestibule. They both stopped, aghast, as he pointed the gun at them in turn.

'Stand still,' he said, as calmly as he could. 'Now turn that way. Now walk ahead of me. I mean walk, not run.'

They obeyed, looking horribly frightened, and he followed them at a distance of eight feet. Keeping command, staying in absolute control, was everything. They crossed the vestibule and went down the next corridor. Two more nurses were emerging in masks and gowns from the sterile supply room as they approached. He gestured at them with the machine-pistol.

'Back inside.'

He herded them all into the room and shut the door. He glanced through the window into the theatre, where several members of the surgical team had already assembled. Either the room was soundproofed or the noise of the shot had been so muffled that they had paid it no attention. Only one of them had to glance this way to know that something was wrong, however; only one of them had to run to the exit door and sound the alarm.

The three women and the man were watching him intently. He waved at the airtight door leading into the theatre.

'Stand in a line, facing that way. We're all going in there, one by one.'

They formed themselves into a line. He motioned with the gun. The first of them went through the door and the others quickly followed, Marriner bringing up the rear. As he entered the cool silence of the theatre and levelled the gun the anonymous gowned figures were already backing away, their eyes above their masks widening with shock.

36

Eight o'clock.
  Through the glass door of the scrub room Dr Rose saw Lincoln Kumalo being wheeled past from the anaesthetic area to the theatre. He had finished scrubbing up and he put out his hands for the sterile towel that a nurse held ready for him. Another stood by with rubber gloves newly cut from their wrapping. As he was drawing them on the door swung violently open and Colonel Prinsloo marched in, a protesting theatre sister caught in his wake.

'Doctor, I want your patient out of there. Now.'

'Are you mad?' Rose demanded. 'What are you doing in here?'

'Didn't you hear me? Kumalo is coming with me. There will be no operation.'

'This is preposterous! He's already under anaesthetic.'

'Doctor, your clinic is about to be attacked by a mob. What you do about that is your own affair, but the security of Kumalo is mine. Either you get him out of that theatre or I will. Do I need to bring a dozen policemen in here to make my point?'

Louis Rose drew himself up to his full, imposing height, but this time there was no facing down the raw anger and determination of Prinsloo. 'Let's be clear about one thing,' he said. 'I'm not agreeing to this. I'm doing it under a threat. I take no further responsibility for this man's condition. Now please get out of here. This is a sterile area.'

'I give you two minutes. Bring him round to the reception area. There'll be a truck waiting.'

Prinsloo strode away. Dr Rose looked at the nurses and got sympathetic shrugs of the shoulders. Impossible man. He left the scrub room and walked to the main doors of the theatre. He pushed them open, entered, and then stopped.

He could not believe what his eyes told him. The patient was not on the operating table, but still lay on the trolley which had brought him in, unconscious from the sodium pentothal injection. The tube which the anaesthetist had passed through his mouth into his trachea had been removed. The theatre staff were not gathered around the table where they should have been, but were lined up against the wall, together with three other nurses and a technician, faced by a man with a lethal-looking gun. He appeared to have been waiting for Rose, and he motioned at him calmly.

'Over there, please, with the others. I'm not going to harm anyone, just as long as you do everything you're told.'

Dr Rose stood his ground. This was his territory that had been invaded, and he was incapable of taking two insults to his dignity in a row. He said: 'What is the meaning of this?'

'The meaning of this, Dr Rose, is that I'm taking Kumalo away from here. I wouldn't be doing it unless it was for his own good.'

Rose took a step forward, anger still masking his fear, but stopped when the man swivelled the weapon towards him. The man unnerved him. The man was well spoken and intelligent, and it was difficult to connect him with any violent behaviour, yet there was a polite, controlled menace about him that suggested he meant exactly what he said.

'I repeat, Dr Rose, stand over there. We have a few minutes to wait, and I want you all to remain very calm.'

The marchers were close to the riverbed when Brakpan cut across their path, scattering dust and pebbles as the Saracen touched forty miles an hour on the precarious slope. A couple of young men broke ranks to run out and hurl petrol bombs at it, but they fell hopelessly short, exploding with gushes of orange flame in the grass. At the head of the procession Duma halted for a moment to grin and wave.

Where the banks levelled out and the river reached its shallowest point Brakpan took the vehicle across, axle-deep in water, before beginning the climb up the opposite slope. Lightning, abandoning his prisoners, had already made his way along the bank, and Brakpan slowed for just long enough to take him on board, scrambling up the cowling and jumping in through the turret. The drivers of the other two Saracens, seeing where Brakpan had crossed, swung down the hill and followed him.

Up the slope, Younis had also left his position, and they picked him up on the move. Then Nicky Flynn, darting from his cover at the edge of the wood, jumped on board as well, settling in the turret and manning the machine-gun.

The wood was a couple of acres of old pine plantation that had run wild over the years, and the Saracen ploughed easily through the growth of saplings, Brakpan picking his way around the solider trees as Nicky directed him towards the weakened section of fence. They bumped over the stream-bed, wide and shallow at this point, and then they could see the fence, with Carver behind it signalling them forward, lining them up, and Brakpan barged towards it.

Inside the perimeter, all the reinforcements had been deployed along the eastern fence, directly facing the marchers. The rest of the guards were staring, some even hypnotically moving, in the same direction. The anti-tank crews had stayed where they were, however, six pairs of men crouched over the box-like Entac launchers, each of their tubes loaded with a wire-guided missile that could pierce the thickest armour and explode behind it. Fish had been watching the nearest two teams, positioned thirty yards inside the southern fence, and knew that they were the greatest danger. He had seen them pick out the Saracen as it headed for the trees and confer suspiciously as they waited for it to emerge again. The new serial number painted on its side and the presence of other similar vehicles might have confused or fooled them until now, but they would be in no doubt once it came through the fence.

As Carver stood back and began signalling, Fish saw the men stiffen up. They had spotted the Saracen, still lurking in the wood but moving towards the fence, and they were turning the launcher towards it, one of them peering down the sighting scope and fingering the swivel stick that would control the flight of the missile, the other holding a second rocket ready.

Fish aimed his rifle and shot the gunner in the head.

The man slumped back from the launcher and rolled away just as the Saracen tore through the fence, slapping down the mesh and shoving through the gap between the pines, Carver still urging it forward. The number-two man on the launcher looked up, startled, then stood and raised his hands in premature surrender. Fish's gaze was on the second crew now, but Brakpan had already seen them and swung the Saracen towards them, charging down on the launcher just as its tube was pointed towards him. The front bumper of the vehicle knocked the weapon aside, mangling the tube. One of the gunners managed to roll aside; the other screamed as the Saracen's wheels crushed his legs. Brakpan halted again, letting Carver and Fish scramble in through the doors Younis had opened for them, then turning back on course and heading for the operating theatre.

The diversion had cost them a precious twenty seconds' worth of surprise. The anti-terrorist police who guarded the theatre were alerted now and they closed in around the building, taking cover behind its corners, knowing better than to waste ammunition by shooting at the Saracen. It had only one vulnerable spot, and that was the man exposed in the turret.

Nicky Flynn had almost forgotten the machine-gun that was in his grasp. Now he began firing blindly, long bursts of shots that chipped bits out of the brickwork at the corners of the buildings, going nowhere near the police but at least forcing their heads down.

In the reception area, Prinsloo had been waiting impatiently for Kumalo to be brought out when he heard the shooting: one crack from a rifle and then several bursts of machine-gun fire.

He could see nothing from where he stood and he thought the troops must be firing warning shots over the heads of the advancing crowd.

The two minutes he had given Dr Rose were up. Behind him Judith stood tensely by the desk, as though she too had something to wait for. After a few moments he could no longer contain himself and he left the building, going around the waiting truck to the nearest corner.

In utter disbelief he saw a Saracen armoured car, with different markings from the one that had gone missing, slew to a halt with its back towards the rear doors of the operating theatre. As he watched, it reversed sharply into the doors, breaking them inwards with a mighty crash, wedging its rear end solidly in the opening. The vehicle's front visor-flaps were down. It seemed to have no human dimension apart from the head of a turret gunner, now swivelling his weapon towards Prinsloo.

He ducked back behind the wall. He understood now exactly what was happening. He shouted to the soldiers on the truck to follow him and he ran back into the building, racing towards the operating theatre. He didn't notice that Judith had vanished.

Within moments of hearing the doors break down, Carver, Fish and Younis had leaped from the back of the Saracen into the vestibule of the building. Jammed into the doorway, the vehicle made an impregnable shield against any attack from outside. They raced down the corridor to the right, turned through the sterile supply room and burst into the operating theatre.

One of the gowned figures lined up against the wall began screaming. Fish and Carver immediately ran to the trolley on which Kumalo lay and started to wheel it towards the exit. Younis, covering the main doors, almost opened fire as they swung inward, checking himself at the last instant when Judith came through.

Marriner, still holding his gun on the theatre staff, saw Dr Rose give a start. He took a step forward, staring at his daughter, until Marriner made a warning gesture.

431

'Judith!' he said hoarsely.

She moved self-protectively to Marriner's side. For the first time her father seemed to recognize Marriner, and the look he gave them both was one of rare bewilderment. 'Aren't you a patient here? Davis? What is this insanity, Judith?'

'You'd better ask him,' she said, pointing to Dr Els at the end of the row. 'I'm sure he knows all about it.' She was breathing fast, as though sucking in courage. 'They're the ones who are insane. They were going to kill Kumalo!'

'Not quite, but possibly worse,' said Marriner. 'They were going to damage his brain. Turn him into a zombie.'

Dr Rose had turned to stare at Els. The frightened look in his eyes above the mask had to do with a deeper predicament than the sudden invasion of the theatre. Now Marriner had to recollect himself: the trolley had vanished through the exit and it was time to follow.

'Go, Judith!' he said, giving her a push, and she ran out without hesitation, without looking back. 'The rest of you can start moving out slowly as soon as we've gone.'

Younis was backing away from the main doors. Marriner reached into the airline bag, pulled out the Very pistol and fired a gas grenade across the room. They fled into the corridor just as the acrid pale smoke began to engulf the theatre.

In the vestibule, Carver and Fish were already heaving Kumalo's heavy recumbent form into the deck space between the rows of seats. In the turret Nicky Flynn was firing short bursts at anyone who poked a head round a corner. Marriner shot another gas shell down the right-hand corridor to halt any pursuit from that direction, then scrambled into the vehicle after Younis and Judith. He slammed the armoured doors behind them and yelled at Brakpan, 'Go!'

The Saracen lurched free of the opening and turned into the driveway, heading for the gates. As it did so, a police sniper who'd been waiting for a clear shot stepped out of cover beside the theatre building. He took careful aim with his R4 rifle at the retreating back of Nicky Flynn's head. He fired.

Inside the wagon they heard a soft thump from the turret, and then Nicky dropped through it and off the seat, flopping into the aisle beside Kumalo, gushing blood down the back and the front of his uniform. The bullet had passed straight through his neck, cutting the spinal cord. Careful Nicky, always filled with doubts about this undertaking, was dead before he hit the floor.

Prinsloo, at the head of the party of troops, pushed open the doors of the theatre and then fell back, coughing and choking, met by an almost solid wall of tear gas. He fought his way back through the confused soldiers, into the corridor at the side, and found that filled with gas as well. The only way out now was back through the reception area, and by the time he got there and ran out on the forecourt the Saracen was a distant dark blob at the far end of the drive, excited police in the foreground taking useless pot-shots at it. Off to his right, the shattered rear doors of the theatre were gushing gas into the sunshine and the surgical team were stumbling out through it.

The army major appeared, looking panic-stricken. Prinsloo had forgotten about the major. He had even been forgetting the crowd beyond the fence.

'I think we need you down there, sir. They're getting close. If we have to open fire, you should be the one to give the order.'

More buck-passing, he thought grimly, but this time he would have none of it. 'You just do whatever you have to,' he said. 'If you want to defuse the situation, my advice is just to tell them that Kumalo is no longer here. Let them know he's escaped. Show them they're wasting their time, then chase them home.'

Prinsloo stalked away, content to leave this chaos to sort itself out. He had other things to think about. He had to stay calm, look ahead. They had got Kumalo out, but now what did they do with him? It was a fair bet that they would head for Rietvlei Farm, yet that wasn't the whole answer, either. They had to have something planned beyond that, some

433

means of moving him to a safer place, maybe out of the country.

Prinsloo had got used to bouncing his ideas off Willemse, and he wondered idly what had become of the bugger.

The Saracen crashed easily through the roadblock just north of the clinic, breaking the iron boom off its hinges and throwing it high in the air, sending police and soldiers scattering. Inside the vehicle there was wholesale disorder, with five passengers being jerked about on the seats in the rear, Kumalo unconscious and Nicky lying dead beside him. The deck was awash with Nicky's blood, and Judith was staring in disbelief at his body. Now she looked up at Marriner.

'We have to stop along here. We have to pick up Nandi Kumalo.'

'What?'

'His daughter. She came to me this morning, asking for help. She wants to go out with him. Your friend Duma arranged it.'

'Bloody Duma! Does he think this is a refugee service?' But he could see from the mute appeal in Judith's eyes that he had to say yes, that he could not refuse to take Kumalo's daughter. 'As long as she understands the risks,' he said, his gaze drawn back involuntarily to the ghastly surprised expression on the face of Nicky Flynn.

The Aerospatiale SA330 Puma was designed as a fast medium-lift transport helicopter capable of carrying into battle a dozen fully equipped troops besides its basic flying crew of two. In its configuration as a gunship, the South African XTP model had the sliding door and two of the passenger seats removed on its port side to accommodate a 20-millimetre cannon pod and a swivel seat for its operator. It was this seat that Rendle occupied, several feet behind the cockpit section where Jumper Cross sat beside the weapons systems officer who was responsible for the helicopter's other main armament of rockets and a forward-mounted Etna

434

machine-gun pack. Conventionally, the WSO was still known as the gunner and the man behind the cannon was called the door gunner – though both titles were purely nominal today, since for the purposes of this aerial display none of the choppers of 19 Squadron was carrying any ammunition.

They had taken off at exactly eight o'clock, paired with another gunship to form part of a flight of six. First they had headed north-east to circle the Voortrekker Monument and the vast crowd gathered around it. Now they were over the suburbs of Pretoria, preparing for a run down Church Street, the main thoroughfare of the city, in advance of the army parade that would pass along it to the west.

Unnoticed by the others, Rendle unstrapped his seatbelt and eased himself out of the swivel chair, clipping the roof-mounted safety line to his harness to guard against any sudden banking movement that might throw him out of the door. He pulled the damaged Uzi gun out of the duffel bag beside him and crawled forward. With his free hand he reached between the two cockpit seats and yanked out the leads that connected the VHF radio to the headsets built into the crew's helmets. Even as Jumper turned a startled face towards him, Rendle jammed the muzzle of his Uzi in the back of the gunner's neck, just below the rim of his helmet. The man went rigid in his seat.

'Sorry, Jumper. I'm taking over now.'

'Frank! Have you gone berserk?'

'Never saner, Jumper!' They had to shout at each other over the scream of the turbine engines. 'You do exactly what I tell you now, or this guy gets it in the head!'

'I don't believe you, Frank!'

'You'd better start trying. No more games. I'm deadly serious. I want you to keep formation until I tell you otherwise, and then follow my instructions to the letter.'

Jumper was turning his head back and forth, trying to see Rendle's face and at the same time hold the Puma's position behind and above his partner's. For the first time he got a proper look at the Uzi.

'Hey, that gun is wrecked! You can't frighten me with that!'

'It's got one round up the spout, Jumper, and one is all that I need. I'm betting on it firing. Are you prepared to bet against it or are you going to do what I tell you?'

Jumper turned back to face the front. 'I don't know what you're up to, Frank,' he muttered, 'but you're a lousy ungrateful fucking bastard!'

'I'm sorry, pal.'

Menacing though the crowd still appeared from behind the fence, it had lost some of its tight coherence. Instead of thrusting forward in a sharp narrow line it had begun to spread out, approaching the eastern boundary of the clinic on a broad front, sensing that this obstacle would not be crossed with any ease. A hundred riflemen faced them from beyond the wire mesh, and although a massed charge would no doubt have broken it down and carried them into the clinic this would have required a suicidal desperation that the crowd did not possess. Instead they stopped twenty yards short of the fence, spreading out in a line, beginning a deep-voiced chant: 'Ku-*ma*-lo! Ku-*ma*-lo!'

The Saracens and Hippos had caught up with them. Content to flank the marchers for a while, their drivers now seized the chance to move into the gap, cruising threateningly between the fence and the front row of people. Some words of warning were being bawled at them through a megaphone – no doubt the ritual orders to disperse – but they were almost drowned by the voices of the crowd.

Responding to their mood, Duma turned to face them and lead them in the chant. Suddenly he was aware of a ripple of excitement starting somewhere to his left, spreading rapidly towards him, some news that moved like a wave through the ranks of people, stunning them into silence at first and then making them erupt in bursts of cheering. Somehow a message had slipped through the fence: Kumalo had been spirited away from the clinic. Kumalo was free!

The news swept over those nearest to Duma, and they

were all caught up together in a great clinch of hugging and kissing and crying. What had been a latently hostile crowd was transformed in a few moments into a festive, emotional one, singing, stamping and even beginning to dance, township jive and tribal rhythms mingling in spontaneous displays of joy. Again the army officer with the loud-hailer was warning them; again nobody paid any attention. A crowd of women seized Duma and swept him off his feet with wild dervish yells, whirling him in a circle among them.

A Very pistol cracked, and tear gas began to mushroom at the farthest edge of the crowd. Even this did not dampen their mood, and as they fell back they were laughing and crying at once, like children caught playing some happy prank. The women went on dancing Duma about, and only when more gas shells were fired and one burst close to them did they break ranks and run, still shrieking with jubilation. In front of them some people fell and were trampled. Duma remembered the panic at Elizabeth Kumalo's funeral and knew there were dangers to this hysteria. More in irritation than in anger, he drew the Makarov pistol from his waistband and fired it three times in the air.

The shots had no effect. They were indistinguishable from the bangs of the gas-pistols, and the crowd went on surging past him, more of them falling under the feet of others, all of them still manic with delight. The throng forced him back, and he let them carry him along until suddenly there was another crack and he felt a violent blow between his shoulder blades. For an instant he didn't connect it with the sound. He thought someone had struck him in panic, or kicked him. He felt no pain, but a paralysing numbness began to spread through him, shooting up into his skull and down his spine, and now he knew with a dreadful detached certainty what had caused it. His legs were no longer working, but for a few moments the crush of bodies on either side still supported his weight. Then he fell on all fours. He tried to call out for help, but the sound was choked by something that rose in his throat and he knew it was blood. People went on racing past him, still shouting in triumph, as the blackness crept over him. He thought of Nandi reunited with her father. He thought how ridiculous it was going to be to die now. His mind spiralled down a dark vortex, and he fell over slowly, rolling on his side.

The police had standing orders to shoot anyone seen armed with a gun or a petrol bomb. Staring over the sights of his rifle from fifty yards behind the fence, the marksman still couldn't be sure whether he'd hit the man he had been aiming at. Many people had fallen in the stampede. Most were staggering back to their feet, but a few still lay on the rocky slope while the crowd scattered towards the river, followed by the drifting clouds of gas.

It was Dr Els who found Warrant Officer Willemse.

Els had been the last to flee the operating theatre ahead of the gas fumes, and as he groped his way with streaming eyes down the corridor he had an overwhelming urge to hide himself away. There was no logic to this impulse. Nobody was going to protect him now: not his profession, not his employers and certainly not Hoeksma and Van Straaten. He would be disgraced and disowned. Hardest of all to bear in the immediate sense, however, would be the contempt of Dr Rose and the rest of the surgical team. If he could somehow slip away from the clinic, that at least could be avoided. In the meantime he needed somewhere to conceal himself, somewhere safe from the gas. Instead of following the others out of the building he opened the door to the air-conditioning plant.

The door seemed pretty airtight. As he closed it behind him he heard stertorous breathing in the room, over the hum of the machinery, and when he turned on the light he saw the policeman lying on his back. His eyes were closed, and pale frothy blood was bubbling from his mouth: the certain sign of a lung wound, and at a guess there was a bullet buried in his shoulder as well. They would have a patient for their operating theatre after all. It was only now that Els noticed the gun lying in the far corner of the room, and almost without thinking he went and picked it up, slipping it into his pocket.

The gun was a portent. It gave a sudden clear and fatalistic certainty to his intentions, and when he judged it safe to leave the room a few minutes later he knew exactly what he was going to do.

He found that most of the gas had been cleared by the air-conditioning. There were policeman milling about the building, but the medical staff seemed to have remained outside. Having discarded his theatre gown and mask, Els reached the reception area without being recognized, and there he told a distracted-looking nurse about the wounded man down the corridor.

Outside there was even more confusion, and when he walked out through the gates of the clinic a minute later nobody even noticed him leaving.

37

Marriner tossed a smoke grenade out of the Saracen and watched the grey billowing cloud envelope the road behind them. They took another corner at an alarming tilt, and suddenly the wail of pursuing sirens ceased. For the moment. Brakpan was holding the wagon on its maximum speed and, although that was unusually fast for a vehicle of its size and weight, it wasn't half what a powerful motorbike or car would make. For that reason they had planned this course along a succession of country roads, flanked most of the way by fences, banks or ditches, where overtaking was impossible and pursuit could be hampered.

He turned to glance again at Nandi and Lincoln Kumalo.

The young woman had nodded a breathless greeting to Judith and the others when she'd scrambled aboard, but now nothing could remove her attention from her father. She knelt beside him on the narrow deck, touching him hesitantly, with a kind of wonder in her gestures, listening to his shallow breathing. Only now did she finally look up at Marriner.

'Is he all right? Really all right?'

'I gather he'll come round in about ten minutes.'

'You mustn't worry,' Judith told her. 'Sodium pentothal is a short-acting drug. It wears off quickly. He'll be quite floppy and a bit confused for a while, but he'll be fine.'

She spoke with an assurance that Marriner wished he could share. Now that they actually had Kumalo with them he seemed a terrifying responsibility. The young soldiers watched him with a mixture of awe and concern, the cause and the instigation of all this now lying there oblivious to it all, his hospital nightgown stained by Nicky Flynn's blood.

From behind them they heard a fresh scream of sirens. Marriner picked up the first of the spikeboards and, holding one rear door of the Saracen slightly open again, dropped it out on the road, ready to shred the tyres of anything that followed. They had to expect further roadblocks ahead, but with luck there would not have been time to set up any with enough strength to halt the Saracen. There might well be aircraft soon observing their movements, too, which was why he had planned a period of invisibility between ditching the Saracen and boarding their own chopper.

All that depended on what was happening at the farm.

He told Younis to get up into the turret and take Nicky's place on the machine-gun. Then he picked up his walkie-talkie.

'Unit Five. Do you hear me?'

Blikkies Steyn did not reply.

Blikkies sat perfectly still in the thick bush on the slope thirty feet behind the farmhouse. The morning air was filled with the calls of birds and the humming of insects; deeper into the bush, he no longer had to be so careful about being overheard talking on the radio, but this close to the house he needed absolute silence.

After all the hours of waiting and observing, it was time to make his move.

He stood up. He held his panga and his radio in one hand and he lifted his kitbag with the other, making sure the drawstring was pulled tight. He began to pick his way carefully down the slope.

Ever since the police had settled themselves in around the farm, he had known that the key to outwitting them lay in controlling the house. It was the two cops in there who were in contact with their base and gave orders to the others. Their names were Brink and Smit. Brink was the one who did all the talking on the radio. Blikkies would have to enter the house from behind, since the front was overlooked by other men across the clearing. He would have to act swiftly and silently, without risking any shooting or other sounds of alarm.

Keeping to the cover of the bush, he moved up to the rear wall and pressed himself against it. Apart from a small kitchen alcove to one side the house had only two rooms: a main living area and a bedroom that led directly off it. Each had a narrow window at the rear and both of them were open to catch any cooling breeze that was going. A swift glance into the living room told him that the two policemen were still settled where they had been since daybreak, on two chairs beside the windows that looked out on the clearing and the track. Their backs were towards him; they had their jackets off, and he saw that Smit wore his pistol in a shoulder harness. Brink's gun lay on the table beside him, together with his radio.

Blikkies had to get them out of that room briefly, away from the windows, away from the radio.

He crouched beside the wall and loosened the drawstrings of his kitbag. He opened it just wide enough to encourage the snake lying coiled in the bottom of the tough canvas bag to slither out.

It was a real beauty of a snake, a puff-adder nearly five feet long, and he had caught it an hour ago when it emerged from its hole to bask in the early sun. As its head emerged from the bag now he caught it in the same way, pinning it by the neck with the flat of his panga blade, then grasping it tightly behind the head between thumb and forefinger. The snake hissed, and its sleek grey-brown body swelled in anger. He stood up, shaking it loose as it tried to coil around his arm. He peeped into the room again and saw the men still seated,

441

still facing away from him. He reached in, holding the puff-adder head-down, and let it fall silently to the floor.

Blikkies moved to the other window, carrying his radio and his panga. He hoisted himself quickly through the opening into the bedroom. He crossed in silence to the door that led from the living room and stood behind it, listening, hardly breathing.

Blikkies knew more or less what the snake would do, and more or less what the men would do. The puff-adder was an aggressive species as snakes went, quite as likely to defend itself as to flee if it was attacked. Its sharp primitive senses would tell it it was exposed, endangered. There was little or no cover for it in the sparsely furnished room, and it would slither round the base of the walls seeking a crevice large enough to hide its fat body. Almost certainly it would travel down the darker side of the room, away from the sunlight, getting itself between the policemen and the front door before they realized it was there.

The men's behaviour was even more predictable. Most people had a quite irrational fear of snakes. Not even a puff-adder would attack a man unprovoked; it would never strike except in self-defence – but try telling that to someone trapped in a room with one.

He did not have long to wait. He heard a chair scrape sharply on the floorboards and then overturn, a muffled curse, a shout of alarm.

'*Here Jesus! Slang!*'

'*Kom weg! Gou!*'

If the men had had time to consider their reaction they might have tried to kill the snake, or even opened an escape route for it, but the instinct in the first few seconds was always to get away. Sergeant Brink backed hastily into the bedroom, and Blikkies stepped from behind the door and struck him with the panga, a backhand blow across the throat so clean and swift that it didn't stop him moving, merely propelling him faster across the room. Before he had hit the opposite wall Blikkies was through the door, raising the panga again. Smit had also backed off but had stopped in the middle of the

442

room, trying to tug his pistol out of its holster as he stared at the snake coiled against the door with its head raised, ready to strike.

Smit became aware of the movement behind him and made a terrified half-turn just as Blikkies swung the heavy steel blade. It caught him on the side of the neck instead of the back, a blow strong enough all the same to sever the tendons and the carotid artery, sending him gasping and reeling across the room. He clutched his neck and fell against the door. He fell on top of the snake, which darted its head forward and struck him twice on the arm, through the fabric of his shirt, before writhing out from under him.

Smit lay panting and making gurgling noises, choking on his own blood. Blikkies had meant it to be cleaner than this and now, shaking in the aftermath of the violence, he couldn't bring himself to finish the poor bastard off. He went to check on Brink. The sergeant had probably been dead before he fell, his head half-severed by the razor edge of the panga. Blood was everywhere. Blikkies picked up his radio and returned to the other room, where the snake had slithered into the far corner and was coiled up again, watching him through its black button eyes. Smit's breathing was slower and shallower now, the puff-adder's deadly venom accelerating his slide through unconsciousness to death.

Blikkies was about to switch on his radio when the other one, the one lying on the table, crackled suddenly into life.

'Brink?' demanded a gruff voice.

He picked up the set, hoping he knew how to work it.

'*Brink, jou hel! Prinsloo hierso.*'

He found the right button for transmitting. '*Verskoon, Kolonel. Hier praat Smit.*' He knew the name of Prinsloo from the conversations he had overheard; now he was relying on Smit's voice being unknown to him.

'*Smit, waar de duiwel is Brink?*'

'*Hy't net so 'n bietjie buite gaan rondkyk, Kolonel.*' Brink was looking around outside. How long could he keep that story alive?

'*Gee vir hom 'n boodskap, hoor jy?* I haven't got time to repeat all this, so listen well. . . .'

Blikkies sat down on the chair vacated by Brink, concentrating hard on Colonel Prinsloo's message, hearing of the raiders' success at the clinic, listening to the plans for dealing with them. When the transmission was over he looked at the snake looking at him, and a slow grin spread across his face. This would be better than he had expected. This would give those city boys out there a real run-around. He reached finally for his own radio and switched it on.

Five hundred feet below them the Puma's crew could see the pale smudged faces of the crowds turned up to watch them from the pavements along Church Street. They had crossed Church Square and continued westwards, the centre of Pretoria dwindling quickly behind them, giving way to featureless suburbs, and now they were drawing level with the small hill surmounted by a water tower which was their marker for a turn to the south.

Rendle said, 'Be ready for it, Jumper,' and to emphasize his point he nudged the frightened gunner again in the back of the neck with his Uzi.

Jumper Cross had been flying in a sullen silence for the past few minutes, woodenly obeying Rendle's orders. Now he said, 'You must know this is crazy, Frank. Being off the air . . . everybody will already know something is wrong.'

'No news is good news, Jumper. Do it now!'

As they came level with the water tower they watched the lead helicopter banking and heading into the turn. Instead of following, Jumper eased the control column forward and suddenly throttled up, losing height and gaining speed simultaneously, making a stomach-lurching drop out of the formation and surging forward.

'Down some more, Jumper! Do it like you meant it!'

The Puma dropped again, to a hundred and then to fifty feet, and now it was racing over the low suburban sprawl at a hundred and thirty knots, a huge shadow charging ahead of it. At this height the downthrust from its big rotor blades raised a storm of unsuspected dust from the streets, making pedestrians turn away and even run in fear. The rest of the six-chopper flight was long since lost to view.

Jumper was right, of course. Ground Control at Zwartkop would have been concerned at the loss of radio contact, but by now they would be in a panic. They would be doing everything they could to keep track of the helicopter by its IFF radar signal. On the other hand, they could not possibly have any clear idea why it had gone astray, and it was Rendle's guess that they weren't going to shoot an expensive new chopper out of the sky until they had a good reason.

'Down again!' he yelled.

'Come on, Frank . . .'

'Jumper, I've seen you shaving fur off the backs of rock-rabbits in one of these things. Down!'

In a dizzying minute or two they had left the suburbs behind and now they were out in the scrubby bush country that stretched westwards towards the Magaliesberg. There was no chance of hitting power lines or television aerials out here, and Jumper, now in a rashly defiant mood, took the chopper down to fifteen feet and even less, contour-flying over the low treetops, getting them as far under the radar as possible.

In the distance ahead Rendle caught a flash of dark gleaming blue in a cleft between the brown hills: the Hartbeespoort Dam. Soon he would be able to see the Pelindaba smokestack that was the marker for their landing.

They had weaved their way steadily past the straggling outskirts of Johannesburg and then cut north-westwards across open country, dropping rapidly from Highveld into bush. All the way they had stuck to the narrowest roads, with brief jolting overland short cuts, and they had shaken off all pursuit. For the final leg to the farm, however, there was no avoiding the major national road running westwards from Pretoria to Hartbeespoort. It was about a mile along this stretch that they encountered the roadblock.

Younis in the turret saw it first, and shouted a warning

down to the cab. Brakpan slowed the Saracan for a couple of seconds while he sized it up, then charged confidently forward again. It was obvious that the barrier had been set up in some haste. Two police vans standing across the outside lanes reduced the traffic to a single narrow line, and three cars parked at staggered intervals beyond these forced it to make a crawling, twisting manoeuvre around them. It was an adequate roadblock for all normal purposes. It would stop almost anything except ten compact tons of armoured steel bearing down on it at forty-five miles per hour.

Younis opened up with the MAG when they were a hundred yards short of it, forcing the police to dive for cover. Brakpan went for the gap between the vans, guessing that the Saracen's eight-foot width might make it by a whisker. It didn't. The right edge of its reinforced-steel bumper caught the front of one van, slamming it out of the way but sending a horrible jolt through the wagon. He slowed momentarily to gear down, then smashed into the first of the patrol cars broadside-on, overturning it and sending it tumbling along the road. He drove in a straight line between the next two cars, hitting them fore and aft, knocking them easily aside. Then the road was clear ahead except for a single policeman who had broken from cover and was deftly flinging a spiked chain across in front of them.

Brakpan was going too fast to stop, and there wasn't much point in stopping anyway. All six of the Saracen's wheels went over the spikes, and almost at once the tyres began to soften and the vehicle became more sluggish.

In its gloomy interior, Lincoln Kumalo sat in the centre of a row of seats, supported on one side by Nandi, on the other by Carver. He was still very drowsy from the anaesthetic, barely more than semi-conscious, but he knew enough to understand what was going on and now the jerking and crashing had revived him a little more.

'Trouble?' he murmured.

'No trouble,' said Carver, gripping his arm. 'We got run-flat tyres. They'll slow us down, but they'll take us a long way yet.'

'We also got a busted radiator,' Brakpan called from the front, 'and that *is* trouble.'

Marriner, sitting opposite Kumalo, looked up in alarm. One or other of the collisions at the roadblock must have dented the armoured grille sufficiently to hole the radiator, and steam was gushing from the Saracen's nose. It had also lost speed and was rumbling and vibrating on its flattened tyres; suddenly it no longer seemed the indestructible battle-wagon it had been.

'How much further?' he called anxiously to Brakpan.

'Three, four k's. I guess we can just about make it.'

Marriner's watch said ten to nine. They were just nicely inside their schedule. He picked up his walkie-talkie and spoke briefly to Blikkies again, and then addressed the others.

'Listen, everybody. They're waiting for us at the farm, but Blikkies is in charge there and he's going to try to draw them off. It means we have to make a diversion as well. We can't go in on foot now, the way we planned it. We're going in through the back door.'

'What back door?' Judith asked.

'We're going in through the nuclear reactor plant.'

He leaned back in his seat. He and Blikkies had already discussed this hastily revised plan in as much detail as time would allow. He knew what kind of reception awaited them, and he knew how with luck they could avoid it. Yet everything still hinged on Blikkies and Rendle.

Across the aisle Kumalo's daughter held on to him tightly, watching him every moment as though afraid he might vanish if she took her eyes off him. Kumalo himself was looking at Marriner. Kumalo had worked out who was in charge of all this and he gave Marriner a faint, wondering smile.

'I'm asking you for the last time, Smit. *Where is that man Brink?*'

'To tell you the truth, sir. . . .' Blikkies hesitated. 'It's like this. He's got a bad case of the shits. He keeps having to go out back. It's kind of embarrassing for him.'

447

There was a brief suspicious silence from Colonel Prinsloo. Then he barked, 'I'll give him the shits when I get hold of him! Now listen; this can't wait. The missing helicopter has definitely been hijacked by this man Rendle. The helicopter and the Saracen are both heading straight towards you. You men are not equipped to stop the Saracen: that can be dealt with by the reinforcements who are about to surround the farm, but you blokes must stop that helicopter at all costs. Stop it landing, stop it taking off, I don't care. It must not be allowed to rendezvous with the people from the Saracen. Got it?'

'Got it, Colonel.'

'The reinforcements will be shooting at anything that moves, so keep your heads down. Inform me of every development. Out.'

Blikkies sat and stared for a few moments across the room, at the snake still watching him from one corner and the body of Smit lying in the other. Prinsloo was still buying his act. Even more amazingly, the cops staked out in the bush had bought it as well, though he'd confined himself to two brief conversations with them, relaying fictitious orders from Brink to stay put. Now the deception would be put to its ultimate test. He pressed the button that linked him to the detectives on the second channel of the radio.

Constable Smit had stopped making his ghastly noises just after half-past eight. It still seemed weird, even faintly sacrilegious, to have taken over a dead man's personality and to speak lies on his behalf, but in other respects Blikkies was quite enjoying himself. He had realized early on that this radio with its two independent channels was the essential link between Prinsloo at his headquarters and the detectives out here on the ground. Neither side could communicate directly with the other, so Blikkies could give contradictory information to each without the other being any the wiser.

Now he was listening to the same babble of complaints and questions he had heard earlier. How much longer would they be stuck out here? When would they get some food? Why couldn't they talk to Brink?

Blikkies spoke up. He could only hope that Smit's voice wasn't readily familiar to any of them.

'I told you, Brink has the runs. He's not well. If you'll all just listen, I'll tell you the good news. Orders from Colonel Prinsloo. There's apparently no chance of anybody showing up here for several hours yet, so we're pulling out now.'

'About time,' said someone.

'A helicopter is coming in with fresh men. You can ignore the helicopter. Just make your ways separately to the river-bank and move down to the road. You'll be met there. Go now, and go quietly!'

'What about Brink?' asked another voice.

'Brink and I will follow. Over and out.'

He switched off the set with finality. He stood up and went to the front window, standing just far enough back to be in shadow. Across the sun-drenched clearing he could make out the men rising from among the thorn trees, beginning to move away towards the river. They'd be in for a shock when they met the reinforcements head-on about five minutes from now. Well, serve the bastards right. They would have killed him without any qualms. Brink and Smit would have killed him if he hadn't got to them first.

To one side of him Smit's body was already beginning to hum with flies. From the other corner the snake still watched him impassively. The snake had done its work, and he would be sure to let it go. You always knew where you stood with a snake.

Marriner threw out the last two spikeboards just after they had turned on to the short spur road leading to the reactor, and followed it with the last of the smoke bombs. The bevy of police cars following them at a healthy distance promptly disappeared from sight. Belching steam, losing speed, grinding its way up the slight rise with its wheels flattened almost to their rims, the Saracen must have looked to the guards on the gates like some monstrous old railway engine that had run off its tracks. Younis in the turrret fired a couple of short bursts over their heads, and then the wagon was banging its

449

way through the flimsy mesh gates and turning right, heading over the smooth parkland in front of the reactor building towards the southern perimeter fence, its wheels gouging tracks across the lawn. Guards scattered like ants around it as it steamed up the slope leading to the drop into the valley. At the very moment it crested the ridge, its overheated engine finally seized up.

There was a great clunking noise as the pistons jammed in their cylinders and the whole transmission system locked with a shudder. The vehicle slithered to a halt, and for a few moments there was a sudden unnerving quiet, broken only by the hiss of escaping steam and the cursing of Brakpan as he tried to work the engine out of gear. The cab was filled with the stench of hot oil and burnt rubber.

Brakpan declutched a couple of times, letting the Saracen roll forward, and then it sprang out of gear and began free-wheeling down the slope. Lumbering slowly at first, it gained speed rapidly under the momentum of its ten-ton weight, and in a few moments it was moving at an astonishing rate towards the barbed-wire fence. It was moving too fast even for Brakpan's liking, and Marriner saw him pumping the brake pedal and getting almost no response, and the realization seemed to strike them both at once that no power meant no power brakes. Among the passengers the momentary relief of moving again was quickly overtaken by the knowledge that the vehicle was quite out of control, and now they were hurtling towards the fence at a terrifying speed, the steep bushy slope of the valley falling away beyond it.

From fifty feet above it, Rendle saw the Saracen bowling over the smooth grass of the reactor plant, coming from quite the opposite direction to the one he'd expected. Then it was lost to sight as the helicopter made a steep banking turn to orbit the clearing in front of the farmhouse. He could see Blikkies near the edge of it now, waving them down, the grass flattened around him by the wind of the rotor blades. There was no sign of anyone else, though he'd caught sight of a line of troop carriers parked at the edge of the road about a mile away.

450

'Take her down, Jumper!'

The nose of the Puma lifted as it lost its directional thrust and went into hover. Jumper eased down on the pitch control and the chopper descended gracefully to the middle of the clearing, landing with scarcely a bump, settling down on its undercarriage as the rotors slowed. Blikkies was running towards it, shielding his face from the dust storm.

'Out we go, Jumper.'

The pilot throttled back his engines, and he and the crewman resignedly unfastened their seatbelts. Rendle covered them with the Uzi gun until they had climbed out through the cockpit door and hopped to the ground, and then he unclipped his safety line and followed. In spite of the racket from the chopper there was an uncannily peaceful air about the farm, like somewhere at the still centre of a hurricane.

'You made it, thank Christ!' Blikkies was yelling ecstatically.

'Sure I made it,' said Rendle, professionally nonchalant. 'What was all the fuss?'

'The fuss is moving in on us right now. We've got maybe five minutes. You see any sign of the others?'

'They're just over there.' Rendle pointed to the hillside behind the house. 'But how they intend to get down, I don't know.'

The Saracen broke through the fence with a scream of tearing wire, uprooting the iron posts on either side of it. The strands of tough wire dragged at it before snapping, slowing it down, but now it was bouncing blindly into the bush and over rocks, throwing the passengers off their seats, Brakpan fighting to steer some kind of course through the thick screen of vegetation. The wagon mowed down the bushes and all but the toughest trees; these he tried to cannon off, to retard the downward plunge, wrenching the wheel this way and that, taking them in a lunatic slalom down the hill. Something they hit made the back doors bang open and Nicky Flynn's body, already thrown to the rear, tumbled out.

Suddenly the bushes parted in front of them and the farmhouse was right ahead and below, surrounded by its collection of junk. The Saracen lurched into an outcrop of rock, almost came to a stop and then cruised down the gentler slope to the right of the house, smashing aside bedsteads and oil drums, knocking one of old Meiring's Chevrolets off its blocks. Losing speed rapidly on its buckled wheels, it rode across the edge of the clearing, dipped its nose into the Crocodile River and stopped.

The back of the cab was a shambles of overturned bodies and entangled limbs. Marriner was the first to extract himself, dropping to the riverbank on wobbling legs. Blinking the scene around him into focus, he saw Blikkies running towards them; in the background, like an apparition, the great helicopter sat framed by the trees in a flood of sunshine.

'Come on, come on, we've got to move,' Blikkies said without ceremony, urging the passengers out, dragging at their clothing to hurry them along as they tumbled one by one through the doors. 'Anybody hurt?'

Nobody seemed to be hurt. Marriner lifted Judith to her feet and Carver gave Nandi a steadying hand, but everyone's concern was really for Kumalo.

He was the last to be helped out, Nandi at once going to his side. Whatever lingering effect the anaesthetic had had must have been shaken clean out of him in the last few minutes, for he stood upright without assistance and gazed around him. He was unsteady on his feet, but his eyes were clear and he was obviously alive to everything. It had not been noticeable before that he was taller than any of them, a helpless invalid transformed into a commanding presence. Quite suddenly he gave a huge grin that made his features come to life. He was looking at Brakpan, wading round from the steaming front of the Saracen. He said: 'Man, you are some driver!'

'Can we for Christ's sake get going?' Blikkies demanded, not charmed by any of this, and even as they began moving off there came a rattle of gunfire from some way down the river.

'What's that?' Marriner asked in alarm.

'Cops shooting at each other, with any luck. But it won't last.'

They went in a shambling line towards the clearing. The Puma's two crewmen stood watching them from one side, disconsolate, hostile, but not quite succeeding in hiding their curiosity. Rendle was paying attention to none of them. He had climbed back into the helicopter and out on the sill of the cockpit door, and was using a hatchet from the emergency kit to smash off the stubby little IFF aerial above the windscreen; without it the radar trackers would have trouble identifying the aircraft.

Now that they had all met up there seemed a bewildering number of people to keep track of: ten of them besides Rendle. On Marriner's instructions they scurried one by one beneath the moving blades to the gun door on the port side, pulling themselves into the cabin, finding seats wherever they could. Marriner went last, and he had just scrambled through the doorway when he realized Judith wasn't with them. Judith was still outside, standing close to the cockpit, shielding her face from the downthrust of the blades and watching Rendle. As soon as he had dealt with the aerial he dropped to the ground and she ran forward and passionately embraced him.

It was the kind of embrace that a woman could give only to her lover, full of relief and excitement and wanting. There was something so perfectly ridiculous about the scene, and at the same time so logical, that Marriner did not know what he ought to be feeling. He couldn't be shocked or jealous or angry. He supposed he should have seen this coming and yet in some way he had seen it and refused to recognize it. Judith, so distant from him lately and so stricken with guilt, had found the justification that she needed for running away. She was running away with Rendle.

They separated, Rendle climbing into the cockpit and Judith running to the gun door. She avoided Marriner's eye as he helped her over the sill, but when he went on watching her she couldn't help giving him a fleeting glance: no longer

453

guilty, a little defiant, ready to defend herself but hoping she didn't need to. They'd both been telling him something with that kiss, offering him a choice of responses. He realized that if he was hurt at all it was in his vanity, not in his pride. He smiled at her wryly and she smiled back with relief. He went forward to strap himself in beside Rendle in the cockpit.

Rendle was embarrassed, making much of checking out the switches on the overhead panel and then leaning out of the side window to shout something, maybe an apology, to the two airmen they were abandoning in the clearing. Marriner wanted to lean over and tell him everything was all right, but now he was throttling up the two turbine engines, filling the cabin with noise, and employing all the concentration he needed for takeoff: watching his rev counters and rotor speeds, working the cyclic and collective pitch controls. The helicopter lifted, sagged down a little as he got the feel of it, then rose again at the centre of a great storm of dust. They were airborne, the clearing and the farmhouse falling away below them. At a height of thirty feet he eased the stick down and the airframe tilted forward as it gained its directional thrust. He banked sharply to the right, picking up speed, and the dark bush became a blur beneath them. A quarter of a mile along the riverbank, towards the road, they glimpsed a line of heavily armed policemen staring dumbfounded up at them.

It was nine-fifteen when the radio link to the farmhouse suddenly came back to life in Prinsloo's caravan. He went through the motions of taking the headset and talking into it with a curious lack of passion.

'Brink? Smit?'

'Neither, Colonel,' said a new and tense voice. 'Brink and Smit are dead. They've been dead for an hour or more. Looks almost like a mad axeman was at work here . . .'

The voice droned on, Prinsloo grunting acknowledgements at intervals. He wasn't hearing anything he hadn't guessed since the moment Brink and Smit – or whoever was playing Smit – had gone off the air. They had had him fooled, fair and square.

'And you know they got away, of course?' the voice concluded nervously.

'I know they got away. Thank you.'

He dropped the headset and stared through the window, across the grounds of the clinic. He was exhausted, drained of anger, a little light-headed. Kumalo was no longer in his charge, no longer his responsibility. He was in the hands of the brass-buttoned generals busy flying their toy planes over Pretoria, and Prinsloo had a feeling that they had no more control over him than the politicians floating their toy ideas. They'd all got too big for their boots, himself included. They could break up riots, crush dissent, drop bombs over half of Africa, build enough jails to house a hundred thousand Kumalos, and in their hearts they had never believed a thing like this could happen: a stolen helicopter, a stolen Saracen, a ragamuffin crew of troopies had slithered through their great clumsy hands like so many eels. Oh, well, he didn't care any longer. Let them try to blow Kumalo out of the sky if that gave them any pleasure, and this time let them pick up the pieces themselves.

38

The sun beat down on the great concrete bowl of the amphitheatre. Even this early in the day, even in the shade of the awning on the podium, Deputy Minister Hoeksma was feeling the heat. Thank God they always got these things over before the sun rose to its searing zenith, he thought. He could well have done without being here today of all days, but an appearance on these occasions was important for any ambitious politician, and he was also aware of an ill-defined need to distance himself from what was going on at the Woodvale Clinic. With luck, now that he had shown his face, he and his wife could soon slip away. He was anxious to talk to Van Straaten and Prinsloo, eager to hear that things had gone according to plan.

455

Up on the hill to his left, the grey cubiform outline of the Voortrekker Monument was already slightly blurred by the heat haze. In front of him the crowd, a hundred thousand of them or more, sat attentively listening to the speech of the Minister of Justice. Dreary stuff, really; Hoeksma's attention wandered, and his eye was caught by the sight of a helicopter beyond the rim of the amphitheatre. Nothing unusual about that, except that it was approaching very low and very fast. There'd been a dozen military flypasts earlier in the morning; he had assumed they were all over, and certainly none of the planes taking part had flown in this fashion. His interest remained idle, however, until he realized that the helicoper's course would bring it straight over the crowd, and already the whine of its engines was becoming more insistent, growing in volume, beginning to drown the amplified words of the Minister. Heads turned among the crowd; people were standing, pointing and suddenly screaming as the aircraft crossed the top of the amphitheatre and swooped in low with a thunderous noise over the throng, no more than five feet above their heads, chased by a giant shadow as it headed for the floor of the arena and seemed about to hit the podium itself, levelling and banking at the last moment, the wind from its blades flinging dust into the eyes of the dignitaries, lifting the women's summer dresses and blowing off their hats.

Then it was gone, as suddenly as it had arrived, still hugging the ground and now crawling up the hill to the east, the sound of its engines fading and then abruptly ceasing as it vanished round the edge of the monument.

'*'n Skande!* The man must be insane!' The Minister of Justice was down on his knees, trying to gather his scattered notes. The crowd roared in a mixture of anger and bewilderment. Hoeksma's wife had actually been knocked off her feet, but instead of helping her he was staring after the vanished helicopter.

'What is it?' she called to him, but he only shook his head. He couldn't have begun to explain. To him the pilot's action seemed anything but insane. There'd been something ominous about it, something so triumphantly insolent that it had to have a meaning.

'You didn't have to do that,' Marriner said.

'I didn't mean to, exactly. Flying like this, following the contours, you don't always know what's right underneath you.'

Marriner didn't know whether to believe him. He didn't know Rendle well enough to be sure when he was joking, but it could hardly matter now. He had flown with hundreds of chopper pilots, he knew all about their daredevil nonchalance, but he had never come across one like Rendle. He used the big machine with such a delicate, fluid grace that all its movements seemed like extensions of his own. He made it dance, hover, corkscrew and turn on its axis. He flew five and ten feet above the ground at a hundred and forty knots. He used bushes, hills and tree lines for concealment, he dodged behind solid objects such as, now, the granite bulk of the Voortrekker Monument to confuse the low-level radar. It was called nap-of-the-earth flying, and he was the best practitioner Marriner had ever seen.

He was also leaving no doubt about who was in charge of Phase Two. He tossed a plastic-covered chart into Marriner's lap and said: 'I'll be following my nose, but I want you to give me bearings now and then off the directional beacons. I'll show you how to pick them up. Don't want to stray too close to any SAM batteries.'

'Where would they be?'

'From what I recall, they keep them roughly here, here and here.' He dabbed with his free hand at some points along the eastern border. 'Cactus missiles, five-mile range and bloody accurate. Not impossible to evade, but much better just to stay out of their way. I want you to be my eyes and ears, man.'

Marriner glanced back down the cabin, at the other nine strapped into their seats along either side. Air from the slipstream blasted in through the gun door, and beneath them they could see the ground rolling dizzyingly away.

Nandi and Judith were making no secret of their fear, the soldiers were trying to look stoical and Kumalo was enjoying himself hugely, laughing at some joke of his own. Marriner guessed that a lot of things could seem funny after twenty-five years in jail.

In the room they had given him at the Congress camp east of Lusaka, Harry Makibani was still wearing his voluminous silk pyjamas at ten to ten that morning, and thinking about sending the guard for some hot water to shave in. There wasn't much point in hurrying to greet the day around here, since it rarely had much to offer in return. Any distraction was welcome, so when he heard a car pull up outside he naturally went to the window. When he saw that its occupants were Pahlani and Govender, he was not at all displeased. Whatever they wanted with him, they should be good for half an hour's amusement. If they had come for the reason he suspected, then they were about to make his day.

Harry heard the guard, with an important briskness in his stride, leading them down the mud-floored corridor to his room. The spit and polish was all an act: Harry had the run of the camp, for what it was worth, and since the idea of escaping was just slightly less attractive than the idea of staying he had never seriously considered it. Instead he had done the first thing that any prisoner with a regard for his creature comforts would do: he made friends with his guards. He had even persuaded one of them to catch a bus to Lusaka, to buy whisky for him and send an artfully worded, innocent-seeming telegram from the post office.

Pahlani came through the door first, looking as stern as ever and clutching a sheet of paper which he displayed as forbiddingly as a death warrant. Harry did wonder for a moment whether it was some kind of summons to the kangaroo court they were planning to confront him with.

'Good morning, Godfrey,' he said affably. 'Good morning, J.K.,' he said as Govender entered. 'How nice of you both to come so far to visit me.'

458

Pahlani thrust the paper at him. 'Harry, what exactly is the meaning of this?'

'How can I tell until I've seen it? Why don't you sit down?'

A little nonplussed, they seated themselves awkwardly on the two uncomfortable stools beside his small table. Harry did not reach for the paper until he had sat on his unmade bunk, and then saw that it was a telex message. It was from Zurich, and it was signed by Joshua Rosenblatt. It was couched in Josh's stilted accountant's style, and although he understood it at once he pretended to read it again, teasing the patience of the other two. Finally he looked up and a slow grin spread across his face. The grin turned to a laugh, and the more he laughed the more amusing the strained, uncomfortable faces of the others seemed. Pahlani's bluster was all bluff. He was looking at two angry but worried men.

Finally he said, 'You came all this way to ask me what it means? It seems as plain as daylight to me. It seems that little Josh is giving you an ultimatum.'

'Why not just admit that you put him up to it?' Govender demanded.

'Me?' Harry's tone was all injured innocence. 'Why would I do that? How would I do it, from a place like this?'

'Harry, we know how your mind works. This isn't Joshua's doing.'

'You should give him more credit, J.K. He's a stickler for procedure, just like you. I'm sure that all he says here is correct. It's all in line with the constitution of the Congress—'

'You know exactly what it means, Harry! He's threatening the executive. He's trying to blackmail us!'

'Strong words,' said Harry equably. 'All he's done is take an executive decision as the treasurer of the Congress, and if Josh says he has the right to do that, then you'd better believe him. If you want my informal opinion, the effect of this is that he's got the Congress leadership by its black balls from five thousand miles away, and there's damn all you can do about it.'

'Oh, nice!' said Pahlani bitterly. 'And that pleases you, of course.'

'As a matter of fact, yes.' Harry suddenly dropped his

459

geniality. He stood up from the bunk, and even in his pyjamas he made an oddly imposing figure. 'When we talk about the leadership, what we really mean is the two of you and Gumbi, don't we? And that's the way you want to keep things, isn't it? You're looking for any way to squeeze Lincoln out short of actually killing him. "Willing to wound but afraid to strike" – isn't that the expression?' They said nothing. Harry continued. 'Well, let me tell you that without him this movement would be nothing. Trying to run it without his leadership would be lunacy.' He slapped the message against his palm. 'This is an insurance policy against lunacy, my friends.'

'So you did have a hand in it,' Govender said, more resigned now. 'I still call it blackmail.'

'Does it matter? Can't you see that it's for the best? We'll be that much stronger if we can settle our rivalries and present a united front under our Leader.' He grinned again. 'It would be a good start if you arranged to let me out of this place.'

They exchanged a long uneasy glance, and Harry knew he had won this round at least. Pahlani said stiffly, 'We can't speak for Gumbi. He may have his own ideas.'

'And he can't be reached? What's he going to do down there, try to pull rank on Lincoln when he arrives?'

'I don't know. He doesn't share those thoughts with us.'

The dark fleeting thought occurred to Harry then that perhaps Gumbi was the only one who was not afraid to strike.

A little after ten o'clock the helicopter crossed the Escarpment. It was called just that: a steep, dramatic rocky ridge that marked the eastern edge of the Drakensberg range and the limit of the southern African plateau. The land dropped away ahead of them, a great rolling plain of deep, dark green Bushveld studded with citrus groves, ideal terrain for the Puma's ground-hugging progress.

Back over the less friendly grasslands of the Highveld they'd had two close calls, both times with pairs of Mirage F1s that were clearly out to intercept them. The first had been near the town of Witbank, and Rendle had played cat and mouse among the six cooling towers of a big power station, weaving figure eights around them while the jets screamed back and forth, constantly losing sight of the chopper, unable to fire their rockets for fear of an industrial disaster. The second pair had picked them up further east, and Rendle had dived into the deep gorge of the Komati River and plonked the Puma down between two high cliffs, simply waiting for the fighters to go away.

'Like trying to drop bricks on a flea,' he said laconically.

Now, slipping down from the Escarpment, the wheels of the Puma practically brushing the flat tops of the acacias, they could breathe a little more easily. There were no air bases closer than Pretoria, and every mile they travelled took them further from the likelihood of aerial interception. There were still the Cactus missile bases clustered close to the Mozambique border, but in the meantime . . . yes, there were the landmarks Marriner was looking for, the peak of Mount Ngwenya to the left, the Little Usutu River on the right. The Kingdom of Swaziland lay before them.

No outsiders were ever admitted to the inner offices of the National Intelligence Service. If a visitor had an appointment, he would be escorted to an interview room well away from the main working area. If he didn't, he was unlikely to get past the guard at the ground-floor entrance.

This was a quietly insistent visitor, however, well spoken, reasonable and apparently not a crank. He knew the name of the man he wanted to see, and turning up like this on a public holiday he might well be telling the truth when he said he had something important to convey. So the guard reasoned anyway. He asked the man to wait outside and telephoned the duty officer. The duty officer telephoned Tertius Van Straaten.

Van Straaten would have left instructions that he was not to be disturbed if he had thought it likely that he would be. All the immediate anguish was over; the recriminations were still to come. Brooding behind the closed door of his office,

461

he wondered whether he should tender his resignation before it was demanded, for demanded it certainly would be. The choice was not as obvious as it looked; offering to resign could be interpreted as an act of honour or an admission of guilt, depending on who was doing the interpreting. There was no one in the Service, and no one in the Government, who wasn't going to be in an ugly mood over this fiasco, and they didn't even need to look around for scapegoats. He and Hoeksma already had the tethers round their necks, and the high priests were ready to lead them to the precipice, no doubt with Prinsloo on the sidelines sourly muttering, 'I told you so'. The disaster could not have been more complete: they had set out to eliminate Kumalo and instead they had let him escape.

When he was told about the visitor downstairs he cringed a little. He could hardly imagine anyone who would want to see him less, let alone go to the trouble of seeking him out here. Van Straaten decided to turn him away, but then reconsidered. A man in his situation needed all the friends he could get, and although this one seemed an unlikely ally he might just possibly have some information, some insight or counter-evidence that could prove useful.

Van Straaten sent word that he would meet him at the front door. Bringing him even as far as the interview room seemed too much an act of complicity. He left his office and went downstairs.

Across the cool, narrow, shadowed lobby the man was framed in the arched doorway. He stood a few feet outside the door, looking out over the colonnades and flagstoned piazzas of the Union Buildings, the gardens below them and the purple jacarandas of the city. The soft sandstone of the buildings and the stamped gravel of the pathways had a golden glow that was never harsh, even in the strongest sunlight. Van Straaten nodded to the guard at the door and stepped outside. The visitor still faced away from him, gazing at the view.

Van Straaten said: 'Dr Els.'

Els glanced over his shoulder but still did not turn around.

462

He was smiling faintly, and there was an odd unfocused look to his eyes, as though he had just woken from a deep sleep.

'Well? You wanted to see me?'

Finally he did turn, without haste, and Van Straaten saw that he was holding a gun, an automatic pistol, in both hands, raising it, pointing it. Van Straaten was looking into its muzzle, barely six inches away.

His mouth dropped open. He began to raise his hands in a fending movement. He tried to say something, but all that came out was a gulping noise from his throat. Still smiling at him, Dr Els shot him in the face.

The bullet smashed the left lens of his glasses, went through his eye and into his brain. His head jerked back in a little palsied movement. His legs folded under him, almost as though he were doing a slow knees-bend exercise, and he sprawled gently on his back on the gravel path. Els bent over him and shot him again, this time in the centre of the forehead.

The echoes of the shots crashed back from the walls of the building, chasing each other down in harsh warbling whispers right across the gardens. The guard appeared in his doorway, aghast, and ducked back inside. Els made a little conciliatory, beckoning gesture at him, as though urging him not to be afraid, then raised the gun to his own temple and fired again. The bullet passed through his head and buried itself in the wall, followed by a swift jet of blood that threw a vertical pattern of bright rosettes against the sandstone. Dr Els fell sideways and collapsed across the body of his victim.

39

'Now you've seen Swaziland,' Rendle said.

It had taken them half an hour to cross the country, the altitude of the land below falling all the time, until with one last gasp the flanks of the Lebombo Mountains rose ahead of them, marking the eastern boundary of the kingdom and signalling the final drop to the coastal flats. There'd been no sign of any further pursuit, and they could reasonably conclude that the South African radar had lost track of them completely. Nor, apparently, was there any official knowledge of their intrusion into Swazi airspace. They'd listened in to Air Traffic Control at Matsapa and heard no requests for identification, no mention of any strange helicopter sightings.

The rough bulges and depressions of the mountains rolled away under them, rising, levelling and dipping, and once again the character of the land changed sharply. The altimeter crept down gradually to below a hundred metres, and now they were flying over a moist green plain dotted with baobab and umbrella trees.

They let the truth seep in slowly, cautiously.

They were in Mozambique.

They had made it.

Lincoln Kumalo sat just behind the cockpit. Rendle turned to give him a thumbs-up sign, and Kumalo roared the news back to the others. No proper conversation was possible in the helicopter, but in shouted snatches Marriner had told him as much as he could of the background to his rescue, the several ways in which it had nearly failed. Now he gave Marriner that big infectious grin of his and yelled, 'Home and dry?'

'I guess so.'

But one thing was still bothering Marriner.

Their present bearing should bring them to the Indian ocean coast in fifteen minutes or so, close to the Ponto do Ouro lighthouse which was their marker. When Rosenblatt had first mentioned the place, Marriner had wondered why the rendezvous had been arranged so far south, close once again to the South African border. He'd had no time to think about it since, but now it seemed almost nonsensical. A helicopter could land anywhere, within reason. And that story Rosenblatt had repeated about the state of the roads was hard to believe. Unmade roads in these parts were pretty uniformly awful. Why should the one from Ponto do Ouro be better or worse than any other?

Another point: the South Africans kept their borders with Mozambique pretty carefully guarded. Rendle said one of their Cactus missile batteries was stationed permanently in the area, somewhere near Kosi Bay on the North Natal coast. Having got themselves out of the lion's mouth, they seemed to be returning almost deliberately to tweak his whiskers.

He remembered something else Rosenblatt had said. He turned to shout at Kumalo: 'I told you this was all Harry Makibani's idea? They've got Harry under arrest.'

'Who has?'

'Your people. A man called Gumbi?'

'Lawrence Gumbi. I will have to see about this.'

'I think he'll be meeting us.' Marriner guessed it was no time for delicacy. 'Do you trust Gumbi?'

Kumalo chose his words carefully. 'He's an ambitious man, but very sound. I have no reason to distrust him. Why?'

'No reason I can explain.'

He couldn't explain it even to himself. It was not the internal feuding of the Congress leadership that concerned him, but the proximity of those missiles. Come to think of it, there was no reason why they should expose themselves unnecessarily to danger from that quarter. They didn't have to follow their directions to the letter. He gave Rendle a nudge, and in unobtrusive sign language indicated what he wanted. The pilot nodded. Imperceptibly he altered the helicopter's course and put it on a heading to the north-east.

It was 9 a.m. in London when Hannes Koekemoer reached his office and found a small solid parcel waiting for him. He didn't open it immediately. First he went to the phone and dialled the number of Jasper Darries's bedsitter in Holloway again, just in case he might have returned in the last hour. Again there was no reply. Shit, he told himself: I am breaking all my own rules. It could happen so easily at a time like this, all those nice precautions blown to glory because the one thing you'd never reckoned on had happened, because an agent had disappeared without trace.

Well, it was true that he'd always known Jasper would cut

465

loose on him one day, but Koekemoer's instincts told him that wasn't the way of it. He hadn't been too concerned when the young man didn't make the Wednesday meeting in Fulham, but then when he didn't respond to the dead-letter drop the same afternoon, or the telephone signal yesterday morning, the spiders in Koekemoer's stomach had started scuttling around. They had staked out Jasper's building, staked out the Congress office. His sandy-haired young assistant, now his newest recruit in the London station, had got into the bedsitter on some pretext and found all his possessions intact. Including the bank deposit book with its forty-five thousand pounds in it, concealed under a floorboard.

Koekemoer remembered his parcel. He picked it up, studying its outer details out of habit. Brown Jiffy envelope, sealed with Sellotape. Typed label, addressed to him in person but impersonally, in the English manner: *H. Koekemoer, Esq*. No postage stamp or franking mark, so hand-delivered. Something dense but pliable inside it. A book. Not a book-bomb anyway; the security staff would have seen to that . . .

A book.

With hands that seemed suddenly clumsy he ripped off the Sellotape. It was Hain's one-volume Persian–English dictionary, rubber-stamped on the endpapers to leave no one in doubt that it was the property of Camden Borough Council Libraries. And in the special slit, his own last message to Jasper, carefully refolded in a new way to show it had been found.

Hannes Koekemoer felt a strange numbing sensation that he recognized as the beginning of grief. Not worry any longer, but grief. Like a man whose son has gone missing, irrationally impelled to phone hospitals and police stations, he had to know. He did something he would never have dreamed of doing. He picked up the phone, dialled the number of the People's Congress and asked for Jasper.

'Jasper Darries?' The woman who answered repeated the name in a blank tone that suggested she didn't admit to knowing it. 'He . . . isn't here.'

'Where is he?'

'Are you a friend of his?'

'Yes.'

He realized she wasn't suspicious of him, merely hesitant. An English voice, an office functionary, probably quite harmless. She said, 'I'm afraid I have some very bad news for you. Jasper has . . . passed away.'

The euphemism infuriated him for some reason. 'What do you mean, "passed away"?'

'He had an accident. He was drowned. Up at Highgate Ponds, you know, near to where he lived? He was only found early this morning, but apparently it happened a couple of days ago. He'd called in to say he was sick, so nobody missed him. I'm terribly sorry . . .'

'How did he get drowned at Highgate Ponds?'

His blunt tone offended her. She said: 'I understand that you're upset, but so are we all. Nobody seems to know. It's assumed he went for a walk up there, somehow fell into one of the ponds and banged his head—'

He slammed the phone down on her. Oh, yes, he thought bitterly, he could see Jasper going for a walk to Highgate Ponds, Jasper who never walked anywhere if he could help it, and certainly not in mid-winter. Much easier to see him being dragged up there at midnight, the bang on the head coming before they threw him in. After calling in sick, with a gun at his head or a knife at his throat, to give them time to work on him first. How the hell had they found out about Jasper? The missing cheque was a possibility, but only one of many. It was pointless to speculate. He supposed he ought to tell himself that Jasper knew the risks, like anybody else, but the truth was that he didn't. Jasper had thought he was going to live for ever.

They were still flying very low, so they didn't see the ocean until they were half a mile from it, the sudden sweep of brilliant blue, the creamy surf, the fringe of palms and tropical shrub straight off a travel poster. Like most inland-dwelling South Africans, the young soldiers got a childish excitement out of seeing it.

The helicopter had reached the coastline eight miles north

467

of where they were expected, and now Rendle turned south and flew parallel to it. The shore was broken here and there by muddy lagoons, but was otherwise straight, the country just inland from it swampy, flat and almost uninhabited: the kind of land that is always coloured an unhealthy shade of green on the map and looks much the same from the air.

Mariner had chosen this approach from the north because it made the Puma a far less tempting target for the missiles across the border. Although it would still bring them well within the five-mile range of the Cactus rockets, it avoided crossing their path at a much closer distance. It meant the helicopter's radar would also give earlier warning if a missile should be launched at it.

'No big chance of that,' Rendle had said. He seemed less concerned than Marriner was by the prospect. 'Flying at this height, we won't make a blip on their screens. Even if we did, they couldn't be sure it was us without a signal from our IFF antenna. They could be zapping some weekend pilot in his Cessna.'

He had dropped speed once they'd turned south, and at less than a hundred knots they seemed to be practically coasting. Within two or three minutes, however, they had spotted the lighthouse in the distance ahead, a single white finger pointing up through the smoky sea haze. A short way this side of it a jumble of low pale buildings set among the shrub must certainly be the site of the rendezvous.

They flew on. They had got within half a mile of the buildings when Rendle gave a start.

'Jesus, will you look at those crazy bastards?'

Mariner peered forward and saw what he meant. The erstwhile holiday camp that Rosenblatt had described was a collection of crumbling thatched rondavel huts built around a clearing. Parked in the centre of this supposedly deserted spot, drawn up with military precision, were six big olive-coloured trucks, with dozens of figures swarming around them. As if all this didn't make their presence obvious enough, there was also a flagpole at the edge of the site on which the gaudy colours of the People's Congress had been hoisted. They were perhaps a mile from the South African border, and they were advertising their arrival like a circus come to town.

'What kind of lunatics are we dealing with here?'

'Back off for a minute,' Marriner said suddenly. 'Put us down somewhere. I want to think.'

The figures in the clearing had spotted the helicopter and some of them were waving. Rendle banked rapidly out over the sea and circled inland again, looking for a firm landing in the marshy ground. He found one a couple of hundred yards from the shore, a patch of baked earth with broken fenceposts around it that might once have been a cattle kraal. He hovered above it, put the chopper down easily in the middle of it and slowed the rotors. He looked at Marriner.

'Well? What are we getting ourselves into?'

The others in the cabin strained forward, trying to catch their exchange, looking about them uneasily.

'There's something so illogical about all that,' Marriner said, 'that there's got to be a good reason for it. They may be attracting attention to themselves, but they're also attracting it to us.'

'I don't follow, man. Spell it out.'

'Look, you say the South Africans can't tell this aircraft from any other on their radar. But they can certainly identify that roadshow. They're probably watching it from across the border right now. That would make it a fair bet to them that anything approaching that place with the right size, at the right speed, is the helicopter they've been told to look out for. This one.'

Rendle was watching him stonily. 'So if we'd come from the other direction, if we'd been at a more conventional height, we'd have got a Cactus up our arse?'

'I'm not saying it was arranged that way. I think somebody hoped it would happen.' He turned to Kumalo. 'Somebody who wouldn't mind seeing you out of the way, even if he wouldn't dare to eliminate you himself.'

'Are you accusing Lawrence Gumbi?' the black man said. 'I hardly think you have any evidence for that.'

469

'I'd rather let you be the judge. All I know is that whoever arranged this state reception for you is either very crazy or very smart. All he'd need to know is that one of those missile batteries is within range of this spot and he could reckon on a fair chance of them downing you on the way in. Not his fault. Just the fortunes of war.'

'Well, we are safe now, and nothing can be proved. Maybe I'll ask Gumbi about it and see if it embarrasses him.'

Marriner was incredulous. 'What do you mean, "safe"? We're talking about a man who could be trying to kill you. Backed up by perhaps a hundred of his guerrilla fighters!'

'Not his, Mr Marriner,' said Kumalo, watching him calmly. 'Ours. I have nothing to fear from any Congress soldier, and I doubt I have much to fear from Gumbi.'

'Listen, there is one way to be sure,' said Rendle. 'That's to take the chopper up and give them a target. If they're willing to fire blind, just on the basis of a radar blip, then your theory will check out.'

'Have you gone mad?' Marriner said angrily. 'You want to risk the lives of eleven people—'

'Not eleven. Just one. Mine. The risk isn't that bad; I've done it before. One trick I never got the chance to show you.'

Marriner realized he was actually serious. 'It just isn't worth it, not to prove a point—'

'If the point matters enough, why not? Now, why don't the rest of you hop out and start walking? Go give this Mr Gumbi a nice surprise while I get up there and see what happens?'

Marriner glanced back at Judith. Luckily she was seated well to the rear of the cabin and couldn't hear what they were saying. He shrugged resignedly. 'It's your skin, I suppose.' He said to Kumalo: 'Are you up to walking half a mile or so?'

'Ten times round the exercise yard. Done it every day for twenty-five years.'

'OK.' Marriner called down the cabin to the others, and they started unbuckling their seatbelts, still exchanging puzzled shrugs and frowns. He undid his own harness, climbed out between the seats and turned once more to Rendle.

'I still say you're out to lunch. But good luck.'

Rendle grinned at him. Marriner followed the others out through the gun door, and in a minute they were all assembled by the edge of the kraal. 'What's happening?' Judith mouthed at him over the rising scream of the engines.

'We walk, he flies,' Marriner said. 'Let's get started. I'll explain on the way.'

They set off in a line, picking their way through the waist-high bushes, Marriner turning to watch Rendle take off, hover and then swing out over the ocean, gaining height. He swung resolutely away, deciding he wasn't going to gawk, chivvying the others along a vague footpath that meandered through the shrub.

The heat was wet and the sun beat down on them fiercely. As the sound of the Puma receded they could hear shouting from some way ahead of them. When they reached a gap in the vegetation they saw a crowd of Congress soldiers who'd been moving northwards along the edge of the beach, coming to see where the helicopter had landed, no doubt wondering why it had turned away from the rendezvous. Now they had stopped in renewed confusion, seeing it airborne again, and stood watching to see what direction it would take.

Unnoticed, the passengers plodded on. Only Judith had been keeping her gaze firmly on the chopper, and now she waited for Marriner to catch her up and stopped him with a hand on his arm, an uncomfortable frown on her brow.

'What's he *doing* up there, Patrick?'

'He—'

There was suddenly a gigantic bang that seemed to come from everywhere and nowhere, and Marriner knew it was the sonic boom of a rocket. Judith gasped, and he felt her nails dig convulsively into his arm. In desperation he looked up, around, into the furnace of the sun. He spotted the helicopter hovering like a tiny lost bird, perhaps a mile out to sea and four or five hundred feet high, and then he saw the missile streaking towards it from the south, black and needle-nosed, chased by the white heat of its afterburn, moving almost faster than the eye could follow as its built-in radar locked electronically on to its target. The helicopter seemed totally still, pasted to the sky, helplessly awaiting its doom, and then suddenly it dropped like a stone, falling straight down to the sea, and Marriner found himself waiting to see the splash. Perhaps ten feet above the swell it seemed to come to life like a diving bird, rising and then banking so steeply that its airframe was almost horizontal as it looped further out to sea.

The rocket still chased it. The rocket's flight-path curved sharply downwards as it continued to seek and find its target, but all at once Marriner understood what Rendle had accomplished with that alarming, perfectly timed fall. By forcing such a swift change in the missile's trajectory he had reduced its slant range and dramatically limited its ability to manoeuvre, and now it couldn't veer sharply enough to match the tightly turning, corkscrewing movement of the helicopter. Marriner watched in disbelief as the rocket became visibly confused, wobbling this way and that and then streaking past the Puma in a long uncertain arc, diminishing and then vanishing against the glare from the sky, finally marking its own death with a tiny white splash two miles out to sea.

The whole thing had taken perhaps ten seconds. Judith let go of Marriner's biceps, and only now was he aware of how painfully strong her grasp had been. She looked at him with the same shocked incredulity that must have been showing on his own face. Along the footpath the rest of the group stood mesmerized as well, Kumalo at their head, staring at the helicopter as Rendle danced it from side to side in a victory roll. Down along the beach there was cheering as the Congress soldiers began to understand what had happened, and now some of them had spotted the group among the bushes and were running to meet them.

With a shake in her voice Judith said: 'Is that why he went up there? Because he knew that would happen?'

'I told him he was a crazy bastard. That's what you've got on your hands, Judith, a crazy bastard.'

Rendle had picked up altitude again and was hovering a

472

couple of hundred feet above the glittering sea, almost as though inviting another rocket to play games with him. Marriner turned to see the first dozen Congress soldiers swarming up from the beach to greet Kumalo, stopping for a moment in awe and then closing in to surround and seize and hug him, breaking into nervous excited laughter. The rest of the group came forward, and the black soldiers began grabbing the white ones and embracing them, too, and kissing Nandi and Judith. More and more of them came running up, forming a rapturous milling throng around the newcomers, gabbling, laughing and cheering until Kumalo raised a hand to silence them.

A tall, lean black man in olive-drab fatigues had appeared at the edge of the beach, twenty yards away. He stood there alone, as though he couldn't quite bring himself to join in the fun. His bearing was aloof and dignified; at another time it might have been quite commanding, but now it contrasted oddly with the expression on his face. To Marriner, and as surely to Kumalo, that expression said everything. It was nervous and knowing. The man was staring at the scene as though still trying to swallow his disbelief.

'Lawrence!' Kumalo called. 'Aren't you going to say hello?'

Lawrence Gumbi seemed to recollect himself. He managed a smile and walked forward. The soldiers around them parted silently, sensing something strange about this encounter, but Kumalo embraced Gumbi warmly as though nothing at all were the matter. He held him by the shoulders and looked him in the face.

'You seemed almost surprised to see me, Lawrence.'

· 'It has been a long time, Lincoln. I . . . could hardly believe you'd made it.'

'We nearly didn't. As you saw. If it hadn't been for the wisdom of my friends here, choosing a different route to this place, there might have been a most unlucky accident at the last moment.' Kumalo paused. 'Maybe this wasn't such a good place to choose, so close to the frontier.'

Gumbi's eyes flicked away for an instant. 'Maybe it wasn't, Lincoln.'

'In fact it was a bit foolish, Lawrence.'

'I agree, it was foolish. I . . .' He stopped himself saying more, perhaps offering some excuse that he knew wouldn't be believed. In the way they looked at each other now there was complete understanding, and some of it seemed to reach out to the soldiers around them, some hint of treachery and conflict approaching a resolution. Watching them exchanging glances, uneasily fingering the slings of their rifles, Marriner knew they sensed a choice confronting them, and he knew which way they would choose. Kumalo had been right. Kumalo would only have to snap his fingers and they would kill Gumbi here and now.

But Kumalo clapped him on both shoulders instead, and grinned.

'All right, Lawrence, we all make mistakes. It's not good for us to chastise each other, punish each other, for each and every one. We have a common enemy to fight. We bury our differences, we work together. We all have our own jobs to do and we don't become ambitious for ourselves. That's the worst mistake of all. Right, Lawrence?'

'Right, Lincoln.'

'Wait your turn, Lawrence. In time it will come.'

Now Gumbi could smile with genuine relief, and the feeling spread at once to those around them. The tension had gone. The black soldiers surged about Kumalo again, clamorous in their welcome. They hoisted him to their shoulders and began carrying him along the footpath. Nandi still hovered anxiously by his side, and Marriner, Judith and the others, already half-forgotten, traipsed along behind. The helicopter came swooping in from the sea and charged ahead of them towards the lighthouse. Kumalo raised his fist in the Congress salute. The Leader had come home.

40

'He froze them,' said Harry.
   'He what?'

'He froze the funds. Little Josh. Hey, are you listening to me or not, man?'

Marriner had been only half-listening. Through the open french windows he had caught sight of Judith and Rendle, in their borrowed bathing suits, crossing the lawn. They had just emerged from the back door of the house after what they called their siesta. The old-fashioned black two-piece was a bit on the loose side, and it made her pale breasts wobble in a way that sent an unexpected pang of yearning through him.

'Just imagine little Josh, sitting in Switzerland like some South American general with seven million dollars of other people's money in his hands. And dictating terms for releasing it.' The thought still gave Harry pleasure. He chuckled and leaned back contentedly in the rickety bamboo couch, sipping warm gin out of a teacup.

It was Monday afternoon, but it still felt like Sunday afternoon. There are places like that, Marriner thought. It had something to do with the heat and the stillness outside, and the melancholy feeling that hung around the crumbling colonial villa and its neglected old garden.

The safe house was in the Polana district of Maputo, once the retreat of wealthy Portuguese *colonos* on the heights overlooking the bay. The garden was a wilderness of overgrown tropical plants – oleander, frangipani, hibiscus – but it boasted a cracked old swimming-pool which Rendle had managed to half-fill with water from a hose. They were heading towards it now, arm in arm, talking and laughing softly, Judith pausing to plant a kiss on Rendle's powerful tanned shoulder. They would know they could be seen from the drawing room as well as by the guards around the fence, but they were oblivious to everything except themselves, the way they had been for the past three days.

Maybe Judith was not quite oblivious. He almost wanted to think not. He remembered the jaunty, self-satisfied walk she had put on for Rendle's benefit after the first night she had spent with Marriner, and he wondered whether it was only the gingerly way she had to step through the coarse grass that prevented her repeating it.

Who had backed off from whom? It was hard to remember. Why was he only now feeling a twinge of jealousy?

'So I'm sitting in this damned camp, nothing to do all day but worry about Lincoln and what they're trying to do to him, when I remembered this loophole in the Congress constitution. I managed to smuggle a message out to Joshua. There he was, still holding in trust nearly all the money he'd raised after the Algiers conference. Seven million dollars, all in his own name – just about our entire budget for the coming year!

'There's this provision that when the treasurer believes the proper voting procedure won't be followed on the disposal of funds he's entitled to freeze them. That means no income for the Congress. No money to feed and pay our soldiers, apart from anything else. We could have had a mutiny on our hands. Josh with all of it under his mattress, somewhere in Zurich – they didn't even know where to find him. Cutting and running with it, for all they knew, that loyal little whitey they'd always taken for granted.'

They sat facing each other in the drawing room, waiting for the car to arrive. It was a big stone-flagged room, sparsely furnished and mercifully cool, a thing for which Harry seemed grateful. After bustling around town all weekend he had finally turned up half an hour ago, hot and bothered, equipped with the paperwork Marriner would need for his journey: emergency passport, exit visa, air tickets. This wasn't the kind of bustling he enjoyed. The glory-train of the People's Congress leadership, with Lincoln Kumalo at its head, had swept northwards to Lusaka within a day of its arrival, leaving Harry to tie up a lot of loose ends: running to

476

and fro with papers, arguing with consular officials and bureaucrats. Getting Marriner out was no real problem, but the South Africans – Rendle and Judith staying here, the rest of the squad holed up in a villa of their own across the bay at Catembe – would need to be granted refugee status before they could move on. More red tape, even though the Mozambicans were making it as easy as they could.

All this had not improved Harry's temper, but the bottle of gin, procured from God knew where in this import-starved country, was having a mellowing effect. He leaned forward and poured himself some more.

'I guessed that the three of them – Pahlani, Govender and Gumbi – were going to find a way to keep me and Josh out of circulation and vote Lincoln out of office. I decided to do a bit of ballot-rigging myself. You see, under this constitutional rule, no decision of the executive on the disposal of that money could be validated without the vote of the President, provided he was free to participate. Well, Lincoln Kumalo was our President and from last Friday, theoretically anyway, he would be free.

'So what Josh told them was that he was simply holding on to the money until Lincoln had been reinstated with full presidential powers. It was all in the rulebook. Well, more or less. Without the money the Congress would be helpless. Without Lincoln we'd be more than helpless. They could have both together, or neither. They began to see sense after that. I wasn't to know that Gumbi was pulling a stroke of his own, but even he has fallen into line behind Lincoln. We are all united again. Until the next time an old lion starts looking frail.'

Marriner smiled. 'I remember you telling me once about your faith in the power of money.'

'That's right, Patrick. You and me, drinking gin like this, in Ireland. How does it feel to be rich?'

'It hasn't sunk in. I suppose that's what they all say.'

They heard a car draw up at the front, doors slam, the voices of the guard at the entrance and the Mozambican soldiers who would be his escorts. It was going to be a long, zig-zagging journey back to Europe, avoiding exposure to unfriendly eyes. At least he could be thankful that the press hadn't picked up his name, the South Africans with too much of their own to hide having smothered all the details they could.

They stood up. They shook hands. He had said goodbye to Judith and Rendle earlier, and would only be disturbing their absorption in each other by doing it again. To his surprise, perhaps as a final nod to their former intimacy, she had shown him a letter she was writing to her father: a first attempt at reconciliation, possibly the start of a friendship that would prosper better from a distance.

He took one more look at them, sitting on the edge of the pool, as close together as they could get. He felt a last whisper of regret, a dying flicker of desire. Back home there would be the Widow Swanson, evenings by turf fires, days in the damp green fields, some contentment, some restlessness. And always the same faint flickering of unease at the sight of a strange car nosing down the avenue at Ballygarron.

PANGOLIN
by Peter Driscoll

THE PLACE: the teeming streets of Hong Kong.
Alan Pritchard has just turned forty and he has nothing much
to lose: his wife has long gone, his son is dead, his lover has
married another man. And what remained of a promising
career in journalism has ended with a redundancy payment of
12,000 Hong Kong dollars.

THE PROJECT: the perfect kidnapping.
All that is open to Pritchard is to turn a bar-room fantasy into
chilling and deadly reality.

THE TARGET: the CIA's top operative in South East Asia,
codename **PANGOLIN**

This is Peter Driscoll's brilliant, breathtaking novel of
explosive action and searing suspense.

0 552 132195

THE WILBY CONSPIRACY
by Peter Driscoll

'A first-rate, high-powered thriller' *Desmond Bagley*

'The setting is South Africa; the headlong action moves from
Cape Town to Johannesburg to the bush, in a high-tension
game of political intrigue . . . The plot is gripping and superbly
ingenious'
New York Magazine

'The best chase story I have read for a long time'
Eric Ambler

'Immensely exciting' *Sunday Telegraph*

'A first-rate action story' *Sunday Times*

0 552 132187

A SELECTED LIST OF FINE NOVELS AVAILABLE FROM CORGI BOOKS

The prices shown below were correct at the time of going to press. However Transworld Publishers reserve the right to show new prices on covers which may differ from those previously advertised in the text or elsewhere.

ORDER FORM

All Corgi/Bantam Books are available at your bookshop or newsagent or can be ordered direct from the following address:

Corgi/Bantam Books,
Cash Sales Department,
P.O. Box 11, Falmouth, Cornwall TR10 9EN.

Please send a cheque or postal order (no currency) and allow 60p for postage and packing for the first book plus 25p for the second book and 15p for each additional book ordered up to a maximum charge of £1.90 in UK.

B.F.P.O. customers please allow 60p for the first book, 25p for the second book plus 15p per copy for the next 7 books, thereafter 9p per book.

Overseas customers, including Eire, please allow £1.25 for postage and packing for the first book, 75p for the second book, and 28p for each subsequent title ordered.

NAME (Block Letters) ....

ADDRESS ....

....